PRETTY I

PRE

DANGEROUS

By Stephen Haughan.

Published by Stephen Haughan.

'neque femina amissa pudicitia alia abneurit'

'A woman, having lost her virtue, will hesitate at nothing'

Prologue

Thrown together by circumstance, three young girls forge an unbreakable friendship during their deprived upbringing on a run down Essex estate, learning to duck and dive at an early age to survive on the mean unforgiving streets. Tougher than most boys their age, the girls endure a brutal catholic education to emerge as young adults intent on building a better life for themselves and their families at all cost, legal or otherwise.

Shamelessly brazen and untamed, the three friends and their dismissive respect for authority embark on a life of petty crime to fuel their retail addiction, a life that would rapidly spiral out of control and bring them face to face with wealthy Arab Sheiks, government ministers, South London mobsters and a Psychopathic Japanese war lord.

Deborah Dawson or Dee Dee as she likes to be known, with her fight not flee approach to life leads her two cohorts on an alcoholic roller coaster ride of sex and violence that would shake the criminal underworld and the British government to it's very core.

PRETTY DANGEROUS©

CHAPTER ONE.

The Taster.

Monday morning, a little after nine and the staff at Shooze on the Romford high street were busy preparing for the days trading. Maizie and Trisha, two tanned teens nursing horrendous hangovers struggle to keep it together while Julie, the store manager and self confessed bitch stood staring at the door, occasionally checking her watch and tutting through clenched teeth. 'Where is she then?' she asked the two girls who ducked down behind the sling backs 'You heard me!' she added, 'I know she was out with you two all weekend, if she's not here within the hour then she'll be looking for another job, i'm fed up with her attitude and her blatant disregard for my authority!'.

Julie was referring to Deborah Dawson or Dee Dee as she liked to be called, a nineteen year old trainee at Shooze and close friend of Maizie and Trisha, all three having attended the Sisters of the divine challis catholic school for girls.

They had grown up together on the run down Bircham estate Goodmayes, a dilapidated tower block built in the nineteen fifties, now listing dangerously to one side and long overdue for demolition, with peeling paintwork, racist graffiti and the stench of stale urine in the stairwells. Maizie and Trisha's parents had eventually managed to escape the monstrous monolith and relocate several streets away, leaving a handful of less fortunate residents including Dee Dee and her mother stuck in an endless cycle of rotting refuse, rent arrears and ever increasing threats from loathsome loan sharks.
Although enduring the harshest of punishments inflicted by the sisters and mother superior during their years at school, the unruly girls could not be tamed, neither could their crude urban tongues be broken. Trisha, also nineteen, but the youngest by a month and a half had frustrated her teachers the most with her inability to grasp the simplest of subjects, leaving her with an IQ of someone several years her junior. Instead she, along with many of her friends focused much of her attentions on the opposite sex, namely the boys of St Benedict's who's playing field bordered their own. Trisha stood out from her peers due to her flowing flame red hair and spectacles which she would lower to the end of her nose whilst beckoning provocatively to the lusty lads. They in turn would scramble up and over the fifteen foot chain link fence that separated them and wrestle one another for her affections, the chosen boy would then be dragged by his school tie into the shrubbery where Trisha would subject him to a full oral examination, male anatomy and sex ed being the only subjects to hold her attention in class.

'Where is she Maize?' Trisha asked, peering over the shoe rack at Julie's furrowed brow before ducking down once more 'She's gonna av a bleedin hissy fit if Dee don't turn up again'.
Maizie took her mobile from her pocket
'You keep that bitch talkin, i'll give Dee a bell' she said, heading for the staff room.
'Just goin for a piss Jules!' she called out.
Julie stood bolt upright, looking around the store for any sign of a customer. 'Maizie i'll thank you not to use that language in this store, now if you need to use the staff facilities i suggest you do so quickly'. Trisha approached the counter to avert Julie's attention while Maizie disappeared out of sight, feverishly tapping at her blackberry. 'Thassa nice blouse Jules, d'ya get it on the market?' she asked, stroking the lapel of Julie's top.
Julie hailed from Collier Row and considered herself above the likes of Trisha and her friends, the product of a private school education and privileged upbringing due to her father's multi million pound plastics empire, she hadn't had to endure the same hardships as her unruly subordinates, that is until recently when her father and founder of Pearson Plastics, once famed for having clad one in three of all Essex homes in upvc left Julie and her mother and fled the country with his twenty two year old PA Briannah and every penny in the family account for a life of lust and luxury on the Greek island of Corfu. Julie blushed and pulled away 'Er no!' she said, striking an elegant pose, 'This is a Vivienne Westwood original from a Camden Boutique i'll have you know'.
'You sure?' Trisha asked, taking a closer look, 'Me uncle Davey floggs them on iz stall for a fiver, e got a

load of em daan Dagnam off black Mickey who nicked em out of a Somali sweat shop in Stepney, eez a fucker that Mickey ya know, e got banged up last week for nicking Tottenham's coach at West Ham and shitting in the manager's hat'.

Julie turned her nose up and attempted to change the subject 'What is she doing in there?' she said, looking in the direction of the staff room.

Maizie, the eldest of the three having just turned twenty meanwhile was pacing up and down in the ladies with her phone to her ear 'Come on Dee answer the fuckin phone will ya!' she cursed, then hearing the dripping cistern she crossed her legs and realized she had to pee. At that moment Dee Dee answered 'Ello Dee, where the bleedin ell are ya?' Maizie asked whilst attempting to wriggle out of her thong. She lowered her bottom onto the cold porcelain seat and immediately lost the signal, 'Ello, ello Dee can you ear me?' she said, springing to her feet.

Dee Dee answered in a week rasping voice, 'Fuckin ell Maizie' she croaked, 'Ar been up all night bangin the bouncer from Benjy's, ar'm bolloxed mate'.

Maizie pricked up her ears, 'Who Terry, you lucky bitch, e's well fit' she said lowering her backside once again, 'Ello, ello, fuck it!' she cursed, leaping up again,

'Ar keep losing ya but arm breaking me neck for a piss, ang on!' Maizie kicked off her skimpy thong, stood astride the pan and began to pee whilst standing, the sound of which reverberated around the room. 'Woss e like?' she continued, 'Judging by the size of im ar bet e's ung like an orse'.

Dee Dee looked over her shoulder at the naked body beside her, face down with a criss cross of scratches on his back resembling the London tube map, she then slapped his firm muscular buttocks but failed to rouse him, 'E's all rock and no cock!' she replied angrily, 'Bleedin lightweight! e passed out after free an arf hours so i ad to finish meself off wiv me rabbit, ar'll teach im to leave me gaggin!' Dee Dee smiled as she peered over to get a glimpse of the sex toy firmly lodged in Terry's backside.

Maizie, still peeing was now gyrating her hips trying to wash one of her pubic hairs from the side of the pan. 'Gottcha!' she laughed, finishing her pee with two short squirts. 'Dee you gotta get in ere mate!' she said flushing the loo, 'Jules is doin her nut, iss arf nine!'

Dee Dee glanced bleary eyed across the room at her Westlife wall clock, 'SHIT!!' she yelled, leaping out of bed, knocking over three empty vodka bottles and planting her left foot squarely in a half eaten carton of chicken Madras, 'Oh Fuck, fuck, fuck it!' she cursed, hopping on one leg out onto the landing and into the bathroom where she plunged her curry clogged toes into the toilet and pulled the chain,

'Are you pissin an all?' Maizie asked.

'Not exactly!' Dee Dee replied, still clutching her phone, then to her horror the water in the pan turned a deep royal blue and reeked of disinfectant, 'SHIT SHIT!' she again cried, wrenching her foot clear, but it was too late, her skin had been stained and no matter how forcefuly she scrubbed with her mothers bath robe the colour remained, 'Oh thas just bloody marvlus' she said looking down at her miss matched feet.

'You alright Dee!' Maizie asked whilst wrestling one handed with her thong, but the lacy lingerie had become entwined around her stiletto 'Bugger!' she

said, tugging as she staggered across the room until there was a ripping sound and the thong tore in two. 'Ar don't bloody believe it!' she said, holding up the shredded remains before tossing them into the toilet, 'Ar'll av to go commando naah!'.
Dee Dee trudged back into her room where the sleeping bouncer lay snoring loudly, 'Tell the bitch ar'm on me way' she told Maizie before hanging up the phone and gathering her scattered clothes from around the room.
Squeezing into a skin tight halter neck top which accentuated her more than ample breasts, Dee Dee rummaged through her pockets, 'Bus fare, bus fare!' she said to herself checking the bedside table, 'Come on, come on!' she added franticly. Dee Dee then spun round and looked directly at the condom machine she had mounted behind her bedroom door 'Bingo!' she cried, emptying the coins from its cash drawer and turning to leave. Stopping in the doorway she looked over her shoulder at the rabbit she had rammed into Terry's rectum as he slept having failed to satisfy her limitless desires. A mischievous smile crept across her face as she inched closer, reached out a hand and turned the dial on the end of the sex toy full on and stood back. The vibrator whirred into life and Dee Dee roared with laughter as Terry opened his eyes and sprang to his feet,
'WHAT THE FUCK!!' he screamed, hopping around the room clawing at his backside, 'DEE WHAT THE FUCK HAVE YOU DONE TO ME?'
Dee Dee held her stomach in fits of hysterical laughter 'Fuck me Tel, you look like the ever ready bunny wiv a battry up iz arse!' She then left the room and a frantic Terry and made her way along the hall, toying with a tear in the dated magnolia woodchip in

passing.'Laters loverboy!' she called back before slamming the front door behind her.
Hearing the commotion, Dee Dee's mother Pearl, a forty year old asthmatic chain smoker emerged from her bedroom coughing and spluttering wearing nothing but a threadbare Bon Jovi Tee shirt and clutching a can of cider in her smoke stained fingers.'Woss goin on?' she said, peering into Dee Dee's room to see Terry bent over in front of her daughters mirror attempting to retrieve the nine inch rubber rabbit, but it was stuck fast, 'You dirty bastard!' she cried 'You sick fucking dirty bastard, get the fuck outta my ouse!'. Terry grabbed a pillow in an attempt to muffle the buzzing sound, 'Sorry Misses D!' he stammered 'It's, it's not what you think!'.
'NOT WHAT AR FINK!' Pearl yelled, swigging the last of her cider and hurling the empty can at the buzzing bouncer, 'YOU GOT MAR DAUGHTERS DILDO ANGIN OUT YER ARSE, AR TELL YA WHAT AR FINK YOU PERVY PONCE, AR FINK YOU BETTER PISS OFF BEFORE AR KICK THAT FING SO FAR UP YOUR BACKSIDE YOU'LL BE TALKIN LIKE ROBBIE THE FUCKIN ROBOT!'. Pearl turned and lumbered back to her room where the fizzing sound of another opening can of super strength cider could be heard before kicking her door closed and collapsing amongst the drunken debris and photos of her former husband Billy strewn across her flannelette bedspread.
Childhood sweethearts, she and Billy had been inseparable until one September morning at the breakfast table, out of the blue with a mouth full of Cheerio's he announced that he no longer loved her and that there was somebody else. Billy promptly moved out and into the flat directly below hers with

her best friend Sandra, and it was the constant sound of their headboard pulverizing the plastered wall beneath her that drove Pearl to her eventual drunken reclusive state.
Terry, unable to retrieve the throbbing toy dressed tentatively with a strained expression etched on his face and after plucking his car keys from beneath a pile of cast off condoms he made his way, penguin like out of the flat and onto the landing. It was there that the true gravity of his situation began to sink in, he was on the sixth floor, the lift hadn't worked since nineteen eighty three and there were some two hundred and forty steps to the ground floor. Clenching the handrail tightly with beads of sweat forming on his forehead the muscular man mountain and former minder lowered one foot after another, each time letting out a pitiful whimper as the trembling toy tweaked his g spot.
Dee Dee meanwhile had paused on the second floor clutching her stomach and rocking back against the wall upon which was scrawled the words 'PAKIS OUT' a racist reminder of the riotous eighties on the Bircham estate which had seen many immigrant families driven from their homes by a mindless menacing mob. In recent years neighboring children as young as four had queued on the stairs to prove their worth by attempting to urinate as high as the famed 'fifth step' and gain their right of passage into the 'Bircham boys' a gang of anarchic adolescents that plagued the residents of the estate and surrounding areas, stealing anything left unattended to fuel their skunk and candy addictions. Consequently the third and fourth steps were constantly swimming in stagnant pee, and with the stench of ammonia stinging her nostrils Dee Dee

bent over double gagging violently. Suddenly a jet of projectile vomit gushed from her mouth and splattered the floor at her feet with a cocktail of madras and mojito's from the previous night. Moaning she spat out the remains of the partly digested chicken that were lodged between her teeth and stepped gingerly over the steaming pile, wiping the stinking drips from her chin and flicking them onto the wall, 'God, never again!' she said, trembling.

Dee Dee rummaged in her handbag as she made her way queasily to the ground floor, pulling out an empty cigarette packet, 'Fuck it!' she cursed, eager for something to take the sickly taste away, she then noticed two boys no older than ten or eleven skulking by the dustbins coughing and spluttering as they passed a lit cigarette back and forth between them, taking clumsy puffs and fanning the smoke from their streaming eyes.

'Eeya!' Dee Dee called out, approaching the lads, 'Gissa fag!'.

The two startled boys stood rigidly to attention, hiding the cigarette behind them. 'What fag?' one of them said nervously, 'We aint got no fags!'.

Dee Dee looked one of the boys in the eye, 'Ar know you, your Jimmy Donnley's boy!' she said, pulling the hand with the cigarette from behind his back 'If e knew you was smoking e'd beat the fuck outta ya, now gissa fag and ar won't say a word!'.

The boys friend whispered in his ear and the pair began giggling 'Show us ya tits first!' he said, cheekily.

'What?' said Dee Dee, taken aback momentarily.

'Yeah!' the other lad added 'If ya wanna fag you gotta show us ya tits!' he waved half a packet tantalizingly in front of Dee Dee's face.

'You cheeky little bastard's!' Dee Dee smirked checking that the coast was clear 'I ain't got time for this shit!' she added lifting her top and bra allowing her pert breasts fall free.

'Corrrr!' the two boys said simultaneously, raising their hands to cop a feel with their eyes and mouths wide open.

'No ya don't ya dirty little scrotes!' Dee Dee snapped, wrenching the cigarette packet from the boys hand and banging their two heads together 'Now piss off and pull ya puny little pecker's ya pervy little gits!'. Leaving the letcherous lads reeling Dee Dee marched out of the tower block lighting a cigarette and laughing at the boys audacity.

Terry clawed at the rail hand over fist as he descended with his eyes clenched shut and an expression somewhere between ecstasy and agony on his reddened face. But on reaching the second floor himself he suddenly lost his footing and slipped on Dee Dee's freshly deposited vomit, his legs sliding from beneath him,'OH FUCK NO!' he cried losing his grip on the rail and crashing to the floor landing firmly on his backside in the stinking spew. Terry let out a blood curdling scream as the impact of his fall pushed the lengthy love toy further inside him rendering it irretrievable without segical intervention.

'OOOH FUCK, NO NO FUCK!' he cried, thrashing around and thus coating himself in the foul combination of Dee Dee's stomach contents and rancid pee. His woeful cries could be heard way up on the nineteenth floor where the Bircham boys were fighting over a well thumbed copy of the top shelf classic 'Fat and Fifty'.

'FUCKIN ELL! LOOKA THAT!' one of them gasped on seeing the center spread, a mountainous monster of a woman in nipple tassels and crotchless panties,
'That ain a bloody beaver!' another said, gawping at the thick thatch of hair between her legs 'Thas a fuckin grizzly bear!' The boys then teased their youngest gang member who attempted to conceal his fledgling erection,
'OY AVA LOOK!' one of the older boys chuckled, 'Bazza's got a bleedin ard on!' Young Barry peeled away from the crowd and pulled his coat down over his knees,
'NO I AINT!' he protested 'AR BLEEDIN AINT ARE TELL YA!' the remainder of the gang leapt on the red faced youth and rubbed the magazine in his face, 'Av somma that!' they yelled as he struggled to break free,
'Get off! get offa me will ya!' Barry squealed.
Just then the door to number two thirteen opened beside them and an overweight, unshaven slob of a man stepped out onto the landing, with a grubby big toe sticking from a hole in his right bedroom slipper and his stomach hanging way down below his crotch, stretching his sweat drenched vest to near bursting,
'Why don't you lot piss off and play somewhere else i carn ear the fuckin telly!' he yelled, waving a fat drenched bacon sandwich in the air.
The boys wriggled out of his reach and sat defiantly ridiculing the man, 'Or what?' one asked 'What ya gonna do fatso, sit on the lot of us!'.
The insenced resident flew into a rage, discarding his sandwich and whipping the leather belt from his trousers, lunging at the lads, 'YOU CHEEKY LITTLE FUCKERS AR'LL FRASH THE FUCKIN LOTTA YA!' but in doing so, his loosened trousers fell around his

knees revealing a soiled pair of baggy pants that looked as though they'd been worn repeatedly for several weeks, the once white Y fronts were now a pale grey with hints of yellow and brown and stains of a more sordid nature. Grappling with his trousers to hide his embarrassment as the children, some heaving and some hysterical looked away in disgust, the furious man charged at the boys like a bull elephant with all three of his chins rippling on his chest.

The Bircham boys leapt to their feet and made a dash for the stairs, gesturing behind them with their hands as they fled

'Wankaaa!' one of them cried.

Having lumbered no more than five yards their persuer stopped, clutching his chest, wheezing as though he'd just completed a grueling marathon, grimmacing he turned and stooped, snatched up the magazine and returned to his flat, slamming the door shut hard against it's rotting frame, 'Little cunt's!' he snarled, collapsing onto his couch, opening the magazine and leering at the large lurid ladies. Reaching into a bowl beside him he then crammed a handful of wotsits into his gaping mouth before thrusting his orange hand into the aging pants beneath his stomach, jostling his genitalia.

Dee Dee sat at the bus stop at the top of her road enduring the endless honking of horns from the 'Chadwell chavs' as she called them, mindless morons in jacked up hatchbacks with a boot full of speakers belting out tuneless trash that could be heard streets away. She sat slumped with a finger in the air as one by one the chavs slowed to lower their smoke glass windows and as though in some bizarre mating ritual, court her with their ridiculous street speak.

Yo Bitch! come pour ya booty in me ride!' a youth who looked barely old enough to breast feed let alone drive called out to her while straining his neck to see over the steering wheel of his suped up Skoda.

'GET FUCKED!' Dee Dee replied, much to the delight of the seven hooded tots crammed inside with him in his tiny car.

'She dissed you bad, blud!' one of them laughed, slapping the driver's oversized cap, he responded by taking a water pistol from his waistbandand holding it on it's side pointing it in her direction, but only succeeded in soaking the passenger beside him when his ridiculous replica leaked it's contents into his lap,

'WHAT THE FUCK MAN!' his friend cried, dabbing at his crotch, 'Diss is embarrassing blud!'

The belittled driver put his foot to the floor in a bid to reassert his masculinity, spinning his rear wheels in the middle of the road sending plumes of white smoke rising into the air, 'Das what arm talkin bout!' he snarled as the screeching grew louder. Turning his stereo to full volume he never took his eyes off Dee Dee until suddenly there was a deafening bang like gunshot and the prop shaft dropped with a resounding clang from beneath his car which immediately lost all power and sat lifeless with it's occupants lowering their caps to mask their humiliation. Passers by laughed and pointed as the lads clambered sheepishly from the car and proceeded to push it into a side street where they stood squabbling and shoving one another apportioning blame.

Dee Dee, still reeling from a weekend of excess could barely manage a smile, her head pounding like a drum. Stubbing her cigarette out on a poster of Peter Andre at the bus stop she stood up a little too sharply to hail the number eighty six and staggered back holding her head with one hand and steadying herself with the other, 'Shit!' she said, waving the bus down. Climbing aboard Dee Dee rummaged in her bag 'Single to Romford mate!' she slurred, hurling a handful of coins into the tray and wincing at the clattering sound, 'Do me a favor Stellios!' she said to the plump Greek driver, 'Take it easy will ya, me gut's are playin me up summink chronic!' she then felt a rumbling in the pit of her stomach, an unearthly sound that thundered through her small intestine and belched out of her backside at break neck speed, culminating in what could only be described as a brass band crescendo. The colour immediately drained from Dee Dee's cheeks as the noxious vapor rose into the air, 'Fuck me thas dire!' she said, leaving the scene quickly whilst fanning her bottom.
Trapped in his cab and with tears streaming from his eyes the bus driver opened and closed the doors several times to dilute the stench, finally letting an elderly lady onboard. With her bus pass in one hand and a Yorkshire terrier wearing a paisley waistcoat and bandana in the other the octagenarian frowned at him in disgust, assuming the acrid cloud of gas had emanated from his trousers. Cupping her hand over her nose the lady fled to the rear of the bus and dropped into the only seat available, beside Dee Dee.
As the bus made it's way along the busy high road her wrinkled nostrils began to twitch as she looked

Dee Dee up and down, the remnants of the ghastly guff were still seeping from her knickers.
'A repugnant wretch like you my dear!' she snapped, inching away 'Should not be aloud on public transport!'. Dee Dee was not fazed by her outburst, she calmly grabbed the woman by her fake fur lapels, looked her straight in the eye before burping loudly and blowing the proceeds into her face, which in comparison was equally as vile as her earlier flatulence. The elderly woman wrenched herself free, turning up her nose in disgust, her face would have been less contorted if she'd licked the backside of her pampered pooch. She leapt from her seat clutching a lace hanky to her lips and rang the bell repeatedly until the driver relented and opened the door whilst at the traffic lights. Several passengers around her also opted for an early exit as Dee Dee, lifting one buttock, let rip once more whilst changing her facebook status on her phone to 'God i'm so fucked'.
The bus finally arrived at the end of Romford's paved precinct and Dee Dee alighted, taking out the last of her cigarettes she tossed the empty packet unashamedly into the occupied pram of a preoccupied mother, smiling as the tiny tot burst into tears, 'Bleedin rugrats!' she sneered, having vowed never to have children, unlike her cousin Chantelle who at the age of fourteen gave birth to twins, fathered by a penniless pot head with no desire to work, the sobbing snot nosed girls Katie and Kaliegh were often forced to walk bare footed from the supermarket alongside their double buggy laden with 'Betterbuys' branded beer and value vodka.
Before setting off along the high street Dee Dee, in full view of a disgusted coffee shop queue,

proceeded to finger the trapped g string from between her buttocks, 'MAWNIN!' she called out to the startled onlookers then tottered off, her high heels clattering on the granite cobbles. Part way along the precinct Dee Dee had to run the gauntlet of a gang of irish laborers waist deep in a hole in the road wrestling with a gas main, but amid the sexist comments and wolf whistles one blue eyed boy caught her eye, 'Ello ansum!' she said, stooping to get a closer look at his rippling torso and strong manly hands and in doing so giving him more than a glimpse of her heaving cleavage.

'How you doing missy?' he replied in a broad Belfast brogue 'Sure your a grand sight on a monday morning you are'

Dee Dee was about to reply when the gangs foreman, a fat, fiery Fermanagh man with his jeans typically bearing way too much backside cleavage threw his hard hat at the young man and squelched towards him in the boggy trench.

'WHAT THE FECK AM I PAYIN YA FOR YA LAZY FEKIN FEKKER' ,he barked red faced 'NOW GET FEKKIN DIGGIN AND DON'T YOU STOP TILL I FEKKIN TELL YA, YA USELESS FECKIN FEKKA!'.

Annoyed at his outburst Dee Dee stood bolt upright and took a long drag of her cigarette until the tip was glowing red, then seeing the bullies backside beneath her, dropped the burning butt between his spotty cheeks where it lay smouldering in his underpants for a second or two before he stopped wide eyed in his tracks, then leapt around the hole screaming at the top of his voice, 'BE FEK BE JESUS, ME FEKKIN ARSE IS ON FEKKIN FIRE'. The gang and Dee Dee fell about laughing as the floundering foreman rolled around in the sodden mud in an attempt to douse his denims. The blue eyed boy grabbed a CO2 extinguisher and emptied it's entire freezing contents onto his bosses backside leaving him shivering in a frosty featal position beneath a cloud of sub zero gas. The lad then took Dee Dee's hand and planted a kiss on her counterfeit Cartier ring, God blessya me darling!' he said, winking 'That bastard's bin roidin my fekkin arse all mornin!'.

Smiling Dee Dee took an eyebrow pencil from her handbag, crouched and scrawled her number across the chest of his high viz jacket 'Gissa bell sometime!' she said, then seeing the tell tale bulge in his trouser pocket added 'Oooh gissa fag will ya, ar give me last one to paddy the Popsicle there!'. The young man took the packet from his pocket and they both watched as the frost bitten foreman clambered from the trench, his teeth chattering uncontrollably,

'Ggg get dddddiggin ya fe fe fe fekkin b bastards!' he stammered, climbing into his transit van and slamming the door shut. Accepting a light from her new friend Dee Dee then walked the short distance to the shoe store and stood outside finishing her cigarette stamping on a newspaper as it blew by she laughed out loud at the picture of black Mickey on the front page with the Tottenham managers tainted trilby inset.

On seeing her friend, Trisha came rushing from the store, 'Dee where the fuck av you bin iss arf ten and Julie's as got the right arse!'.

Dee Dee held out her shaking hands, 'Ar dunno if ar can face it Trish, looka me ar'm still pissed for fuck sake!'.

Trisha took Dee Dee by the arm and dragged her toward the door, 'Ar'm angin off an'all mate' she confessed, coaxing her friend inside 'But we carn afford to lose this job, we need the money for Magaloof!'.

For the previous three years the girls had holidayed at the raunchy resort, an annual hedonistic pilgrimage of drink and drug fueled debauchery that had once landed them in hot water with the local authorities, but after each performing a lewd oral act on the chief of police in the back of his car all charges against them were dropped. 'Come on Dee ar make you a coffee!' Trisha added.

'Fuck me mate you look dog rough!' Maizie laughed on seeing her friend, 'Mind you i aint bin too cleva meself, ooz idea was it too av large donna's on the way ome, ar been up and daan to the khazi all bleedin night, ar tell ya me arse is angin in tatters, ar reckon ar know what a bleeddin baboon feels like now!'.

Julie suddenly caught sight of Dee Dee

'DEBORAH, MY OFFICE, NOW!' she yelled, marching to the back of the store. Maizie and Trisha hurried about their business while Dee Dee, tutting and raising her eyebrows, followed the seething manager.

'Can i elp ya?' Maizie asked a mother who was browsing with her teenage son in tow,

The mother plucked a pair of black leather loafer's from the rack and thrust them at Maizie, 'Help him with these?' she said, rudely.

'Yeah course!' Maizie replied, ushering the boy to a chair, 'Now, park yer arse daan there for me!' she added, crouching down on her knees and removing the boys trainers, 'Right ear we go!' she said, loosening the laces on the left shoe, 'Slip ya foot in there for me!' .But the young boy had become distracted by the sight of Maizie's bare bottom beneath her skirt reflected in the mirror behind her.

'Come on, shove it in will ya!' she said, losing her cool. It was then that she noticed a growing bulge in his school trousers and followed his gawping gaze.

'You dirty little fucker!' she said, pulling her skirt down over her rosy cheeks before flicking the boys erection with her shoe horn as hard as she could. The schoolboy bent over and cried out clutching his crotch,

'WHAT'S GOING ON?' his mother yelled, 'Daniel dear, what's wrong?'

'E'z got trouble with the orn!' Maizie chuckled as the boy rocked back and forth on the stool.

'I BEG YOUR PARDON!' his mother stormed.

'The orn!' Maizie said, brandishing the horn. The boy clasped one of his pumps over his privates and ran teary eyed from the store, leaving his mother glaring at Maizie who, tongue in cheek, offered her the loafer's, 'Can i intrest you in any of our cleanin products madam?' she asked, in a rare display of professionalism 'We got a two for one promotion fingy at the moment!'. The mother knocked the shoes from Maizie's hands and barged past her, muttering obscenities under her breath.

'Fanks for shoppin at Shooze, do come again!' Maizie called after her, slumping onto the stool herself, 'Ar don't need this shit!' she sighed, then catching sight of herself in the same mirror she raised her skirt and called out to Trisha opposite,

'Eeya Trish, dya reckon i oughta av a brazillian or a landin strip?'. Trisha looked up for a moment, 'Ar'd av it all off babe if ar was you, me sister'll wax it for ya if ya want, she done mine!'

'Fuck that!' Maizie replied, dropping her skirt, 'I ain into pain, anyway blokes don't like the stubble, that geezer last week wouldn't go daan on me coz e reckoned itta be like snoggin George Michael!'.

Maizie's comments were a welcome break for Trisha who was having problems of her own, the lady whose feet she was currently sizing had a distinct hygiene problem, especially down below which turned Trisha's stomach, each time she opened and closed her legs her flowing skirt would waft the bodily odour into the young assistants face until she could stand it no longer, 'Fuck it! ar don't get paid enough for this!' she snapped, 'Look love we ain't got nuffin in your size, now take this and do one!' she thrust a can of foot powder into the woman's hand and pointed at the door.

'Foot powder!' the woman replied, quizzically 'But, but whydo i?'.

Before she could finish, Trisha walked away, 'It ain't for ya feet iss for ya fanny ya smelly bitch!' she called out before joining Maizie. They both looked at each other and said simultaneously 'Fuck this!'.

Dee Dee meanwhile was standing quietly taking Julie's volley of abuse, the pounding in her head and gurgling in her gut making her feel nauseous and giddy.

'I've given you enough chances Dawson, heaven knows i have!' Julie ranted, 'You and your good for nothing friends show me no respect at all, i've worked hard to get where i am!'. By now Dee Dee had switched off and Julie's barking was just jumbled blurb as far as she was concerned.

'And another thing!' Julie continued whilst straightening her managerial certificate on the wall. 'Mr Sanjeef isn't happy, oh no not happy at all, i've

told him all about you three in my staff appraisals and he's informed me as store manager!' she puffed out her chest 'That i have the authority to sack you all!'.
Dee Dee came to her sense's on hearing the word 'sack' 'What?' she said in disbelief, 'But, but!'
A knowing smile crept across Julie's face, she had these impudent girls in the palm of her hand and maybe now she would gain the fear and respect she believed she so rightly deserved. 'Deborah Deborah you can but me all you like!' she said smugly.
But Dee Dee in her nautious condition had heard enough, 'Ya right, ya stuck up slag!' she snarled, lurching forward, 'Ar can butt you all ar like!' Before Julie realized what was happening, Dee Dee head butted her square on the bridge of her nose, breaking it instantly, sending a torrent of blood streaming down her face. The startled manager cupped her hands to her face and fell to the laminate floor screaming frantically whilst Dee Dee stood menacingly over her, 'Put that in ya fuckin staff appraisal ya dozy bitch!' she snapped before ramming her fist through the glass of Julie's framed certificate.
Dee Dee was usually a docile girl but in times of extreme stress the wolverine within her would manifest itself and as a frightened Julie wriggled into a corner she kicked open the staff room door and stormed out into the store. 'Oy you two!' she called to her friends, 'Come on! less get the fuck out of here!'.
Trisha and Maizie looked at each other then at Dee Dee,
'What you gone and done Dee?' Maizie asked 'Where's Julie?'.
Dee Dee wiped a smudge of blood from her forehead and made for the door, 'She was doin my ed in so ar

nutted er!' she replied, 'We don't need this poxy job, you comin or what?'.
Maizie and Trisha looked at each other again then hurried after Dee Dee, 'But Dee!' Trisha squealed, 'What about Magaloof?'.
'Ar'll finka summink!' Dee Dee replied, striding defiantly along the High street with her friends scurrying behind, 'Right naah though ar need an air o the dog, less av one in Wiverspoons!'.
'Yeah but Deeee!' Maizie stressed looking over her shoulder 'Thas the fird blinkin job we've ad in free mumfs, what am ar gonna tell me mum?'
Queuing at the bar of the Stag and Hounds Dee Dee, Trisha and Maizie rummaged through their purses,
Ar got two paand seventy, ow much you two got!' Trisha said, spilling her change onto a beer mat,
'Don't look at me!' Maizie replied, holding open her empty Gucci purse, 'Ar done sixty quid on booze last night, then i ad to give me mum that score that ar ponced off her on friday!'.
Trisha shoved Dee Dee's shoulder 'See Dee, ar told ya we needed that blinkin job, naah what we gunna do, we carn even afford a pissin drink!'.
'Ar told ya ar'd fink of summink!' Dee Dee snapped counting her own meager coins, she then smiled on seeing the blue eyed irish lad and his friends coming in for their lunch, 'What you two avin?' she asked Maizie and Trisha who both looked at their paltry pile
'A panda pop and free straws by the looksa fings!' Trisha sighed.
'Leave it to me!' said Dee Dee putting two fingers in her mouth and whistling loudly
'OY OY SAVALOY!' she yelled,

The lad waved dragging his friends to the bar to join the girls, ‘I was just tinkin about you sure i was!’ he said before introducing himself and the others,
‘I didn’t catch your name earlier but i’m Duncan, this here’s Ryan, that’s Dougal, Jim, Willy, and Tyler!’
The girls looked the beefy boys up and down, ‘Blimey Dee!’ Trisha gasped, ‘Where’d ya find this lot?’.
‘In an ole in the graand!’ Dee Dee chuckled, ‘Thas Trish, this is Maizie and ar’m Dee Dee!’ she explained.
The boys crowded round, eyeing the three teenage hotties, ‘You tree are gorgeous sure you are!’ Willy chirped up, ‘Like, like feckin angels you are, listen this lot are all gay, i’m the only heterosexual here but i’ll take you one at a time or all at once!’.
‘Blimey e’s a cocky little fucker ain e!’ Trisha laughed.
The others then set about Willy, twisting his nipples and playfully punching his ribs,
‘Ya cheeky little fekka!’ Dougal laughed, ‘You wouldn’t fekkin know what to do your a feckin virgin sure you are!’.
Duncan clasped his hands together ‘Royt girls what’ll ye be havin!’.
The three girls smiled at each other, ‘Ar’ll av a wicked’ said Trisha, sitting at a nearby table,
‘Me an’all!’ Maizie added ‘An a baga pork scratchins!’.
‘Two blue wicked’s an a JD an coke!’ Dee Dee told Duncan while staring into his dreamy eyes, ‘Oh an a bag of toe nails for er!’.
Duncan and the others huddled at the bar giggling like children, ‘Oyd loyk to fook the arse off the tree a dem!’ Jim joked.

Tyler tossed a beer mat at his head 'You always were a greedy cont Jim Duggan!' he said as he and his friends fell about laughing.
'SCUSE ME MISS!' Duncan called out to the long haired barman who frowned back,
'Mister!' the tender snapped.
Duncan then got Willy in a headlock teasing his friend 'Well little Willy here doesn't care if your a miss or a mister!' he joked, 'He just wants to know if your free on friday noytt!'.
The barmen glared at the hysterical boys,
'What do you want to drink i've got people waiting!' he said angrily.
Duncan composed himself 'Sorry!' he said, elbowing jim in the ribs to silence him, 'Can oy have six pints of Guinness, a JD and coke, two blue wicked's and a bag of pork scratchings!'
'Will ya get me a bagga nut's!' Willy butted in, but was dragged from the bar by the others,
'No ya can't have a bagga nut's ya greedy fek!' Dougal said, shoving him into a chair opposite the girls, 'Just sit the fek down and don't leer at the ladies or i'll be telling them all about your little problem down below!'. Willy spun round pleading with his friend
'Oy told you that in the strictest confidence Dougal, you promised you wouldn't say a word!'. The rest of the boys wiggled their little fingers at Willy who sank into his seat,
'Sure i only told the lads!' Dougal replied, 'Don't worry they won't tell a soul!'
'Well i told me maa!' Tyler chirped up with his hand in the air,
'And i told father Riley!' Jim added 'Oh and Sister Catherine, their gonna ask the congregation to pray

for you on Sunday!'. Soon all the boys hands were raised as they reeled off the names of everyone they'd informed of Willy's erectile dysfunction.
'There you go ladies!' Duncan said, setting the drinks down, 'And pork scratching's for the lovely Maizie!'
'Fanks!' Maizie replied, tearing open the bag and popping one into her mouth,
'Anyone want one?' she gargled offering the bag around while crunching the crispy treat, but each of them backed away.
'For fuck sake Maize, turn it in will ya!' Dee Dee said, feeling a little queazy,
'Me nan gives them poxy fings to er Shitzu Sophie but she don't make arf as much bleedin noise as you!'.
'Ar carn elp it!' Maizie squawked with her mouth full, 'It was ya nan that got me into these in the first place, ar do love your nan she's such a laugh!'.
Trisha tugged Dee Dee'a arm, 'Eeya that bitch pissed up mar bleedin leggins!'
'Who!' asked Dee Dee 'Me nan!'.
'No stupid!' Trisha laughed 'Er little shit thing! them leggins was brand new an'all, ar was well pissed off!'.
Duncan and his friends listened intently to the girls insane ramblings,'Sure you girls are as mad as fek!' he said, sinking his pint, 'Royt, who's for another!'.
'We ain't got no dough!' Maizie replied, pouring the crumbs from her bag into her mouth.
Dee Dee kicked maizie's leg, 'What she means is, we aint bin paid yet so we can't get a raand!'.
Jim leapt from his seat, whipping out his bulging wallet, 'We wouldn't dream of taking your money girls!' he said, heading for the bar, 'same again is it?'.
Maizie and Trisha drained their bottles noisily through their straws, 'Yeah fanks!' they both replied.

'Cheers Jim!' Dee Dee added, spitting an ice cube back into her empty glass, 'And no white mice this time!'. Jim stopped in his tracks with a puzzled expression, 'White mice!' Dee Dee repeated, jangling the ice cubes around in her glass.
'Ohhh!' Jim said as the penny dropped, 'White mice, ice, very good, i suppose you'll be wanting a fresh fairy's arse!'
Now Dee Dee looked puzzled, What the fuck are you on about!' she asked.
'Fairy's arse, glass!' Jim said 'Apples and toads and all that Cockney shite!'
The three girls roared with laughter while the Belfast boys looked on bemused, 'You paddy's crack me up!' Dee Dee chuckled, 'Yeah ok Jimmy cricket ar'll av a JD in a fairy's arse wiv no white mice mate!'.
Dougal joined Jim at the bar, 'Hey guys what about a shot to go wid it?' he asked.
Trisha pricked up her ears 'Oooh yeah Sambuca's mar favrit!'.
Soon the table was laden with drinks, bottles, pints and shot glasses which were emptied and refilled in succession, and as the alcohol began to take effect so the subject of conversation deteriorated.
'Can i ask you's girls a personal question?' Duncan said, feeling a little more sure of himself, 'What's your favorite position?'.
Without hesitation Trisha chirped up 'Ar love it doggy me!'.
The rest of the party fell about the place, 'Why's that Trish?' Dee Dee asked, tongue in cheek 'So you aint gotta look at the ugly fucker!'
'No, no course not!' Trisha replied over the laughter, 'Iss so ar can watch X facta at the same time, ar like flashin me tits at Simon, e'z gorgeous e is!'

'What about you Maizie darlin?' Willy asked, 'I bet your a feisty one, sure you are!'. Maizie downed her Sambucca and beckoned to Willy who leaned forward as she whispered in his ear. 'I fekkin knew it!' he gasped, wide eyed as she told him of her love of leather and nipple clamps, 'She's a fekkin dirty bitch this one!'.

Dougal looked over his friends shoulder and gestured to the others to look at at Willy's crotch,

'Will you look at that, young Willy's got a fekkin woody!'. Jim and the others leapt on Willy,

'Ya horny little bastard!' Tyler yelled, grabbing Willy's erection and twisting it through his jeans.

'GET OFF ME YA CONTS!' cried Willy, bending over double, 'OUCH, I FEKKIN TOLD YOU THEY WERE GAY!'.

Duncan looked Dee Dee in the eye, 'And what about you me darlin?' he asked, winking provocatively, 'What floats your pretty litte boat?'.

'Folla me an ar show ya!' replied Dee Dee leaving her seat, 'Arm goin for a piss!' she told her friends before heading for the ladies. Duncan, seeing that his friends were preoccupied, watched by Trisha and Maizie, left the table moments later and made for the toilets himself. Looking around firtively he crept into the ladies and was instantly taken aback by the sight of Dee Dee sat in an open cubicle with her skirt and thong around her ankles,

'Ar really did need a piss!' she said over the sound of trickling water.

Duncan immediately turned away shielding his eyes 'Sorry i'll er!' he stammered 'I'll come back later!'

'Shut up!' Dee Dee said, 'Arm finished naah, get yer arse over ere!' she stood wiping herself then tossing the paper into the toilet, flushed it away and lifted one foot onto the pan with her back to the wall. Duncan stood rooted to the spot in abject disbelief 'Oy paddy!' Dee Dee said impatiently, 'D'you wanna shag or what!'. Duncan loosened his belt and hurried into the cubicle where he was grabbed and had Dee Dee's tongue forced into his mouth, kicking the cubicle door closed she grappled with his jeans, pushing them and his emerald green boxers down to his knees before sinking her manicured nails into his buttocks, Dee Dee pulled him towards her aggressively taking his manhood with ease.

Duncan was used to taking the lead when it came to fornication but on this occasion he found himself powerless as Dee Dee ground her hips into his, undoing his shirt and sinking her teeth into his hard nipples. 'JESUS GIRL!' he screamed 'I'M NOT INTO PAIN!'

'Shut it you fuckin lightweight!' Dee Dee snapped, her backside banging on the cubicle wall, 'And don't you even fink about blowin ya load yet i aint done!'.

Duncan was now merely a tool to be used for Dee Dee's insatiable pleasure, hanging on tightly whilst she grappled and groped him, 'Thas it, right there!' she said wrenching the toilet roll holder from the wall in the heat of passion. Suddenly the door opened and the pair heard footsteps outside, Duncan attempted to pull away but Dee Dee was about to climax and nothing was going to stop her.

Stop will ya!' Duncan whispered, attempting to break away 'Someone's comin!'

'Yeah me in a minute!' Dee Dee gasped, wrapping her leg around his waist and thrusting harder, 'Oooh fuck yeah!'.

The door to the adjacent cubicle opened and they heard a familiar voice, 'Is that you in there Dee?'

asked Maizie, she then hopped up onto the pan and peered over the top, 'Fuckin ell Dee!' she cried, looking down on the two of them, 'Woss e like, any good?'

'Ang on a minute Maize!' Dee Dee said, seconds before her shuddering orgasm. Duncan let out a shrill cry as Dee Dee's nails pierced his buttocks, he was then cast aside like a rodeo rider thrown from a bull. While Dee Dee stood panting slumped in the corner, 'Not bad mate!' she said, looking up at her friend, 'D'you wanna go!'.

Duncan quickly dressed himself and ran from the cubicle rubbing his bottom, 'I er, i gotta get back!' he said sheepishly. He turned and watched momentarily as Dee Dee stood wiping herself once again and Maizie with the door wide open also, hitched up her skirt and lowered herself onto the pan passing wind as she did so, which made the two girls howl with laughter,

'You dirty bitch Maize!' Dee Dee chuckled.

Maizie looked around her cubicle 'Oh fuck it!' she cursed, 'Dee you got any bog roll in there?'. Dee Dee joined Maizie next door handing her the roll complete with holder,

'Fuck me Maizie that proper pen and inks girl!' she said holding her nose, 'She's got a rotten arse aint she!' she said turning to Duncan, but the breathless blue eyed boy had seen enough and left in a hurry, scampering back to his friends who jeered him knowing full well what he'd been up to,

'Sit yaself down ya dirty fekker!' Jim said pulling out a chair.

'No, no i'll stand boys!' Duncan replied, his reddened rear now throbbing.

Dee Dee washed her hands and joined them back in the bar, ‘Right Willy boy, what we avin naah?’ she asked. his friends pushed him toward the bar
‘Yeah get em in ya toyt fook!’ Tyler joked, slapping him around the head.
Maizie returned moments later and sat at the table, ‘If ya need a piss Trish!’ she said to her friend, ‘Ar’d give it a minute or two if ar was you mate, ar just dropped a proper rotten log!’.
A further two hours of heavy drinking passed with the girls were faring rather better than their newfound irish friend's,
‘Jesus i’m wankered!’ Dougal said, rolling back in his seat. Willy in the meantime was slumped forward blowing bubbles in the spilt sambucca. The girls laughed as one by one the burly boys drifted in and out of consciousness, but then suddenly the doors flew open and in marched their furious foreman, ‘WHAT THE FEKKIN FEK DO YOU FEKKIN FEKKERS TINK YA DOIN?’ he barked, grabbing Duncan by the scruff of his neck, ‘LOOK AT THE FEKKIN STATE A YEEZ, YA LAZY DRUNKEN BASTARDS, GET THE FEK OUT THERE AND GET FEKKIN DIGGIN!’ HoistIng Willy and the others from their seats the red faced foreman manhandled them out the door, but the fresh air only made matters worse as the zombie like gang staggered toward the trench and one by one fell in landing in a giggling heap in the bottom with a heaving Willy straddling them.
‘Willy ya baaastard!’ Jim slurred as he and the others were showered with Willy’s stomach contents.
Their foreman stood glaring into the hole ‘YA NO GOOD USELESS SHOWER OF FEKKIN SHITE!’ he yelled, ‘YA FEKKIN SACKED, THE FEKKIN LOTTA

YEEZ!' he stormed back to his van and sped away leaving the boys reeling in the rancid trench unable to clamber out.

Dee Dee, Maizie and Trisha gathered up the discarded drinks and sat for a while reflecting on their day, 'Ahhhh they was nice weren't they!' Trisha said tasting a Guinness for the first time, 'Eeeya thas not bad that! try that Dee!'

Dee Dee took a sip and immediately spat it out, 'Ar'd rarva drink me own piss than that shit!' she said, sinking a sambucca to take away the taste.

Maizie tossed the small change from her pocket onto the table, 'So what are we gunna do for dough Dee, were proper potless remember!'

'Yeah!' said Trisha, 'And what about Magaloof!'

Dee Dee thought long and hard while her two friends reminisced about their spanish exploits, 'Will you two shut the fuck up about Magaloof!' she snapped, 'Ar'm tryna fink!' she then had an idea, 'Trish mate ow much was in the petty cash tin at work?' she asked. Trisha looked confused 'About sixty quid, why?' she replied.

'Thatta do for starters, come on drink up!' Dee Dee said, downing the last of the shots.

Trisha and Maizie looked at each other, bemused, 'What you on about Dee?' asked Trisha 'We've bin sacked remember, and the shops shut naah, iss arf seven for gawd sake!'.

Dee Dee took a bunch of keys from her bag, 'It don't matter ar still got a key to the back door ain i!'

'Dee we can't just go and nick it!' Trisha said, hesitantly 'We ain't burglar's!'

'We'll ave to Trish!' said Maizie, slinging her bag over her shoulder, 'We aint even got the blinkin bus fare ome!'.

Dee Dee dragged Trisha to her feet and thrust her handbag into her hands 'Come on, ow ard can it be!'. It was dark by now as the three inebriated girls tottered out into the near deserted high street,
'This way!' Dee Dee said, leading her friends to the service road that ran behind the stores, with few street lights to light their way they picked their way between the refuse bins and discarded boxes trying to distinguish which of the unmarked building was the Shooze store.
'Ar fink thas Primarni!' Maizie said straining her eyes 'And that must be Ann Summerz coz there's all the dildo boxes!'.
Dee Dee smiled, remembering where she'd left her rampant rabbit, 'Yeah thas right' she agreed 'There's the Carphone whatsit and that must be Greggs!'
'Oooh ar love their pasties, don't you Dee!' Trisha said, walking into a wheelie bin, 'Ow me bleedin foot!' she cried.
Dee Dee glared at her as Trisha hopped on the spot,
'For fuck sake Trish!' she whispered, 'Keep it daan will ya!' she then saw the rear entrance to Shooze with the bucket brimming with cigarette butts smoked during her frequent breaks. 'Ere we are!' she said, taking the keys from her bag. Huddled together, Trisha and Maizie watched as Dee Dee tried several keys in the lock, 'Ar can't see fuck all!' she said fumbling,'Woss the alarm number Maizie?'.
Maizie held her head trying to think while Trisha stood with her legs crossed,
'Oh urry up you two ar really need a piss naah! she moaned clenching her thighs tightly together and bobbing on the spot.
Maizie thought for a moment 'Is it four two free one or free four two one!' she mumbled.

'Oooooh!' Trisha squealed 'Come on!'.
Maizie took out her phone 'Shall ar ring Julie?' she asked.
Dee Dee snatched it from her hand, 'No for fuck sake!' she snapped 'What ya gonna say, oh hi Jules we're breakin into the shop can we av the code!'
'Oh yeah ar see what ya mean!' Maizie replied, 'Sorry!'. Dee Dee eventually found the right key and opened the door to the sound of the alarm beeping, 'Ar try bofe!' she said tapping in both sets of numbers until the beeping stopped,
Trisha then barged past her and ran into the toilet,
'Sorry ar'm bustin!' she cried slamming the door closed behind her.
'Keep ya fuckin noise daan!' Dee Dee called after her friend closing the rear door and she and Maizie crept into the staff room,
'There it is!' Dee Dee said, taking the petty cash tin down from a shelf.
Maizie could hardly contain herself 'Oooh this is exitin Dee, iss like oceans eleven, but wiv free of us, an iss a shoe shop not a casino and Brad Pitt aint ere, ar wish e was though e'z dead orny!'.
Dee Dee looked round at her friend 'What the fuck are you on about Maize?' she asked, then opening the tin the two of them peered in and both said simultaneously 'What the fuck!' Dee Dee took out a five pound note and a few coins 'Seven paand firty!' she gasped, 'Seven paand fuckin firty, OY TRISHA GET YOUR ARSE OUT ERE!'.
Trisha emerged moments later 'Thas betta, woss up Dee?' she asked, straightening her skirt.
'Woss up?' replied Dee Dee angrily, 'Ar fought you said there was sixty quid in ere!'

'There was this mornin!' Trisha replied 'But i ad to go out and get milk and tea bags, oh an ar borra'd a few quid to get Jordan's new book and a Take That cd, ar'm so glad Robbie's back aint you!'.

Dee Dee grabbed Trisha by the arm, 'Why didn't you tell me that ya stupid cow!' she growled,

Trisha pulled away 'Ar fought everyone new Robbie was back!' she replied, innocently.

Dee Dee threw her hands in the air and walked away,

'Maize, tell er to shut up before ar fuckin slap er good an ard!' she said, fuming, 'Seven paand firty, seven fuckin paand firty ar don't fuckin believe it!'.

While Dee Dee paced the room seething Trisha switched on the kettle, 'Wanna cuppa tea Dee?' she asked.

Dee Dee lunged at her hapless friend but Maizie leapt in the way, 'No ar don't wanna cuppa fuckin tea!' she yelled.

Maizie wrestled with her friend 'Dee leave er, you know what she's like!' she said ducking Dee Dee's flaying arms, 'She's fick as fuck!'.

Trisha attempted to defend herself, 'No i aint!' she replied, 'Ar got free C's an a B in maffs!'

Maizie turned and laughed 'You only got that coz you let Mr Pervis feel you up in detention!'

'Who, pervy Pervis?' Dee Dee added dropping her clenched fists 'That nonce text me a picture of iz nob once, the dirty git!'

'Really!' Maizie gasped, 'What did ya do!'

Dee Dee smiled 'Ar sent im a picture of me uncle Davey's pit bull chewin a pair of pants, ar fink e got the message!'. Dee Dee then noticed the stores safe tucked in the corner of the room, 'Old up you two,

ava look!' she smiled running her hand along the cold steel door 'Ar bet there's a few quid in ere!'
'How the ell we gonna get in that Dee!' Maizie scoffed 'We ain't tooled up and we ain even proper burglar's!'.
Dee Dee rummaged through the drawer beside her but only managed to find a plastic spoon and a stapler, 'Bloody Marvlus!' she grunted.
Maizie pointed at Trisha 'Are spose if silly bollocks adn't av spent all the petty cash we could've bought some plastic explosives or summink!' she laughed,
'Come on Dee let's get out of ere!'.
But Dee Dee was staring at the security camera in the corner facing the safe, 'Maize what day does Mr Sanjeef bank iz money?' she asked
'Fursday ar fink!' Maizie replied, 'Why?'
'E was ere on Friday' Dee Dee explained 'Ar see im stick a fist full of fifties in this bleedin fing so the doughs still in there, come on, elp me look for fridays tape!'
The girls thumbed through the many video cassettes beside them until Trisha plucked one out, 'Ar got it!' she said, looking pleased with herself, 'Friday the fird, that was our Billy's birfday, e'z free naah, ar got im a West am kit an a ride on tracta, the silly little sod went daan the stairs on it though an ed butted me muvva's enry oova, you wanna see im, e looks like e'z got an ard boiled egg on iz ed!'.
Dee Dee snatched the tape from her hand, 'What the fuck are you on about, just gimme that will ya!' she barked, shaking her head.
Turning on a portable tv Dee Dee popped the cassette into the recorder and the three watched as an image of the safe appeared.

'Can ya turn it over Dee!' Trisha asked 'X facta's on in a minute!'.
Dee Dee flew into a rage, 'TRISHA!' she yelled 'FUCK OFF AWAY FROM ME WILL YA!'.
Trisha hung her head and sat on the opposite side of the room swinging her legs, 'I only wanna see Louis creamin imself over Dermot, iss so obvious e want's to kick iz back door in!'.
Dee Dee and Maizie did there best to ignore her,
'Forward it a bit Dee!' Maizie said, watching the timer.
Dee Dee slowed the tape at the moment Julie entered the staff room followed by Mr Sanjeef, then watched in horror as Mr Sanjeef began groping his willing manageress, 'What the fuck!' Dee Dee gasped, 'Maize ava look!' They watched in disbelief as the randy retailer stripped Julie to her underwear before bending her over the safe.
'Eeeya Trish look!' Maizie said 'Mr Sanjeef's doin er doggy, the dirty fucker!'. The three girls watched the pornographic video showing the Bengali boss locked in the steamy embrace for nearly ten minutes with Julie occasionally reaching behind to slap his bare bottom,
'The dirty bitch loves it don't she!' Maizie laughed. When the pair had finished, Mr Sanjeef took out his wallet and handed a grateful Julie seventy five pounds,
'Fuckin ell, she's on the game!' Dee Dee gasped,
Julie composed herself and left the room while Mr Sanjeef pulled up his trousers and turned his attention to the safe.
'Ere we go!' said Dee Dee watching closely. They could clearly see the dial as the owner turned it to the right then left, Dee Dee mimicked his actions until to

there complete surprise, with a click the safe door swung open,
'Fuck me Dee, we did it!' Maizie squealed clasping her hands together. Inside amongst the files and folders were two piles of crisp fifty pound notes,
'Fuckin yes!' Dee Dee said, grabbing one and fanning the notes in front of her face. Maizie took the other and after hurriedly counting their loot, threw their hands in the air,
'Two an arf grand!' Dee Dee shrieked, 'We're proper fuckin minted!'.
Sharing the cash equally between them Dee Dee and the others wiped their fingerprints from the safe, took the video cassette showing them entering the room and left the shot of Mr Sanjeef mounting Julie paused on the screen.
'E won't report it!' Dee Dee said, smiling 'Not now e knows someone's seen im bangin that slag!'. Closing the door behind them the three delighted friends hurried from the scene and hopped onto the night bus, sitting at the back staring into their bulging purses.
'Ar'm gonna get botox an air extensions tomorra, an a new pair of straighteners,' said Maizie thumbing the notes.
'Arm gonna get vajazzled!' Trisha said, rubbing her crotch.
'What the fucks that?' asked Dee Dee.
'Iss the latest fing!' Trisha replied, 'They shave ya bits bald and stick little crystals all raand it!'.
Dee Dee roared with laughter 'Ar spose they ang a bleedin chandelier out ya arse an'all!'. They rode the rest of the way home elated with their achievement, planning to hit the shops the very next morning to splash their ill gotten gains.

Maizie and Trisha got off a stop before Dee Dee, 'We'll meet you in KFC about arf nine!' Maizie called from the bus stop as the pair waved Dee Dee goodbye.
Looking up at the squalid tenement that had been her home for as long as she could remember, Dee Dee sighed, wondering if she'd ever escape such a place or one day die in poverty like so many of it's previous occupants. Climbing the stairs to the sound of barking dogs and screaming babies Dee Dee had to step aside quickly as a man sped down past her, his raging wife leaning over the handrail above with a bawling babe in arms,
'GO ON FUCK OFF BACK TO ER YOU USELESS CUNT!' she screamed at her cheating hubby, 'AR DON'T FUCKIN WANCHA!'.
Letting herself into her flat Dee Dee peered into the darkened living room, just making out the figure of her mother slumped in an arm chair with several empty cans at her feet. Taking a large coat from a hook on the door she covered her snoring mother, running her fingers through her hair remembering the days when Pearl was once a vibrant beauty with everything to live for.

CHAPTER TWO.

The Plan.

The next morning Dee Dee was woken by the sound of raised voices, donning her pink track suit she gingerly stepped out into the hall to investigate,
'Ar can't pay ya, i aint got no money!' Pearl could be heard explaining to a beefy bailiff who, with his foot firmly wedged in the open door was having none of it.
'Well madam!' the man replied, showing her the court order on his clipboard 'I'm authorized to removed goods from the property to help settle your debt, it's right here in black and white so if you'll kindly let me in!'.
Pearl was frantic, 'Ar can pay ya next week when ar get me disability!' she begged, but to no avail.
'I'm sorry madam!' the bailiff insisted 'I have to have something from you today, now can i come in and take a look around!'. Pearl had no choice but to let him in, but within moments of entering the dilapidated flat it soon became evident to the debt collector that what little possessions she did have were of no value at all. The television had three buttons missing and her furniture was some twenty years old.
'Oy ar got summink for ya!' Dee Dee called out, 'Leave it to me mum, ar'll sort it!'
'You sure love!' Pearl replied before opening another can 'Ar pay ya back love, honest ar will!'.
The bailiff, asuming that Dee Dee may possess a valuable stereo system or flat screen tv made his way to her room, but once inside and having had the door closed behind him he looked around in disgust,
'There's nothing here to interest me!' he said, turning to leave.
Dee Dee blocked his path 'What about an and job?' she asked guesturing with her wrist,

'Do what?' the bailiff asked taken aback by Dee Dee's brash remark at first, but looked her up and down all the same, and then at his watch, it wouldn't be the first time he had been offered and subsequently taken up sexual favor's as part payment on a debt. 'Yeah go on then!' he said, putting his briefcase down, dropping his trousers and sitting on the end of the bed. Dee Dee sat beside him, rolled up her sleeve and got to work, causing the bailiff to moan and tense with pleasure, after several minutes of vigorous hand work he eventually cried out and ejaculated over Dee Dee's hand,

'Where's the bathroom?' he said, leaping to his feet and tugging athis trousers.

'First on the left!' Dee Dee replied, watching him scurry from her room. Looking round for a tissue Dee Dee noticed the man's lunchbox tucked inside his open case, with a devilish grin she removed it and popped open the Tupperware lid. She took out one of the ham sandwiches inside and wiped the residue from her hand across the whole meal bread before returning it.

The bailiff returned looking a little flushed, picked up his case and left in a hurry, 'I want the money next week!' he called out, 'Or you'll both be out on your ear!'.

Dee Dee joined her mother in the lounge,

'What d'ya give im Dee?' Pearl asked, swigging her cider.

'A taste of iz own medicine!' Dee Dee chuckled.

Pearl set down her can and took her daughters hand 'Fanks love!' she said forlornly 'ar'm sicka livin like this, no wonder ya dad buggered off and left us!'.

Dee Dee dropped down on one knee beside her mother 'Mum, dad left us coz e'z a no good twat!' she

said, stroking her hand, 'Thingsa be different one day, you wait and see, ar get us out of ere!'. she then took a hundred pounds from her pocket and thrust it into her mothers hand, 'Eeya, get yaself summink nice mum!'.
Pearl looked at the money as though it were thousands, 'Blimey Dee ar can't take that from ya love, ar get me benefits next week, ar be alright!'.
'You take it mum!' Dee Dee replied, getting up to leave, 'Just don't spend it all on booze though, get yourself a new coat itta be winter soon and you know how ya feel the cold!'.
Pearl stooped for her can and took another sip and popped the cash into her cardigan pocket, 'Well there is a nice one in the charity shop, iss only got one button missin!'
'No mum, get yaself a new one!' Dee Dee pleaded, 'When was the last time you bought yaself sumink new?'.
Pearl thought long and hard looking round the room, 'Ar bought that picture from the paand shop, nice ain it!' she pointed to a tacky print of two kittens in a flower pot, 'Oh and a new bog brush set for the loo, iss green so it matches the pan!'.
Dee Dee shook her head in despair and headed for the bathroom to freshen up.
Meanwhile the bailiff had climbed into his car where his boss, Derek was waiting, 'D'you get the money?' Derek asked, then seeing the bailiffs expression added 'You didn't get it did ya, your too bleedin soft that's your trouble, i'll go next time and if they haven't got it i'll drag em out into the street and sling all their shit out as well!'.
Derek was a nasty piece of work, having evicted dozens of poverty stricken families without batting

and eye 'Lunch time' he said checking his watch 'Fank fuck i'm starving!'.
His colleague, eager to win back his bosses approval took out his lunchbox, 'Here have one of these!' he said, opening the box.
'Don't mind if i do, cheers' Derek replied, taking out the soiled sandwich and taking a large bite, 'Mmmm!' he mumbled wiping the semen from the corner of his mouth, 'Very nice, the hams a little salty but apart from that their spot on!'.
'Seeya mum!' Dee Dee said, popping her head into the living room in passing,
'Tadaa love!' replied pearl, waving from her chair, 'Av a nice day, where ya goin, anywhere nice?'
'Ar'm gunna meet Trish and Maizie up taan!' Dee Dee said, heading for the door.
'Give em mar love won't ya!' Pearl called after her whilst delving into a packet of sherbert lemons.
Leaving the block Dee Dee suddenly noticed her father crossing the car park and heading her way, 'Oh fuck!' she said, changing direction and pulling her hood up over her head,
'Dee there you are love, ar was oping ar'd run into ya!' he said stepping in Dee Dee's path, 'Ow are ya babe?'.
Dee Dee tried to side step him and carry on with her head down but he took hold of her arm,
'Dee babe just ang on a minute will ya!' he pleaded, 'Ar know ya mad at me and all that but ar bin worried about ya, are you alright, and ow's ya mum?'.
Dee Dee pulled away, wrenched her hood from her head and looked him in the eye, 'WHAT IS THIS?' she yelled, 'You don't give a toss about me or me mum, if you must know you wrecked er fuckin life and

mine, we don't want nuffin to do wiv ya, now get outta mar way ya prick!'
Her father attempted to hug her but Dee Dee shoved him aside,
'DON'T TOUCH ME!' she screamed, 'DON'T FUCKIN TOUCH ME!'.
In an attempt to coerce his daughter Dee Dee's estranged father reached into his pocket and produced a number of ten pound notes, 'Eeya take this Dee!' he said thrusting them toward her hand, 'Get yaself summink nice!'. Dee Dee looked down at the money, cleared her throat and spat into his open hand then barged past him and fled towards the bus stop.
'DEE! BABE DON'T BE LIKE THIS!' he called after her, shaking the spit from his hand,'DEE AR STILL LOVE YA BABE!'.
'FUCK OFF AND DIE!' Dee Dee called back before hopping onto a waiting bus and making her way to the rear, her mortified father stood looking in her direction,
'Tosser!' she said to herself before turning away and dropping into a seat.
Maizie and Trisha were already seated in KFC tucking into chicken nuggets and slurping on milkshakes when Dee Dee arrived, 'Where ya bin Dee?' Trisha asked, pulling a seat out for her friend, 'Me and Maize av bin ere ages!'.
'We ad the bailiff bangin on the bleedin door again this mornin!' Dee Dee replied,
'Oh no!' Maizie gasped 'What appened?'.
Dee Dee looked at her hand and smiled, 'ar sorted im out, ar just ope e likes mayo!'
Trisha and Maizie looked confused, 'What you on about Dee?' asked Trisha.

'Never mind!' Dee Dee replied beckoning to her friends who leaned closer, 'Listen ar bin finkin, fuck workin for a poxy minimum wage, we need to earn some serious dough, and after last nights caper ar reckon we could do it again, only next time bigger, a bank or summink!'.

Trisha and Maizie sat speechless for a moment, 'A bank!' Maizie finally gasped, 'Fuckin ell Dee thas a bit strong ain it!'

'Yeah Dee!' Trisha added, finishing her shake noisily, 'We aint even propa robbers!'

'Listen you two!' Dee Dee snapped, 'ar'm gonna do it wiv or wivout ya, ar'm sicka livin like a rat in a fuckin cage, ar want the good life an ar don't care what i av to do to get it so your eeva wiv me or you aint!'

'She's right Trish!' Maizie agreed, 'What we got to lose, ar'm in Dee, besides ar've decided ar wanna live like Paris ilton and get me wunna them little am bag dogs!'.

Trisha was a little more hesitant, 'Yeah but what if we get caught?' she asked, 'We could get banged up in Olloway wiv all them rug munchin lezzer's!'

'Ar don't give a fuck!' said Dee Dee 'We ain't gonna get caught though, if we're careful, iss all in the plannin, ar'm gunna go and see black Mickey in Pentonville lata, e'z the biggest feef ar know, e'll elp us, e owes me a favour, now ar you'z two in or what?'.

Trisha relented and nodded her head, 'Yeah ok Dee ar'm up for it, but i aint avin no mutt crappin in mar bag, iss Gucci!' she proudly held up her leopard print handbag.

'Gucci my arse!' Dee Dee laughed 'Thas a snide!'

'No it aint!' Trisha replied, clutching it to her chest, 'Me ex bought it for me!'.

'Well for a start!' Dee Dee pointed out 'Gucci aint spelt wiv two O's and a Y!'
Trisha looked closely at her bag which did in fact have the word 'Goochy' in gold letters on it. 'You sure?' she asked, 'E said it cost im free undred quid!'
Dee Dee and Maizie both burst out laughing, 'Fuck me Trish!' Maizie chuckled, 'Ar fought you was fick mate but thas takin the piss!'.
Trisha looked despondent 'Bleedin ell, ar let im shag me in the back of iz transit for this an'all, it done mar back in layin on that poxy plasterboard!'.
Dee Dee couldn't stop laughing, 'Fuckin ell Trish you crack me up!' she said, holding her stomach, 'Ar don't wanna know what you ad to do for ya dodgy Jimmy Choo's!'.
Trisha looked down at her feet, 'Don't tell me they're fake an'all!' she cried, 'Ar'll bleedin kill im when ar see im!'.
Dee Dee helped herself to Trisha's chicken nuggets while she scrutinized her footwear, 'Right listen!' she said, fanning her mouth 'We're gonna need a mota but none of us can drive, ar mean we carn exactly leg it out of a bank wiv a bag full of cash, all the fuckin alarms goin off then wait for the bleedin bus can we!'.
Trisha put her hand up as though at school, 'Ar know Dee!' she said excitedly, 'We could get a cab!'.
Dee Dee and Maizie looked at their dim witted friend in disbelief, 'A cab!' said Maizie, 'Are you sure?'.
Dee Dee put her head in her hands, 'Trish mate, if we left it to you we'd all be big Mamma's bitches at Olloway in no time!'.
'Me bruvver's got a mota!' Maizie said, turning to Dee Dee, 'E's only just passed iz test but e'z bin drivin for years, e won't say anyfing neeva coz e knows ar'll

beat the shit out of im, me and Trish can go and see im while your up the nick!'.
'Right thas sorted then!' Dee Dee said, taking out her wad of notes, 'Less go and flash some cash!'.
Leaving the fast food restaurant the girls first saw Mr Sanjeef sprinting from his shoe store being pursued by a furious Mrs Sanjeef wielding a video cassette above her head, 'You dirty bastard!' she screamed, her sari flowing behind her, 'I'll make baji's from your bollocks if i catch you!'. Julie then crept gingerly from the store and hurried off in the opposite direction.
'Ooh err!' Dee Dee laughed 'Ar don't reckon she fought much of iz bollywood blockbuster!'.
'Looks like Julie's is out of a job an'all!' Maizie remarked, 'Serve's er right the dirty bitch!'.
The girls spent the next couple of hours in and out of every boutique in the High street trying on clothes they never could have afforded before, emerging laden with brightly colored bags,
'Ar could get used to this Dee!' Maizie said with the broadest of smiles, 'Ar feel like a bleedin millyonair!'
'Can we go in ere?' Trisha said, standing outside an adult store, 'Ar gotta get meself some new naughty knickers, i ad a coupla pairs of them edible likrish ones, me ex said it was like going daan on Bertie basset!'.
Dee Dee and Maizie followed her inside, gawping at the size and shape of the numerous sex toys on offer, 'Fuck me Trish, looka that!' Dee Dee said, stroking a lengthy black dildo, 'Iss like an orses cock!'
'Woss this for?' Maizie asked, toying with a short rubber object.
'Iss a plug!' Dee Dee replied, picking up another.
'What! for the bath?' Maizie said examining it closely.

'No stupid, for yer arse!' Dee Dee laughed, 'Iss a bleedin butt plug!'.
Maizie screwed up her face tossing the toy back onto the counter, 'Oooh thas disgustin!' she said, wiping her hand.
Trisha had disappeared to the rear of the shop where she thumbed through the rails of revealing lingerie,
'What'dya fink of this Dee?' she called out, holding a lurid latex leotard in front of her with holes cut in various places, 'Ar quite like a bitta rubber!'.
'Ar wouldn't if ar was you!' Dee Dee replied, 'Apart from you sweating like a pig, when e'z givin you one, it'll sound like a clown tryna make a poodle outta two balloons!'.
Trisha returned the garment in favour of a lacy basque and fishnet tights, 'Thissa do!' she said, heading for the checkout.
Meanwhile Dee Dee had caught sight of the holy grail of vibrators 'The G 1000' a nine inch nickel plated love toy, so named because of it's reputation for hitting the G spot at a staggering one thousand RPM and boasting nought to orgasm in less than a minute. With five speed settings, forward and reverse gears and a built in LED flashlight this titanic toy was at the top of every wanton woman's wish list, and as her previous vibrator was having to be surgically removed from the bouncers bottom, Dee Dee had to have it.
'Blimey Dee!' Maizie gasped, 'The neighbours'll fink your being rodgered wiv a road drill!'. The giggling girls left the store and walked the short distance to the taxi rank.
Dropping Maizie and Trisha off first, Dee Dee leaned out of the window, 'Don't forget to see ya bruvva!' she called after them, 'The Bircham estate please

mate!' she then told the driver, who raised his eyebrows at the mention of thisnotorious no go area, 'I'll drop you at the end of the road!' he said, daring not to go any further, the Bircham boys had been known to clamber all over a car like baboons at a safari park wrenching off wiper blades and wing mirrors.

Dropping her bags in her room Dee Dee made her way into the kitchen, 'What we got to eat muvva ar'm starvin?' she called through to the lounge where her mother sat in an intoxicated stupor,

'Av a look in the fridge love!' Pearl replied, kicking the empty cans from around her feet.

Dee Dee took a box from the top shelf, 'Ar do meself a burger in the George Formby alright mum!'

Pearl scrambled to her feet 'OH ANG ON!' she yelled, but before she made it to the kitchen Dee Dee lifted the lid on the portable grill and stepped back in shock, 'What the fuck!' she gasped, 'MUVVA!'. Inside the grill were a steaming pair of threadbare knickers,

Sorry love!' Pearl said, removing them, 'Ar was dryin out me gusset, the eatin's on the blink again!'.

Dee Dee then noticed her mothers socks draped over the toaster 'Bleedin ell muvva' she sneered 'This ain exactly igenic is it!'.she tossed the box of the burgers back into the fridge.

'Ar do you a sandwich love!' Pearl said taking out the cheese.

'No fanks mum!' Dee Dee replied, opening a packet of crisps, 'Ya'v probly got ya bleedin bra in the bread bin!'

'No i aint Dee!' her mother replied, pointing at the oven 'Thas on a bakin tin wiv me gammon rashers!'.

Dee Dee threw the remainder of her crisps into the pedal bin in disgust and left the kitchen, 'Ar get

sumink out later!' she said, leaving her mother placing another pair of soggy knickers under the grill and closing the lid.
Meanwhile Trisha and Maizie were sat in Maizie's bedroom with their new clothes strewn around them and the deafening sound of drum and bass music coming from the next room. It was Maizie's brother Bradley, spinning his decks and beat boxing badly into his microphone.
'Come on Trish!' Maizie said, leaving her room 'less go an av a word wiv Brad!'. The pair stood outside his room with their ears pressed to the door listening to the wannabe rapper and laughing into their hands,

'I aint J zee and i aint no Fiddy
I aint no Dappy and i aint P Diddy,
My name spells danger, i'm like the lone ranger
listen to my lirics, coz there gettin stranger,
i strive for the riches, livin on the street
dreamin of the bitch's that i just wont meet,
Britney baby listen when i say i miss you
all i got now is my dick and a tissue
my dick, my dick, my dick and a tissue'

Opening her brothers bedroom door Maizie was shocked to see him grabbing at his crotch, standing in just his baggy boxers, a heavy gold chain around his neck and a cap tipped to one side, 'What the fuck?' she laughed.
'Fuckin ell sis!' Bradley shrieked, dropping his headphones around his neck and covering his crotch with a porn magazine, then realizing what he had in his hand covered that with a copy of his favorite motoring weekly, his walls were adorned with posters of semi naked girls draped over the bonnets of hot

hatchbacks or wetting one another's t shirts with hoses whilst washing and waxing. 'Get out will ya!' he said, kicking a copy of 'Bums n Boobs' under his bed.
'We wanna word wiv Ya' Maizie said, sitting on the end of his bed, then hearing a cracking sound reached under her bottom and produced a broken bong, 'Ooops!' she said, 'Sorry bruv!'
'Oh nice one sis!' Bradley snapped, taking the two pieces from her, 'Thas proper fucked now innit!', Bradley always said he was a black man trapped in a white body, idolizing gangster rappers and dreaming one day of owning his own Beverly hills crib with a gleaming Hummer parked outside.
'Me Trish and Dee need a driver bruv!' Maizie explained 'And your the only one wiv a mota!'. Bradley's pride and joy was a ten year old white Vauxhall Nova that he was gradually restoring and adding a few extravagant sporty features, nitro injectors, bucket seats, a rear spoiler and a neon light underneath to name but a few.
'You mean the 'Supernova' sis?' Bradley proudly replied, 'Dat cars so phat man, me and me bredrin Jase are fittin a bangin bass box in the boot at the weekend!'.
Maizie and Trisha had trouble deciphering Bradley's urban speak, 'Look bruv!' Maizie proceeded to explain, 'Us free yeah, we're gonna do a few jobs that aint exactly legal if you know what are mean!'. Bradley smiled and tried to click his fingers together,
'You'z gonna be ho's thas wicked man!' he said excitedly, 'Yeah ar don't mind pimpin your booty, you'll av to give me some petrol money though coz me'z don't get me jobseekers till friday!'.

'We aint goin on the game ya twat!' Maizie said, throwing a pillow at Bradley, 'We're gunna rob a few places, banks, jewellers an all that!'

Bradley burst out laughing, 'You'z free girls!' he chuckled, 'Dat's da funniest ting me heard all day blud, You'z aint gonna be no robbers, look at you'z man, you'z like barbie dolls innit!'.

Maizie tossed a handful or receipts onto the bed from her earlier shopping spree, 'We bought all that lot today!' she told Bradley, 'Wiv the dough we nicked last night, two an arf grand bruv'.

Bradley binned the broken bong and thumbed the receipts 'You'z robbed Two an arf grand, fuckin ell sis!'

'Yeah!' said Trisha waving the remainder of her cash 'And we're gunna rob a shit load more an'all!'

'You can av ten percent of whatever we nick!' Maizie added, 'All you gotta do is drive us around, but if you aint intrested ar find someone else!'. The two girls got up to leave.

'Woah woah, ang on sis!' Bradley said, imagining what he could do to his beloved car with the extra cash. 'Maybe i'z could take you round in me ride, me leave de babylon standin man when me puts me boot to de floor!'.

Trisha shook her head, 'Woss e on about Maize?' she asked.

'I aint got a bleedin scooby Trish' Maizie laughed 'Iss like talkin to a flippin alien arf the time' she then looked across at Bradley's decks, 'Woss all that Dappy Diddy shit about anyway bruv!'.

Bradley donned his headphones and began scratching and mixing, 'AR WANNA BE ON BRITAIN'S GOT TALINT INNIT!' he yelled over the

hip hop beats. 'AR COULD BE THE NEXT DIZZY RASCAL'
'Dozy bastard more like!' Maizie said to Trisha as they turned to leave,
'Woss that sis?' Bradley asked, exposing an ear
'Nuffin!' Maizie replied Pushing Trisha out of the door 'Just keep ya phone on, we'll bell ya when we need ya!'. The two girls left Bradley jerking from side to side puffing and popping into his microphone and grabbing at his crotch.

CHAPTER THREE.

Tooled up.

'Gissa fag muvva!' Dee Dee asked on her way out 'Ar'm gaspin!'
Pearl held a crumpled packet in her shaky hand, 'Eeya love, and take one for lata!' she said, coughing into her opposite hand 'Thas a nice top is it new?' she added, looking Dee Dee up and down, 'Oh ar do like them boots an'all, they're lovely they are!'.
Dee Dee spun on her heels, 'Fanks mum, ar got meself some new clobber up the igh street, ar'm off out again, ar see ya lata!'

'Ok, bye love!' Pearl replied, rummaging down the side of her chair for a discarded toffee.
After changing busses twice Dee Dee finally got off at the Caledonian road and walked the short distance to Her Majesty's prison Pentonville, arriving just in time as the queue of visitors began filing through the fortified gates.
'NAME!' a guard said sternly as Dee Dee reached the desk.
'Dee Dee!' she replied, 'Oh ar mean Debra, Debra Dawson!'
'The prisoner's name Miss!' the guard barked.
'Oh yeah!' Dee Dee said, a little unnerved by his tone, 'Er, Black Mickey!'
The guard took off his glasses and glared at Dee Dee, 'Black Mickey!' he snapped, 'Black Mickey, do you know how many Prisoners by the name of Michael of Afro Caribbean descent we currently have in this Prison!'. Dee Dee shook her head. 'I'll tell you shall i!' he continued, tapping at his computer. 'Here we are, thirty four, so if you could elaborate a little i'd be extremely grateful, what's this Black Mickey in for?'
'Shittin on a Tottenham coach!' Dee Dee replied.
The guard smiled and tapped at his keyboard once again 'You mean Mickey Spencer, one of our more frequent visitors, he's quite the celebrity with the West Ham boys in here after that little turn out, ok and your Miss Deborah Dawson, sign here and follow the others to the end of the corridor!'.
Dee Dee was led to the visitors room and seated at a table,
'Wait here miss!' another guard told her, 'We'll let the prisoner your here!'.

Mickey Spencer, a six foot Rastafarian with a thin gaunt face and a marijuana leaf tattoo'd on his neck was lying on his bunk reading Nelson Mandella's autobiography, feeling more and more angry and oppressed with every page.

'Spencer you got a visitor!' a guard said, tapping the cell bars with his night stick,

'Fuck you man!' Mickey replied angrily 'You don't own me!'

'Look do you want this visitation or not Spencer?' replied the now irate guard, 'Or shall i leave you on lock down!'.

'Who is it?' Mickey asked, 'Is it me mum wiv me curried goat?'.

The guard opened Mickey's cell door, 'Quite frankly Spencer!' he said angrily 'I don't give a shit if it's your sister with an ard boiled dog, just get your scrawny arse down to the visitors room!'

Mickey followed the guard along the landing singing a rousing anti oppression song at the top of his voice 'THE HIGHER YOU BUILD YOUR BARRIERRRRS, THE TALLER I BECOME!'

'Shut it Spencer!' growled the guard, brandishing his stick.

Mickey barged past him and carried on singing, 'SOMETHING INSIIIIDE SO STRONG!'.

'Ello Mickey!' Dee Dee said as he dropped into the seat opposite 'Ow ya doin?'

'Blimey Dee ar didn't expect to see you!' Mickey said, rocking back 'Ar fought it was me mum man! how you doin anyway, hows your mum?'. Mickey was an old friend of Dee Dee's family having stayed with them for several years when he was younger while his mother received treatment for her methadone addiction.

'Still on the piss Mickey!' she replied. Just then a large bald man visiting the prisoner on the next table put his fist in the air, a hammers tattoo clearly visible on his forearm,

'Oy Mickey mate!' he yelled, 'Fuckin respect man, your the bollocks ar tell ya, they're singin about you on the terraces at Upton Park, your a legend Geez!'

'Cheers man!' Mickey said, a life long West Ham fan himself, he then leaned across the table and planted a kiss on Dee Dee's cheek, but then felt a guards stick digging into his ribs,

'No contact Spencer, you know the rules!' the guard said menacingly.

Micky slumped back into his chair giving the guard a defiant finger 'Iss nice to see you babe!' he told Dee Dee, 'But what you doing coming to a place like this?'.

'Ar need yer elp!' Dee Dee said, leaning forward and lowering her voice, 'Me and me mates wanna do some robbery's' a smile crept across Mickeys face,

'Don't laugh Mick ar'm serious!' Dee Dee said, looking over her shoulder at the guard, 'We done one last night and got Two an arf grand, we wanna do some more, wiv your elp that is, ar need to earn some serious dough Mick, the council's gonna kick us out the flat soon, eever that or mum's gonna drink erself to deff!'. Having a soft spot for the family, Mickey eventually agreed to hear Dee Dee out,

'Listen Dee!' he said finally, 'Ar'm gonna go down for six years, the old bill planted a kilo of coke at my place coz they was supposed to be guarding Tottenham's coach and ar made em look like pricks!'.

'Bastards!' Dee Dee gasped.

'One bastard in particular Dee!' Mickey explained 'Detective inspector Pritcher, Jack Pritcher, remember that name, he's a slippery bastard man!'

Micky told Dee Dee how the D I had a personal vendetta against him ever since he was a young boy, stopping him in the street at every opportunity and subjecting him to humiliating searches. Mickey was no choir boy though, he'd stolen just about everything that could be stolen in the east end of London, cash, cars and gems. known for his love of big American cars, Mickey would turn heads wherever he went in his beloved powder blue nineteen fifties Cadillac, that is until D I Pritcher had it crushed leaving Mickey heart broken and vowing to get even one day. 'You know where mar sister Marcie lives don't ya Dee!' Mickey whispered.

'Yeah are fink so!' Dee Dee replied, 'Is she still in Seven Kings, raand the corner from the lybry?'

'Thas it!' Mickey nodded, 'Number seventeen, above the kebab shop, Go see her Dee and tell her to give you mar bag from the loft, apart from all mar blaggin tools, there's a note book with dates and times of security van drop offs, addresses of banks and building society's with shit security, it's all in there Dee, don't lose it and please be careful, after your first blag Pritcher will be on your case so you gotta stay one step ahead of the slag, oh and one other thing Dee, promise me you won't go south of the river, me and Billy Tibbs and his Bermondsey firm have got an agreement to stay out of eachuvver's manor!'.

Dee Dee agreed 'Fanks Mickey' she smiled watching the other visitor's filing from the room 'Ar be in touch babe'

'Come on Spencer back to your cell!' the guard behind Mickey barked.
'Later'z Dee!' Mickey said, leaving the table, he was then led from the room singing at the top of his voice once more 'THE MORE YOU REFUSE TO HEAR MY VOICE, THE LOUDER I BECOME!'. Dee Dee smiled, waved and left with the others.
Once outside Dee Dee telephoned her two friends and arranged to meet at hers that evening before hopping onto a bus bound for Seven Kings.
Some thirty minutes or so later Dee Dee alighted outside the library, and turning the corner she looked up at the row of flats above the shops 'Seventeen' she said to herself standing outside the kebab shop. Dee Dee rang the bell on an adjacent door and waited, a moment or two later a voice on the intercom asked, 'Who is it?'.
Dee Dee moved closer, 'Iss me Marcie, Dee Dee!' she replied, 'Mickey sent me!'.
There was silence for a few more moments before Marcie replied in a nervous tone 'Hi Dee, er look iss a really bad time right now, can you come back tomorrow or something babe!'.
Dee Dee was a little frustrated at Marcie's response having come so far, 'Ar won't be long Marcie mate!' she said, 'iss really important, please hun' she looked up and saw the curtains above twitching,
'MARCE MATE!' she yelled up at the window, 'IT IS IMPORTANT!'. After a minute or two Dee Dee heard footsteps descending the stairs inside and the door opened just enough for Marcie to peer round,
'Ar told ya iss a really bad time Dee!' she said, 'You'll have to go!' she glanced nervously along the road.
It was obvious to Dee Dee that she'd been crying and a bruise was beginning to appear below her left eye,

'Woss a matter Marcie mate ?' she asked, 'Who done that?'.

'It don't matter Dee' Marcie replied, physically shaking, 'Please mate you better go!'.

But Dee Dee was having none of it, pushing the door open she barged past her petrified friend and stormed up the stairs to the flat above, 'Who was it, who it ya?' she growled, clenching her fists.

Marcie looked along the street once more before closing the door and scurrying after Dee Dee. 'Iss alright Dee iss nuffing onest' she said, following Dee Dee into the lounge which had been ransacked, the television was on it's side on the floor surrounded by broken glass and picture frames,

'Don't look like nuffin to me!' Dee Dee replied, picking up the pieces of a smashed vase, 'Ar reckon some arseole's done this to ya, now who was it Marcie, eh?'.

Marcie had no choice but to tell her, 'Iss me boyfriend Kelvin, he drinks ya see, he's a nice guy when he's sober, but when he's drunk!'.

'E'z a proppa arseole!' Dee Dee said interrupting her.

'Well yeah!' Marcie replied, looking out of the window with trepidation, 'You better go Dee, he's only nipped out for some more beer!'. But it was too late, the pair of them heard a key being turned in the lock downstairs and then the door slam shut.

'WOMAN!' Kelvin yelled, 'GET IN THE FUCKING KITCHEN AND DO ME A PIZZA, AND GET ME SOME NUTS AN'ALL!'

Marcie stood petrified in the corner of the room, unable to speak.

'Leave this prick to me!' Dee Dee said stepping out onto the landing just as Kelvin reached the top of the stairs.

'WHAT THE!' he gasped, 'WHO?'.
Before he could finish Dee Dee grabbed him by the throat, 'You wanna fuckin nut!' she snarled, 'Ar got a fuckin nut for ya you slag!'. Dee Dee butted the startled drunk as hard as she could on the bridge of his nose and because he had a carrier bag full of beer in each hand he was unable stop himself falling backwards and tumbling heavily to the bottom of the stairs, his head colliding firmly with the front door. Dee Dee sprinted down after him and put the heel of her boot onto his throat, 'You listen to me you fuckin low life!' she growled as Kelvin nursed his bloody head, 'You betta fuck off and don't even fink about coming back!'
'ALRIGHT!' Kelvin nodded, assuming Dee Dee must be psychotic. 'Let me get me beers' he said gathering up his cans before ducking out of the door, but once out in the street he felt a little braver,
'AR'LL BE BACK YOU BITCH!' he shouted up at at a frightened Marcie, 'AR GOT A FUCKIN KEY INNIT!'. but as he pulled the key from his pocket a plastic bag containing a large quantity of heroin came out with it and dropped to the pavement, this was seen by two policemen who were dealing with a minor traffic incident in the road beside him,
'Shit!' Kelvin said, scrambling at his feet, then seeing the approaching officers attempted to make his escape, but in his drunken state he was no match for the policemen and was soon apprehended and cuffed
'Arll av that Key you ponce!' Dee Dee said snatching it from his hand as he struggled to break free. 'You can add assault to this slag's offences she told the arresting officers, she then looked Kelvin in the eye, 'Thas right you prick' she smiled 'She will be pressing

charges, see you in twenny years ya fuckin loser!'. Kelvin was bundled into a squad car and driven away from the scene at high speed. The polices zero tolerance stance against heroin meant that kelvin was looking at a minimum of fifteen years for his sizable stash and with an additional assault charge Dee Dee's estimation of twenty years wasn't far astray.

Closing the door behind her Dee Dee skipped up the stairs grinning, 'That tossa won't be givin you any more grief!' she told Marcie who threw her arms around her, sobbing uncontrollably.

'Thank you Dee, are really mean it babe!' she blubbed, 'Ar'v been a prisoner in here for the past three weeks!'.

Dee Dee went through to the kitchen, 'Come on Marcie ar make you a nice cup of tea!'. she said, putting on the kettle. The two girls sat and chatted, with Dee Dee repeatedly reassuring her friend that everything would be ok and that Kelvin was gone for good, she then helped straighten the room, vacuuming the broken glass and replacing the scattered sofa cushions 'Ar bin to see Mickey today' she explained.

'Oh how is he?' Marcie asked, 'I hate it when he goes inside, he's always looks after me ya see, since dad died!'.

'He's alright babe!' Dee Dee replied, 'You know ya bruvva, a bitta bird never bovvered im'

'I hope he's not in long this time Dee!' Marcie said, taking Dee Dee's hand, 'I feel so much safer when he's around!'.

'I er, ar need to get iz bag out the loft!' Dee Dee said, looking out into the hall, 'Is there a ladder or summink?'.

Marcie got a stick from behind the door and lowered the loft hatch, 'Yeah Dee just pull it down!' she told her 'There's a light on the left next to the Christmas tree'

Dee Dee scrambled up into the loft banging her head on one of the low beams, 'Fuck, fuck, fuck shit, fuck it!' she cursed, rubbing her forehead.

'You ok Dee?' Marcie asked at the foot of the ladder.

'Yeah!' replied Dee Dee, turning on the light, 'Ar just banged me bleedin nut thas all!'. Rummaging around amongst the boxes of decorations and redundant kitchen gadgets Dee Dee came across a large black holdall, 'Bingo!' she said, sliding open the zip, there inside was an array of lock picking equipment, balaclava's, crow bars and maps and as promised, the all important notebook which she quickly thumbed through. Sure enough, contained within the book were addresses of vulnerable banks, building societies and jewellers.

'You got it Dee love?' Marcie asked.

'Yeah!' Dee Dee replied, turning to leave, but then something caught her eye, a cloth bag about half a meter long jutting out from beneath the loft insulation. Pulling out the bag Dee Dee untied a strap around it and gasped on opening it, inside was a sawn off twin barreled shotgun, 'Fuck me!' she said, brandishing it 'Now we're talkin!'.

Dee Dee, balancing on the timber joists, held the gun as any would be robber would, 'Give us ya fuckin money!' she said, aggressively, but suddenly she lost her balance and her right foot slipped from the narrow beam and went crashing through the bathroom ceiling, at the same time Dee Dee's finger tightened on the trigger and to her horror the gun went off with a deafening bang, blasting a gaping

hole in the roof tiles, 'FUCK!' she screamed, he ears ringing and her leg dangling.through the broken plastered ceiling, her boot had fallen to the floor below revealing her stained right foot.
'DEE ARE YOU OK?' Marcie yelled, rushing into the bathroom, 'What happened?'.
As Dee Dee dangled precariously she quickly rolled the shotgun back into it's cloth back and tucked it into the holdall and hoisted her leg back up into the loft,
'Ar'm alright Marce' she called down, 'A'r fink it was a bleedin meteorite or summink!' she replied, poking her head out of the hole in the roof, 'Ar see this program right! where a turd fallin from a jumbo jet khazi flattened a lollypop lady in Luton, whatta way to bleedin go eh! smuvvered in shit!'.
'Sorry Dee what was that?' Marcie asked, helping Dee Dee down the ladder, 'And what's with the blue foot?'.
Dee Dee looked down at her bare foot, 'Oh er, ar was tryna wash chicken madras out me toes!' she said, hunting for her missing boot, 'Fuck me' she gasped, looking at the devastated bathroom, 'Sorry Marce' Marcie merely smiled and put an arm around Dee Dee, still immensely grateful for her earlier intervention, 'Don't worry about it Dee, ar'm insured!' she explained, 'As long as your alright babe!'.
'Ar gotta be goin Marce!' Dee Dee said, pulling her boot from the wreckage and shaking the debris from inside, 'Ar'm meetin Maizie and Trish later, you member them don'tcha?'
'Yeah course!' Marcie replied, following Dee Deeto the foot of the stairs, 'Tell em ar said hi!' she added, 'Oh and give your mum my love, ar keep saying ar'll pop round and see how she is one of these days!'.
Dee Dee gave Marcie a peck on the cheek and a

reassuring rub of the shoulder, 'You'll be alright babe, that tosser's out ya life now' she said, turning to leave, 'You take care mate, ar see ya later!'

'Yeah seeya Dee!' Marcie replied, waving, 'And thanks again!'.

'Owd you two get on?' Dee Dee asked, dropping the bag in the hall and joining her friends in the lounge with her mother.

'Alright Dee, we've sorted a mota' Maizie replied offering Dee Dee a can of cider, 'Eeya mate, get ya maaf raand that!' she added, swigging from her own can, 'We've bin avin a right laugh wiv ya mum'

'Yeah!' Trisha chirped up holding a handful of photographs, 'She showed us all yer old baby phota's!'. Pearl fingered a bunch of dog eared photographs in a shoe box on her lap,

'Bleedin ell muvver!' Dee Dee said after a long gulp of cider, 'What'dya get them out for?'

Pearl would often have a nostalgic moment with her box of memories, sitting in floods of tears and remembering times gone by when they were a happy united family, long before her husbands roving eye destroyed her world. 'Oh ar do love this one of you Dee!' she said, showing the girls a crumpled picture, 'You ad a nappy full of shit but you was as appy as Larry!'.

Maizie burst out laughing, 'She's always like that Misses D!' she chuckled, 'When we was in Butlins we was doing shots in the chalet and she farted and followed fru!'

Trisha put her hand in the air, 'And what about that time Dee' she laughed, 'When there was a blowback from the septic tank in Benidorm and it pebble dashed our barfroom!'

Maizie screwed her face up in disgust ‘Corr! fuck me yeah!’ she said, ‘That was bleedin chronic wurrnit!, mind you it wern all bad, ar copped off with that plumber what was iz name Manuel or Miguel or summink!’
‘Manuel ar fink!’ Trisha replied, ‘And it weren’t just the khazi e was roddin eh Maize!’
Dee Dee dragged Maizie to her feet, ‘Right come on you two!’ she said, ‘Ar’ve seen Mickey and we’re sorted!’
‘Who, Black Mickey?’ Pearl asked, ‘How is e Dee love?’
‘Banged up again Mum!’ Dee Dee replied,
Pearl removed a faded photograph of Mickey at Dee Dee’s christening from her box, ‘Ahhhh never mind!’ she said looking lovingly at the snap, ‘Give im mar love when ya see im again!’
Dee Dee picked up the holdall and led the other two to her room,
‘What you got in there Dee?’ Trisha asked. Closing the door behind them.
Dee Dee reached inside and pulled out the gun, ‘Is this the bollocks or what?’ she asked, cocking the weapon.
Maizie and Trisha leapt back, ‘Fuckin ell Dee!’ Maizie gasped, ‘Woss that for?’
Dee Dee aimed the empty gun at her friends ‘For robbin ya dozy cow, wod’ya fink iss for!’ she snapped,
‘What we spozed to do do, old up a bank wiv an air dryer or summink, now look!’ she rummaged through the bag emptying it’s contents onto the bed, ‘We got everyfing we need here, but we gotta practice on somewhere small first before we it the big time, you two got any ideas?’

Maizie and Trisha looked at each other 'Ar dunno Dee!' Trisha replied, 'We aint never robbed anyone before!'

'Thas why we need the bleedin practice ya doughnut!' Dee Dee barked, 'Anywhere that might av a few quid and ardly any security!'

'Ar got it!' Maizie said excitedly, 'What about a doin charity shop?'

'Shut up Maize!' Dee Dee laughed, 'What we gonna get from a bleedin charity shop, two bob, a bleedin rubiks cube and a smelly coat!'

'No listen Dee!' Maizie explained, 'Some of em take bundles, me nan used to work in the cancer shop in Epping, they took free an arf grand one Saturday!'

Dee Dee's ears pricked up, 'Ar'm listenin!' she said, sitting on the edge of her bed with the shotgun on her lap.

'Well!' Maizie continued, 'There's an animal welfare one on the Rainham road, ar've seen it from the bus, some edgeog charity or summink, well the old dears were queuing to get in there Dee!'

Trisha smiled, 'We ad an edgeog in our garden' she said, daydreaming, 'Lovely little fing it was, me mum used to put a saucer of milk and a cheesy biscuit out for it!'

Dee Dee looked at Trisha in despair, 'Trish mate' she sighed, 'Shut up about friggin edgeogs and pay attention will ya!'

'Sorry Dee!' Trisha sulked 'E was lovely though wiv iz little pointy nose, ar called im Brian after Brian from Westlife coz e was so cute' Trisha rambled on, 'Ar fink next doors Staff musta got im coz e aint been back for iz cheesy biscuits in ages'

'TRISHA FOR FUCK SAKE!!' Dee Dee snapped 'We're tryna plan a fuckin robbry and you and your bleedin edgeog aint elpin!'
'Yeah shut up Trish' Maizie added, 'Your doin mar bleedin ed in'
Trisha sat like a scolded schoolgirl on the edge of the bed, 'Ar do miss im though!' she said under her breath.
Maizie and Dee Dee looked over at their mumbling friend, 'SHUT THE FUCK UP!!' they both yelled.
'Right what about the mota?' Dee Dee asked.
'Sorted Dee!' said Maizie giving the thumbs up, 'Me bruvva's gonna do it but we av to give im some petrol money first!'
'Yeah whatever!' Dee Dee replied, raising her eyebrows, 'Just make sure e knows what e's doin thas all!'
'E's a good driver Dee!' Maizie said, reassuringly, 'E'z only ad one accident, e backed over the Pizza ut delivery boy, made a right mess of iz bike e did, e got out to elp, see the boy was alright and buggered off wiv iz deep pan pepperoni!'
Dee Dee put her head in her hands, 'Can we just stick to the fuckin plan and stop goin on about pizza's or bleedin edgeogs!' she snarled, slamming her hand down on the bed, 'We'll hit the shop tomorrow lunchtime, all the old gits would've bin in with their pension money by then, you two be raand ere by arf eleven, and don't be late!' Dee Dee handed Maizie forty pounds, 'Tell ya bruvva to fill the mota up, and tell im if e fucks me about!' she slipped the gun back into the back, 'Ar'll blow iz fuckin bollocks off!' Dee Dee then took out her new 'G 1000' love toy and

stroked it's shaft, 'Now if you two don't mind!' she added, wriggling up the bed, 'Ar need some me time!' 'Oh er, yeah right!' Maizie said, awkwardly 'We'll see ya tomarra then Dee, enjoy!'.
Trisha and Maizie left the room and said their goodbye's to Pearl on the way out while Dee Dee turned her pulsating toy up to maximum throttle and lowered it between her legs, Trisha and Maizie were half way down the stairs when they heard Dee Dee cry out 'FUCKIN ELL, YEAH BABY!!'

CHAPTER FOUR.

The hit.

After a night of orgasmic passion and three battery changes, Dee Dee lay slumped in the corner of her room, toy in hand. Only stirring when her bedside alarm clock sprung into life belting out Diana Ross's classic 'Where did our love go' 'What, what the fuck?' she said, rubbing her eyes, Dee Dee scrambled to her feet and looked lovingly at her toy before tucking it under her pink fluffy pillow 'Shit!' she cursed noticing the time, it was eleven o'clock and Maizie and Trisha were due in half an hour. Peeling off the rest of her clothes she ran through to the bathroom and hopped into the shower where she spent the first few minute scrubbing at her blue foot again but to no avail, 'Fuck it!' she cursed, giving up and soaping the rest of her body, but suddenly the luke warm water turned to an ice cold jet, 'Fuck, fuck, fuckin fuck!' she yelled leaping from the shower and standing shivering, head to toe in lather, 'MUVVA! THERE'S NO FUCKIN OT WATER!' she yelled along the corridor.

A voice from her mother's bedroom replied, 'Yeah sorry Dee.love ar fink the boilers on the blink again!'

'Fuckin great!' Dee Dee said toweling the foam from her body and dragging a brush through her tangled hair, 'Ar gotta get out of this shit ole'

Dressing in jeans, trainers and a hooded top, buttering herself a slice of toast Dee Dee took a sip from a carton of milk from the fridge but then gagged immediately and spat it out into the sink, 'Shit what the!' she said, pouring the lumpy contents out of the carton and holding her mouth under the cold tap, spitting the cheesy morsels from her teeth. Before she had a chance to complain to her mother yet again Dee Dee heard the screeching of tyre's in the car park below, 'Who the fuck?' she said, peering out of the window, it was Bradley and the girls in his pimped up Nova spinning round the car park in doughnut fashion with white smoke pouring from the rear end and a deafening hip hop beat banging from the bass box, 'Woss that twat doin?' Dee Dee asked herself.

'OY OY DEE!' Maizie yelled from the passenger window, 'YOU COMIN OR WHAT?'

Dee Dee slammed the window shut, grabbed the bag and marched down the stairs. 'What the fuck are you doin?' she barked when Bradley skidded to a halt

beside her, 'D'you wanna get us nicked before we bleedin start you prat!'
'Be cool woman!' Bradley replied, flashing a fake stick on gold tooth and dressed from head to toe in a white and gold track suit with matching cap 'Me knows what me doin!'
Dee Dee hopped into the back and slammed the door shut, 'For one, don't tell me to be cool!' she barked 'Two, i aint your fuckin woman, three you better know what your fuckin doin and four, TURN THAT FUCKIN SHIT DOWN!!'
Bradley turned his stereo down a notch 'Dat aint shit Dee!' he said looking in the rear view mirror, 'Das urban blud, das the street vibe man!'
'Just drive you nob!' Dee Dee snapped, hugging the holdall.
Bradley sped from the car park and out onto the high street nodding his head in time with the music, 'Ar mixed diss one meself, wodya fink sis?' he said, turning to Maizie before singing along with the vocals,

'Don't diss me man coz i got no class
gonna bust a cap in your candy ass
Don't curse me blud for the way i roll
for the shit i smoke and the money i stole
i live my life and i aint lookin back
and all i say is i shoulda bin black
shoulda bin black, shoulda bin shoulda bin, shoulda bin black'

Maizie and Trisha sang along too 'Shoulda bin, shoulda bin, shoulda bin black!' Maizie turned to Dee Dee 'Thas quite good ain it Dee, catchy ar mean!'

'Yeah!' said Trisha attempting a big box little box hand jive, 'Iss like fifty cent an all that gangster rappin stuff ainit!'
Dee Dee tipped her head back and looked at the roof of the car, 'No Trish!' she said calmly, 'Iss shit!'
Parking three doors from the animal welfare shop the three girls and Bradley sat observing the door, 'Dass it?' Bradley scoffed 'Dass what ya gonna rob, a flippin charity shop, man this is fucked up, you'z aint gonna get nuttin in there blud ar tell ya!'
Dee Dee tapped Maizie on the shoulder 'Shut im up will ya' she insisted 'E'z doin mar bleedin ed in!'
'Iss alright bruv!' Maizie said, tapping Bradley's knee, 'These coffin dodgers take shit loads of dough, believe me!'
Dee Dee handed the bag to Trisha and flung open the car door 'Right you two go and do the business, ar'm gonna wait ere with Dippy Rascal in case e fucks off wivout us!'
'What us?' Maizie asked, 'Ain't you comin in Dee?'
'Iss a fuckin charity shop!' Dee Dee barked, 'Iss a piece a piss, now get in there, get the money and get out!'
Maizie and Trisha left the car with a degree of apprehension, 'But Dee!' Trisha said, leaning in the window.
Dee Dee grabbed Trisha by the collar, 'Look you dozy cow!' she snarled, 'If you don't wanna be sellin chicken nuggets or cleanin Kharzi's for the rest of ya life ar suggest you get in there and get the fuckin money!'
Maizie tugged Trisha towards the shop door, 'Come on Trish she's right!' she said, peering in the window, 'Iss the only way were ever gonna make some serious dosh' Trisha relented and the pair opened the

door and stepped inside. The air was musty and smelt like an old folks home, two elderly ladies in horn rimmed spectacles stood pricing nik naks behind the counter and hadn't noticed the girls enter,
'Woss that smell?' Trisha said, turning up her nose.
'Moff balls!' Maizie replied, looking round the shop
'Me nan puts em in er knicker drawer!'
An ageing gentlemen in a long creased raincoat and cloth cap stood thumbing through a pile of second hand trousers, a large dew drop teetering on the end of his nose. Maizie and Trisha shuffled along the aisle pretending to browse the chipped crockery and romantic novels, but stood out somewhat in their designer sportswear. After blowing his nose loudly into a floral handkerchief the old man eventually left empty handed and the girls approached the counter, looking over their shoulders at the door,
'Right ere goes!' Maizie said, reaching into the bag in Trisha's hand and pulling out the shotgun. 'Give us the fuckin money!' she said, menacingly whilst pointing it at the women who barely acknowledged their presence 'Ar said give us the money!' Maizie reiterated, 'Come on, and it over!'
Both ladies were profoundly deaf and only looked up when Maizie tapped the guns barrel on the glass counter, 'Oy ar'm talkin to you!' she added.
'I'll be with you in a moment dear!' one lady said, taking very little notice of the gun, 'Now where did i put that pen!' Maizie and Trisha looked at each other in amazement as the two old ladies went about their business, 'I don't know dear, here have mine' her friend replied, taking her own pen hanging on a piece of string around her neck and handed it to her. 'Oh no Mavis dear you know i always write in black' she

replied, 'Yours is red dear, you know i never write in red!'
'Oh i am sorry Dolly dear!' Mavis said, looking around the counter, 'I've seen it here somewhere!' The two elderly ladies rummaged amongst the leaflets and lace doilies discussing the pro's and con's of writing in red and black ink oblivious to the impending danger stood before them,
Maizie then notice a similar piece of string around Dolly's neck with a black pen tied to the end, 'Iss angin raand ya neck ya dozy bitch!' she said, gesturing with the barrel of the gun.
Dolly hadn't heard a word and continued looking, growing more and more frustrated, 'Heavens Mavis i can't find the darn thing!' she cursed.
Maizie, losing her cool reached over the counter, grabbed the pen and held it inches from Dolly's nose, 'Ere's ya bleedin pen ya doddery old cow!' she snapped.
'Oh there it is!' Dolly said gratefully, 'Thank you dear, now what can i do for you!' she then noticed the gun for the first time, 'Oh i'm sorry dear we don't buy firearms!' she added, 'Company policy dear, you understand, you might like to try the Badger's Trust in Wood lane, i've heard they'll buy anything!'
'No no Dolly dear!' Mavis said interrupting, 'The Badgers trust is in Cherry tree lane, next to Waitrose, i'm sure of it!' The two ladies then began a heated discussion on the whereabouts of the Badgers trust ignoring Maizie and Trisha once again.
'OY! FOR FUCK SAKE SHUT UP WILL YA!' Maizie yelled, 'THIS IS A FUCKIN ROBBRY, SO GIVE US THE FUCKIN MONEY!'
Meanwhile Trisha's attention had wandered to a rack of tiny hand knitted hedgehog blankets, 'Ahhh aint

they sweet Maize, ar might get one in case Brian comes back!'
Maizie turned to her friend, 'What?' she asked, totally confused by now, 'What are you on about Trish, were supposed to be robbin the bloody place!'
Trisha held up a tiny blanket, 'Ar wonder if they do booties to match!' she said.
Maizie snatched the blanket and threw it in Trisha's face, 'Shut up about fuckin edgeogs and blankets and pay attention will ya!' She then thrust the barrel of the gun under Dolly's chin, 'READ MAR LIPS!' she snarled, 'THIS IS A ROBBRY, SO GIVE US THE BLOODY MONEY!'
'Oh Mavis dear it's a robbery!' Dolly said turning to her friend,
'A what dear?' Mavis asked, cupping her hand to her ear,
'A robbery dear!' Dolly repeated, 'They want the money!'
Mavis looked over the top of her glasses, 'Oooh a robbery, how exciting, are they going to tie us up dear, i'll get some string i'm sure we have a ball somewhere, if i could just remember where i put it!' she opened several drawers and delved inside while Dolly opened the till 'I'm sorry dear we banked the money this morning!' she said, holding up a five pound note and some change,
'WHAT!' Maizie screamed, 'YOUR FUCKIN KIDDIN ME!' she ran behind the counter and pulled the tray from inside the till, 'You banked the bloody money already you dozy cow!' she snapped. Maizie snatched a guide dog collection box from the counter and shook it vigorously 'There's a few quid in ere!' she said handing it to Trisha and heading for the door

'Get the rest of the money and let's get the fuck out of ere!' she added, leaving the shop.
Trisha snatched the five pound note from Dolly and was about to leave when she spotted a standard lamp in the window, 'Oooh how much is the lamp?' she asked, 'Mar nan'd love that!'
'It's twenty five pounds dear!' Mavis replied, retrieving the lamp 'It's real tortoise shell you know!'
'Ahhh!' Trisha sighed, 'We ad a tortoise once, but me bruvva fought it was a turtle and drowned the poor fucker in the bath!' Trisha handed Mavis the five pounds back and took a further twenty from her pocket,
Dolly then peeled a badge with the words 'i helped a hedgehog' from a strip and planted it on Trisha's chest, 'Thank you dear, do come again!' she said, holding the door open. Trisha staggered out of the shop with the large lamp in one hand and the collection tin in the other.
'What the fuck av you got there?' Dee Dee asked, leaning out of the window, Maizie sat in the back not daring to tell Dee Dee that the robbery had been a complete disaster,
'Iss a lamp Dee!' Trisha replied proudly 'Nice innit!'
'Ar can see iss a fuckin lamp you dozy mare!' Dee Dee yelled, 'What the fuck are you doin wiv it and where's the bleedin money?'
Trisha held up the collection tin, 'Don't worry Dee!' she smiled, 'Ar got the money an'all!' Trisha opened the boot of Bradley's Nova and wrestled with the lamp, turning it this way and that in an attempt to fit it inside. Just then a voice from behind her said, 'Would you like a hand with that madam?' she turned to see a strapping policeman in a high viz jacket looking over her shoulder.

'Shit!' said Dee Dee, seeing the officer in the door mirror and sinking down into her seat 'Iss the old bill!'
Trisha merely smiled and handed the bobby the collection tin, 'Oh fanks!' she said, fluttering her eyelashes at him, 'Just old that for me will ya!'
Dee Dee cringed in her seat 'What is that stupid bitch doin?' she gasped.
The policeman looked down at the tin, 'Oh i see your collecting for our prickly friends!' he said reaching into his pocket,
'What' Trisha replied, struggling with her lamp,
'Hedgehogs' the officer said, dropping a pound into the tin, 'Charming little creatures!' then seeing Trisha had won her battle with the lamp and the car boot, handed her the tin back, 'Keep up the good work Miss!' he said before heading off along the street.
Trisha joined the others in the car 'Ahh e was nice' she said handing Dee Dee the tin.
'Woss this?' Dee Dee barked, 'Where's the bleedin money?' Maizie sank down into her seat and hid her face.
'Well!' said Trisha 'I ad a fiver but ar spent it on the lamp!'
Dee Dee broke open the tin and emptied the contents into her lap, 'Free paand twenty!' she said angrily 'You mean to tell me all you got was free paand twenny and a poxy lamp!'
'Well it is real tortoise shell Dee!' Trisha said, pleased with her bargain 'Ar got it for me nan so she can see to do er jigsaws!'
Bradley fell about laughing 'Me told ya blud!' he said, clicking his fingers, 'You aint gonna get nuttin from no charity shop innit!'
Dee Dee sat quietly seething at the thought of failure and worse still the thought of never ever leaving her

grubby council flat and mundane existence, but as many had lived to regret, she was at her most dangerous when cornered in this way.
'Gimme that fuckin gun!' she said, wrenching the bag from Maizie, she took out the shotgun, a handful of cartridges and a ski mask.
'What ya gonna do Dee?' Trisha asked, looking across at Maizie, 'Maize woss she doin?' Maizie shrugged her shoulders.
'WAIT ERE!' Dee Dee barked, tucking the gun inside her jacket and flinging open the car door once again, 'AND YOU, SHIT FOR BRAINS!' she yelled at Bradley, 'KEEP THIS FUCKIN MOTA RUNNIN!' Dee Dee slammed the door shut and marched across the road with gritted teeth towards a branch of the Provincial Alliance building society and without hesitation donned the ski mask, pulled her hood over her head and flung open the door,
'EVERYBODY ON THE FUCKIN FLOOR!' she yelled, whipping out the weapon and brandishing it menacingly. Three startled customers in a queue spun round with a horrified look on their faces and stood rooted to the spot while the two young female cashiers looked at each other not knowing what to do, 'I SAID ON THE FLOOR YOU FUCKERS!' Dee Dee told the builder and two middle aged women who immediately fell to their knees with their hands in the air. She then grabbed a shopping bag from one of the women and emptied it's contents of fruit and tinned goods onto the floor before thrusting it between the security glass, 'FILL THE BAG YOU SLAGS!' she barked, then out of the corner of her eye she noticed the heavily tattooed builder edging towards her, in a flash Dee Dee brought the butt of the gun down hard on the side of his face, 'GET

DOWN AND STAY DOWN YOU CUNT!' she screamed. The two women by his side were crying hysterically, covering their heads, 'FOR FUCK SAKE SHUT UP! Dee Dee snarled 'IF YA BEHAVE YASELF I WONT FUCKIN URT YA!' one of the cashiers then reached for a button at her side, 'OY!!' Dee Dee yelled before cocking the shotgun and discharging it with a deafening bang into the ceiling. The blast ruptured the sprinkler system sending a shower of freezing water down onto their heads, Dee Dee aimed her weapon at the cashiers once again, 'You gonna fill that fuckin bag now or what!' she growled. The two girls quickly opened their cash drawers and began stuffing bundles of twenty and fifty pound notes into the carrier bag while Dee Dee stood in the deluge watching the door and the captives at her feet. 'Thatta do!' she said, seeing the bag was almost full, snatching it from the counter and backing away towards the door Dee Dee looked the cashiers in the eye, 'If i ear any fuckin bells goin off in the next five minutes!' she snapped, 'Ar'll come back in ere an ar'll shoot the fuckin pair of ya, you got that!'. The frightened girls nodded in agreement and edged away from the counter while the two women huddled together on the sodden carpet. The builder lay motionless, the sprinklers washing the blood and plaster from his face. Dee Dee thrust the gun inside her jacket and backed out of the door, taking off the ski mask when she was out of sight, then with her bag brimming with cash she ran to the waiting car leaving a trail of puddled footprints and leapt into the passenger seat, 'FUCKIN DRIVE!' she screamed, but Bradley seemed more concerned with his new bucket seats,

'Yo bitch!' he said shoving a dripping Dee Dee 'Ar just bought dem dere seats!' he moaned 'Dem's real levva man, dat shits gonna stain!'

Dee Dee took out the shotgun and thrust the barrel hard into Bradley's crotch, 'Ar SAID DRIVE YOU USELESS CUNT!' she screamed, while Maizie and Trisha sat in the back looking nervously over their shoulders. Bradley, fearing for his manhood quickly put the car into gear and attempted to pull away but immediately stalled. Dee Dee looked in the rear view mirror and could see two uniformed bobbies strolling in their direction, cocking the gun she rammed it even harder between Bradley's trembling legs, 'GET THIS PIECE OFF SHIT GOING!' she said, checking the policemen's proximity once more 'OR AR'M GONNA BLOW YOUR FUCKIN BOLLOCKS OFF!!' Bradley composed himself for a second, slipped the gearstick into first and edged out into the road,

'Nice and easy!' Dee Dee said looking over her shoulder as they rounded the corner hearing the building society's alarm bells start up and watching the two policemen sprint across the road, 'Less get the fuck out of ere!' Dee Dee said, clutching the bag of notes.

Bradley parked the car in the garage of his parents town house and closed the door behind them, 'Shit man dat was wicked!' he said wrapping his knuckles on the roof of the car, 'We'z real robbers man!'.

Dee Dee leapt from the car and pinned Bradley to the garage wall by his throat, 'You listen to me you prick!' she snapped, 'Your just the fuckin driver, thas all you are, and from now on you do what ar say, when ar say it, you got that!' Bradley nodded and Dee Dee released her grip, 'Ar don't give a fuck if ar shit on ya seats!' she added 'If ar say drive you fuckin drive!'.

Maizie and Trisha climbed from the rear 'Bleedin ell Dee your soaked!' Maizie said, squeezing the water from Dee Dee's sleeve, 'Come on ar sought you summa mar clothes out!' Dee Dee followed the others up to Maizie's room and dumped the bag onto her bed, she then stripped to her underwear while Maizie rummaged through her wardrobe, Bradley couldn't believe his luck, he was finally in the same room as a semi naked girl and clasped his hands over his twitching trouser pocket,

'Ar got summink in mar room that might fit ya!' he said thrusting his groin towards her.

Dee Dee looked him up and down whilst slipping into a pair of Maizie's leggings and sweater 'Dream on you little scrote!' she scoffed.

Trisha leaped up and down clapping her hands excitedly 'Ow much we got Dee!' she asked, 'Looks like shit loads!'. Dee Dee grabbed the bottom of the bag and emptied the bundles of crisp notes onto the bed.

'Blimey Dee!' Maizie said wide eyed 'There must be faasands ere!'.

Dee Dee arranged the bundles into similar amounts counting in her head as she did so, 'Fuck me!' she gasped, 'There's undred and forty five grand ere, what a fuckin result!'

'Bloody ell Dee!' Maizie said, slumping down on the bed, 'We're bloomin minted we are!'. Dee Dee handed Bradley ten one thousand pound bundles which he duly counted, 'Dis aint no ten percent!' he moaned, 'Ar fought mar cut was ten percent man!'. Dee Dee prodded his chest with a firm finger, 'Your lucky to get that you fuckin idiot!' she said, backing him into a corner, 'You do as your told and you'll get your ten percent, alright!'

Bradley nodded and stuffed his cash into his baggy joggers, 'Sweet!' he replied, ducking away from her. Dee Dee took another ten thousand from the pile and divided the rest into three equal portions, 'Thas ten grand for Mickey and just over forty grand a piece for us, you two alright wiv that!'
Maizie and Trisha picked up their share and held it tightly to their chests, 'Yeah course Dee!' Maizie nodded with a huge grin on her face, 'I aint never seen this much dough in all me life!'.
Trisha skipped around the room holding her cash in the air, 'Ar fill like ar won the bleedin lottry ar do!' she cried.
Dee Dee dropped her cash into the holdall, 'This is just the start!' she said, zipping the bag and tossing it over her shoulder, 'Iss gonna get bigger and better you wait and see, but tonight we're going up west to celebrate!'
'China whites?' asked Trisha, barely containing her excitement, 'Thas where all the footballers go!'
'Maybe!' replied Dee Dee, 'We can go anywhere we want with this much dough!'
'Ar've always wanted to be a wag!' Trisha added, 'The closest ar got was being banged by the Billericay back four after a charity match wiv Saafend United!'
'Billericay!' Maizie laughed, 'They're ardly Man United are they Trish, anyway that makes you a slag not a wag!'.
Dee Dee turned to leave 'Ar'll pick you'z two up in a cab at eight!' she said, opening the bedroom door. Bradley then began beat boxing before pointing at Dee Dee and breaking into his own version of a Clash classic,

'Mar Dee Dee was a bank robber
she never hurt nobody
she just loved to live that way
and she loved to steal your, money'

Dee Dee couldn't help but laugh as she made her way downstairs listening as her two friends joined in amid raucous laughter

'Mar Dee Dee was a bank robber
she never hurt nobody
she just loved to live that way
and she loved to steal your, money'

Dee Dee returned home to find the bailiff and his boss stood at her doorstep attempting to gain access yet again,
'Ar told you i aint got it!' Pearl could be heard pleading, 'Just leave us alone will ya!'.
Dee Dee flew along the landing, swiping one of them with her bag 'Oy what the fuck's goin on?' she asked, standing between them and the door.
'We are in possession of a court order young lady!' Derek said, straightening his tie, 'The outstanding amount has not been paid by the due date so we are well within our rights to seize property or in your case as your property would in no way cover your debt we can indeed serve an eviction notice, now if you'll please stand aside!'
'Ow much is it?' Dee Dee asked, looking the men in the eye.
'Excuse me!' one of them replied, looking down his nose at Dee Dee.
'You erd!' Dee Dee replied angrily, 'Ow much is the fuckin debt!'

The two men laughed knowing full well that Dee Dee or indeed her mother could hardly scrape together even a third of what was owed.
'If you must know madam!' the bailiff scoffed, 'The outstanding balance on your account is one thousand three hundred and forty two pounds, now if you'll please stand aside we have work to do!'
Dee Dee reached into her bag, thumbed though the notes and thrust a bundle into the startled bailiff's hand, 'One an arf grand to leave us the fuck alone!' she said, crossing her arms defiantly.
The two men looked at each other in amazement before flicking through the banknotes, 'Oh well er!' Derek stammered, slipping the cash into his pocket, 'Yes er, this brings your account up to date Miss Dawson, it's been a pleasure doing business with you!' he then put a lecherous arm around Dee Dee and whispered in her ear 'I've heard how accommodating you can be, is there er, any chance of a repeat performance, maybe for the two of us!'
'GET FUCKED!' Dee Dee yelled, 'YOU GOT YA FUCKIN MONEY NOW DO ONE YA PAIRA CUNTS!' The two men were taken aback by Dee Dee's aggressive stance and backed away along the landing, 'Just er, just keep up your rent payments!' Derek called back 'And we won't be bothering you again!'
Dee Dee held her middle finger in the air, 'Do ar look fuckin bovvered!' she replied escorting her mother inside
Pearl collapsed into her chair and reached for a tin 'Dee love where d'ya get all that money?' she asked 'Your not on the game girl are ya?'
'No muvver ar'm not on the bleedin game!' Dee Dee said flinging her bag onto the sofa and flopping

beside it, 'Ar just ad a win on the orses thas all, eeya fancy Chinese, mar treat!'
'Oooh yeah!' Pearl said, rubbing her hands together, 'We aint ad a chinese in ages, can i ave chicken balls, ar do like chicken balls, ar want curry sauce though, none of that sweet and sour shit!'.
Dee Dee pulled a menu from between the sofa cushions and took out her mobile phone, 'Av what ya like mum, ar get ya crispy duck an'all if ya like!'
'Oooh no!' Pearl said shaking her heard, 'Thas well dear Dee, ar just ave me balls and noodles!'
'Your avin duck muvva!' Dee Dee said defiantly, 'An a pankake roll an'all!'
Pearl licked her lips 'Oh fanks love!' she smiled, 'Shall we av a night in, strictly's on later wiv your favorite judge, Craig wass iz name?'
Dee Dee turned her nose up, 'Muvva you know ar can't stand that smug bastard' she said, calling the Golden Dragon, 'Ar just wanna smack im in the face wiv a wet packet of shit every time ar see im, anyway ar'm goin out wiv Maize and Trish tonight, we're goin up taan, yeah ello mate can I order a takeaway?'.
Pearl pulled herself forward in her chair and took Dee Dee's hand, 'You be careful love!' she said, squeezing tightly, 'Them fancy fellas are only after one fing ya know, keep yer and on yer aypney thas what me nan used to say!'
Dee Dee smiled, remembering her nan fondly, 'Thas not all she said Muvva!' she laughed, 'She told me to piss me knickers if ar'm ever caught out in the cold!'
Tucking into their oriental feast a short while later, Dee Dee and her mother laughed telling tales of their grand and great grandparents colorful past, like the time Dee Dee's grandfather George Dawson, a wing commander in the RAF, bombed a German whore

house sending it's occupants fleeing into the night with their trousers round their ankles and visible blackened bottoms.

When dinner was over Dee Dee carried the plates out into the kitchen, 'Ar gotta get ready naah mum!' she called through to the lounge, 'You gonna be alright on yer own?'

'Yeah course ar will!' Pearl replied, 'Don't worry about me love, you go and enjoy yaself!'

Dee Dee rummaged through her drawers for her favorite 'fuck me' knickers as she called them, a tiny blue lacy pair with pink velvet hearts.

Once dressed in a strapless top and heels she straightened her hair and applied the last of her glossy make up, stuffed a handful of twenties into her purse and headed for the door, 'Don't wait up mum!' she said in passing, 'Ar got me key!'

'You look lovely Dee love!' her mother said, choking back the tears, 'Ar used to dress like that for ya farva'

Dee Dee paused and joined her mother in the lounge, 'You'll meet someone one day mum' she said stroking her hair, 'You just gotta get out of this rut, why don't ar make you a nice cup of tea before ar go eh, instead of that beer'

Pearl cradled her can and shook her head, 'Ar need it for me nerves love' she said taking a sip, 'Besides, it elps me sleep' Dee Dee looked down in despair, thinking back to a time when her mother would take pride i her appearance and turn all the heads on the estate, making her father the envy of every man in town. 'Go on, off ya go love!' Pearl added, reaching for the television remote which had been crudely repaired with super glue and sellotape 'Corrie's on in a minute an ar got arf a bag of revels ere somewhere!' she reached into her sewing basket and

plucked out the sweets, 'Oh thas the bloke!' she said, having a brief eureka moment.
'Who?' asked Dee Dee with a puzzled expression. Pearl chuckled holding up her bag of sweets 'Im offa strictly, Craig revel whatsit!'
Dee Dee turned to leave 'Don't remind me muvva' she said, holding her stomach 'Ar'm avin trouble keepin me bleedin chow mein down as it is'
Dee Dee descended the high rise stairs daintily in her heels, pausing momentarily, crossing her legs as her stomach gurgled, 'A taste of the orient my arse' she cursed, wishing she hadn't eaten so much.
Dee Dee hobbled into a nearby cab office, 'Can ar use ya Karzi mate?' she asked, holding her stomach 'Ar'm touchin cloff ere!'.
The Indian controller held up his hands, 'I am sorry miss i am not understanding you, what is it you are wanting?'
'The khazi!' Dee Dee snapped, holding her bottom, 'The shitta, the bog, the bleedin loo, oh fuck ya ar'll find it meself!' she stormed to the rear of the office and eventually found a door marked WC, 'Fank fuck!' she said flinging open the door. There inside was an elderly balding Indian man with his trousers round his knees and a copy of playboy on his lap,
'GET OUT! GET OUT!' he yelled, covering his privates with the magazine, but Dee Dee was a desperate woman and reaching in grabbed the mans collar and hoisted him off the pan and out into the office, his trousers falling around his ankles,
'Go an av a Thomas the tank somewhere else ya dirty git!' she said, leaving him fumbling with his underpants in front of a queue of waiting passengers.
Dee Dee ducked inside the toilet slamming the door and looked down at the rancid pan, 'filfy fuckers!' she

said, then in desperation hitched up her skirt, pulled down her knickers and attempted to hover above the putrid porcelain seat, at one point she lost her balance, grabbed a rotten venetian blind that hung over the window and tore it from the wall, 'FUCK IT!' she screamed as her bottom came to rest on the cold pee stained pan, 'Fuckin great!' she cursed.

After squeezing and straining for a full five minutes, Dee Dee finally stood up and pulled the entire roll of paper from the wall, scrubbing her backside over and over, 'Ar'll get aids of the arse in this shit ole!' she said, ramming handful after handful of paper down the toilet.

Hitching up her knickers and straightening her skirt, Dee Dee pulled the chain and watched the pan fill with water, but to her horror instead of draining away it continued to fill until it was close to the rim, 'Shit, shit!' she cried, fumbling with the door. Her stinking bowel contents and soggy paper overflowed, dripped to the floor and inched towards her, finally Dee Dee wrenched open the door and sprinted into the office with the toxic tide behind her, 'Ya might wanna get yaself a plunger mate!' Dee Dee said to the controller in passing, she ran out into the street, pushed an elderly man aside and dived into his waiting taxi, 'Up there mate!' she said pointing along the street, 'Second left, fird right!'

On the way to Maizie's house Dee Dee's bloated turkish cab driver leered at her out of the corner of his eye, occasionally scratching his balls with his free hand, 'You are lovely lady!' he said, wiping the drool from his chin, 'Perhaps you would allow me to buy you a drink!'.

Dee Dee looked him up and down and laughed, 'Dream on geeza!' she said, checking her make up in the mirror, 'Ar don't trust you oily bastards, me nan shacked up wiv an eighteen year old lad she met in Marmaris on a saga oliday, the little fucker took er to the cleaners and moved six of iz wives into er two bed semi'

Maizie and Trisha were waiting outside when Dee Dee's cab arrived, Maizie wore a lime green boob tube and hot pants while Trisha opted for a leopard print figure hugging halter neck dress,

'Where ya bin Dee?' Maizie asked as the pair hopped in the back, 'Some pervert just tried to pick us up in a bleedin ice cream van!'

Your kidding!' Dee Dee laughed, 'Wod'ya tell im, you wanna sixty nine not a ninety nine!' the three girls burst out laughing, but then Dee Dee caught sight of the perverse driver looking at her friends shapely legs in the rear view mirror, 'Oy Abdul!' she said, slapping his arm, 'Keep ya bleedin eyes on the road ya dirty old git, right take us to Piccadilly and urry up'

As the cab pulled away Maizie produced a bottle of apple sourz from her handbag and handed it to Dee Dee, 'Eeya Dee get that down ya' she said, handing out condoms also, 'Bag it up girls eh!' she laughed.

Passing the bottle between them they soon got in the party spirit and Dee Dee rummaged through the drivers glove box, 'You got any tunes in ere or what!' she said, taking out a cd and popping it into the player, 'Woss this shit!' she said, when a traditional turkish goat herders song began. Winding down the window Dee Dee tossed the cd out into the street much to the annoyance of the driver, but he felt a little intimidated at this point and said nothing.

Maizie also noticed the drivers lustful eyes staring at her in the mirror and, nudging Trisha first, she lifted her boob tube giving him a quick glimpse of her tiny bra. The two girls laughed hysterically as the cabbie, whilst groping his crotch, veered across the road narrowly missing a street sweeper.

'For fuck sake Maize!' Dee Dee yelled, clinging to her seat belt, 'Whateva ya do don't show im ya muff you'll fuckin kill us all!'

The girls continued drinking and teasing the driver during the journey, asking him how big he was and when was the last time he'd even seen it beneath his hulking belly, but he took this attention entirely he wrong way and slid a groping hand over onto Dee Dee's knee,

'Oy get off me you fuckin nonce!' she said, bringing the bottle down firmly on his fingers, causing him to cry out in turkish.

Maizie leaned forward 'E'z a dirty fucker aint e Dee' she said, as the car came to a halt in central London, 'E aint gettin a bleedin tip thas for sure!'

Arriving in the bustling capital Dee Dee noticed a Metropoltan policeman approaching and had an mischievous idea, 'You two get out ar'll sort the cab' she told her friends. Maizie and Trisha stood at the side of the road looking round at the bright city lights while Dee Dee slid her hand onto the cabbies lap. Thinking his luck was about to change he leaned back in his seat and unzipped his trousers. In an instant Dee Dee wiped out his manhood and leapt screaming from the car, 'NO AR WONT SUCK IT YA DIRTY BASTARD!' she yelled attracting the police officers attention, furious the portly driver prised himself from the car and gave chase forgetting that he was still exposed.

Seeing an apparent damsel in distress the policemen immediately tackled the driver and wrestled him to the ground, 'You do not have to say anything sir!' the bobby said, slipping on the handcuffs, 'But anything you do say will be taken down and used as evidence!' Dee Dee blew a kiss to the struggling driver and then showed him a defiant middle finger, 'Come on girls!' she said taking Maizie and Trisha by the arm, 'Less go and get wankered!'.

CHAPTER FIVE.

The big take.

Having trawled many of the west ends lesser known clubs, Dee Dee and her two friends finally found themselves outside Soho's most exclusive venue The Lion Bar, a place frequented by Saudi princes and premiership playboys alike,
'Fuck me Dee!' Trisha gasped, seeing the queue of hopefuls disappear around the corner, 'We aint never gonna get in there!'. Admission was strictly by invite only or first come first served for any remaining tables. Scantily clad revelers jostled for the attention of the musclebound doorman guarding the entrance.
'Leave it to me!' Dee Dee said, grabbing her friends by the hand and marching to the head of the queue.

'OY!' yelled one teen hottie behind them in a lycra catsuit, 'We were here first!'
Dee Dee stepped on the girls toe with her six inch stiletto and looking over her shoulder growled, 'Shut it you slag!'. The society girl, fearing for her life, shrunk back into the queue nursing her throbbing foot.
'Sorry were full!' a burly bouncer said, lowering a crimson rope barrier in front of Dee Dee and the others,
'Ar told ya!' Trisha said turning to leave, 'Less gaan ava look in the sex shops!'
Dee Dee yanked her friend back in line, 'Ar said leave it to me did'n i!' she snapped, she then clicked her fingers 'Scuse me mate we're dead famous we are' she told the doorman 'See er' she said tugging Maizie forward 'She's off of Emerdale an ar'm in Eastenders'
The bouncer looked them up and down and then across at Trisha 'Oh yeah and what about er?' he asked 'Ar suppose your gonna tell me she's offa Coronation street are ya'
'Naah' Dee Dee chuckled 'She's wunna the flippin Tweenies'
The bouncer and his associate roard with laughter 'Ar've erd some bullshit in mar time' he said almost choking 'But thas fuckin quality that is, go on then in ya go, just for being such cheeky fuckers'
The girls hurried inside giggling and then stood in awe at their luxurious surroundings, diamond encrusted italian marble lined the walls, gold painted nude waitresses carried bottles of the finest champagne while three white lions wearing silver studded collars paced up and down in a huge cage behind the bar,

'Bloody ell' Maizie gasped, 'I aint never seen nufink like it in me life Dee, iss gawjus, proper gawjus'
Trisha strained her eyes to make out the faces in the dimly lit booths 'Eeya!' she said, tugging Dee Dee's arm 'Aint that im off the telly, you know, the one thas bin shaggin iz bruvva's misses, oh woss iz name?' she then spotted another familiar face, 'Fuckin ell, ava look!' she said, nudging her friends once again, 'There's that news reader bird, woss she doing, ar don't fuckin believe it, she's snortin charlie off a midgets arse, ar fought she was such a stuck up bitch an'all!'
'Come on!' Dee Dee said, making her way to the bar, 'Ar fancy a cocktail!' Holding a fifty pound note in the air Dee Dee whistled to the barmen, 'Oy over ere mate!' she yelled, 'Ar'll av free of them!' she pointed to a cocktail in the hand of a leather clad lovely standing beside her,
'Are you sure madam?' the barman asked, 'It is rather expensive'
Dee Dee took offence to his remark and glared at him, 'Course ar'm fuckin sure' she said angrily 'Ar got money sunshine don't you bleedin worry about that'
'Very well madam!' the barman replied, taking three glasses and a cocktail shaker from the shelf. Moments later he slid three large lime green drinks across the bar, each had a platinum straw and a slice of pineapple on one side, 'Daan the atch!' Dee Dee said sinking her drink in one then choking on what she thought was a stone, 'You could've told me there was a bleedin olive in it, ar fuckin ate olives!' she coughed and swallowed the obstruction.
'That'll be three thousand pounds madam!' the barman said, offering Dee Dee the bill.

'OW BLEEDIN MUCH?' Dee Dee screeched 'Your avin a bleedin laugh aintcha, free grand for that shit, and ya tried to choke me wiv that bleedin olive!'
'Madam that was no olive!' the barman replied, handing Dee Dee a cocktail menu, that was a Cartier diamond ring valued at seven hundred and fifty pounds'
'You what?' Dee Dee said clutching her stomach. Maizie and Trisha fished around in their drinks and plucked out the rings, 'Fuckin ell Dee!' Maizie cried, 'E's right look!' The two girls licked them clean and slipped the rings on their fingers,
'Corr blimey!' Trisha said, polishing hers on her dress 'Thas proper bling that is!'
Maizie laughed and tugged Dee Dee's arm 'Eeya mate, ar tell ya what' she chuckled, 'I aint lickin your bleedin ring thas for sure'
The barman then coughed and thrust the bill closer 'If you would madam' he said,eager to serve a queue of waiting customers, 'We take all major credit cards'
Dee Dee rummaged through her bag muttering under her breath, 'Free fuckin grand' she then felt a hand on her shoulder,
'Please, allow me to get these!' a voice said, she looked up to see a tall handsome man at her side. After a second or two Dee Dee said, 'Ar know you dun i'
Maizie and Trisha were a step ahead of Dee Dee and were whispering to each other, 'Yeah it iz im!' Trisha said, covering her mouth with her hand,
Dee Dee finally caught on 'Eeya your that bleedin gooner aincha!' she said slapping his chest with the back of her hand, 'You can get fucked mate, me grandad'd turn in iz bleedin grave if e knew ar was drinkin wiv you lot'

The premiership footballer was stunned at first by her outburst , 'Well if you mean that i play in midfield for Arsenal then yes your right' he said, straightening his tie 'But i am on loan from West Ham'
'Well fuck me, why didn't you say!' Dee Dee laughed, pushing him toward the bar 'In that case mate we'll av anuvver one of these!' she handed him her glass and looked around for the barman who was serving at the opposite end, 'OY FREE MORE OF THEM GREEN WHATSITS GEEZ!' she yelled.
'What's your name?' the player asked, offering Dee Dee his hand, then catching the barman's eye, 'Whatever these girls want, just stick it on my tab' he told him.
'Me names Debs!' Dee Dee replied, shaking his hand with a manly grip, 'You can call me Dee Dee, thas Maizie and the dippy ones Trish'
'Oh fanks!' Trisha protested, slurping the last of her drink, 'I aint stupid though' she then tossed a peanut into the air and stood with her mouth open, but the flying cashew was caught by the whirring fans blade above her head and propelled at high speed across the club and into the eye of one of the nations best loved daytime tv presenters who reeled back hitting their head on a marble column, 'Oooh shit' Trisha said ducking out of sight while the celeb was carried from the bar bloodied, dazed and confused into the flashlights of the waiting paparazzi.
'I'm' the player was about to introduce himself when Dee Dee intervened
'Ar know who you are!' she said, fishing the ring from her second drink and popping it onto her finger 'Peter wasizname'
'That's right' the player replied, 'Would you like to join me and my friends in the vip room?'

Dee Dee winked at her two friends and slapped Peters bottom 'Does the Pope wear a silly at' she laughed 'Course we bleedin would!'. The girls sipped their cocktails as Peter led them through the crowded club to a door guarded by yet another bouncer who quickly stepped aside and held the door open, 'Cheers mate' Dee Dee said, raising her glass.

Once inside Peter led them to a large circular sofa surrounding a smoke glass table loaded with bottles of the finest bubbly, vintage Cognac and silver goblets brimming with expensive chocolates, 'You'll recognize many of the faces here' Peter told the girls who looked around at the seated guests, Three boy band members, a celebrity chef, two supposedly waring premiership managers, an ex Prime Minister and a Kuwaiti business man flanked by two bodyguards.

'Alright!' said Dee Dee and the others, looking round the lavish room.

Peter gathered the girls together 'This is a personal friend of mine, Sheik Abdullah Hussain' he said, introducing his Arab associate, 'Abby this is Dee Dee, Maizie and' he thought for a moment, 'Sorry what was your name darling?' he asked Trisha.

'Iss Trish' she replied abruptly, 'Or Trisha, whateva ar don't mind'.

The Sheik took an instant liking to Trisha and ordered one of his guards to stand, 'Please won't you join me' he said patting the seat beside him, 'What can i get for such a radiant jewel, champagne, fine wine maybe' Trisha nestled in beside him soaking up the adoration. The Sheik then produced a silver snuff box with what appeared to be cocaine inside, 'Maybe something to help you relax' he said, offering it to Trisha,

‘Nah ar don’t touch that shit’ she said pushing the box away, ‘Me cousin went loopy on that gear, fought e could fly, jumped off the fifteenth floor of our block and landed ed first in a wheelie bin, e’z drinkin minestrone fru a straw and shittin in a bag naah, poor fucker’.
Everybody sat in stunned silence at Trisha’s tale until Dee Dee squeezed herself between the chef and the ex PM, ‘Eeeya!’ she said slapping the chefs knee ‘Mar mum loves your programme, she’s a shit cook though, she tried to do your bleedin minted lamb, got pissed fell asleep and burnt an ole in the bakin tray’.
Maizie sat between Peter and the boy band she had followed since their talent show rise to fame,
‘Hi i’m Jermaine’ one of them said, offering his hand,
‘Ar know’ Maizie blushed, ‘Ar got all your cd’s, loada ya posters and the duvet cover’ Maizie raised her glass to the other two boys ‘Alright Tyrone ows it goin?’ Tyrone nodded and smiled flashing his trademark gold tooth while the youngest member of the band Antoine sat in silence. ‘Oy Ant!’ Maizie said catching his attention, ‘It aint true is it mate?’ she asked, ‘Tell me you aint gay for fuck sake, ar bin friggin marself stupid over you since you dueted wiv Mariah, that video was so orny’ Antoine said nothing, sinking down into his seat.
‘He’s just going through a difficult time at the moment that’s all’ Jermaine said, diverting Maizie’s attention, ‘So what do you think of the new album?’
Iss alright’ Maizie replied nonchalantly, ‘Not as good as the last one, me and Trish went to the Mobo’s and see you perform wiv Aleysha, oh ar love that one tho’ Maizie closed her eyes and burst into song

‘Every time that ar see your face

you take mar heart to a higher place,

'That's our favorite too' Jermaine said, smiling 'I'm glad you enjoyed it, we had such a blast that night'. Maizie looked across at Trisha who was calmly fending off the Sheiks pawing hands, 'Yeah we had a great time' she added, 'We was right up the front, ar fru mar french knickers at ya!'
'We do get a hell of a lot of underwear thrown on stage' Jermaine said, sipping his margarita 'Some skimpy and some you could fit the three of us in'. Maizie laughed and whispered in Jermaine's ear while giving his knee a playful squeeze 'Mine was the pink lacey ones wiv me number in the gusset'
she then looked across at Antoine 'Ar spose you just get shitty pants slung atcha naah do ya?' she asked the recently outed singer who again said nothing, 'There's always one though aint there!' she continued, 'Boyzone ad one, New kids on the block they ad one, even N Sync ad a poofta in the band, ar'm not sayin there's anyfink wrong wiv it though!' she then turned to Dee Dee, 'Dee your uncle David's queer as fuck aint e'
Dee Dee swallowed her belgian chocolate before replying 'Jesus you aint wrong Maize!' she said, wiping her mouth, 'You seen im mincin up and daan the Barking road wiv them pink poodles of iz, what a fuckin sight'.
As the drinks flowed and the party got into full swing Trisha found it increasingly difficult to fend off the lusty Sheiks advances, 'Look ar'm sure your a very nice bloke' she said removing his hand from her knee, 'But i aint intrested mate'
Sheik Abdullah stroked his long black moustache and flashed his bulging money belt, 'I am an exceedingly

nice man' he replied, eyeing Trisha's chest 'I am also a very generous man, i have the penthouse suite at the Dorchester if you'd care to join me later, in fact i have the entire floor if your friends would like to join us'

Trisha was about to refuse when Dee Dee, smelling an opportunity, intervened 'Yeah we'll av summa that' she said raising her glass 'Won't we Trish!' Trisha relented and flashed a half smile at the Arab Sheik.

Several drinking games followed, which in particular fashion, Trisha duly lost and had to endure such forfeits as retrieving a cocktail sausage from the ex PM's underpants, licking Baileys from Peter's chest and simulating sex with the reluctant Antoine. 'Why is it always me?' she said whilst eating a chocolate eclair from the chefs navel 'You aint done nuffin yet Dee or you Maize'

Her two friends laughed, 'Coz your shit at this sorta fing Trish' Dee Dee chuckled 'Thas why'

It wasn't until the early hours of the morning that the party began to wind down and several of the guests were escorted out the rear of the building to waiting taxi's. Sheik Abdullah clapped his hands and one of his henchman disappeared, returning moments later, 'The car is waiting your excellency!' he said, bowing his head.

The Sheik was helped from his seat and beckoned to the girls 'Come, please be my guests' he said leading the way. Maizie and Trisha trotted behind admiring their diamond rings while Dee Dee said her goodbyes to Peter

'Seeya lata love' she said, tweaking the footballers bottom. She then turned her attentions to the ex Prime Minister sandwiched between two bare chested lap dancers 'And as for you mate' she said, pointing a nagging finger 'If you and the rest of them feevin fuckers adn't swindled faasands off the workin class for ya flash mota's and fancy ouses you might still be in a job, just a fought' she then hurried after the Sheik and her two friends leaving the Minister open mouthed. He had indeed been recently embroiled in a damaging expenses scandal that had seen him removed from office and had rocked the entire British government.

Sheik Abdullah's driver held the door of his Bentley open for Trisha and the others 'Ooh ta' Maizie said when a glass of pink champagne was thrust into her hand 'Ar feel like a bleedin celebrity ar do'.

Dee Dee couldn't help but notice that one of the Sheiks men had a snakes skin attache case cuffed to his right hand and sat looking nervously over his shoulder and out of the side window as they made their way towards Park Lane.

Once inside the hotel lobby the Sheik and the others were ushered by hotel staff to a private elevator which only stopped at the penthouse, 'Please make your self at home' Sheik Abdullah said, taking a key from around his neck and freeing the case from his minders wrist, it was then deposited into a safe beside a huge circular bed and locked with the latest fingerprint technology. Dee Dee dragged her two friends toward the toilet 'We're er! we just gonna freshen up Abby alright!' she said, pushing the two of them through the door.

Trisha shrugged herself free 'Dee ar'm alright mate!' she said, heading back out the door 'I ad a dump at the club!'

Dee Dee wrenched her back inside, 'Shut up ya dozy mare and listen!' she snapped, 'We gotta get our ands on that case, there's gotta be shit loadsa the shifty Sheiks dosh in it'

'Ow we gonna do that Dee?' Maizie asked, touching up her make up in the mirror, 'E stuck it in the safe and besides we aint got no gear wiv us'

Dee Dee thought for a second, 'One of us is gonna av to shag im to wear im out' she then looked at Trisha 'Ang on ar'll rephrase that, Trish your gonna have to shag im, and when e falls a kip we stick iz and on the safe and leg it wiv the loot, simples, as them mangey meerkats say'

'Bleedin ell Dee' Trisha said, stamping her foot, 'Ow come i av to do it, e'z got ands like a fuckin octopus'

Maizie and Dee Dee pushed Trisha into a corner of the plush toilets, 'Coz e likes you Trish thas why!' Dee Dee said, 'If e ad the ots for me ar'd bang im, wouldn't you Maize?'

'Oh yeah!' Maizie nodded, 'Course ar would, look Trish we've all ad a taste of the good life and ar dunno about you but ar want some more, so get out there mate and take one for the team'

Dee Dee put a reassuring arm around her friend 'Itta be alright mate!' she said, giving Trisha a squeeze

'Anyway it aint the first time you give it up to get what ya want is it, ar mean don't tell me that spotty geek in the phone shop give you a brand new blackberry for nuffin, wody'a give im in return, an and job or a tit wank or summink!'

'No ar never' Trisha said defensively 'Ar can't tell ya anyway iss embarrassin'

'Come on Trish' Maize said pinning her to the sink, 'Tell us what you did'

'Well' Trisha said, hanging her head, 'I ad to dress up as an alien and blow im and a couple of iz trecky mates'

Dee Dee and Maizie fell about laughing, 'Your avin a fuck laugh aintcha!' Dee Dee roared 'You give captain berk and the clingon's a bj!'
'Well yeah' Trisha said, shamefully 'But ar did get an extended warranty'
'Well thas alright then' Maizie added, 'So you wont mind shaggin the Sheik then will ya'
Trisha finally relented and agreed to help out for the cause, pushing her chest out and spraying some perfume between her legs she prepared herself, 'Right less do it!' she said, having psyched herself.
'Good girl' Dee Dee said, leading her out into the bedroom, 'Oy Abby me and Maize are gonne av a drink on the balcony' she told the Sheik who was lounging on the bed having removed his robe and headdress, 'We'll leave you two alone, nart ar mean'.
Trisha took a large gulp of champagne before Dee Dee snatched the bottle from her and headed for the door,
'We have plenty more my dove' the oily Sheik said, popping open a bottle at his side, 'Come, join me!' He then clapped his hands and summoned his guards, 'Leave us now!' he barked, 'I will see you in the morning'
'But your excellency!' one of them pleaded, 'Your fathers orders were to not leave your side!'
The Sheik flew into an immediate rage and hurled a bronze figurine in their direction and screamed 'I said leave us you insulent dogs or i'll have you trampled by a thousand stinking camels!'
The two guards bowed and backed out of the door, 'Yes your excellency' the other groveled 'Please accept our apologies for offending you, goodnight sir, and sleep well'.

Once alone with Trisha the Sheik ran his hand down her spine, 'Ooh that tickles' she said, pouring two large glasses of bubbly and handing him one, 'Ar don't wanna rush Shakey love, why don't we av a few more drinks first'
At first the Sheik agreed but soon became impatient 'Come my dear' he said placing Trisha's hand between his legs 'Feel how my passion burns for you'
'Ooh er' Trisha said, blushing, 'Your a big bugger aintcha'
Sheik Abdullah began to maul Trisha, showering her with compliments, 'You are more beautiful than any of my seventy wives, your eyes would put the rarest emeralds to shame'
'Cor blimey!' Trisha swooned, 'Your a smoov talkin fucker an'all'
Eventually as her two friends were popping corks and living the high life on the balcony Trisha could contain the Sheiks advances no longer and seeing that he was growing weary from the alcohol and persistent petting she loosened her clothing and let it fall to the floor before slipping beneath the satin sheets, 'At last' the Sheik said, flinging the last of his robes across the room and joining her, there then followed a period of grunting and groaning as the Sheik fumbled awkwardly beneath the bed sheets,
'Left a bit' Trisha said, wriggling to the side and wrapping her legs around his waist 'Come on for fuck sake woss up wiv ya!'
After several moments of sweating and cursing in arabic the Sheik finally got into his stride and Trisha did her level best to appear to be enjoining his efforts, 'Ooh yeah thas it! she said, admiring the elaborate crystal chandelier that hung in the centre of the room. Due to the Sheik's massive alcohol intake

during the course of the evening, after almost an hour he was no nearer to climaxing, Trisha meanwhile had drifted off into her own little world gazing around the room oblivious to his hideous moaning. Soon the Sheik began to tire and Trisha noticed his eyes slowly closing until he finally collapsed on top of her snoring loudly. Grunting she tried to push his slumbering body off of her but his dead weight made it virtually impossible, 'Psssst!' she whispered, attempting to gain her friends attention 'Dee Dee, Maize, give us an and!' but her two friends were swaying arm in arm having downed a further two bottles of champagne singing 'i will survive' at the tops of their voices. Trisha stretched her arm out and just managed to claw a fountain pen from the bedside table which she threw across the room at the balcony window.

'What was that?' Maizie asked, peering into an empty bottle,

'Must be Trish' Dee Dee replied, opening the door and peering cautiously inside. She could just make out her friends arm waving from the gigantic bed,

'Dee urry up' Trisha beckoned, 'Get this fucker offa me will ya!' Dee Dee dragged Maizie into the room and the two of them carefully pulled the sleeping Sheik off of their exhausted friend,

'Fuckin ell!' she said, slipping her clothes back on, 'The randy git nearly put me back out'.

The Sheik was on the opposite side of the bed to the safe so Dee Dee rallied her friends 'We'll all av to drag im closer' she whispered 'Maizie you get iz leg'

The three girls took hold of the slumbering Sheiks arms and legs and heaved with all their might but only succeeded in moving the his hulking body a few inches,

'E'z too bleedin evvy' Trisha said letting go.
Dee Dee looked at the circular bed and had an idea, 'Give us an and!' she said, turning it on its rollers,
'Nice one Dee' Maizie replied, gripping the mattress. Having rotated the bed a full one hundred and eighty degrees the Sheik was now within a couple of feet of the safe. 'Elp me get iz arm' Dee Dee said, taking hold of his wrist 'Come on you two!'
Maizie urged Trisha to help and the three of them, puffing and panting slid his naked body across the remainder of the bed,
'Thatta do' Dee Dee said offering the Sheiks palm up to the safe, but before his hand made contact, Sheik Abdullah stirred and opened one eye,
'What, what the?' he said, coming too.
'Oh shit!' cried Dee Dee, having absolutely no explanation for their actions. 'We gotta go seeya lata!' she shook his hand and turned to leave with Maizie and Trisha close behind but the Sheik, realizing what was going on, leapt from the bed.
'STOP!' he yelled, reaching beneath the bed and producing a long curved razor sharp sword. 'In my country we cut off the hands of anyone who dares to steal from another. but you dare to steal from me, Sheik Abdullah, you will pay with your heads!' the Sheik, still naked lunged at the girls, swiping his sword inches from them,
'Fuck, LEG IT!' yelled Dee Dee, throwing open the door and sprinting out into the hall with the other two girls at her side, Trisha slamming the door behind her. This just infuriated the Sheik even more and he hacked wildly at it, wrenching it open, meanwhile Dee Dee was frantically pressing the elevator button but on the Sheiks earlier orders it had been disabled until the morning. 'What we gonna do Dee?' Trisha cried,

hugging her friend as the seething Sheik flew at them slicing the heads off two stone statues in his path,
'I'll cut you into a thousand pieces and let the buzzards feast on your eyes!' he snarled, now foaming at the mouth. Dee Dee and the others fled into an adjacent bedroom with the angry arab in hot pursuit, hacking at the bed sheets as the girls leapt over tossing anything they could lay their hands on behind them in an attempt to slow their persuer down.
'ELP, ELP!' Dee Dee and her friends cried, banging on the windows as they fled, but there was little chance of anyone hearing their cries on the twenty first floor.
The wafer thin blade of the Sheiks ceremonial sword penetrated deep into anything it came into contact with, slashing the expensive drapes and priceless works of art with ease. Soon Sheik Abdullah had the girls cornered and paused to savor the moment, 'You have nowhere to run now my little doves' he panted, pulling a single hair from his head and splitting it on the swords edge, 'I can promise you all a speedy death, but i cannot promise it will be painless'
Dee Dee and her friends huddled in the corner of the room trembling and frantically looking for a way out. Sweating profusely the Sheik raised his sword and inched towards them relishing the thought of the kill, in his homeland he had put many a peasant to the sword for the slightest of offences, even looking in his direction during the fasting period when he would be particularly touchy, and having their remains buried in unmarked graves out in the Kuwaiti desert.
Dee Dee stood in front of her terrified friends in a vane attempt to protect them, 'Less talk about this Abby!' she said, hoping for a diplomatic solution, but

soon realized by the crazed look in his eye that this was futile, she then winced at the sight of his overly hairy genitalia dangling in front of her and at once had a momentary flash of inspiration. In an instant Dee Dee brought the point of her patent leather stiletto up sharply, making perfect contact with the Sheiks right testicle, so hard in fact that it pierced his scrotum and pushed the dangling ball up inside his stomach. Sheik Abdullah immediately stopped in his tracks and bent over double, first letting out a pitiful whimper and then an agonizing scream. Maizie, seizing her chance, picked up a heavy porcelain vase of gardenia's from the table beside them and after handing Trisha the flowers, took a deep breath and brought it crashing down onto the back of the Sheiks skull sending him and the shattered remains crashing to the floor,

'Nice one Maize' Dee Dee said, stepping gingerly over his body,

'Fanks mate' Maizie replied, giving the Sheik a wide berth 'Ar was shittin flippin meself'

As Trisha followed, the dazed Sheik grabbed her right ankle and fumbled behind him for his sword whilst screaming obscenities in his native tongue, 'Arrrgh get offa me ya fucker!' Trisha cried, beating the Sheik around the head with the flowers until they were completely shredded, but the Sheiks grip grew tighter as he pulled himself up off the floor, 'DEEEE ELP!' Trisha cried, desperately.

Dee Dee quickly stepped on the Sheiks hand as he grappled with his sword, wrenching it from his fingers she swung it wildly above her head, 'Oy Sinbad, cop this!' she yelled, bringing the blade down and severing the arm that clung to her friend before flinging the weapon across the room. Sheik Abdullah fell back in a state of mortified shock clutching his stump which spewed blood from the pumping arteries across the granite floor.

Trisha ran screaming from the room followed by Dee Dee and Maizie, 'TRISH WAIT!' Dee Dee yelled trying to stop her hysterical friend who darted from room to room in a blind panic, she finally ran head long into Dee Dee and Maizie beside the elevator,

'We cut iz arm off, we cut iz arm off Dee!' she rambled, 'Dee we cut iz fuckin arm off!'

Dee Dee shook her friend, 'Ar know we did you dozy cow!' she said, pointing down at Trisha's leg which still had the Sheiks hand clinging to it,

Trisha leapt up and down shaking her leg 'Arrrrgh get it offa me, get it offa me!' she screamed 'Elp, get it offa me please Dee!'

'STAND STILL FOR FUCK SAKE!' Dee Dee yelled, taking hold of the arm and prizing the fingers loose then flinging the lifeless limb across the hall. The three of them stood petrified for a moment before looking round at the bedroom door where the Sheik lay dying having lost the majority of his blood,

'D'ya fink e'z dead?' Maizie asked, not daring to look, 'Av we killed im Dee?'

'Wait ere' Dee Dee said, tip toeing toward the room. Maizie and Trisha held each other tightly, 'What we gonna do Maize?' Trisha winced,

'Ar dunno Trish' Maizie replied, watching Dee Dee, 'Just shut up for a minute will ya'.

Dee Dee peered over the bed at the Sheiks naked blood spattered body and looked closely for any sign of movement,

'E'z bleedin dead alright!' she said rejoining her friends.

Trisha flew into a panic again, 'Oh shit Dee what we gonna do?' she cried, tugging at Dee Dee's arm, 'Maize for fuck sake we've killed im!'
Dee Dee shook herself free, 'Shut up and let me fink will ya!' she snapped, 'E'z dead, we can't do nuffin about that, we just gotta get the fuck out of ere thas all' she then looked down at the severed arm, 'Maizie get Abby's and' she told her friend,
'Oooh no Dee ar couldn't' Maizie cringed backing away 'It might grab me like one of them edless chickens'
Dee Dee raised her eyebrows and gingerly picked up the amputated arm and carried it through to the master bedroom,
'What ya doin Dee?' Trisha asked, trotting behind 'We gotta get out of ere!'
'Shut up a minute' Dee Dee said, holding the limp limb up to the safe and pressing the finger tips against the screen. There was a loud click and the door swung open, 'Ere old that' she said thrusting the arm into Trisha's hand,
'Oooh ar don't wonnit!' Trisha cried handing it to Maizie, who in turn flung it onto the bed,
'Don't give it to me!' she cursed, wiping her hands on the sheets.
Dee Dee peered inside the open safe and gasped 'Fuck me!' she said, plucking out several huge bundles of fifty pound notes and handing them to her gob smacked friends before retrieving the attache case,
'Bleedin ell Dee!' Maizie said ,holding the money up to her nose 'There's a shit load of dough ere!'
Dee Dee sat on the edge of the bed with the case on her lap and slowly undid the clasp, Maizie and Trisha

leaned forward as Dee Dee reached inside and took out a long black velvet box,
'Woss that?' Trisha asked craning her neck.
Dee Dee looked the box over before popping a clip at one end and lifting the lid, 'Fuuuuck me!' she gasped, 'Ava look!' she turned the box and showed her friends it's contents, an elaborate diamond and emerald encrusted chain with a flawless ruby the size of a duck egg attached.
'Fuckin ell Dee!' Maizie said, staggering back, 'Thas gotta be werf a bleedin fortune!'
Trisha turned and headed for the door 'Dee less just take the money and get out of ere' she said, with an anguished look on her face, 'Thas far too big for us!'
'She's right Dee' Maizie added, 'What we gonna do wiv summink like that'
'I aint leavin it' Dee Dee replied, closing the box and slipping it back into the case, she then pulled a pile of papers from the safe with the heading 'Al Jahara pipeline'
'Woss that all about Dee!' Maizie asked,
'Ar dunno' Dee Dee replied, stuffing them into the case with the ruby, 'Ar'll ava look lata' she held the case out in front of her, 'Right you two, put the dough in ere'
Maizie and Trisha dropped the bundles into the case and looked around the room, 'Ow we gonna get out of ere Dee?' Maizie asked, peering out of the window, 'The lift don't bleedin work and there aint no stairs, we're stuck Dee, proper stuck mate'
Dee Dee paced the room, deep in thought.
'We could phone the police' Trisha said, joining Maizie, 'Tell em it was self defence or summink'
Dee Dee held the bag in the air and glared at Trisha 'Are you fuckin mad?' she cursed 'We got a bleedin

fortune ere and you wanna call the old bill! Maize sort er out before ar fuckin slap ere one!'

Trisha sat sulking 'Well what are we gonna do then Dee?' she said, shrugging her shoulders, 'Jump out the bleedin winda'

Dee Dee ran to the balcony 'Thas it!' she cried, throwing open the doors.

Trisha looked at Maizie 'Woss she on about?' she asked 'Dee ar was bleedin jokin mate'

Dee Dee peered over the side at the balcony below, 'We gotta get daan there!' she said looking around the room, 'Maize get me them sheets!'

'But Dee!' Maize replied, thinking the idea preposterous 'Thas ridiculous mate, we'll bleedin kill ourselves!'

'JUST DO IT!' Dee Dee shouted, 'AND YOU TRISH, URRY UP!'.Maizie and Trisha pushed the Sheiks arm onto the floor and gathered up the bed sheets, 'Tie em togeva!' Dee Dee said, taking one end and fastening it to a chrome column on the balcony's edge, she then thought for a moment, 'Oh bugger!' she said remembering the sword, 'Wait there ar'll be back in a minute!' Dee Dee then ran back to where the Sheik was lying and hunted around the floor eventually fishing the sword out from beneath the bed. Emptying a pillow from it's case Dee Dee then meticulously cleaned the weapons handle and laid it back down before running back through to the other room.

'Iz e still dead?' Trisha asked, clasping her handsto her face.

Dee Dee looked at her friend in disbelief 'Of course e'z still dead ya dopey cow!' she snapped, shaking her head 'Fuck me Trish are you fick or what, we fuckin killed im so e'z dead, proper dead, well dead, in fact e can't get any fuckin deader than e iz right naah, ok!' Trisha nodded and looked down at the floor.

Dawn was fast approaching as Dee Dee lowered the make shift rope over the side and tugged on the tethered end 'That should old' she said, cocking a leg over the edge, 'Ar go first'

Trisha covered her eyes as her friend descended slowly 'Is she alright Maize, ar can't look' she said clinging to Maizie's arm 'There asta be anuvva way daan surely'

'There aint!' Maizie replied, watching Dee Dee scramble onto the balcony below 'Come on Trish you go next'

Trisha ran back inside and backed against the wall 'Maize ar can't do it mate!' she said trembling uncontrollably, 'You know ar can't stand ites, member what ar was like in the juniors mate, ar used to piss meslf every time ar went on the big slide'

Maizie dragged Trisha back out onto the balcony 'Just old on tight and don't look daan!' she said, handing Trisha the sheet 'Come on mate we gotta get the fuck out of ere!'

Trisha climbed onto the ledge and peered over, 'Ar can't Maize onest!' she said wiping the tears from her eyes, 'You go, ar stay ere'

Maizie shook Trisha firmly 'Look Trish, Dee Dee done it, iss safe as fuckin ouses!' she said, nudging her friend, 'Just get down there will ya!'

Dee Dee leaned out and looked up at Trisha 'For fuck sake urry up will ya!' she yelled, then opened the patio doors and peered inside the apartment, 'Result!' she said on seeing it was unoccupied and turning on the light.

Trisha closed her eyes and lowered herself down, gripping the sheet as tightly as she could,
'Thas is Trish!' Maizie called down, 'Nearly there!' Dee Dee took hold of Trisha's feet and guided them onto the balcony's edge before helping her down, 'Bleedin ell Dee!' Trisha said, hugging her friend 'My arse was goin there ar tell ya!'
Maizie followed close behind and the three girls made their way to the apartment door. 'Iss all clear' Dee Dee said leading the way out into the hall, 'This way! she added, heading for the service elevator. 'Basement, thata do' she said pressing the button and breathing a sigh of relief.
Once inside the three girls smiled at first then burst out laughing at the thought of their escapade,
'Mar bleedin arts paandin' Dee Dee said, clutching her chest, 'What a fuckin rush' but then to their horror the elevator ground to a halt on the fourth floor,
'Oh mar gawd, oh mar gawd!' Trisha cried 'We're proper fucked Dee!' The girls held their breath as the elevator doors opened, but instead of the police or security there was a maid attempting to push a trolly loaded with cleaning products into the lift. Dee Dee put her foot up and stopped the trolley, much to the annoyance of the maid who began ranting in an eastern european accent. Dee Dee held up the attache case and tapping it barked at the maid 'Oy bitch ar got one word to say to you, immigration, now bleedin do one!' The maid who had very little grasp of the english language knew this word only too well and pulled her trolley clear and hurried away as Maizie closed the door.
Reaching the basement level the girls peered sheepishly out of the elevator into a deserted kitchen, 'Come on' Dee Dee said, leading the way between

the stainless steel worktops and industrial cookers. 'Oooh!' Trisha said passing a giant gateau and scooping a finger full of cream from the top, 'Oh thas lush, try summa that Dee'
Dee Dee and Maizie both spun round and stared at Trisha 'What?' Trisha said wiping the cream from her top lip 'Thas the nuts of a cake'
Maizie grabbed her by the wrist and dragged her away, 'Trish pay attention will ya!' she said, following Dee Dee to the back door 'We ain't got time for bleedin cake!'.
Ducking between the refuse bins, Dee Dee led her friends away from the hotel and down one of London's many back streets 'Eeya quick!' she said, raising her hand and stepping out into the road 'TAXI!' she yelled, hailing a black cab, 'Romford mate' she told the driver as the three of them hopped inside and flopped on the back seat,
'What a night!' maizie said, gazing out of the window at the many department stores brimming with designer goods.
'Bin clubbin av ya?' the cockney cabbie said, sliding open the glass screen between them, 'Ar used to come up ere when ar was your age!'
'What?' said Dee Dee, in no mood for small talk.
'Clubbin!' the cabbie said again, 'Ar get all the clubbers in mar cab me!'
Dee Dee had heard enough and leaned forward 'Listen mate!' she said angrily 'Before ya bleedin start ar don't give a toss who you've ad in this fuckin cab, in fact ar couldn't care less if ya'v ad Mickey Mouse, Donald fuckin duck or the pissin power rangers in ere, you got that!' she slammed the window shut and sat back clutching the case. The disgruntled cabbie

meanwhile, turned off his interior light and fixed his eyes on the road ahead.
The three girls sat in silence for much of the journey, physically and mentally drained from their ordeal until Trisha piped up, 'E wern a bad shag are spose!'
'Who?' Dee Dee asked, not having a clue what her friend was talking about,
'Sheik Abby!' Trisha added, crossing her legs and resting her chin on her hands 'E ad some blinkin stayin power ar tell ya, are you sure e'z dead Dee?'
Dee Dee flew into yet another rage, lunging at Trisha wildly having to be restrained by Maizie, 'Course e'z fuckin dead you stupid bitch!' she growled, 'Ar mean it , if you ask me that once more ar swear Trisha ar'll punch your bleedin lights out!'
'Calm daan Dee' Maize said, taking hold of Dee Dee's flaying arms, 'She don't mean it, do ya Trish?'
'Naah couse not' Trisha replied innocently 'Ar was just tryna make conversation thas all'.
Dee Dee wriggled free of Maizie's grip and sat seething in the corner of the cab, 'Well don't make conversation' she snapped, 'In fact, don't talk to me for the rest of the bleedin day, d'you ear me'
Trisha nodded and sat staring into space for several minutes before adding, 'It was funny though!'
Both Dee Dee and Maizie glared at her, 'WHAT?' they both yelled.
Trisha raised her arms and brought them down in a slashing motion,'Oy Sinbad, cop this!' she chuckled.
No matter how mad Dee Dee and Maizie were with their friend they couldn't help but see the funny side and soon all three were in fits of hysterical laughter.
It was daylight when the taxi finally pulled up outside Dee Dee's tower block, 'Ar'll give you two a ring lata' she told her friends then tossed a fifty pound note

through the drivers window, 'That should cover it geeza!' she said, tucking the case under her arm and waving to Maizie and Trisha as they were driven away.

Approaching her front door Dee Dee could hear voices coming from inside and as her mother rarely entertained visitors she froze on the landing, then peered through the letter box. But unable to see or make out the voice of the mystery guest Dee Dee slipped her key quietly into the lock and eased the door open in an attempt to sneak in unseen, forgetting the aging door had a distinctive creek,

'Is that you Dee love?' Pearl called out from the living room, 'You'll never guess who's ere'

'Bugger!' Dee Dee cursed, in no mood for company, 'Ar'm knackered mum ar'm gaana bed' she added, poking her head around the door, she then stepped back in amazement, 'Mickey, what the bleedin ell are you doin ere?'

Black Mickey was sitting on the sofa with a bowl of cornflakes in his hand, 'Alright Dee!' he said, raising his spoon, 'Ar just popped round for breakfast'

Pearl smiled at Dee Dee, 'They let im out on good behavior apparently'

Mickey winked at Dee Dee and she knew instantly that wasn't the case.

'Oh thas a result' she said, 'Eeya muvva gissa fag'

Pearl offered Dee Dee a cigarette then hoisted herself from her chair 'Ar'll put the kettle on love, make you a nice cuppa tea!' she said heading for the kitchen, 'Mickey d'you wanna nuvver one?'

'Yeah cheers Misses D!' Micky replied, tipping the last of his cereal into his mouth.

Dee Dee sat down beside him and first checked that her mother was out of earshot, 'Good behavior my

arse!' she laughed, 'You bleedin broke out aintcha'. Mickey nodded 'Yeah last night' he whispered, 'Ar couldn't go to Marcie's Dee coz it's the first place they'd look, ya mum said ar could stay ere for a coupla days'
'Yeah course Mickey' Dee Dee replied, putting the case onto her lap 'Ar got summink to show ya anyway, not ere though' As Pearl came back into the room Dee Dee took her teas from her, 'We'll av this in me room mum' she told her, 'Ar'll sort Mickey out a duvet and that'
'Oh ok love' Pearl said, switching on the television 'Ar do ya both a bacon sandwich lata'. Dee Dee led Mickey through to her room and closed the door behind them, 'This is for you first!' she said, taking a bundle of notes from under her bed, 'Iss ten grand from our last job'
Mickey looked gobsmacked 'Jesus Dee, you were serious about blaggin then' he said, pocketing the cash 'That'll tide me over nicely till ar get back on the street'
'Thas nuffin' Dee Dee said, emptying the case onto the bed and handing Mickey one of the larger bundles of fifty pound notes 'Eeya, thas from last nights caper'
'Blimey Dee!' Mickey gasped, 'Ar can't take all this!' Dee Dee picked up the velvet box 'Yeah ya can Mick' she said springing the catch 'Coz ar need yer elp floggin this'.
On seeing the giant gem Mickey immediately clasped his hands to his head 'No, no shit!' he cried 'Dee babe where did you get that?',
Woss up Micky?' Dee Dee asked surprised at his reaction 'We robbed it off some Arab geezer last

night, why woss wrong, iss gotta be werf a few quid ain it'

'Nine and three quarter million to be exact Dee' Mickey said, sitting on the end of the bed with his head in his hands.

Dee Dee's mouth fell open, 'Fuck me!' she said, sitting down in a daze 'Nine and free quarter million, eeya owd you know that Mick?'

Mickey stood up and paced the room shaking his head 'Coz thas the red sea ruby Dee, the second biggest ruby ever faand'

Dee Dee leapt to her feet, 'Well thas good ain it?' she asked 'All we gotta do is flog it and we'll be set for life!'

'No Dee thas bad actually! Mickey said, stopping her in her tracks, 'Remember ar told you about Billy Tibbs and his saaf London firm'

'Yeah!' Dee Dee replied, 'But we aint bin saaf of the river, we nicked it up west'

'Listen to me Dee' Mickey said, resting his hands on her shoulders, 'Billy's been plannin to blag this stone for mumfs, the Arab was due to visit a saaf London mosque next week and thas when they was gonna snatch it, Dee e put a shooter to my head and told me to stay away from it, when e finds out i broke out of Pentonville last night e'z gonna know ar got something to do wiv it, this is bad Dee, real bad'.

Dee Dee tried to calm Mickey, 'Look surely all we gotta do is flog the ruby and bugger off before anyone finds out'

Pearl then called out from the lounge 'Eeya Dee, looka this!' Dee Dee and Mickey went back to join her mother in front of the tv, 'They just faand some Arab bloke wiv iz arm cut off in an otel!' Pearl told them, 'Some sorta robbery they fink'

'Shit!' Mickey muttered under his breath, 'We aint buggering off nowhere naah'

Chapter six.

The fence and the South London firm.

..The top floor of the Dorchester had been sealed off while forensic teams surveyed the scene, D I Pritcher and two of his detectives arrived in time to see the body of Sheik Abdullah being stretchered out, 'Wait!' he barked, unzipping the body bag and looking the Sheik and his severed limb up and down, 'Jesus!' he said, looking away, he then began examining the many slash marks in the walls and furniture, 'What we looking at?' he asked one of the scene of crime's officers 'Ninja's, Triads or what?'
'It's too early to speculate sir' the man replied, busily dusting for prints. 'We er, we did retrieve the murder weapon though sir' he added, handing the DI an evidence bag containing the sword, 'We think it's Arabic sir'
'Of course it's fucking Arabic!' the DI snapped, 'It's the victim's own bleedin sword you idiot, how long have you been in forensics?'
'Just over a year sir' the officer replied sheepishly,
DI Pritcher pointed to an inscription on the blade, 'Well tell me what that says?' he asked.
The officer took the sword from him and read the inscription out loud 'Presented to Sheik Abdullah

Hussain by his excellency Sheik Fayahd the Emir of Kuwait, yes it's definitely Arabic sir'
'Just get it to the fucking lab!' the DI barked 'Do we know what's been stolen!' he added, seeing the open safe,
'Not yet sir!' Detective Chris Marsh replied, pointing to the Sheiks two guards sitting quietly against the wall, 'These two gentlemen we believe are the victims personal bodyguards and possibly the last people to see him alive, but they aren't talking sir'
'What do you mean they aren't talking?' the DI said, losing his temper, 'Tell em this is a bloody murder investigation dam it, and they can be banged up for obstructing justice!'. The DI was about to question the guards himself when the elevator door opened and the Sheiks father entered the room in traditional Arab dress, flanked by several armed guards,
'What the fuck?' said the DI standing in their way, 'This is a crime scene gentlemen, I'm gonna have to ask you all to leave' One of the menacing guards pushed the Detective Inspector aside uttering the words 'Diplomatic immunity'
Sheik Mohamed, Abdullah's father and his men surrounded the two seated guards and began a heated conversation in Arabic, the two guards appeared to be pleading for their lives and blaming Abdullah for sending them away, but Sheik Mohamed was furious, pointing to the safe and slapping the two men about the head. The Sheik then barked an order at his henchmen and the two guards were dragged to their feet begging for mercy and marched towards the elevator.
'HEY! HEY!' the DI shouted, 'Those two are my witnesses for god sake!' but the terrified men were

bundled into the elevator to a more sinister fate than the British legal system.
While DI Pritcher and his men were pondering what had just happened, the elevator returned, this time to their complete surprise Lord Fitzroy, the current Foreign Minister stepped out with several members of the MI5 top brass and approached the Sheik,
'Sir! sir may I remind you this is a crime scene sir!' the DI said, trying to make himself heard, 'Will somebody tell me what the fuck's going on!' but this time it was the MI5 officials that pushed him aside, 'This is a matter of national security detective' one of them said, with his hand on the DI's chest,
'Detective Inspector actually!' The DI replied abruptly, 'Detective Inspector Pritcher, and you are?'
The MI5 official prodded the DI with a firm finger and glared at him 'Who I am isn't important right now Detective Inspector Pritcher' he snapped 'What is important is that you do your job and find whoever's responsible for this and return the Sheik's property to me, or you could find yourself directing traffic, do I make myself clear'
Sheik Mohamed and the foreign minister began a heated conversation concerning the stolen documents, 'This would never have happened in my country!' the Sheik said, waving his arms in the air 'I trust you are doing everything in your power to bring those responsible for this to justice!'
'Trust me Sheik Mohamed' Lord Fitzroy said, trying to calm the situation 'I'll have every man in the force scouring the length and breadth of the country until the perpetrators are caught' Sheik Mohamed leaned forward and whispered in the Ministers ear, 'Surely I don't have to remind you that if those documents fall into the wrong hands they could start a civil war in my

country, and i'm sure, for your part Lord Fitzroy it would be the end of your political career and possibly your entire government'

The documents in question that Dee Dee had taken as a mere after thought refereed to a secret deal between the Kuwaiti Sheik and Great Britain to run an oil pipeline through Iraq to neighboring Syria where it would then be transported to the West, with both parties sharing in the wealth, but Saddam Hussain would need to be removed from power for this to happen, so the whole 'Weapons of mass destruction' affair was concocted, and the rest is history.

'You have my word' Lord Fitzroy told the Sheik 'No stone will be left unturned' He then turned to the detectives 'Who's in charge here?' he asked.

'I am sir!' the DI replied 'Detective Inspector Pritcher sir, would you mind telling me what's going on sir?'

'I'm afraid it's classified Detective Inspector, all I can tell you is that a large ruby necklace has been stolen, this one in fact' he then produced a photograph of the necklace from his inside pocket, 'As you can see it's very distinctive and would be very difficult for anyone to sell on the open market, also more importantly some highly sensitive documents belonging to Sheik Mohamed must be found, put every man you have on it and as soon as you have anything, report directly to me at once, is that clear'

'Crystal sir' the DI replied 'Was anything else taken sir?'

'Yes' said the minister, gathering the MI5 officials together and herding them towards the elevator 'Around four hundred thousand in cash I believe' They were followed by Sheik Mohamed and his entourage leaving the DI and his men bemused.

'What the fuck was that all about?' he said, scratching his head, 'Marsh, tell me what we got so far'

Detective Marsh thumbed through his notebook, 'Well sir' he replied, 'According to hotel staff It appears the Sheik returned to the hotel around two fifteen accompanied by his guards and three young ladies'

'Tarts?' the DI asked 'Did anyone get a good look at em?'

Detective Marsh shook his head, 'I'm afraid not sir, apparently the hotels cctv system is undergoing refurbishment at present so isn't in use!'

'MARVELOUS' DI Pritcher yelled, throwing his hands in the air 'Three slags waltz in and out of one of the biggest hotels in London and nobody sees a bleedin fing! well I want em found do you hear me!'

'Sir one other thing' the second detective said, a little nervous at having to break the news, 'It may or may not be relevant sir but, but'

DI Pritcher lost his temper at this point 'I'll decide if it's relevant or not Henshaw' he yelled 'Now what the fuck is it?'

'It's er, it's Mickey Spencer sir' detective Henshaw said, backing away.

The DI raised his eyebrows and shook his head 'No Henshaw it's not Spencer, that toe rags in Pentonville where I put him'

'Not any more sir' detective Marsh added, 'He broke out last night!'

'WHAT?' the DI yelled 'I thought i'd got that black bastard once and for all, well I want him back behind bars asap do you hear me, I want his family and all known associates leaned on, I wanna know who visited the slag while he was banged up and I want

that fucking Minister off my back, d'you hear me, I know Spencer's mixed up in this somehow, I can feel it!'
Detective Marsh interrupted his DI 'Spencer's a thief sir but he's no murderer'
'JUST FIND HIM!' the DI yelled 'And I want those three whores as well!'. The two detectives scurried to the elevator leaving the DI seething and deep in thought.
News of the robbery and Mickey's escape had also reached Billy Tibbs at the office of his families funeral directors just off the Tower bridge road in Bermondsey. Tibbs undertakers, established in the late eighteen hundreds had long been a front for their gangland activities with kidnapping, extortion, armed robbery and drugs trafficking to name but a few. Billy, who looked every bit the gangster in his Savile Row suits and extravagant jewellry, with a scar over his right eye from a recent assassination attempt had recently taken his rightful place as head of the family after his father Alfie Tibbs, a psychopathic bare knuckle fighter in his day, feared by many rival gangs from the Kray's to the Richardson's recently passed away. Billy's twin younger brothers Jimmy and Roland sat at his side. Roland or Rolly as his close friends called him because of his hulking frame brought on by his love of the local delicacy, pie and mash, constantly chewed gum between meals of up to fifteen such pies in one sitting. His suit, in contrast to his older brothers exquisitely tailored outfit was stretched to near bursting point and he was continuously mopping beads of sweat from his forehead with a silk handkerchief. Jimmy, in comparison was in no way an identical twin, looking thin and gaunt from years of cocaine abuse, his

orange tinted gold rimmed glasses forever sliding down the bridge of his nose, which he sniffed repeatedly. The youngest member of the Tibbs family, Laura ran the legitimate side of the business in the front office dealing with grief stricken relatives who would often part with their money unaware that on many occasions rival gang members would be buried in the same casket as their loved ones. Laura, a twenty eight year old lesbian kept her distance from the families criminal activities, stating the least she knew the better, but did however enjoy the financial rewards which afforded her a riverside apartment, a sporty convertible Mercedes and a substantial weekly allowance which meant she could frequent as many gay and fetish venues as she so desired.

Producing their own hardwood caskets, Tibbs undertakers would import the timber direct from the Brazilian rain forest with a more sinister cargo concealed between the mahogany planks, raw uncut cocaine in vast quantities supplied by the Colombian drugs cartels, ready for processing in a warehouse off the Jamaica road before flooding the city streets.

Seething at the radio broadcasters revelation Billy grabbed his brother Jimmy by the lapels and yelled into his face 'Ar fought ar told you to put the fuckin word out about that stone, the fuckin Arab was mine you twat!'

'Ar did Bill!' Jimmy said, squirming and straightening his glasses 'Every blagger in London got a visit ar swear!'

Billy threw his brother down into his seat 'So ow come the fuckin Arab's dead and mar bleedin stone's bin nicked, eh!'

Jimmy shrugged his shoulders 'Ar dunno bruv' he replied, 'D'ya reckon Black Mickey ad anyfing to do wiv it, word is e'z busted outta Pentonville'
Billy took an eight inch switchblade from his jacket pocket and thrust it into his desk 'If e did e'z fuckin dead!' he growled, 'Ar warned that cunt ar'd cut im if e ever fucked wiv mar business, take fat boy ere and go find im'
Roland threw his hands in the air 'But Bill bruv I aint ad me dinner yet!' he said, his stomach rumbling.
'Ar don't give a toss!' Billy snapped, 'You find that slag and bring im to me, alright, and you tell every fucker out there, no one, no one makes a mug outta Billy Tibbs!'.
Jimmy took a snuff box from his pocket and snorted a pinch of cocaine before hoisting his brother to his feet, 'Come on Rolly we got work to do!' he said wiping the residue from his top lip.
Reluctant to leave Roland pleaded with his older brother 'But Bill carn ar just av a coupla pies first, ar'm starvin!'
Billy kicked his swivel chair across the office in a fit of rage, 'NO YOU FUCKIN CAN'T YOU USELESS FAT FUCK!' he shouted with the veins on his forehead bulging, 'GET THE FUCK OUT THERE OR AR'LL BEAT THE BLOODY SHIT OUTTA YA!'
Both Jimmy and Roland knew never to cross their older brother, having witnessed the savage beatings he'd inflicted on many who had opposed him, some meeting an untimely death in a frenzied knife attack earning the blood lusting gangster the nickname of Billy the blade.
'WAIT!' Billy yelled as his brothers were leaving the office 'Pay Nikos a visit an'all'

'Nick the bubble?' Jimmy Replied, stopping Roland in his tracks 'Why's that bruv?'
'Fink abaat it you prat!' Billy snapped 'That Greek nonce is the only fence in London that could shift a stone like that'
Nikos Papageorgiou ran a modest run down back street jewellers in Hackney selling cut price gold and silver, but this was merely a facade to fool the authorities, because behind the scenes Nikos or Nick the bubble as many in the underworld called him, an oily olive skinned man with thick black eyebrows and moustache to match ran a highly lucrative operation laundering money and locating buyers for high value stolen items amongst his numerous contacts around the world. Rembrandt's, Monet's, Da' Vinci's and even Elizabeth Taylor's jewellry had passed through his hands at one time or another, many of the pieces finding a home in the vault's of Japanese businessmen. Nikos had one solitary vice, not drink or drugs but rent boys, young pretty rents boys which he picked up in select bars in the heart of London and drove to the flat above his pawn brokers. Billy Tibbs despised Nikos because of his sordid sexuality and always referred to him as Nick the nonce, but as there was no alternative, he was forced to tolerate him no matter how much it stuck in his throat to do so.
At the same time Jimmy and Roland Tibbs were leaving the undertakers, Mickey was filling Dee Dee in on Billy's dangerous dealings 'E'z a nutter Dee' he told her, 'We're as good as dead if e get's old of us, there's only one way aata this and that's to give im the ruby and ope e let's us live'
'Like fuck!' said Dee Dee, shaking her head 'That rocks mar ticket aata this shit ole an I aint about to let

some saaf London wanker take that away from me, no Mickey there must be somewhere we can flog it'
'Well Dee if your serios mate, but don't say ar didn't warn ya, yer only ope is Nick the bubble' Mickey said, thinking aloud, 'No one else'd touch a stone like that'
'Right, Nicky bubble it is then' Dee Dee said taking out her phone, 'Ar'll get us a lift and we'll go and see im' she then dialed Maizie's number, 'Maize, iss Dee, get that bruvva of yours to come and pick me and Mickey up from mine, yeah Black Mickey', she paused for a moment while Maizie bombarded her with questions, 'Look shut up Maize!' she added, 'Ar know e was banged up, I aint got time to explain, just get that bloody mota raand ere, alright!'
Maizie stood with the phone to her ear watching Trisha galloping towards her tv to simulate bowling with a games console remote in her hand, 'Maize look ar got a strike!' she shrieked, leaping up and down and in doing so knocking the television set from it's stand, 'Oh shit sorry Maizie!' she said, cupping her hand to her mouth.
'For fuck sake Trish!' Maizie yelled, then turned her attention back to Dee Dee, 'Sorry Dee iss that doughnut she's just trashed me bleedin telly, ar'll av to bring er wiv me mate she's a bloomin liability ere'
'Just urry up' Dee Dee replied, hanging up.
Trisha managed to lift the now broken television set back onto the dressing table before Maizie dragged her away unaware that the tv's power cord was wrapped around her foot, 'Oh bugger!' she cried, tugging the tv onto the floor once more,
'Ar got it Maize don't worry!' Trisha said wrestling with it for a second time.
'Trish leave it will ya!' Maizie snapped, 'Iss probly shagged now anyway'

Trisha set it gently back down onto the floor while Maize slipped her foot out of the loop of cord, 'Me dad's mate Ronnie's good wiv telly's' she told Maizie 'E fixed mar portable when ar spilt sambucca daan the back, e'z gorgeous an'all, ar couldn't elp starin at iz arse crack while e was bent over, iss dead firm Maize ar reckon e could crack conkers wiv them cheeks'

Maizie had heard enough and dragged Trisha from the room 'Come on Dee's waitin!' she said angrily.

Banging on Bradley's bedroom door Maizie marched straight in, catching her startled brother masturbating on the end of his bed with a copy of the freeman's catalogue on his lap, open at the swimwear page, 'SIS!' he screamed, tugging his tee shirt down over his knees, 'Get aat will ya!',

Maizie grabbed the catalogue from him 'What you doin wiv this ya dirty bastard!' she said, showing it to Trisha.

Bradley's face was crimson as he stammered 'Ar, ar, ar was looking for some new flippers!' he said, thinking fast.

Trisha looked over Maizie's shoulder at the bikini's then at his prominent bulge, 'Well you've already got ya snorkel aintcha' she joked.

Bradley grabbed a pillow and tossed it in their direction 'Get aat the paira ya!' he yelled.

'Alright keep yer air on' Maizie laughed, she then noticed that pages one hundred and ten to one hundred and fifteen, the women's underwear section were gummed together and stiff as a board, 'You need to get yaself a girlfriend ya pervy little git' she said, tossing the catalogue back at him, 'Or you'll snap that fing off one of these days' She then turned to leave, 'Oh, we need the mota so be daanstairs in five minutes, alright!. They left Bradley folding over the corner of the page he'd been ogling and tucking it under his pillow, he then begrudgingly pulled on his baggy jeans and hoodie.

Outside Nikos Papageorgiou's shabby Hackney jewellers 'PAPAS PAWN' there was a screech of brakes and a flurry of feeding pigeons took to the sky. Jimmy and Roland stepped out of a gleaming black S type Jaguar and stood straightening their suits, Roland donning a pair of black Ray Ban's, looking every inch the mobster. Jimmy dipped his finger into his snuff box yet again and rubbed a quantity of the class A drug onto his gums before trying the door. 'Where the fuck is e?' he snapped, pushing hard against the locked door. The pair then peered through the grimy window, rapping it with their knuckles, 'NIKOS OPEN UP!' Jimmy screamed, kicking at the door.

With his nose pressed to the glass Roland then noticed a shadowy figure ducking behind the counter at the rear of the shop, 'E'z in there bruv' he told Jimmy who bent down and prised opened the letter box,

'You open this fuckin door naah you ponce!' he yelled pushing his glasses back along his nose 'Or ar'll drive mar mota fru the fuckin winda!'

Nikos appeared from behind the counter with his hands in the air, scurrying towards the door 'Ok, ok!' he yelled, sliding two bolts back and opening the door, 'Sorry fella's' he said, nervously, 'Ar was just stock taking and didn't hear ya, please come in'

'Don't gimme that bollocks' Jimmy snarled, shoving Nikos aside and marching inside 'Ar told ya before what'd appen if you ever fucked us araand' he then knocked a crystal dolphin from a display cabinet and

watched it shatter on the floor, 'Fings get broken' he said grinning, 'And not just yap oxy china, you get mar drift?'
Nikos darted behind his counter and lowered the flap, 'Fella's, fellas!' he pleaded, 'There must be some misunderstanding, please have a cigar' Nikos first retrieved a box of cut price Havana's from under the counter, but then seeing their disapproving look produced a more expensive brand. Jimmy and Roland emptied the box in two handfuls and stuffed the cigars into their breast pockets while Nikos looked on in despair,
'Cheers!' Roland said, taking a silver plated lighter from a stand and lighting one of the cigars then popping the lighter into his pocket, 'Billy sent us' he added, blowing the smoke into Nikos's face.
A look of dread crept across the jeweler's face as he mopped his streaming brow, 'Billy' he gasped, 'Why, why would Billy send ya, ar've always been straight wiv Billy, e know's that, and he's always had a fair price from me, ar'd never av im over ' His eyes flashed around the room as he cringed, not knowing whether to run or stand and face whatever was coming.
Just then a door at the rear opened and a teenage lad appeared, 'Ar'm off now Paps' the boy said, lifting the flap on the counter, 'See you at the club later yeah'
Nikos took a few notes from his pocket and stuffed them into the boys hand 'Get yaself those trainers you wanted' he said, watching the boy leave. 'My er, my nephew' he told the Tibbs brothers, 'He's staying for a couple of days'
Jimmy knew better and lunged at Nikos across the counter 'E'z a fuckin rent boy you lying nonce!' he

growled, shoving Nikos against the rear wall, 'Naah sit daan we wanna word' Nikos dropped into his leather chair and sat like a condemned man, 'Woss this all about boys, ar'm sure we can straighten this aat' he took his snake skin wallet from inside his coat and thumbed through the notes.

'Put ya fuckin money away!' Jimmy yelled, 'We aint ere for that, you eard about the robbery at the Dorchester?'

Nikos tucked his wallet back inside his coat nodding his head, 'Yeah, yeah course, the red sea ruby, have you got it, can ar see it?'

'No we bleedin aint!' Roland said, 'We' he was then interrupted when an elderly lady entered the shop 'Excuse me dear' she called out 'I was wondering if I might be able to get my bracelet repaired?'

'WE'RE SHUT!' Jimmy yelled,

The lady approached the counter and took a lace handkerchief containing the broken jewellry from her pocket, 'Oh but the door was open' she added, holding out her hand, 'It was a wedding present from my late husband you see'

Jimmy knocked the handkerchief from her hand and looked her in the eye, his face inches from hers, 'AR SAID WERE FUCKIN SHUT, NOW PISS OFF!' he shouted, then watched her turn tail and drag her shopping trolley out of the shop as fast as her arthritic legs could carry her,

'Oh well I never' she mumbled as she left in a state of shock.

'As ar was sayin' Roland continued, 'We never nicked the stone, some uvva toe rag blagged it, which as you can well imagine as upset my older bruvva, you could say e'z devastated by the sheer lack of respect the criminal underworld has shown im in this matter'

Jimmy slammed his hand down on the counter 'E'Z FUCKIN LIVID IS WHAT MAR BRUVVA'S TRYNA TELL YA!' he yelled, he took a moment to compose himself 'Every two bob firm in London knows that blag was iz, so it must be an outside mob, maybe them scousers av grown a set of bollocks and ventured daan saaf, eeva way a stone that big'd av to go fru you Nikos, your the only fucker that could shift it'

Nikos held his hands in the air, 'Lads, lads ar've not erd a fing onest!' he groveled, 'Ar knew Billy was planning somefing big and when I erd the ruby was in taan ar just assumed e'd got it, onest thas the troof'

'Well e aint got it!' Roland barked, 'So what your gonna do Nikos me old son iz tell us the minute some fucker try's to flog it, you got that, or me and Jimmy ere are gonna pay you anuvva visit and when we leave the only fing on display in this shit ole will be your internal fuckin organs, do ar make meself clear, oh and keep yer eye aat for Black Mickey an'all'

'But Mickey's in Pentonville boys, everyone knows that!' Nikos replied, 'E'z lookin at six years I heard!'

'Well e'z aat!' Jimmy barked, 'Got on the fuckin roof and jumped over the wall onto a lorry load of spuds, king Edwards ar fink, anyway if the scousers never done it you can bet that slag did, so keep an eye out for im'

'Yeah, yeah course boys' Nikos said, visibly shaking, 'As soon as I hear anyfing i'll let you know straight away, you av mar word!'

Jimmy took a card from his pocket then grabbing a silver letter opener from it's case thrust it through the card pinning it to the counter, 'You can reach us on

that number' he said, grabbing his brothers arm and heading for the door.
A Rolex wrist watch in a glass cabinet caught Roland's eye on the way out, 'Is that a snide?' he asked a trembling Nikos who shook his head, 'No, no thas the genuine article' he said stepping through the counter, fumbling in his pocket for the cabinet key, assuming he was about to make a sale,
'Good' Roland replied, putting his fist through the glass door and slipping the watch onto his wrist, 'Ar don't wear fakes'. The two boys left Nikos clasping his hands to his head in disbelief and climbed back into their car.
At that very moment Bradley rounded the corner with Dee Dee, Mickey and the others, 'Shit, keep going, keep going!' Mickey said, ducking down in the back of the car.
'Why woss up?' Bradley asked.
'Just go will ya, or we're all dead!' Mickey yelled, shoving Bradley in the back.
Bradley put his foot to the floor and wheel spun past the Tibbs's Jag looking Jimmy in the eye in passing.
'Tosser' Jimmy snarled, pulling away in the opposite direction.
Mickey peered nervously over his shoulder watching the brothers disappear out of sight before sitting up in his seat,
'What is it Mick?' Dee Dee asked 'Who was that?'
Micky clasped his dreadlocks, shaking his head, 'The bleedin Tibbs's Dee, we're fucked naah'
Maizie tapped Dee Dee's shoulder 'Who are the Tibbs's Dee?' she asked 'Woss goin on?'
'Never mind, turn this mota raand!' Dee Dee told Bradley, 'Ar'll go see this Nick the bubble geezer' Mickey leaned forward and tugged at Dee Dee's top

'You can't Dee!' he said, looking across at the jewellers, 'The best fing we can do naah is disappear for a while, we got enough money to last a few mumfs'.
Trisha and Maizie looked on not knowing what was happening as Dee Dee stepped from the car, 'Ar'm just gonna av a word wiv im thas all!' she told them.
Dee Dee opened the door of Nikos's shop to find him on all fours with a dustpan and brush sweeping up the broken cabinet glass, 'Alright!' she said, letting the door swing closed behind her, 'Are you Nikos?'
'Yes, yes' the pawnbroker replied, straightening his back with a strained expression 'What can ar do for ya young lady, a belly bar is it or maybe a tongue stud, ar've got these ultra violet ones that glow in the dark for all you clubbing types'
'Naah fuck that' said Dee Dee, strolling behind the counter and making herself at home in his chair 'I aint ere for that shit'.
Nikos didn't know what to make of her at first, 'Excuse me girly' he said emptying the broken glass into a basket 'If ya'd care to wait on this side of the counter ar'd be only too happy to serve ya'
Dee Dee rocked back and forth in his chair 'You've just ad a visit from the Bermondsey firm aintcha' she said, looking Nikos in the eye.
Nikos looked confused a first, 'Sorry!' he said, heading for the door, 'Ar dunno know what your talking abaat, ar'm gonna av to ask ya to leave'
Dee Dee wrenched the letter opener from the counter and examined the card, 'Friends of yours are they?' she asked, tossing Nikos the card.
'They're er, they're acquaintances of mine thas all, not that iss any business of yours' he replied,

approaching the counter, 'Look who are you and what do you want?'
Dee Dee picked at her nails with the point of the letter opener, 'It don't matter who I am right naah Nicky boy' she said looking him in the eye 'What does matter is that me and you are gonna do a bit of business, you see ar got the ruby'
'You!' Nikos gasped, 'What, how?' he stammered, 'This is some sorta joke right, who put you up to this?' he then beckoned to Dee Dee, 'Come on, aat, I aint got time for games young lady'
'Iss the red sea ruby' Dee Dee said, remaining seated 'Iss angin on a diamond and emerald chain, iss werf nine and free quarter million and ar nicked it off Sheik Abby the uvva night'
Nikos stood in stunned silence for almost a minute, 'Young lady' he eventually said leaning across the counter 'if you av Indeed nicked stone, which ar find very ard to believe then ar fink you'll find your in a whole eap of trouble' he warned her, 'Your'e right, two of the the Tibbs brothers were just ere, and a proper nasty pair they are too, but iss their older bruvva Billy who'd really give ya nightmares, ar've never come across a more unhinged individual, my advice to you girly is if you av got it give im the stone and pray to god that he don't kill ya, ar'd be only too appy to act as the go between'
'Ar bet you would ya slippry bastard!' Dee Dee said, joining Nikos at the counter, 'Naah let me tell ya what ar fink shall i, plan A, you find me a buyer for the stone, we both make a shit load of dough and fuck off somewhere where the Tibbs's can't find us' she looked around Nikos's dilapidated shop 'Or are you gonna tell me you got some emotional attachment to this dump' Nikos was about to reply when Dee Dee

continued 'Or there's plan B, ar take the ruby to Billy boss man, tell im ar nicked it off you and that you were gonna fuck im over, now e may or may not believe me, but if e'z arf the nutter you say e is ar fink e'd av to pay you a visit to find aat, wod'you' reckon?'.

Nikos paced the shop realizing Dee Dee had him in a corner, and knowing full well that if Billy Tibbs had the slightest of suspicions about his loyalty he would kill him in a heart beat to save face amongst his fellow criminals. 'Do you realize what a dangerous game your playing young lady' he warned Dee Dee, 'This aint Ken and Barbie and a plastic flippin tea set, these are real gangsters with real guns, you could get seriously urt, or worse'

Dee Dee stood her ground, 'Lemmy tell ya summink' she said, glaring at him, 'Ar'm a proper bitch, in fact ar'm the worse kinda bitch, ar'm an ormonal bitch wiv nuffin to lose, ar come from nuffin an ar got nuffin, this is mar chance to get the fuck off these streets and I aint gonna let you or Billy the kid get in mar way'

Nikos stood speechless, never having heard such language from someone so young, let alone a girl, but greed soon got the better of him, 'Let's just say for argument sake' he said, going over the facts and figures in his head 'Ar was insane enough to go against the wishes of the Tibbs brothers, and ar were to find you a buyer, of which there are many interested in that rock, woss in it for me, considering the fact that ar'd undoubtedly have to relocate, possibly abroad'.

Dee Dee knew she had his attention, 'Well ar want nine mill!' she said abruptly, 'Anyfing above that is yours'

Nikos's eyes lit up, knowing that the Japanese and Americans would be bidding furiously to own the ruby, possibly pushing the price well over ten million pounds. 'Well thas a very attractive offer my dear' he said, stroking his moustache, 'You'll want that in cash no daat?'

'Yeah, cash paand notes' Dee Dee replied, rubbing her thumb and forefingers together 'And iss all gotta be ush ush nart ar mean'

'My dear girl' Nikos replied, 'Between them, my clients have a combined wealth of billions, much of which accumulated from the purchase and sale of priceless antiquities stolen from around the world, so I assure you their discretion can be guaranteed'.

'Thas alright then' Dee Dee said, heading for the door, 'Ar be in touch'.

Nikos hurried after her wringing his hands 'But what about the ruby?' he asked, 'When do ar get to see it?'

Dee Dee laughed at him 'Ya don't fink ar'm stupid enough to bring it wiv me do ya, like ar said, ar be in touch, you just get the Japs and the Yanks wavin their wonga and then we'll talk, ar'll bell ya later' she then noticed a ladies gold Rolex in a display case, 'Is that a snide?' she asked.

Nikos frantically rummaged in his pocket, 'No, wait, wait!' he yelled, producing a set of keys and fearing yet more broken glass, 'Here, take it!' he said, opening the door and handing Dee Dee the watch. 'Oh fanks!' she replied slipping it into her pocket'Ar'll give it to me muvva 'She's never ad a real one, she always wear fakes ya see'. Dee Dee opened the door and disappeared out into the street leaving Nikos dazed and confused as to what had just happened.

'Blimey Dee where ya bin?' Maizie asked as Dee Dee climbed back into the car, 'You've bin in there for bleedin ages'
'Yeah woss appnin Dee?' Mickey added, nervously 'Are we gettin rid of the stone or what?'
Dee Dee patted Mickeys hand reassuringly 'Yeah, don't worry Mick' she told him, 'Ar made Nick the bubble an offer e can't refuse, e'z gunna flog it for us wivout the Tibbs's knowin'
'That's a hell of a gamble Dee' Mickey said, rocking back in his seat and shaking his head, 'Ar just ope you know what ya doin!'
Trisha raised her hand 'Will somebody tell me who the Tibbs's are?' she asked.
Mickey looked her in the eye, 'Believe me babe' he said with a shaky tone 'You don't wanna know'
Dee Dee slapped her hand down on Bradley's thigh 'Right, back to mine boy blunder!' she laughed 'And take it easy, your not Jenson fuckin Button ya know'
'Iss the mota girl innit!' Bradley said, stroking the dashboard 'Since ar got me new carbs and injectors man iss just like shit off a stick' He then popped a cd into the player and cranked the volume up, 'Listen to me new mix' he added, nodding his head to the throbbing bass line 'Ar'm sendin it to Louis Walsh blud'
'Ar'll send it for ya!' Dee Dee said, cringing, 'Air mail!' she ejected it from the player and tossed it like a frisby from the moving car.
'Arghhh no maaan!' Bradley cursed, looking over his shoulder 'Dat woulda gone platinum ar swear it, ar bin workin on me lyrics, tell me what ya tink' Bradley launched into yet another cringe worthy display of inferior beat boxing, covering his steering wheel in

spit in the process, and if that wasn't bad enough, the rapping soon followed.

'You can go to hell bitch ar'm tellin you iss over
nuttin comes close to mar pimped up Nova,
Ar don't give a fuck if ya say ya wanna blow me
if ya fink ar give a shit then ya really don't know me,
Ar got ten more bitch's, to take your place
they're sittin on mar dick and they're sittin on mar face
So fuck you bitch in ya granddads rover
nuttin comes close to mar pimped up Nova
nuttin, nuttin, nuttin comes close to mar pimped up Nova!'

While Dee Dee, Maizie and Trisha sat in shocked silence Mickey bounced up and down in his seat , 'Yeah man that shit is cool bro!' he laughed, giving Bradley a high five, 'Maizie babe ar fink ya bruvva's really got summink!'
'Yeah' Maizie replied, 'E always says e'z the gifted one in the famly!'
'GIFTED!' Dee Dee laughed, 'Your avin a fuckin laugh aintcha, ar mean Einstein, e was gifted, Willy Shakespeare, e was gifted, even that bird on youtube that fires ard boiled eggs out of er muff, she's gifted, but silly bollocks ere aint gifted, e'z a pork pie short of a fuckin picnic thas what e is!'
Maizie laughed and added to Dee Dee's insults 'E'z one brick short of a full load' she chuckled.
Trisha then attempted a witty one liner but failed miserably 'Yeah!' she said excitedly, 'E's a tea bag short of a cuppa!'
Dee Dee and Maizie both looked at their half witted friend and said , 'Shut up Trish'.

DI Pritcher paced his office within the Mets serious crimes unit, his telephone to his ear attempting to calm an irate foreign Minister, 'I assure you sir we are doing all we can' he said, feeling the heat, 'Ar've got a dozen officers working round the clock, trust me Minister we'll have a result very soon ar'm sure of it, yes sir ar'm well aware of the political implications and no sir ar don't relish the thought of walking the beat again, iss taken me a long time to get where I am' the DI held the phone away from his ear for a moment while the Minister vented his frustrations, 'Yes sir, yes sir!' the DI said, eventually getting a word in, 'Ar wont rest until those documents are found you have mar word, yes sir ar'll call you the minute I have some news, good bye sir!'. The DI breathed a sigh of relief after replacing the handset, 'Stuck up twat' he muttered, but was then interrupted when detective Marsh entered the room.

'Sir we have a lead on the red ruby case' he said, waving his notepad under the DI's nose. 'I've just come from Pentonville sir, it seems Spencer did have a visitor just before his escape, it was logged by the duty officer sir'

The DI's eyes lit up, 'Excellent Marsh, who was it?' he asked, praying for a speedy conclusion.

Detective Marsh thumbed through the pages of his notebook 'Yes sir it's here somewhere' he said, turning page over page, 'One moment sir' he could see that the DI was beginning to lose his cool, 'No that's not it! he said fumbling.

'Marsh for gods sake!' the DI barked 'Just tell me who the bloody visitor was you idiot!'

'Here it is sir, a Miss Dawson!' Detective Marsh said, holding up the pad, 'According to the duty log Miss Dawson was Spencer's only visitor during his stay,

and thankfully sir all visitors are required to give their full address as well as their name'
'Nice one' the DI smiled, 'Where does this Miss Dawson live?'
'Essex sir! Detective Marsh replied, 'Goodmayes in fact, on the Bircham estate'
'Get a car over there right now and pick her up' DI Pritcher told his Detective 'And don't screw it up Marsh, this Dawson girls all we got at the moment'
'I took the liberty of sending a car already sir' Detective Marsh added, 'They should be there any minute'
'Good work Marsh' the DI replied, 'Let me know the moment they bring her in' Detective Marsh left his DI and hurried back into the incident room where a ten strong team of officers were busy sifting through the police records of every armed robber that had ever been in custody and all their known associates.
Bradley drove onto the estate with one hand on the wheel and the other dangling from the window, rocking to a fro in his seat, toying with his cap whilst checking out a bunch of gum chewing school girls hovering on the corner,
'Ar be back for you ladies lata yeah!' he said in passing. One of them raised her middle finger and after popping her gum yelled, 'Get lost you freak!' her friends then spat their gum into their hands and hurled it at his car 'Yeah sod off limp dick!' another called out, wiggling her little finger in the air.
'Friends of yours!' Dee Dee chuckled, looking back. Bradley then slammed on the brakes seeing the police car parked outside Dee Dee's block.
'What the fuck are you doin you nob!' Dee Dee cursed, lurching forward.

'Iss the filf innit!' Bradley said reversing behind a large builders van 'Ar gotta be careful coz ar nicked me tax disc off me nans mobility scoota'.

Dee Dee and the others watched the officers make their way along the landing and knock at her mothers door. 'Shit!' Dee Dee said, 'What the fuck do they want?'

'They must be on to us Dee' replied Mickey 'Where's the stone?'.

Dee Dee held her head 'Oh fuck, iss in the case under me bed, opefully me mums too pissed to answer the door' as the words left her mouth Pearl could be seen opening it and asking the men inside.

'Fuck, fuck, fuck, the dozy cow!' Dee Dee yelled, thumping the dashboard.

'Miss Dawson we're here on a very serious matter' one of the officers told Pearl, 'We understand you visited a Michael Spencer in Pentonville prison recently!'

'No ya silly arse' Pearl laughed, 'You must want Debs mar daughter'

The officer looked confused 'So your not Deborah Dawson I take it?' he asked, checking his notes. 'Course not' Pearl laughed taking a can from the mantle 'Ar'm er muvva, why woss wrong?'

The officer looked around the room, 'Nothing for you to worry about madam, is er, is Deborah home?' Pearl shook her head and ripped the ring pull 'Nahh she's out wiv Mickey!' she said, burping loudly.

The two officers looked at each other, 'Mickey Spencer!' one of them asked 'He was here?'

'Yeah course!' Pearl replied, offering the officers a can, which they bluntly refused. 'Ar said e could stay ere for a bit' she added.

'Madam!' one officer said taking out his handcuffs 'I'm placing you under arrest for harboring a known fugitive, anything you do say will be taken down and used as evidence'
'What, ay?' Pearl shrieked, struggling as she was cuffed, 'What ya doin i aint done nuffin!'.
'We'll let the judge decide shall we' an officer replied, yanking her from her chair and wrenching the can from her hand, 'What time are you expecting your daughter and Mr Spencer back?'.
Pearl was livid at this point and kicked one of them in the shin 'I aint tellin ya nuffin ya fuckers!' she cursed, trying to break free, 'Get off me!'. Pearl was consequently marched out onto the landing with her hands cuffed behind her.
'Shit they got me mum!' Dee Dee said, seeing her frog marched to the stairs.
'You' wait here!' one of the officers told his colleague 'Keep an eye on the flat in case the girl comes back'
Pearl was escorted to the police car and bundled in the back, then driven away at high speed.
'Get daan!' Mickey yelled as the squad car whizzed by.
'Now what?' Maizie said, looking up cautiously. 'This is bad Dee, they nicked ya mum'
'She'll be alright don't panic' Dee Dee said, reassuringly 'She's a tough old bird me mum, she done six mumfs in borstal when she was twenny one'
'What for Dee?' Trisha asked, 'Was she out robbin an'all?'
Dee Dee shook her head, 'Naah nuffin like that, a police orse run over me aunt Reeny in the poll tax riots, so me muvva rolled up her news of the world and shoved it up the fuckers arse'

'Best place for it' Mickey laughed, 'So what appened to the orse?'

Dee Dee couldn't speak for laughing at first, 'Well' she chuckled, 'It bolted into Arrods wiv the screamin copper on it's back and chased Al Fayed fru the knicker department' Everyone in the car burst out laughing at the thought of the Harrods boss fleeing hysterically through the lacy lingerie.

'Apparently' Dee Dee added, 'E legged it into a changing room and got a black eye from an arf naked Dutch dyke'

Bradley then seized the opportunity to brag about his non existent sex life 'Ar done it wiv a coupla lezzers once!' he said puffing out his chest, 'It was well good, we ad a sex sandwich an everyfing'

'You lying bastard!' Maizie said, slapping the back of his head, 'You probly ad a wank and a cheese sandwich ya flippin virgin'

'WHO YOU CALLIN A VIRGIN!' Bradley yelled, looking at his sister in the rear view mirror, 'Ar done it five times in one night once!'

'Ar know' Maizie said, almost wetting herself with laughter, 'Mum ad to snap ya bed sheets in arf and fro em away ya filfy little git, and she said if you kept on tuggin ya todger she was gonna put ya back in mittens'

Bradley sat red faced with his bottom lip quivering,

'Bitch! he muttered under his breath.

Dee Dee thought for a moment, looking up at the guard outside her door 'Ar gotta get that case!' she said, strumming her fingers on the dashboard,

'Are you mad Dee!' Mickey said, 'Less just leave it and get out of ere'

'No fuckin way!' Dee Dee snapped, 'I aint goin fru all this for fuck all' She climbed from the car and

slammed the door, 'Ar'll sort it aat, you lot sod off ar catch up wiv ya lata'
'Ok Dee, if ya sure' Trisha said, leaning out the window, 'Ar need to go to mine anyway, ar gotta av a shower me feet are chuckin up summink chronic'
'Don't ar bleedin know it! Maizie said, fanning her nose, 'They're proper makin me gag Trish onest'
'You know ar've always ad Bad feet Maize' Trisha replied, looking down at her shoes, 'Ar fink ar get it from me granddad, e got foot rot in the war and ad to av em both chopped off'
'That aint a bad idea' Maizie laughed, 'Do they do that on the national elf'
'Shut up!' Trisha said, flopping back in her seat and crossing her arms, 'They aint that bad'
'Naah course not!' Mickey added, winding down his window and taking a deep breath of fresh air. 'Ar need to pick up some tings from me flat as well Dee, so we'll catch ya later, be careful yeah'.
Dee Dee looked at Bradley sitting at the wheel looking morbidly depressed, 'Oh for fuck sake cheer up' she said, trying to raise his spirits, she then took a hundred pounds from her pocket and tossed it into his lap, 'Eeyaa take that' she told him 'Get yarself raand to Albert street, knock on the green door, number seventy two, tell Janice ar sent ya, she's an old mate a mine, one of er girls'll sort you aat, don't get Julie though, unless you like being trussed up like a chicken in a rubber mask wiv jump leads on yer arse cheeks'
Bradley's eyes lit up at the thought of finally being alone with a real woman, dominatrix or not. He stuffed the money into his pocket and hurriedly started the car. 'Albert street yeah?' he asked, champing at the bit 'Number seventy two ya say'.

'Yeah thas it' Dee Dee replied, winking at her friends in the back, 'Free doors along from the bookies, if there's a lava lamp in the winda, they're open for business'.
Mickey took a blue pill from his wallet and offered it to Bradley, 'Ar don't need no viagra man!' Bradley said, pushing his hand away 'Ar can go for days, in fact by the time ar've finished bustin that bitch's booty she gonna need six mumfs of Physio, nart ar mean blud!' Bradley sat grunting whilst thrusting his groin back and forth.
Maizie snatched the pill from Mickey and tapped her brother on the shoulder, 'OY BRUV!' she yelled, 'Just take the bleedin fing will ya'. Bradley snapped out of his fantasy and while thinking more realistically, popped the pill into his mouth and swallowed it.
'No not yet you idiot!' Mickey cried, thumping the back of Bradley's chair, 'Your supposed to take it arf hour before!'
'Really!' Bradley shrieked, looking at his watch, 'We gotta go Dee, see ya lata!' He sped away leaving Dee Dee by the side of the road and roared out of the estate, 'Ar drop you and Trish off first Sis!' he said, continuously checking the time, 'Where do you live Mickey?'
'Gallows corner man' Mickey replied 'Just off the roundabout'.
'Shit!' Bradley said, looking down at his crotch, not knowing what to expect , 'Thas nowhere near Albert street!' Bradley barely stopped the car for more than a few seconds to let his sister and Trisha out before speeding off once again,'Shit! shit!!' he cried, jumping a red light and feeling a twitch in his trousers, 'Iss kicking in Mickey, what do I do man?',

Mickey, sitting behind Bradley, covered his mouth with his hand trying not to laugh, 'Try not to fink about it man' he chuckled, 'You'll just make it worse!'.
'Yeah, yeah course!' Bradley replied, desperate to delay the inevitable, but to his horror the first thing he noticed was a young lady bent over at a bus stop tying her laces, and in doing so flashing the majority of her white lacy thong, 'No, no!' he cursed, averting his eyes and clenching his legs together, but then a wonder bra billboard on the side of Woolworths caught his eye, 'Oh come on man gimme a break!' he cried. To make matters even worse the traffic ahead ground to a halt while a delivery truck reversed across the road, 'Come on, come on!' Bradley said, beeping his horn several times. He then leapt from his car to get a better view ahead, unaware that he now had a prominent erection straining the crotch of his trousers. It was only when he heard giggling and looked round to see a group of women in the post office queue pointing in his direction,
'EASY TIGER!' one of them yelled.
Bradley quickly hopped back into the car and looked round at Mickey, 'Ar'll av to drop you off ere Mick!' he said, with a strained expression on his face, 'Ar'm gonna bust uvverwise!'
'No worries man' replied Mickey, getting out of the back, 'If you do a left ere and cut fru the supermarket car park, Albert street's about five minutes from there, come and get me when your done, number four Tyson avenue bruv'
'Yeah, yeah!' Bradley said, pulling away, 'Just off the roundabout, right!' He sped into the side street with only one thing now on his mind, doing it and doing it and when he'd finished doing it, doing it some more.

After ten agonizing minutes hurtling through the streets of Romford, narrowly missing pedestrians and other road users, Bradley skidded to a stop several doors along from the brothel, leaping from the car and wrenching the cash from his pocket, 'Green door, green door, seventy two!' he said to himself, scanning the houses until he was standing outside, 'Fucking sweet!' he shrieked, seeing the lurid lava lamp on show in the window. Bradley looked around furtively before sprinting to the door and leaning on the bell,

'Come on!' he said squirming on the spot. The door then opened and Janice, the madam peered out, 'Yeah, can I help ya!' she said, brushing the hair from her eyes.

Bradley waved the notes in front of her, 'Ar got money ar wanna do it!' he said excitedly, 'Ar wanna see Julie, yeah, yeah Julie, is she in?' Janice looked him up and down disapprovingly 'Are you old bill?' she asked, 'I aint seen you before'.

'No, no Dee Dee sent me, onest Miss' Bradley pleaded, peering over her shoulder hoping to catch a glimpse of a naked girl.

'Oh Debs, well why didn't ya say' Janice said, holding the door open, 'Go on up iss the fird door on the left' Bradley barged past her and flew up the stairs almost bursting with anticipation,

'Come in' Julie called on hearing Bradley tapping at her door. Bradley hurried inside and stopped dead in his tracks on seeing Julie sprawled across her sumptuous divan bed in the finest french lingerie, 'Fuck me!' he said, gawping, never having been this close to a naked woman in his life. The viagra was now having full effect on his manhood which strained to break free.

'What can ar do for you sweetie?' she asked, opening her legs to reveal her crotchless lacy knickers.

Bradley thrust the money in a jar beside the bed and whipped off his baggy trousers, 'All of it, yeah yeah all of it, I want the lot!' he squealed with excitement , 'Blow jobs, toe jobs, cow girl, school girl, leather, rubber, pvc, doggy, are don't care ar wonnit all' Bradley was positively foaming at the mouth by now, 'Ar just wanna do it man, all night yeah, yeah do it, do it!' Bradley began grunting, thrusting his groin toward her.

Julie reached out and slipped Bradley's belt from his trousers and slid the zip down seductively,

'Yeah das it woman' he shrieked, 'Release the beast!'.

Meanwhile Dee Dee had crept unseen to the foot of the stairs where she stood wondering how she was in fact going to get into her flat with a police guard outside. The main door then flew open and several younger members of the infamous Bircham boys, the eldest no more than twelve, came in carrying a set of mercedes hub caps and a condom machine wrenched from the wall of the public toilet, 'Oy you lot, come ere!' Dee Dee said beckoning to them. They immediately stopped in their tracks, attempting to conceal their ill gotten gains, 'We faand em!' one young lad said, wiping the snot from his nose across his sleeve, 'We never nicked em honest!'

'Ar don't give a toss if ya did' Dee Dee replied, taking fifty pounds from her pocket, 'D'you lads wanna earn some real dough?'

Their eyes lit up immediately 'Corr bleedin ell yeah!' another gasped. The boys stashed their goods behind the bins and crowded round. 'What we gotta do?' the lad added, mesmerized by the cash, 'You aint wunna them bleedin peado's are ya, that old fucker on the forf floor offered me a fiver to see mar winkle, so ar kicked im in the nuts, nicked iz money and told me dad, im and iz mates stuck the nonce in iz van and took im out to Eppin forest, we aint never seen im since'

'No I aint a bleedin peado' Dee Dee laughed, 'Listen, there's a copper outside mar flat upstairs, Ar need you lot to get rid of im for me, there's, do that and the dosh is yours'

'No trouble' a cocky lad said, reaching for the money, 'We know ow to deal wiv the old bill'

Dee Dee snatched the money away peeling off half and handing it out, 'Ya can av it when e'z gone' she told them, 'Ar don't trust you little buggers' Dee Dee watched the boys sprint up the stairs chattering like chimpanzees then sat on the step and waited.

The Bircham boys ran to the floor above Dee Dee's and peered over the balcony, soon the bored bobby beneath them did the same, looking round the run down estate shaking his head in disgust. Two boys helped their smaller friend up onto the rail where he dropped he proceeded to drop his trousers and urinate onto the policeman's head below, the startled officers immediate reaction was to look up and in doing so caught an eye full of the chuckling boys pee, 'Wankerrrrrr!' one lad yelled, mocking the dripping policeman with hand gestures.

'YOU LITTLE BASTARDS!' the officer screamed, wiping the urine from his face, 'I'LL FUCKIN KILL YA FOR THAT!'. Leaving his post the bobby ran to the stairs mopping his saturated hair from his face, then turning the corner with one more flight to go he

looked up to see three bare bottoms mooning at him from the top step,
'Kiss this!' one of the lads cried, slapping his cheeks before all three hoisted up their trousers and scurried along the landing with the furious PC in hot pursuit. The Bircham boys ran to the stairwell at the opposite end of the block and darted round the corner, rummaging in their pockets and listening to the officers size eleven shoes clattering towards them,
'Fuckers!' the constable screamed, but on rounding the corner himself he was confronted by the mob of youths each stretching a condom on the end of their thumbs,
'Let im av it!' one brazen lad yelled, the PC was then pelted with an array of ribbed and flavored rubbers fired like elastic bands, striking him about the face,
'You little!' he cried, before choking on one of the lubricated projectiles. Staggering back with his hands protecting his reddened face the officer tripped, striking his head on the rail which incensed him even more, 'I'LL KILL YOU LITTLE SHITS!' he yelled, picking himself up and starting after them once again. The Bircham boys zig zagged down the tower block, running from end to end taunting the seething policeman who lumbered after them intent on dishing out some harsh justice.
Dee Dee leapt to her feet and ducked around the corner, hearing the jeering mob approaching, she couldn't help but smile as the lads ran by and out into the car park with the panting PC close behind.
'Fanks!' the last lad cried snatching the fifty pound note in passing,
'Quality!' Dee Dee said, climbing the stairs.
Outside her flat Dee Dee first peered over the balcony, making sure the police officer had his hands

well and truly full with the loutish lads then slipped the key in the lock and let herself in,'Yes, fank fuck' she said, retrieving the case and checking its contents. She filled a carrier bag with clothes, make up and her straighteners then as an after thought tossed the straighteners to one side and replaced them with her G1000 vibrator, 'Ar can live wiv curly air' she said to herself, 'But not wivout a screamin bed buster'

The police officer had been hounded and harassed to near breaking point by the Bircham boys and had called for backup, Dee Dee watched from the balcony as a squad car arrived, 'Bugger' she cursed. But before the reinforcements left their vehicle the petrified PC scrambled in the back with his uniform in tatters,

'Get me the fuck out of here!' he cried, visibly shaking. The jeering juveniles then pelted the car with begonia's ripped from a neighbours flower bed then laughed as one of them tipped half a gallon of purple paint, retrieved from a nearby skip over the squad cars roof.

'Fuck this!' the driver said, standing on the accelerator and fleeing the scene.

'Nice one boys! Dee Dee laughed, handing the gang leader another twenty pounds, 'There's a coupla quid extra for the entertainment'

'Fanx darlin' one lad said, with a cheeky wink, 'Anytime' the gang hurriedly shared out the spoils and ran off in the direction of the sweet shop to gorge themselves on gum, gobstoppers and enough frozen slush to cryogenically freeze themselves.

Dee Dee cut through the back streets behind the estate, past the dog track and over the railway bridge to Trisha's house. 'Bloody ell Dee you got it' Maizie said, answering the door, 'Come in ar got the kettle on'

While Dee Dee told her friends how the Bircham boys had helped, Mickey had just reached his flat, 'What the fuck' he said, seeing the door had been forced open, assuming he had been the latest victim of a spate of burglaries he ventured inside, bracing himself for the mayhem ahead. Pushing open the creaking living room door, Mickey peered inside to where his Plasma tv usually hung over the fire place and was amazed to find it still in place. Breathing a sigh of relief he took off his coat and hung it on the back of the door, but then a voice startled him,

'Ello Micky! Mickey spun round to see Jimmy and Rolly Tibbs standing behind him, 'Nice of you to drop in'

Mickey was gripped with fear momentarily before making a dash for the street door but Jimmy grabbed a handful of his dreadlocks and yanked him back 'Naah naah Mickey thas not very ospitable' he snarled, 'We came all this way to see ya didn't we bruv'

'Yeah we did Jim' Roland replied, taking Mickey by the arm and flinging him down onto the sofa.

'Look boys' Mickey said, holding his hands up, 'Ar dunno what this is all about, but whatever it is you got the wrong man'.

Jimmy snorted another pinch of coke from his box and paced the room, 'Naah Mickey' he said taking out a six inch hunting knife and casually dragging it across the screen of Mickey's forty two inch tv, 'If there's one fing that really get's mar goat', he then hurled the knife at the floor narrowly missing Mickey's foot, 'ISS BULLSHIT!' Jimmy screamed, wrenching the knife from the carpet and holding it poised at

Mickeys groin, 'So maybe you wanna fink a bit more before you open that big black maaf a yours'
'Jimmy onest man!' Mickey pleaded, retracting his crotch from the blade, 'Ar swear to god man, whatever it is ar'm not involved in it onest!',
Meanwhile, feeling a little peckish Roland had retrieved a tupperware dish from Mickey's fridge 'Woss in ere?' he asked, leaning through the serving hatch.
'Er, thas jerk chicken' Mickey said nervously, 'Help yaself!
'Jerk fuckin chicken!' Roland said, hurling the dish into the bin, 'Jerk off chicken more like, woss up wiv you savages, why can't you eat proper grub?'
Mickey shrugged his shoulder 'We never ad pie and mash in Tobago Rolly' he laughed.
But Roland wasn't amused, 'What did you fuckin say!' he growled, grabbing a leg of lamb from the freezer and marching through to the lounge, 'Insult our fuckin national dish will ya you black bastard!' Roland grabbed Mickey's right hand and slammed it down on the coffee table.
'NO, NO ROLAND IT WAS A JOKE, PLEASE DON'T!' Mickey screamed.
'Well I aint fuckin laughin' Roland snarled, raising the frozen joint above his head and bringing it down firmly on the back of Mickeys hand.
Mickey recoiled, letting out a pitiful cry with tears streaming down his face, rocking back and forth whilst nursing his rapidly swelling hand. 'Please, please boys let me go ar won't say nuffin man honest!' he cried.
'Where is it Mickey?' Jimmy asked, shredding a cushion beside him with his knife, 'What ya done wiv

the ruby?' he proceeded to empty the contents of a four drawer sideboard onto the floor.
'Jimmy man!' Mickey begged 'Ar don't know nuffin about no ruby, tell Billy it weren't me, please bro!' Jimmy turned and glared at Mickey, baring his teeth, 'Firstly you slag!' he said, brandishing his blade, 'I aint your fuckin bro, and secondly you can tell im yaslf coz your comin wiv us!' Jimmy hoisted a struggling Mickey to his feet 'Get up you fucker' he grimaced,

'No please Jimmy!' Mickey cried as he was dragged from his flat and bundled into the back of the Tibbs's car. Jimmy then snatched the mail from a bewildered postman standing at Mickeys gate and threw it on the back seat, 'Eeya, summink to read on the way' he laughed.

With Trisha's parents both at work, Dee Dee and her friends sat at the kitchen table dunking chocolate biscuits into their tea, 'So what appens naah Dee?' Trisha asked, taking her eye off her biscuit for a moment 'Oh bugger!' she then cursed as half of the digestive sank to the bottom of the cup. She fished around with her spoon as Maizie and Dee Dee looked on shaking their heads

'For fuck sake Trish!' Dee Dee said, sliding the cup away, 'Just make anuvva one will ya!'

Trisha made a grab for the cup 'Me nan used to say never waste a good cup of tea' she said, sipping the lumpy liquid, 'She was always droppin er garibaldi's in er'z, ar seen er strain a cup fru the gusset of er stockins once rather than fro it away'

Maizie and Dee Dee both pushed their cups away, having lost their appetite. 'Well' Dee Dee said, taking out her phone, 'Ar left Nick the bubble me number, soon as e rings we'll flog the ruby and bugger off wiv the dough'

'Saands good to me! Maizie said, rubbing her hands together, 'Ar might buy meself an orse like what Jordan's got, and get a tit job like er's an'all' she pushed her underdeveloped breasts together, jostling them in her hands. 'Ar reckon ar'v ad bigger zits on the end of me nose than these bleedin fings'

Suddenly Dee Dee's phone rang, 'Speak of the devil' she smiled, 'Thas probly im naah, Oh mum iss you, are you alright?' she asked, surprised to hear Pearls voice, 'Woss appnin?'

'Ar'm only allowed one call so listen Dee' her mother replied, cupping her hand over her mouth, 'They keep goin on about that robbry up toaa, now I aint stupid, ar know Mickey's probly involved and for all ar know, you are as well, don't worry I aint said nuffin but the shits really it the fan ere, they're on about some papers that was nicked, apparently they're top secret or summink so if it was you lot love, be careful and don't worry about me, they can't old me forever'

The phone then went dead as Pearl was taken back to the interrogation room.

'Ar spose they want the ruby back do they Dee?' Maizie asked, putting a hand on her friends shoulder, 'Ar dont mind mate, big tits'll only fuck me back up anyway'.

Dee Dee sat in quiet contemplation for a few moments before opening the case, 'Naah she never said nuffin about the ruby' she said, sliding the files out onto the table, 'The old bill are after these papers, top secret shit or summink'

'What are they Dee?' Trisha asked, looking across the table 'Some top nob bin caught wiv iz traasers daan!'.

Dee Dee sat quietly reading, gleaning what little information she could from all the political jargon. 'Ar knew it!' Dee Dee finally said, slapping the table, 'Ar knew when we bombed the shit aatta them rag eds it was all about the friggin oil, and this bleedin proves it!'

As the girls sat mulling over the enormity of the situation there was a knock at the door, 'Shit!' Dee Dee said, ramming the papers back into the case, 'Quick ide this!' she handed the case to Maizie and crept to the bay window peering cautiously through the net curtains, 'Oh fuck me iss only Brad!' she added, opening the door, 'Owd'ya get on at Janice's, did they make a man of ya?' she asked their grinning driver,

Bradley bounced in brimming with confidence 'Oh it was well good man!' he said pulling up a chair at the table and tossing his hat onto the side, 'Julie gave me the works blud!'

'You ad Julie?' Dee Dee gasped, 'Fuck me your a brave lad!'

'I ad the rubber, the leather, the Pvc the lot man!' Bradley bragged, 'The only fing was, she ad a flat battry so ad to wire me arse up to the mains, what a rush though man, it made mar bleedin teeth rattle, ar'v always liked bein dominated though, ar was the only kid in our class that used to get a boner during detention'

Dee Dee looked around, 'Oy Brad where's Mickey?' she asked.

Bradley clasped his hands to his head 'Oh shit man yeah!' he cried, 'Ar knew there was somefing else ar was gonna tell ya, ar went to pick im up yeah, and iz ouse was all proper busted up man and there was no sign of im!'

'Shit! shit! fuckin shit!' Dee Dee yelled, 'Them fuckin Tibbs's must av im, this shit's gettin proper aat of and!'.

CHAPTER SEVEN.

Laura's lust.

Detective Inspector Pritcher was becoming increasingly frustrated with Pearl's refusal to cooperate 'Look love, the longer you piss me abaat! he warned 'The longer your gonna be in ere'.
Pearl merely shrugged her shoulders and stared down at the table 'No bleedin comment' she muttered.
The DI then considered a slightly softer approach 'Ok how about a nice cuppa tea, you must be firsty by now!'
'Fuck ya tea' Pearl barked, 'Ar'll av a scrumpy jack an a fagt hough if ya got one'.
The DI flew into a rage and stormed from the room, 'MARSH!' he yelled along the corridor,
Detective Marsh came scurrying from the canteen with a half eaten cheese sandwich, 'Yes sir, here!' he said, binning his lunch.
'Ar want that woman charged with obstructing justice do you hear me!' the DI told him, 'And anyfing else we can pin on er d'you ear me' the DI then paced the corridor 'Now Marsh?' he asked his detective 'Answer me this, if a villain needed to get rid of a rock the size of that ruby, where would he go?'
'There's only one fence who could handle it sir' Detective Marsh replied, 'That greek bloke in Hackney, Papa something or other'
'Correct Marsh' the DI smiled 'Nikos Papageorgiou, we've been after that greasy scumbag for years, but he's good i'll give him that, he comes up squeaky clean every time we pull the fucker in'
'D'you want us to bring him in again sir?' Detective Marsh asked, 'I could send a couple of uniformed guys down there'.

'No, no' the Di replied, 'Ar'll pay Mr Papageorgiou a visit meself and apply a little pressure, you stay ere and deal with that bitch in there'

DI Pritcher left the station and drove the six or so miles through the busy city streets to Hackney in the east end of London. 'Ello Nikos' he said, throwing open the shop door and looking round with an air of distaste 'Ar see your still refusing to move with the times, what ar mean is your shop's still a shit hole' Nikos looked up from the gents watch he was repairing and took a step back, 'Mr Pritcher!' he gasped, 'What the, ar mean to what do I owe the pleasure?'.

The DI examined several items of value amid the general clutter, 'Ar trust you have the relevant documentation for these trinket!' he said, wrapping a gold chain around his wrist 'Ar'd ate to find out these were stolen in any way, coz then ar'd ave to shut you daan and take you in, and that my dear Mr Papageorgiou involves a shit load of paperwork ,and everyone on the force knows that I ate fuckin paperwork more than I ate the orrible cockroaches that profit from the bastards that nicked the gear in the first place' the DI looked directly at Nikos, 'Naah don't get me wrong Nikos me old son, ar'm not saying that your establishment is anytfng but Kosher, Christ no,ar'm merely stating the fact that the criminal element of society would target someone like yourself to offload their ill gotten gains, so you see whenever there's a blag on mar manor ar'm gonna have to come down here and rattle your cage time after poxy time, do you understand, are said do you understand?'

Nikos held his hands up, 'Mr Pritcher ar don't know anyfing abaat any blags arswear it!' he said, holding

up his receipt book, 'Ar run a respectable business ere, no funny business!'
At that moment the door opened and a young teenager in a full length parka popped his head inside to proposition the proprietor 'Got a coupla Zippo lighters and a charm bracelet if ya intrested Mr Paps' Nikos looked mortified with the plain clothed DI in such close proximity, the lad was a regular supplier of goods pick pocketed from unsuspecting passengers on the London underground, he first tried to gesture to the boy to go away but with the DI now showing an interest Nikos yelled at the boy, 'NO AR'M NOT INTRESTED CLEAR OFF!'
The young lad looked confused 'Ar'm only after a score for the lot Mr Paps' he added.
DI Pritcher beckoned to the boy 'Come on in son ar might be interested! he said, holding out his hand, 'Where did you say you got these from?'
The theif finally caught on, looking at Nikos's jerking head movements and backed away 'Er, ar didn't' he said, ducking out the door and sprinting off along the street.
'Friend of yours?' the DI asked Nikos who was feeling a little hot under the collar to say the least.
'No er, corse not' Nikos replied, shuffling furtively, 'Ar told ya Mr Pritcher ar run a respectable business, everyfing above board' then assuming the DI was just another copper on the take he decided to try a little bribery. Nikos took a tray of gold rings from under the counter and held them under the DI's nose, 'Perhaps you'd like to pick somefing out for Mrs Pritcher' he asked 'They're all genuine eighteen carat, you ave mar word on it'.
The DI knocked the tray from Nikos's hand and glared at him, 'Ar wouldn't give that bitch the steam

off mar piss!' he yelled, 'Since ar caught her with a strappon stuck up one of my WPC's she can rot in hell for all ar care!'
Nikos found himself in an awkward situation as the DI unleashed a tirade of venomous abuse
'Fifteen fuckin years ar gave that cow, three poxy holidays a year, a convertible BMW and a platinum credit card and what does the fuckin whore do, moves her fuckin dyke girlfriend into my house and what happens to me, ar'll tell ya what fuckin appens to me, ar'm kipping in one of the cells next door to the ponces and peado's, it aint fuckin fair are tell ya!' after exhaling sharply, having vented his anger the DI turned his attention back to Nikos who stood open mouthed. 'So as you can tell Nikos! he snarled, 'The lack of sleep as made me particularly ratty so ar'm in no mood to be fucked araand by the likes of you, am I making myself clear?' The DI straightened his aching back having spent several sleepless nights on the stiff station bunks while his wife and her lover languished in the luxury of their four bedroom Chiswick town house. 'So NIkos' he continued, 'Ar'm gonna put a question to ya, and if ar don't get a satisfactory answer you can consider yaself right up there on top of mar shit list, which, as many lags now serving hard time'll tell ya, is not a good place to be, d'you know anyfing abaat the disappearance or should I say feft of the so called red sea ruby, now ar know, and ar know the villains know that your the only man with the contacts to shift it, so fink very carefully before you answer!
Nikos did indeed think long and hard, he certainly didn't need the heat that this gem was attracting but the thought of the millions he could make brokering a deal with eager collectors far outweighed the risks.

'Mr Pritcher ar swear to ya if ar knew anyfing ar'd tell ya, ones tar would' he said, lying through his teeth, 'Like yaself ar've erd rumors but nufing more, as god is mar witness'
'Rumors!' the DI barked 'Exactly what rumors have you erd?'
Nikos was keen to divert the polices attentions elsewhere 'Well ar was told, and this is purely a rumor you understand' he said, lowering his voice, 'That the Tibbs brothers had showed an interest in the stone, but that didn't come from me Mr Pritcher so please don't mention my name in your enquiries, not unless you want mar death on your conscience'
'Firstly Nikos' the DI said, grinning 'Ar don't have a conscience, so if you were to turn up knee capped and gutted like a pig it wouldnt change mar life, ar can assure you of that, and secondly as for the Tibbs's ar'll pay em a little visit, but if ar find aat your giving me the run araand ar'll let it slip that you reckon they're a bunch of impotent cock sucking faggots' DI Pritcher turned and left Nikos mulling over what in fact the Tibbs boys would do to him if they heard such a derogatory remark, whatever it was it would undoubtedly involve a savage beating and certain death at their torturous hands.
Mickey Spencer in the mean time had been dragged from the Tibbs's car and taken forcibly to the rear office where Billy sat flanked by several members of his infamous gang, some baring the battle scars from knife and gun battles with South London yardies and drug lords from the Russian mafia.
'Well done you two' Billy said, congratulating his brothers as he rose to his feet and stepped around his huge mahogany desk, 'Mickey, Mickey ar fought you and me ad an understandin' he said menacingly.

'Please Billy!' Mickey replied, whilst being restrained, 'Whatever you fink it is ar've done man, ar'm tellin you it aint true!'
Billy said nothing, instead, in a flash he raised his clenched fist and brought it crashing down on the side of Mickey's jaw, dislodging two teeth which were spewed with a stream of blood onto the floor. Mickey cried out and slumped to his knees but was hoisted back onto his feet. 'Don't tell me what ar fuckin fink Mickey!' Billy snarled, slapping Mickeys swollen face playfully, 'Ar'll tell ya what ar fuckin fink, ar fink you fuckin ignored our little arrangement, went behind mar back, mugged me off and took what was rightfully mine!'
Mickey shook his head and spat out a clot of blood
'Naah Billy man, ar never nicked nuffin' he said, struggling to speak.
Billy hit him again, this time fracturing his jaw and knocking him unconscious, 'WAKE IM UP!' Billy yelled to his brothers who shook Mickey violently until he came too, moaning in agony, 'Good' Billy smiled 'Now that I av your undivided attention again Mr Spencer let me tell you this, if ar let a feevin low life scumbag like you screw me over ar'll av every plastic gangster in London lining up to pull mar pants down and fuck me up the arse, d'you get mar drift?'
Mickey nodded, his lips now badly bruised and spattered with blood, it was all that he could do to gargle let alone speak,
'Ar can't fuckin ear ya!' Billy said, losing his temper, 'What did he say Jimmy?'
'Ar dunno bruv' Jimmy replied, struggling to hold Mickey up, 'But e aint cooperatin is e'.
'No e fuckin aint!' Billy growled , turning to one of his henchman, 'Give us ya piece' he snapped. The man

whose nose had obviously been broken on several occasions took a pistol from his inside jacket pocket and handed it to Billy who, without hesitation, put the barrel against Mickeys right knee and pulled the trigger. There was a deafening bang as Mickey fell from the brothers grasp and collapsed in a heap on the floor, reeling from side to side unable to scream with a throat clogged with congealing blood. Billy tossed the smoking weapon onto his desk and stood over Mickey with his hands on his hips 'Get this piece of shit aat of ere' he said to his brothers, who dragged Mickey across the floor by his jacket, 'Put im in the chiller wiv the stiffs, a few hours in there might loosen iz tongue'.

Mickey was taken to the companies morgue and thrown into a refrigerated room lined with open caskets, in which lay deceased men and women awaiting embalmment. Clutching his shattered knee Mickey huddled in the corner daring not to look at the faces of the dead wondering if he soon would be among them.

As Billy's men mopped the bloodied floor the door opened and his sister Laura stormed in, 'Billy for gods sake i've got a client in the front office!' she snapped, then looked down at the bloodstained cloths, 'Oh for Christ sake Billy do you have to do this sort of thing in here, it's not right, I know it gives you lot a hard on when you get your guns out but have some bleedin respect for the dead!'.

Billy put an arm around his little sister, 'Sorry babe it was just a bit of business thas all'.

Laura broke away from his clutches and pointed to the trail of blood, 'You call that business!' she yelled, 'What shall I tell the poor cow in the front office who's just lost her husband, we have to make sure they're

dead love, so we put a bullet in their in their head, company policy you see!'.
'Calm daan sis' Billy said, stroking her arm, 'Just tell her one of the hearses back fired and that we're extremely sorry if it alarmed her in any way'
'I'm not happy about this Billy' Laura told her brother, 'Dad never brought any of his business back here, he'd turn in his bleedin grave he would'.
'It won't appen again sis' Billy said, trying to keep the peace, 'Now go on back to work, there's a good girl'.
'Don't patronize me Billy' Laura warned her brother as she left the office, 'I'm very sorry madam!' she told her weeping client, 'One of the funeral cars apparently back fired, I do hope it didn't frighten you, I tell you what, why don't i make us both a cup of tea, I know I could certainly do with one, milk and sugar?'
While Mickey's core temperature steadily dropped, Dee Dee and the others sat trying to figure out the best course of action, 'Ar got it blud' Bradley said, pulling an imaginary gun from the crotch of his baggy jeans, 'If the Tibbs's av got Mickey we go daan there yeah, bust up the place yeah, and pop a cap in their sorry arses woja reckon?'
Dee Dee, Maizie and Trisha sat speechless for a moment, 'What fuckin planet are you on you muppet?' Dee Dee finally said, 'Just sit the fuck down will ya, yer not friggin elpin'.
'We need to suss the place aat first Dee' Maizie said, taking out her phone and surfing the net, 'There can't be too many funeral fingy's in saaf London!'. After typing the name Tibbs and funeral into the search engine she was instantly given the location of the families undertaking business, 'Eeyaar' she said, holding up the screen, 'Tanner street, Bermondsey, not far from the river'.

'The river, hmmm' Bradley said, wracking his brain once again.
'Yes the fuckin river!' Dee Dee snapped, 'What d'you wanna do now you prat, sneak up in a bleedin submarine and torpedo the fuck aat of em!'. Bradley thought it best to say nothing at this point at the risk of enraging her further.
'Maizie's right Dee' Trisha added, 'One of us could go in there pretendin a relatives of ours just croaked and av a look raand'
'Thank you Trish' Dee Dee said, patting her back, 'Thas real big of ya'
'What, ay?' Trisha exclaimed 'Ar didn't mean me, what ar meant was'
'You'll be fine Trish, just act natral' said Maizie, siding with Dee Dee, 'We'll be right aatside in the mota'. Trisha's continuous protests fell on deaf ears, eventually leaving her no choice but to agree to the daring assignment. 'Ok ar spose' she said unconvincingly, 'Ar'm probly the best one out of the free of us for this sort of fing anyway, coz ar done drama in year free and got a gold star for me actin in the school play'
'Trish' Maizie laughed 'You was the arse end of Jesus's friggin donkey, that ardly makes you Angelina flippin Jolie does it!'
Trisha sat and sulked 'Ar done lots of stuff ar did, what about the time ar was a pirate in treasure island'
'Oh fuck me yeah' Dee Dee chuckled 'That was ilarious that was, you tripped over ya sword and brought arf the bleedin set daan wiv ya, Miss Gladstone spent free weeks in ospital and freatened to av you expelled'
'You do it then!' Trisha said, defiantly,

'No, no Trish' Dee Dee said, giving her a patronizing hug, 'Maizie and me avn't ad your featrical trainin'.
'Thas what ar was sayin' Trisha replied, gullibly, 'Ya've iver got it or you aint, ar reckon ar could'a bin on the telly by naah if ard'a kept it up'
Maizie couldn't help herself, 'What as?' she laughed, 'One of the bleedin telly tubbies!'
It was all that Dee Dee could do to separate her two friends as Trisha lunged at Maizie 'Your just bleedin jealous you are!' she yelled, shoving Maizie against the fridge, 'You never got picked for the pantomime did ya, no and you know why, coz you aint got no talent thas why, and if you adn't av talked me into smokin and bunkin off, who know's ar mighta bin an ousehold name like Judiff Charmers or, or!' she thought for a moment.
'The toilet duck' Dee Dee smirked.
Trisha broke away and stormed through to the lounge 'You'z two always take the piss outta me' she sulked, staring into space, 'Mar dear old nan believed in me she did god rest er soul, she never missed one of mar shows'
Dee Dee and Maizie began to feel a tinge of guilt at maybe having pushed their friend a tad too far 'We didn't mean it Trish mate!' Dee Dee said, urging Maizie to apologize, 'We was only pissin abaat'
'Yeah' Maizie added, 'Ar fought you was well good in Beauty and the Beast!
Trisha spun round, 'Did ya!' she cried, with a huge grin on her face, 'That was one of mar favorites an'all, mind you ar wanted to be Belle but they made me a flippin tea cup instead'
'Yeah but Trish mate' Dee Dee said, patting her friend on the back, 'You were the bollocks of a tea cup though, how you never got a bleedin bafta for

that is beyond me' Trisha naively agreed and the three were friends again.

Meanwhile Bradley sat scratching his aching groin 'Woss up wiv you?' asked Dee Dee, 'You got a dose or summink?'

'Naah course not man!' Bradley replied, taking a quick peek into his underpants, 'Julie said she was clean so ar didn't bovva baggin it up'.

'And you believed er you soppy bastard!' Maizie snapped, throwing her hands in the air, 'Woss a matter wiv you?'

Bradley now looked a little concerned, 'Shit!' he gasped 'Ar was gonna go back on Friday for an all nighter an'all, she reckons's she's well up for some water sports'

Dee Dee turned he nose up, 'Fanks for that image Bradley, but that ain't gonna appen, coz you'll be stuck at ome pissin puss outta ya pox ridden prick'.

Now Bradley really was scared, he leapt from the table and ran to the bathroom, bolting the door behind him, 'Shit, shit!' he cried, dropping his trousers and grabbing the nearest flannel to hand to scrub his genitals. Applying what he thought was liquid soap from a bottle, Bradley rubbed his groin as hard as he could with the thought of crabs or even aids running through his mind. He then felt a mild tingling sensation which slowly grew in intensity until it began to burn, Bradley threw the flannel and examined himself whilst hopping on the spot, 'What the fuck!' he yelled, checking the bottles label which read 'Feminine hair remover', 'SHIT NO, NO FUCK!' he screamed as the burning became intolerable. Standing on tip toes Bradley tried desperately to dip his privates in the sink, but he was too short, 'SHIT ELP!' he cried, fanning himself with a towel, he then crouched over the toilet and poured handfuls of water over his crotch which mildly alleviated the pain, but he then looked on in horror as clumps of his pubic hair fell out into the pan until all but a few strands remained.

'You alright in there bruv?' Maizie asked, knocking on the door, 'D'you need some elp?'

'NO, NO!' Bradley replied, cowering over the pan, 'LEAVE ME ALONE!' He sheepishly emerged several moments later looking extremely distressed and stood quietly in the corner of the kitchen, occasionally tugging at his pants.

'Right come on super stud' Dee Dee said, beckoning to Bradley, 'We gotta go to saaf London'

Bradley lowered himself gingerly into the seat of his car, wincing as his scrotum became trapped under his right leg,

'You alright son' Dee Dee said, slapping his thigh which increased his level of pain ten fold.

'Fuck, yeah man ar'm fine!' he said, through clenched teeth, 'Just, please don't touch me thas all'

As the four friends set off across town, DI Pritcher had just arrived at the Tibbs's premises, shoving the door open he marched through the office barely acknowledging Laura 'Is he in?' he asked sternly, heading to the rear.

Laura sprang to her feet and made after him 'Wait!' she yelled, 'You can't go back there!' fearing her brothers office would still show signs of Mickeys beating she stood between the DI and the door. 'Oh er, it's you Mr Pritcher' she added, looking him in the eye. Throughout his career, DI Pritcher had cause to visit the Tibbs's on countless occasions, putting their recently departed father behind bars for robbery and

extortion not once but three times totaling some twenty three years in custody.
'It's Detective Inspector Pritcher now Laura' the DI told her, taking out his warrant card, 'I suggest you stand aside before I have you nicked for obstruction!'.
Laura slipped away and returned to her desk. 'I knew you were the smart one' the DI smiled.
Laura was smart, despite growing up within her families criminal empire she had managed to stay on the right side of the law, excelling at school unlike her siblings she achieved a Degree in business studies at the University of London. Even their mother Esther had been a thorn in the side of the London constabulary, the original gangsters moll she eventually died of tuberculosis whilst serving eighteen years for attempted murder, wounding a young police officer in fact during a high speed getaway with Laura's father.
DI Pritcher flung open the door of the rear office where the Tibbs brothers and their associates were sat huddled round the desk, deep in conversation. 'Ello boys!' he smirked, 'Hope ar'm not interrupting anyfing'.
The startled gang members looked up, barring the DI's view as Billy slipped a revolver into the desk drawer. 'Woda you want Pritcher?' Billy growled, 'Come to gloat over the old mans deff av ya?'.
One of Billy's henchman leapt to his feet and lunged at the DI, his fists clenched, 'You fuckin pig!' he yelled, but a lightning fast blow to the ribs and a butt to the bridge of the nose from the Detective Inspector sent him reeling across the room.
Jimmy reached into his jacket pocket, glaring at the DI but was yanked to his senses by his older brother, 'Don't be fuckin stupid!' Billy snapped.

'Thas right Billy' the DI said, straightening his jacket, 'Put a lead on ya mutt' Jimmy was seething but wouldn't dare go against his elder brothers wishes.
Billy rocked back in his seat, 'I ear they made you a DI!' he said, full of loathing, 'Ow many cocks did you av to suck for that then?' Jimmy and the others burst out laughing but the DI merely leaned forward and looked the crime boss in the eye,
'Not as many as your old man did in Parkhurst ar bet, eh Billy!' he said calmly.
'YOU FUCKIN SLAG!' Billy screamed, as Roland and the others did their level best to restrain him, 'AR'LL RIP YOUR FUCKIN FROAT AAT!' he then pushed the others away, 'Get the fuck off me!' he snarled, reaching for the drawer, but then hesitating.
The DI paced the room, 'Naah that I av your attention Billy' he said, smugly 'Ar'm gonna put a few questions to ya, and if ar don't get the answers ar want, there'll be fifty coppers here wivin the hour to take this place apart brick by shitty little brick, board by board and nail by bloody nail do I make marself crystal clear?' The DI toyed with the handle of the door leading to where Mickey was held captive. 'Wod'ya wanna know Pritcher?' Billy asked, diverting the DI's attention.
The DI smiled, 'Thas more like it Billy' he said, returning to the desk, 'You see, fings are so much easier when you all cooperate'.
Billy growled under his breath, 'Just get on wiv it you cockroach' he replied, reluctantly.
DI Pritcher took five pounds from his wallet and thrust it into Roland's hand, 'Fatboy, go and get me and ya bruvva a cuppa tea there's a good lad' he laughed and then gestured to the others 'And take these ladies wiv ya'. They each looked at their boss for a

sign to tear the DI to pieces but were given the contrary,
'Go on you lot, piss off' Billy told them, 'Ar'll deal wiv this'
'But Bill' Jimmy protested, 'Ar should stay wiv ya! Billy lost his temper, grabbing a bust of Rocky Marciano from his desk and hurling it across the room, 'AR SAID GET THE FUCK AAT, ALL OF YA!' he screamed, having little patients for insubordination within the ranks. Jimmy, Roland and the others filed out of the room, grimacing and making idle threats under their breath.
The DI closed the door behind them and pulled up a chair opposite Billy, folding his arms on the desk in front of him, 'Now Billy where were we?' he began. Billy held his hand up, stopping the DI in mid sentence, 'Ar know what ya want Pritcher' he said, taking two bundles of cash from his drawer and tossing them across the desk,
'There's two large there, now piss off and leave us alone'.
The DI swatted the cash back at Billy, shaking his head 'Ar'm not here for ya money Billy' he snapped, 'And even if ar was, a measly two grand'd be a fuckin insult, don't ya fink?' The DI then produced a photograph of the Red sea ruby from his jacket pocket and slammed it down on the desk, 'This is why ar'm here Billy, one of the biggest blags in the last decade, and it don't take a bleedin genius to work aat that you and your firm had summink to do wiv it, you and that scum bag Spencer' the veins on the DI's neck stood out 'Now Billy' he continued, staring his adversary in the eye, 'Even if you've got nufing to say, it's only a matter of time before we nab Mickey, and when he hears the deal ar'm gonna offer

him to give you lot up, ar don't fink he'll be in any position to turn it daan'.

Billy clasped his hands together behind his head and smiled, knowing full well that Mickey was safely locked in his refrigerator 'You aint got nuffin on me Pritcher, your just pissin in the wind as usual' he scoffed, 'Uverwise you'd av a bleedin warrant in yer and instead of this poxy picture' Billy tore the photograph in two and tossed it aside, 'Now if you'll excuse me, officer!' he added, sarcastically, 'Ar got a business to run' Billy then slid his card across the desk, 'Ar usually give a discount to friends and famly' he said with a wry smile, 'But you Mr Pritcher' he paused, looking the DI up and down, 'Ar'll bury you for nuffing' he said menacingly.

DI Pritcher examined the card closely before smirking and tossing it flippantly over his shoulder, 'You might scare arf the pot heads, ponces and pimps on this manor Billy Tibbs' he replied, turning for the door, 'But you sure as fuck don't scare me, ar've shit bigger villains than you son, ar'll be seeing you sooner than ya fink and yeah, next time maybe ar'll av that bleedin warrant'. With this the DI left the back office, slamming the door behind him 'You might wanna fink abaat a career change young lady' he told Laura in passing, 'Coz ar'll be shutting this shit hole down sooner or later and putting those brothers of yours behind bars just like ar did your old man'. Laura didn't look up from her computer monitor, she merely raised her middle finger defiantly. 'Now that's not very nice is it' the DI added, leaning over her desk and eying her cleavage, 'Tell me Laura, are you still dating dykes' he asked sarcastically .

Laura looked at him as though he was something she had just scraped from the heel of her shoe, 'If you

mean am I still a lesbian' she snapped, 'Then yeah, coz the only alternatives are wanker's like you who think that a squeeze of the tit and a five minute fuck is all a woman wants'.
DI Pritcher had no retort for Laura's outburst and turned for the door muttering under his breath, 'Bleedin rug muncher's'. Once outside the DI radio'd back to the station, 'Marsh, tell me you've got something out of that Dawson woman' he said, hoping for a break in the case.
'Not yet sir' Detective Marsh replied from outside the interview room, 'She's a tough old bird sir, hard as nails in fact'.
The DI flew into a furious rage having just been belittled, screaming down the phone in front of crowd of bewildered shoppers, 'LISTEN YOU MORON, AR DON'T CARE WHAT YOU AV TO DO, YOU GET THAT BITCH TO TALK, BEAT THE SHIT AAT OF ER IF YOU HAVE TO, DO YOU HEAR ME!'. The DI had been investigated many times after complaints of police brutality but had thus far evaded a disciplinary hearing.
'Yes sir, right away sir!' Marsh replied, sheepishly, 'I'll get right back in there sir'.
A fuming Di Pritcher stared back at the gawping crowd, 'WHAT?' he yelled. The gathering quickly dispersed and the Di hopped back into his car.
Dee Dee and the others arrived outside Tibbs's seconds after the DI's departure, 'Right ya know what to do dontcha Trish' Dee Dee told her friend, giving her a reassuring pat, 'If Mickey's in there you do whatever it takes to get im aat'
'Ar do me best Dee' Trisha said nervously, psyching herself up, she then put her head in her hands and closed her eyes.

'What the fuck are you doing?' Dee Dee asked, Trisha raised her hand to silence Dee Dee,
'What's she doin Dee' Maize asked 'Bleedin meditatin or summink'.
Trisha tutted and opened her eyes, 'If you'z two must know' she said angrily, 'Ar'm tryna to get into character, all actors do it before a big scene'.
'Your not a bloody actor!' Dee Dee said, shoving Trisha toward the door, 'Or an actress for that matter, so fuck gettin into character, just get in that pissin shop!'. Trisha climbed from the car, muttering to herself and slamming the door behind her, she then stood taking several deep breaths. Dee Dee leaned out of Bradley's car window, 'OY SANDRA BOLLOCK, GET THE FUCK IN THERE WILL YA!'.
Trisha hurried to the door 'Alright ar'm goin, ar'm goin' she said, shoving the brass handle, 'Ello, ello!' she called, once inside. Laura had nipped to the kitchen to make herself another tea and emerged with a packet of biscuits and a tray, 'Oh sorry I was just out back' she told Trisha, taking a seat, 'Please sit down won't you, oh would you like a cup of tea the kettle's still hot?'.
'Naah iss alright fanks' Trisha replied, 'Ar just ad a brew'.
Laura put her cup to one side, 'How can we help you?' she asked, 'Have you recently suffered a bereavement?'.
'A what?' Trisha asked, confused.
'A bereavement' Laura said again, 'The loss of a family member or friend perhaps' Whilst appearing professional Laura couldn't help but find herself physically attracted to Trisha, paying particular attention to her pert lips and drifting off momentarily into an erotic fantasy involving the two of them.

'Oh, oh yeah!' Trisha said, taking a tissue from her bag and appearing to mop tears from her face, 'Me great Granddad's kicked the bucket'.

Laura snapped out of her fantasy at Trisha's remarks, 'You er, you mean the gentleman has passed away' she said, offering Trisha a fresh box of tissues, 'I'm so sorry for your loss, had he been ill for some time or was it a sudden departure, if I may ask?'

'Ar told ya' Trisha said, blowing her nose and milking the part, 'E kicked the bleedin bucket, e's got an outside karzi so e takes a builders bucket to bed for a piss an a dump, well the silly old sod got up in the middle of the night, tripped over the fuckin fing and stoved iz ed fru the wardrobe door, iss Robbie ar feel sorry for though'

'Robbie was your great grandfather?' Laura asked, bemused at such a story.

'No ya doghnut' Trisha laughed 'Robbie's the bleedin tortoise, e was ibernatin under a pile of pants at the bottom of the wardrobe and got the shock of iz bloomin life e did, ar named im Robbie after Robbie Williams coz e'z so cute wiv iz little funny legs an'all' Trisha was now in full swing, chattering nonsensically. 'Ar dunno how they did wivaat im'

'Who, the tortoise?' asked Laura struggling to keep abreast of things,

'No ya nutter!' Trisha said, raising her eyebrows, 'Robbie Williams, ar mean Gary and the uvvers are alright but Robbie, e'z fuckin gorgeous dontcha fink'.

Laura nodded with a half hearted smile, never having found any of the boyband members remotely attractive.

Trisha continued rambling as though the pair were old friends, 'Ar waited free hours outside HMV once just to pinch iz arse, firm as fuck it was, but while ar was coppin a feel some little scrote nicked me ambag'.

By now Laura had totally lost track of the conversation, 'Oh er, i'm sorry to hear that' she said, 'I'm sure it must have been very distressing for you'.

'Not arf as distressing as it was for im' Trisha laughed, 'Ar chased the little fucker into Lillywhites and caught im on the escalator'.

Laura soon found herself unwittingly engrossed in Trisha's tale, 'Did you make a citizens arrest?' she asked, 'Or call for security?'.

'Nar sod that' Trisha replied, clenching her fist, 'Ar give im one up the guts and pushed im fru the perfume caanter, got me bag back an'all'

'Oh i'm glad to hear it' Laura smiled, 'You were lucky'.

'Well ar weren't gonna let it go' Trisha replied, defiantly 'I ad free paand fifty left on me oyster card'.

Laura gathered some papers together, 'So I take it your wanting to make arrangements for you great grandfather, miss?'

'Moore, Trisha Moore' Trisha said, leaning forward, 'Wiv an e like Demi Moore, ar loved er in ghost with Patrick what's iz face dint you, gettin daan and dirty wiv that potter's wheel fingy, me and me ex, Trevor tried it wiv playdo, ar made a shitty egg cup while he kicked me back door in'.

Laura quickly intervened 'Yes, yes I remember the film, it's one of my favorites too', now about your late great grandfather'

'Who?' Trisha asked, forgetting why she was there, 'Oh the stiff, yeah' she added, 'Sorry ar talk a lot when ar'm stressed, it's these places, they gimme the eeby geebies, ar dunno ow you lot do it ar really don't, messin about wiv deadens and that, me uncle Barry used to do it until they caught im and banged im up, the dirty fucker'.

Laura hadn't heard a word that Trisha had been saying for the previous few moments, finding herself completely captivated by her roguish cockney charm.

'Are you sure I can't make you some tea' Laura said, resting her hand on Trisha's 'It may help steady your nerves'.

Suddenly Trisha could sense Laura's advances and the caress of her fingers, 'Oh erm, er, ang on a minute!' she said, making for the door, 'Ar'm just gonna get some air'

'Ok take as long as you like' Laura replied, hoping for her return.

Trisha ran to Bradley's car and leapt in the back seat, 'Well?' Dee Dee said, in anticipation, 'Did ya find aat anyfing'.

'Yeah ar did!' Trisha said, putting on her seatbelt, 'That bird in there's a bleedin lezza and want's to get in mar knickers the dirty cow!'.

'What about Mickey?' Maizie asked, 'Did ya find out where they got im?'

Trisha shook her head 'No ar didn't get that far, ar legged it when she started comin on to me'.

'Well get back in there!' Dee Dee said, angrily, 'Go on, ar don't give a fuck if you av to do the dirty dyke with a double ended dildo, just find out where Mickey is will ya!'.

'Oh Deeee!' Trisha protested, 'Can't someone else do it'.

Dee Dee shoved Trisha back out the car, 'You get the fuck in there, and flash her some tit or summink, fuckin ell Trish it aint the first time you bin wiv another bird is it, member that tart in Torremolinos, you couldn't get enough of er'. Dee Dee was referring to a torrid bisexual one nighter that her friend had after downing two thirds of a bottle of tequila and almost a dozen cocktails.

'But Dee ar was bladdered, you know that' Trisha said, in her defense, 'Ar must admit though, she ad a tongue bigger than arf the dicks ar've ad, and fuck me she knew ow to use it'. At that precise moment two elderly ladies were passing within earshot as Trisha continued, 'She done me with a massive strappon an'all'.

'Oh my word!' one lady gasped,

'Woss up wiv you?' Trisha asked them, 'Come on, don't tell me you two ain't ad a game of dunk the dildo before, all that bible bashin's just a front, you old git's are at it all the time, Maizie's nan's the biggest gash guzzler ar know, her and arf the blue rinse bingo mafia'.

The ladies hurried away, dragging their shopping trolleys behind them, 'Well I never!' one of them exclaimed.

'Ar bet you fuckin did!' Trisha yelled after them.

Dee Dee threw her empty coke can at Trisha, 'Oy silly bollocks' she snapped, 'Forget that shit, get in there and flirt like fuck, take er for a drink or summink, just find aat where Mickey is will ya, me and Maize are gonna bugger off for a while, give us a bell when ya've got summink, and ar don't mean a twelve inch love toy arf way up ya flu'. Dee Dee slapped Bradley's knee sending yet another shudder through his reddened groin, 'Come on ya rampant rapper' she urged, 'Get this crate started and take us ome'. Bradley pulled away, leaving an apprehensive Trisha and swerved out into the path of a refuse truck narrowly missing it by inches,

'JESUS!' Dee Dee gasped, 'You twat, you sure you got a bleedin license?'.
Meanwhile Maizie cowered in the back covering her eyes, 'Ar fink ar might av just shit meslf Dee' she said, peering through her fingers.
'Woss up wiv you'z two man?' Bradley laughed, unaware or the devastation left in his wake, 'I'z never ad no accident'. The dust cart had veered across the road to avoid Bradley's oncoming Nova, mounted the curb and careered headlong into a branch of Starbuks, sending the frightened frappuccnino covered customers diving for cover.
Once their nerves had settled, Maizie had an idea, 'Eeya Dee they got Zumba daan the community center tonight, fancy it?'.
'Zumba!' Dee Dee laughed, 'What the fuck do ar wanna go zumba for, that shit's for sad ponce's who need to get a bleedin life, and line dancing, thas just as bad, dressin up like Billy the fuckin kid and jiggin abaat like crusty the bleedin crab!'.
'Ar take it thas a no then' Maizie asked, 'Iss just that Janice from the CO-OP reckons there's a well fit geezer doin the classes, Miguelle or Manuelle or summink, she said arf the women on the estate go there just to perve at iz arse in a pair of spandex gym shorts'.
Suddenly Dee Dee was interested after all, 'What time's it start?' she asked, eager to see for herself.
'Arf seven ar fink' Maizie said, excitedly, 'Ar could wear me new leggins and that blue top that shows off me tits' she cupped her breasts in her hands 'D'ya know what Dee, ar reckon these are gettin bigger ar really do, ar still wanna get em done though coz blokes like bigguns, don't they Brad?'.

'Shut up please sis' Bradley replied, putting all sexual thoughts out of his mind, 'Ar proper reckon ar got a dose man, diss is so bad'.
'Don't be fuckin stupid' Dee Dee said, in a rare display of sympathy, 'Avin a dose is a good fing, coz it's proves you've done it wiv a real bird instead of knockin one aat to the top shelf totty like the pafetic little virgin you was'.
Bradley thought for a moment, not knowing quite how to take Dee Dee's remarks, then puffed out his chest, 'Yeah blud, ya right!' he smiled, 'Iss like a tag innit, ar bet Snoop dog's ad one, and Dizzy man, with the booty that boy's been bangin e must be riddled wiv it'. Once at home Bradley raced to his room to proudly update his online status to 'I've got an STD man, that's serious testicle damage to all you'z virgins out there' Bradley himself not knowing the true meaning, stepping behind his decks he then began an impromptu rap,

'sittin in mar kitchen
mar girlfriends bitchin
she's given me a dose and ar can't stop itchin,
ar knock er to the floor and ar'm givin er a slap
coz she's given me the pox or she's given me the clap,
ar'm tellin all mar bro's coz they got one too
and given arf a chance ar be givin it to you,
a dose, a dose, get yaself a dose
jerking on a catalogue don't come close,
a dose, a dose, get yaself a dose
jerking on a catalogue don't come close,
a dose, a dose
get yaself a dose'

Dee Dee and Maizie were showered and dressed in no time in readiness for the evenings dancing, 'D'ya fink Trish'll be alright Dee?' Maizie asked, as the two of them left the house, 'Yeah course she will' Dee Dee said, crossing her fingers behind her, 'Ar give er a ring later, see how she's gettin on'.
Along with several other women from the estate, Dee Dee and Maizie filed across the green, dodging the piles of fresh and decaying dog poo to the community center, a run down prefabricated building erected shortly after the Bircham tower blocks were built. Crime and neglect had taken it's toll on the heavily graffiti'd center, with boarded windows, leaking gutters and a stench of urine at the back doors that could not be eradicated. Anything of value had been stripped from it's walls and display cabinets during the countless break-ins by local youths to fund their drink and drug addictions.
Dee Dee tapped on the woman's shoulder in front of her as they queued to get in, 'Alright Shirl!' she smiled, 'Ow you doin?'.
Shirley Thomas lived on the fourth floor of Dee Dee's block with her two son's, her third and eldest son Ryan was serving nine years in Pentonville for armed robbery and assault with a deadly weapon following a post office raid in Walthamstow. 'Oh ello Dee' she replied, spinning with a smile 'Yeah arm alright fanks, hiya Maize, you alright'.
'Yeah armgood fanks' Maizie added, 'Ow's Pete?'. Peter was Shirley's youngest son at seventeen whom Maizie had dated for a short while. 'Still the same love' Shirley explained, 'E won't come out of iz room or talk to anyone, he was devastated when you dumped im Maize, ar'm worried he might do somefing stupid now, ar'v heard im banging iz head

on the wall in the middle of the night, can't you av a word wiv im'.

Maizie shook her head, 'Your bleedin jokin aintcha' shescoffe, 'E'z a flippin fruit loop that boy of yours, ar couldn't wait to get shot of im, d'you know he used to shit in a nappy and ask me to change im'.

'You're fuckin jokin!' Dee Dee gasped, hearing this for the first time,

'Oh yeah'!' Maizie continued 'I ad to powder iz fuckin arse an'all!'

Shirley took a tissue from her bag and mopped a tear from her eye, 'Ar blame me'self' she sobbed, 'Ar breast fed im till e was fourteen and only took iz dummy off im last week, mind you the doctor say's it's just a phase and e'll probly grow aat of it'.

'PHASE MY ARSE!' Dee Dee laughed, 'E'z a fuckin nut job thas what e is, ar mean anyone that crawls round on their ands and knees wiv arf a pound of warm crap in their romper suit wants locking up in mar book'.

Maizie then laughed to herself, 'You shoulda seen im eat Bolognese though Dee it was so funny, e ad it in iz hair, up iz nose, e used to get in a right state wiv it, the bleeda'd be in the bath for ages after that, im and iz rubber duck!'

'Maize!' Dee Dee said, having heard enough, 'Shut up will ya, your freakin me aat' she then turned to Shirley who was grinning like a Cheshire cat, knowing how much peter loved that duck. 'You eard anyfing from your Ryan Shirl?' she asked, steering the conversation away from Peter, 'When does e get aat?'.

'Not for anuvver free years ar fink' Shirley replied, forlornly, 'Ar get a letter from im every now and again, but e's in solitary at the moment though for stabbin that peado bastard that was in the papers last week'. Ryan was halfway through a forty day lockdown in solitary confinement for malicious wounding, and for once his mother and many others had approved of his actions. The majority of the prison's population had been gunning for Jason Lewis ever since he set foot inside. Lewis had been convicted of the abduction and horrific murder of local schoolgirl Katie Bryant, a crime that had shocked the entire nation and lead to one of the largest man hunts on record. Ryan had fashioned a makeshift blade from a sharpened toilet handle and lay in wait for Lewis in the prison laundry, when the guards had turned their backs, some say deliberately, Ryan plunged the blade into Lewis's neck narrowly missing his carotid artery, and as the child killer thrashed around screaming in a pool of his own blood Ryan slammed a heated industrial iron down onto the side of his contorted face shouting 'DIE YOU FUCKIN ORRIBLE CUNT, DIE!'.

Lewis, in severe shock later slipped into a coma and was pronounced dead within days while Ryan was hailed a hero by the prisoners and guards alike. Solitary confinement was merely a formality as he was showered with gifts of cigarettes and porn from admiring inmates and letters of thanks from a grateful public.

'Fuckin good on im!' Dee Dee said, giving Shirley an approving pat on the shoulder 'That slag got what e deserved'.

The queue began to shuffle towards the entrance, many of them craning their necks, eager to get a glimpse of their hot blooded Italian instructor, Miguelle, 'Ar wouldn't mind coppin off wiv im' one enthusiastic lady said, 'I erd e's a fantastic shag'. The

ladies hurriedly changed in a side room, fluffing their hair and tweaking their make up before joining Miguelle in the hall.
'Welcome, welcome lovely ladies!' he said, bowing before them in his tight sweat pants. Being new to Zumba, Dee Dee and Maizie thought it best to stand at the back and copy the others. 'Ok shall we begin' Miguelle said, slipping a cd into his player and gyrating his hips, 'This is a warm up to get you beautiful ladies hot, hot, hot'. While the rest of the class kept in time with their instructor, Dee Dee and Maizie weren't doing so well, 'Tell im to slow daan will ya' Maizie panted, 'Ar'll put me bleedin back aat in a minute'.
Dee Dee wasn't listening, her gaze was fixed firmly on the backside of a huge woman in front of them, her jogging bottoms straining at the seams, 'Jesus Maize looka the state a that will ya' she grimaced, 'The last time I saw a crack like that it ad a farmers arm angin out of it'. She referred to a trip with St Augustine's to an Essex dairy farm to witness a veterinary inspection as part of their biology project,
'Fancy that eh' she added, 'Fistin cows for a livin'. Maizie couldn't help but laugh 'Fuck me Dee that was so funny' she said, struggling to keep in time with the others, 'Ar nearly pissed meself when you stubbed ya fag aat on that bullocks arse'.
Dee Dee smiled 'Yeah, ar don't fink the vet saw the funny side of it though, the poor bleeda, the fuckin fing reared up and bolted arf way to Billericay wiv im angin aat the back end'. Dee Dee then rubbed her backside, remembering the punishment inflicted by the mother superior, 'Ar got six of the best for that, fuckin urt an'all' she added, 'The bitch took a bloomin

run up for the last one and snapped er cane on me arse cheeks, the sadistic fucker!'.

Maizie, along with many other girls attending St Augustine's had also suffered under the sister's brutal regime, 'Ar used to ram arf a dozen pages of the Daily Mirra daan me knickers' she laughed, 'Only trouble was, the bleedin ink used to come off, ar member once I ad Bin Laden's ugly mug on my left cheek and Wayne Rooney on the right'.

'Ooh nasty!' Dee Dee shuddered.

The large lady in front of them spun round and glared at the two girls, 'Do you mind!' she scowled, wiping the strands of sweat drenched hair from her eyes and breathing heavily, 'Some of us here are trying to concentrate'.

Dee Dee nudged her friend, 'Sorry love' she said, sarcastically, 'Tryna lose weight are ya?'.

The woman pulled her vest down over her exposed navel 'As a matter of fact I am' she replied, proudly, 'I've lost a whole five pounds in five weeks, Miguelle says i'm making excellent progress'.

Dee Dee looked her up and down, 'Oh yeah ar can see that' she said, winking to Maizie. The woman struck a confident pose before Dee Dee added, 'But if ya want my advice love, forget the zumba, it's a rolla gaffa tape you want'.

The woman looked confused, 'What ever for?' she asked?.

'Well' Dee Dee went on, trying not to laugh, 'You can stick it across that fat face of yours every time you fancy a bucket of doughnuts ya lumpy twat!'.

The woman stood mortified 'What, what?' she stammered.

'You erd!' Dee Dee growled 'Stop fuckin eatin, iss as simple as that'. The woman's bottom lip began to

quiver before she exploded into floods of tears and stormed out of the hall. Miguelle begged her to stay but she threw open the doors and marched off across the green, taking a chocolate bar from her pocket and tearing off the wrapper, she stood and sobbed beneath a street light devouring the bar in seconds.
'Fat fighter's my arse' Dee Dee laughed, 'Ar'd give er arf a cream cracker a day, tie a dead rabbit to er backside and chase her round the park with me uncle David's greyhound, she'd shit the bleedin blubber off'.
'Like that chubby girl in science Dee' Maizie laughed, 'When you bet er she couldn't lose a stone in a week, poor cow puked all er grub up, ended up bulimic and spent the next free mumfs in a nut house'.
The pair stood giggling at the back of the hall recounting the highlights of their short but colorful lives, 'Eeya!' Maizie laughed, 'Member them blokes wiv that date rape shit'. Dee Dee smiled and nodded. Her friend was referring to the time the two girls ran away from home after Maizie's parents had grounded her for smoking weed. They had spent their collective savings of thirty two pounds fifty on two tickets to London's club land, a chicken doner and a pitcher of vodka redbull.
Wandering the streets later that night amusing themselves by waking as many sleeping tramps as they could and flashing them their breasts, the pair soon attracted the attention of the city's seedier residents,
'Hello ladies, how are you tonight?' a man called out as he and his friend crossed the street to join them,
'Where are you going?'.

Dee Dee barely acknowledged them, simply raising a finger in the air, 'Get lost ya nob', she said, dragging Maizie away.

The men, both Lithuanian, quickened their step, 'Wait wait!' one of them called, 'Would you like to go to a party, music, free drinks, something to smoke if you like'.

Maizie stopped and tugged at Dee Dee's arm, 'Ang on Dee iss a party mate, free booze an'all'.

Dee Dee remained hesitant, 'Ar dunno Maize, we don't know these geezers' she eyed the two up and down, 'What are ya, polaks or summink?' she asked.

'No, no!' one of them protested, 'We are students from Lithuania studying medicine in your country, allow me to introduce myself, my name is Miri and my friend is Arden'. Their story was a complete fabrication, the two were part of an international sex and drug trafficking ring, praying on the naive and vulnerable with promises of a glamourous life and pockets of cash. Their victims, many of them young penniless girls would soon find themselves trapped in a life of sex and violence unable to escape due to their cleverly orchestrated addiction to class A drugs keeping them subservient if not willing.

Maizie tugged again at Dee Dee's arm again, 'Fuckin ell Dee, free booze and somewhere to get our ed's daan, less av it!'.

Dee Dee knew that Maizie could whine and sulk for days if she didn't get her own way, she then quizzed the two men further, 'What are ya, vaj doctors or summink?'.

'I'm sorry' Miri replied, 'What is this?'.

Dee Dee scratched at her crotch 'Gyno whatsits!' she replied struggling for the correct terminology, 'You know, fanny fiddlers' she added, 'If you are, you aint experimentin on me ar can tell ya, the last junior quack that stuck iz and up mar flu got a face full of piss and a jimmy choo in iz lug ole!'.

The two men looked at each other, 'I do not understand!' Arden said, shrugging his shoulders.

Dee Dee eventually gave in to Maizie's pleading, 'Oh alright!' she nodded, 'But their better be some blokes fitter than you two mingers there, coz you look like you both fell out the ugly tree and it every fuckin branch on the way daan'.

The girls were taken by taxi to a large Georgian house off the Holloway road which had been crudely converted into more than a dozen sparsely furnished bedsit's, each secured with a heavy galvanized hasp, staple and padlock which aroused Dee Dee's suspicions. Once inside one of the rooms the two men began speaking in their native tongue, 'Eeya!' Dee Dee said, looking round 'Where's all the uvvers?'.

'Excuse me?' Miri said, breaking from his conversation.

'The uvvers' Dee Dee said again, 'If this is a bleedin party, where the fuck is everyone?'.

'Oh yes' Miri said, taking four glasses from the cupboard, 'Our friends will be along soon. here have some vodka and make yourself at home'. he poured a large measure into each glass and set them down on the coffee table.

Dee Dee nudged her friend, 'Er, where's the bog?' she asked Arden, 'Ar need to powder me nose'

'Yeah' Maizie added, crossing her legs, 'And ar need a pony'

'A pony' Miri said, looking bemused 'What is this pony?'

'A shit!' Dee Dee replied, 'A crap, a dump, drop a bleedin log'. The penny dropped and Arden pointed to a door in the corner of the room. Dee Dee dragged Maizie inside and kicked the door closed,

'Wossup Dee?' Maizie asked, wriggling out of her knickers and lowering herself onto the pan.

'Summink aint right' Dee Dee replied, stooping to peer through the key hole, 'Ar don't trust these shifty fuckers' she then saw Miri take two coloured pills from his wallet and drop them into two of the glasses, smiling to his friend as he did so. 'Ar fuckin knew it!' she snarled, 'The bastards drugged our bleedin drinks' she noted the position of the glasses on the table and turned to Maizie, 'Did you ear me Maize?', But Maizie had a more pressing problem, a serious blockage of the bowel, with a reddened strained expression she bent over double. 'Woss up wiv you?' Dee Dee asked.

'Fuckin ell Dee!' Maizie gasped, 'Ar'm proper bunged up mate'.

'Whatd'ya want me to do abaat it?' Dee Dee laughed, 'Squeeze ya bleedin ed, just urry up will ya we gotta get aat of ere'.

Maizie pushed and strained, gritting her teeth, 'Poxy bleedin kebabs!' she cursed, 'Bleedin ell Dee ar reckon ar need gas and air for this fucker'. Eventually there was a loud splash and Maizie flopped back against the cistern, 'Fuck me' she sighed, the color draining from her face, 'If thas what child berfs like ar'll buy one off Madonna'.

Dee Dee dragged Maizie to her feet, 'Wipe yer arse and get ya kit off' she told her.

'What, what for?' Maizie asked, pulling at the roll of toilet paper.

'Just do it ya silly cow!' Dee Dee barked. The two girls stripped to their underwear with Maizie still none the wiser,
'What we doin Dee, ar don't even fancy em!' Maizie added.
'Shut up will ya!' Dee Dee snapped, 'Just do what ar do and we'll get aata this bloody mess'.
Arden and Miri were seated on a worn leather sofa with the coffee table in front of them when the two girls emerged and stood before them completely naked. The two Lithuanian's sat bolt upright, hardly believing their eyes, usually it would take at least an hour for the vodka and rohypnol to take effect on their victims to get to this stage,
'Less get this fuckin party started then' Dee Dee said, turning on a portable stereo and thumbing through a pile of cd's, 'UB40 thatta do' she said popping a disc in.
Arden and Miri looked at each other in disbelief as Dee Dee began gyrating to Cherio baby with Maizie following her lead. Miri joked with his friend in Lithuanian 'We needn't have bothered with the drugs with these two eh!'
'You may be right my friend' Arden laughed then beckoned to Dee Dee, 'Come, sit' he said, slapping his lap. Dee Dee lowered herself slowly and sensually onto his crotch urging Maizie to do the same. The two then performed a raunchy lap dance, raising the men's blood pressure and bringing them to the point of ecstasy. Miri and Arden gave each other a knowing smile and slumped back, closing their eyes.
Wasting no time, still grinding her body against Arden's, Dee Dee reached behind with one hand and

switched the glasses. 'Less ava drink', she said, slapping Arden's cheek playfully.

'Yes, yes' he replied, reaching forward and taking the two glasses he perceived were safe, handing one to his friend. Dee Dee and Maizie sipped at their vodka and watch the two Lithuanians drain their glasses, and then pour another.

'Dance for us!' Miri said, clapping his hands and clinking his glass with Arden's as though they had hit the jackpot. Dee Dee and Maizie performed their usual dance floor routine which would drive the boys wild in the Romford night clubs.

After several more vodka's the men appeared lethargic, unaware that the powerful date rape drug was coursing through their veins. Miri' was the first to succumb to the toxic cocktail and slip into a semi catatonic state,

'Miri, Miri wake up!' Arden slurred, slapping his friends face, but soon he too fell fowl of the drugs effects, slumping back like a discarded rag doll.

Dee Dee slapped Miri hard across the face but with very little reaction, 'Gottcha you shit bags!' she laughed, 'Right get dressed Maize' The pair hurried back to the bathroom and slipped on their clothes, 'Less get the fuck aat of ere Dee' Maizie said, making for the door, she then turned to see Dee Dee rummaging through the cupboards, 'Dee what ya doin, come on will ya!'.

Dee Dee looked at the two dozing Lithuanians with distaste, 'We gotta teach these fuckers a lesson first, ava look in there will ya' she pointed to a chest of drawers alongside the bed.

Reluctantly Maizie agreed, firstly discarding many of the clothes in the top drawer, 'Bloody ell Dee this shit's mingin!' she said, flinging a stained pair of

knickers across the room, 'Is this any good mate' she added, retrieving a set of hair clippers from the back,
'Fuck me yeah thatta do for starters' Dee Dee smiled, snatching them and plugging them in beside the sofa. She stood behind Miri, jerking his head back, 'Goin anywhere nice this year sir' she joked, shaving his head on the lowest setting but leaving several ridiculous random tufts. She then turned her attentions to Arden who lay motionless with his tongue out to one side. Maizie continued to delve as Dee Dee laughed to herself, 'What'dya reckon Maize?' she said, showing off her handy work, 'Am I the bollocks of an air dresser or what?'. The two men looked as though they had both been exposed to high levels of radiation.
'Ar dunno abaat that Dee' Maizie laughed, 'Ar fink dumb and dumber there might want their money back', she then produced a packet of florescent marker pens, 'You finkin what ar'm finkin Dee?' she said, looking at their balding heads,
'Fuck yeah' agreed Dee Dee. The two set about scrawling obscenities across Miri and Arden's scalp and faces like, Wanka, Homo, Nob and arse wipe to name but a few in several different colors. 'Fuckin quality!' Dee Dee said, stepping back and eyeing the two men.
'Issa bastard to get off an'all' Maizie added, drawing exaggerated eyelashes onto Arden's face.
Producing a pair of nail scissors from her hand bag Dee Dee proceeded to cut one leg off each of their trousers and one arm off their shirts which had Maizie in hysterics, 'Ar gotta get a phota' she chuckled, 'That is so goin on facebook'.
Dee Dee emerged from the bathroommoments later with a bottle of cheap aftershave, wafting it under her

nose, 'Fuck me thas shite!' she said, heaving. she then yanked at the mens trousers and poured half the contents onto each of their manhoods,
'Oh Dee thas just nasty mate' Maizie said, shaking her head.
'Ar know' Dee Dee smiled, 'When they wake up they'll fink their bollocks are on fire'. Dee Dee then noticed a leather bum bag around Miri's waist and slipped it from him, 'Ello ello' she said sliding open the zip and peering inside, 'Fuck me!' she gasped, 'Maizie ava look!'
'What is it?' Maizie asked, craning her neck.
Dee Dee took out a large bundle of notes, fifty's and twenty's. 'There must be bleedin undreds ere!' she said, excitedly. She quickly stuffed the cash into her pocket, 'We'll split it lata Maize' she told her friend, then produced more than a dozen clear plastic bags containing a white powdered substance, 'Oy oy you naughty boys' she said, slapping Arden playfully across the face. Maizie backed away, 'Fuckin ell, drugs Dee' she said, holding up her hands. 'I ain't interested in that shit, just leave it Dee and less get aat of ere'.
'Me neeva' Dee Dee replied, taking out her mobile phone, 'But ar know someone who will be', she dialed nine nine nine and waited, 'Ello, yeah ar wanna talk to someone abaat drugs' she told the police operator, her call was redirected to Inspector Meadow of the drug squad, she recounted the whole story excluding the haul of cash but refused to give her name when asked, merely the location.
'Do you have a description of the two gentlemen' the inspector asked.
Dee Dee looked at the lethargic Lithuanians and laughed, their clothing shredded, their hair mutilated

and their faces smothered in graffiti, 'Well put it this way' she said, kicking Miri's lifeless body, 'If you couldn't pick these two out in a line up your in the wrong fuckin job mate' she then hung up the phone. 'That should do it' she told Maizie, 'Come on less get the fuck aat of ere'.

'Baat time' Maizie replied, opening the door.

On leaving Dee Dee could hear the sound of a child crying, 'Ang on Maizie' she said, stopping her friend on the stairs and putting her ear to an adjacent door to listen closer,

'Dee come on!' Maizie pleaded. Dee Dee tugged at the heavy padlock securing the door then ducked back inside the room where Miri and Arden lay, 'Dee what ya doin?' cried Maize, keen to distance herself from the two men, 'The old bill'll be ere in a minute'.

Inspector Meadow had quickly mobilized his team and were indeed racing to the scene. Dee Dee wrestled with the two delirious drug dealers, rummaging through their pockets until she eventually produced a bunch of keys from Arden's. Darting back out into the hall she frantically tried each key in the lock until it sprang open. 'For fuck sake Dee, leave it!' Maizie cried, turning to leave. But Dee Dee pushed open the door and peered inside,

'Ello!' she called, 'Is anyone in ere?'. The room was dark, the windows boarded, blocking any means of escape, Dee Dee felt her way across the room, her eyes gradually becoming accustomed to the poor light. Following the sound of sobbing she peered behind the bed, and there crammed into the corner was a young girl no older than thirteen or fourteen shaking uncontrollably with her head buried in her hands. 'Hey, you ok?' Dee Dee asked. The girl said nothing, wriggling further into the corner, 'Iss ok' Dee

Dee added ‘We aint gonna urt’cha, we’re gonna get you aat of ere, ya safe naah’. Hearing this the young girl sprung to her feet and threw her arms around Dee Dee’s neck, hugging her so tightly Dee Dee had trouble breathing. ‘Iss ok, iss ok’ Dee Dee said, prizing her arms free, in doing so she noticed several puncture marks on the girls forearms, a sure sign that drugs had been administered, ‘Woss your name?’ Dee Dee asked, but the girl was clearly traumatized and could not speak.

Maizie joined the two of them in the room, ‘What is it Dee?’ she asked, ‘Who’s that?’

‘Ar dunno’ Dee Dee replied as the girl clung to her once more, ‘She ain’t said a bleedin word, gawd knows ow long those bastards av ad er locked up in ere’.

Maizie took a step closer and stared at the girls face, ‘Jilly!’ she said, holding her hand over her mouth in astonishment, ‘Bloody ell Dee iss er!’

‘Who?’ Dee Dee asked, none the wiser ‘D’you know er?’

‘Iss er off the news Dee’ Maizie replied, ‘Jilly Becket, thas right aint it, your names Jilly aint it?’, the girl remained tight lipped.

Jilly Becket had disappeared several weeks earlier whilst on her way home from a friends, her distraught parents had made an emotional plea for her safe return on the nightly news and her photograph had been splashed across the front pages of many of the national newspapers. ‘Bleedin ell it is!’ cried Dee Dee, looking into Jilly’s eyes, ‘Your mum and dad are so worried abaat you mate’. Many had presumed the missing girl dead the longer the fruitless search had gone on.

Maizie ran to the boarded window and peered through a slit at the flickering blue lights of the approaching police cars, 'Old bill!' she said, heading for the door, 'We carn ang araand Dee, ar fink there's a back way aat'.

With her pockets crammed with cash, Dee Dee agreed and lead Jilly out into the hall, 'You go daan stairs Jilly mate' she told the petrified girl, 'The police'll take you to ya mum and dad'. Jilly stood at the top of the stairs and watched Dee Dee and Maizie make their way along the corridor before uttering a solitary word, 'DEE!' she yelled, sprinting after them. Dee Dee turned as Jilly leapt into her arms holding her even tighter than before, wrapping her legs around her waist and planting a huge kiss on her cheek.

'Ar know, ar know' Dee Dee said, fighting back the tears as a lump grew in her throat, 'You go naah Jilly mate, go on and take care darlin'

Jilly kissed Dee Dee once more and ran back to the stairs, descending three at a time, reaching the bottom just as Inspector Meadow and his team burst through the door, 'Jilly!' he said, recognizing her instantly, 'Good god it's really you' he then grabbed a wpc by the arm, 'Get this girl a blanket and take her to the station right away' he barked, 'AND WILL SOMEBODY INFORM THE PARENTS, NOW!'.

Jilly was lead to a waiting car and driven away at high speed while Inspector Meadow's officer's raced up the stairs and into the room where Miri and Arden lay, 'What in god's name?' he gasped, on seeing the state the two were in, some of his officers burst out laughing. Surrounded by a stash of incriminating evidence the two men looked a sorry sight. The room was thoroughly searched and photographs taken before Miri and Arden were dragged to their feet and their hands cuffed behind their backs, 'Get these morons out of here' the Inspector said, 'And search the rest of the building, tear this place apart if you have to!'. This eastern European criminal enterprise had plagued the capitals streets for many years and the removal of these two prominent figures would undoubtedly deal their organistaion a desisive blow.

Dee Dee and Maizie slipped unnoticed out into the night having narrowly avoided the miserable fate that had befallen many young girls previously. Miri and his accomplice Arden were facing lengthy prison sentences with the weight of evidence against them, but as they were being processed back at the station a more pressing problem arose. The affects of the incapacitating drug were beginning to wear off and they both began to feel the burning sensation between their legs from Dee Dee's earlier lotion application. The pair began to squirm cross legged, begging for their hands to be freed so that they may scratch the affected area, but the police officers were having none of it, 'PLEASE MY BALLS ARE ON FIRE!' Miri cried, rubbing his groin against the sergeants leg,

'Get off me you sick bastard!' the officer yelled, pushing Miri away, 'You fuckers'll shag anything won't ya!'. The burning in their trousers grew in intensity, becoming unbearable. Howling like hyena's the two men thrust their hips at one another, pausing momentarily, catching sight of their reflections in a plate glass window which infuriated them.

'I've had enough of this!' the sergeant yelled, 'Take these two parasites to the cells', with their cuffs finally removed, Miri and Arden were thrown into a cell together. Word had spread throughout the police station of the two Lithuanians comical condition and a crowd of officers and wpc's had gathered to peer at them through an observation hatch. The two men immediately dropped their trousers and boxer's and began clawing furiously at their genitals with a look of sheer horror on their ridiculous faces.

'What the fuck?' a wpc cried, jostling with her fellow officers for a closer look, 'That's just gross!'.

The pair each received a fifteen year sentence for their criminal activities, reduced from twenty after agreeing to supply the police with information leading to the arrest of the heads of their unscrupulous organisation. Jilly Becket was reunited with her elated family amid a media frenzy, few of the gangs victims had ever been seen again let alone alive, but during her numerous radio and television interviews Jilly never once revealed the names of her rescuers, stating only her eternal gratitude.

Dee Dee and Maizie spent the remainder of that fateful night in the finest Park Lane hotel ordering the best that room service could provide, finally returning home penniless having purchased hundreds of scratch cards in a bid to increase their wealth, 'A bleedin tenner thas all we got' Maizie laughed, still struggling with the zumba rythem,

'Ar know' Dee Dee laughed, 'We even ad to jump the barrier at Chadwell eaf'.

Maizie stopped dancing and stood with her hands on her hips gasping for breath, 'This is bollocks Dee' she said, wiping the sweat from her brow, 'Me feet are bleedin killin me, ar need a fag an a drink, shall we piss off daan the Welly?'.

The Wellington pub in Goodmayes was a lively local frequented by many of the Bircham estates characters like 'Bobby the bet' an eighty two year old former docker who would give odds on just about any sporting event from the seat at the end of the bar he had occupied for some sixty years, 'Slippery Mick' so called because of his greasy completion and familiar stench of waste cooking oil which he collected daily from fast food restaurants and West Ham Terry a city professional from monday to friday but come the weekend the ardent hammer's fan would get 'Slaughtered' as he put it, on Carlsberg and vodka and entertain everybody time after time with his hilarious chicken leg dance which after countless views was fast becoming a youtube sensation.

Dee Dee picked up her towel and headed for the changing room, 'Yeah ar'v ad enough of this poncey shit an'all' she said, looking over her shoulder at the many dancers attempting to emulate Miguelle. Seeing their departure the prancing instructor skipped rhythmically to the back of the class, 'Ladies, ladies' he called after them, 'We still have another twenty minutes of class'.

'Forget it mate ar'm fucked' Maizie said, grabbing her sports bag and following her friend, 'We're goin for a beer'.

Miguelle barred their way, keen to keep up his class numbers, 'Please wait' he added, eyeing them up and down with a look of approval, having bedded many of his class members, 'The next dance is erotic and sensual, made for two captivating creatures such as you' he caressed their shoulders and flashed his newly whitened teeth, exuding confidence and an overblown ego.

Dee Dee swatted his hand away 'Get offa me you slimy twat' she snapped, pushing him aside 'I aint intrested and neeva is she'.

Miguelle could tell by Maizie's admiring glances that she had other ideas, 'I think you friend would disagree' he said, whispering sexual innuendo's into Maizie's ear which made her tingle with excitement. Dee Dee grabbed her friends arm and pushed Miguelle away, 'Do one you dago dick!' she snarled, 'Before ar proper lose me rag'.

A stunned Miguelle attempted to laugh off his embarrassment 'I love you English' he joked, 'You have such spirit'

'Spirit!' Dee Dee replied, looking him in the eye, 'Your lucky I aint ad no spirit mate, coz after arf a bottle of JD ar can be a proper nasty cunt ar tell ya, aint that right Maize?'.

Maizie nodded in agreement 'Fuck yeah, she gets proper naughty on that stuff she does, ar member that snotty little shit daan the co-op called er a slag coz she wouldn't go out wiv im, Dee pushed im in the chiller and beat the shit aat of im wiv a frozen lasagna'.

Miguelle backed away with his hands in the air, 'Ok, ok my apologies for offending you' he said, returning to his class.

Maizie slipped out of her gym gear, 'He was kinda cute though Dee dontcha fink' she said, freshening up.

'Oh leave off Maize will ya' Dee Dee protested 'Your as dopey as that lot out there you are, well are tell ya that greasy tosser don't impress me, they're all the same that lot, all gob and no nob'. The two girls laughed as they packed their bags and left the changing room. Maizie paused for a moment, her eyes fixed on Miguelle's honed and tanned body glistening with sweat. The pair then watched as he pawed a young woman, grinding his crotch against

her with the pretense of helping her with her dance moves,
'Bleedin ell!' Maizie gasped, 'E might as well be shaggin er'.
Dee Dee shook her head in disbelief 'Thas fuckin unreal that is' she added. But as the two girls watched the near pornographic display the double doors burst open and the woman's husband stormed in, his fists clenched, 'AR FUCKIN KNEW IT YOU SLAG!' he yelled, lunging at the two of them. His wife it seemed had been having a steamy affair with the zumba instructor as had many of his class and her husband Jimmy Vickers, a scaffolder and local hard man had gotten wind of it,
'Jimmy what you doin ere?' his petite wife Karen cried as Miguelle ducked behind her for protection, having been confronted by many an irate partner previously.
'Ar know you been shaggin this ponce' Jimmy growled, trying to get to Miguelle while the other women backed away.
Dee Dee crossed her arms 'This ar gotta see' she smiled.
Jimmy first picked up the portable stereo playing the zumba rhythm and hurled it at the wall before pushing his wife aside, 'YOU GET THE FUCK OME!' he told her, 'AR DEAL WIV YOU LATA!'.
'No Jimmy please don't urt im!' Karen begged, tugging at his arm, 'He's just a friend, honest!'.
Jimmy pushed her away again, 'AR SAID GET THE FUCK OME, NOW YOU DIRTY WHORE OR AR'LL CLUMP YOU AN'ALL!'. Karen ran sobbing from the hall, passing Dee Dee and Maizie on the way,
'Alright Kaz' Maizie said, raising her hand 'Ow ya doin?'.

Dee Dee turned to her friend, 'Ar fink she's been better Maize don't you!' she said, knowing full well what Jimmy was capable of, 'Put it this way' she added, 'Ar wouldn't wanna be in er shoes right naah!'.

Maizie pointed to a frightened Miguelle cowering at Jimmy's feet, 'Ar bet e wishes e'd never been in er knickers an'all' she laughed.

Jimmy grabbed the petrified instructor by the throat and hoisted him to his feet, 'Come ere you dago cunt!' he said, looking him in the eye, 'You fink you can fuck mar misses behind mar back do ya, fink you can mug me off do ya, you little prick'.

Miguelle hung limply in Jimmy's grasp, shaking his head in abject denial, 'No no it's a mistake, it's a mistake!' he pleaded.

'Too right sunshine' Jimmy said, grinning menacingly, 'The biggest fuckin mistake you'll ever make'. Miguelle took a defensive swing at Jimmy, only managing to slap the side of his head. 'Is that all you got?' Jimmy laughed before peeling his right arm back and unleashing a crushing blow to the bridge of Miguelle's nose, 'Not so pretty now are ya!' he laughed as Miguelle screamed in agony, clasping his hands to his face with blood trickling through his fingers,

'Please, please no more!' the groveling instructor cried, dropping to his knees and crawling on all fours towards the corner of the room.

'Where d'you fink your going you slag?' Jimmy said, planting a steel toe capped boot firmly into Miguelle's side, snapping several ribs instantly and causing him to fall face down on the floor, letting out a gurgling scream.

Still seething, Jimmy grabbed the hair on the back of Miguelle's head and dragged him to his feet once again before ramming his face into a vending machine over and over until it ran with blood and a can of cola dropped into the tray at the bottom. Jimmy looked Miguelle in his smashed face, 'If I ever see you on this manor again' he said through gritted teeth, 'Ar'll cut your fuckin balls off and shove em up your arse, you got that!'. Miguelle by now was unconscious and could not respond and was dropped like a rag doll to the floor. Jimmy shook the blood and skin tissue from his hand and turned to leave 'Alright Dee' he said, pausing for a moment 'Ow's ya mum?'.

'Not bad Jimmy' Dee Dee replied, 'Bitta trouble wiv the old bill and the bailiffs but thas nuffin new'.

Jimmy stood chatting nonchalantly for a few minutes while the other women left the hall in a hurry. 'Anyway ar gotta go' Jimmy eventually said, 'Tell ya mum ar said ello will ya'

'Yeah course ar will Jim, see ya lata mate!' Dee Dee replied. Jimmy left the hall mopping the spattered blood from his face.

Dee Dee stepped over Miguelle's lifeless body and retrieved the cola from the machine, 'Cheers geez' she said, toasting his lifeless body, popping the ring pull and taking a huge mouthful, she then belched loudly and turned to leave tossing the can and the remainder of it's contents over her shoulder, inadvertently striking Miguelle's battered head, 'Come on Maize less go daan the Welly' she said, heading for the door, 'Arm gaggin for a beer'.

CHAPTER EIGHT.

The buyer.

Trisha had spent the previous hour or so doing her utmost to glean what little information she could from Laura, revealing an inch or so of flesh in the right places by way of enticement 'Ar could murder a drink' she said, hoping the alcohol would loosen Laura's tongue, 'Fancy one?'.

Laura, seeing this as a sign that Trisha was relenting to her advances didn't need asking twice 'Yes, yes of course' she said eagerly, 'I know a charming little place not far from here, my cars out front'.

'Oh pukka' Trisha squealed 'I ope they do wicked's'

'You hope they do what?' Laura asked, getting her coat,

'Blue wicked's' Trisha replied, 'Looks like antifreeze but after a dozen bottles an ar'm anybody's'.

'Really' Laura smiled in anticipation, 'Well let's just hope they do, shall we go?'.

Looking very pleased with herself, Laura held the door of her Audi convertible open leering at Trisha's legs as she climbed inside,

'Oooh this is nice' Trisha said, running her hands along the walnut dashboard, 'Ar bet it dun arf go an'all'.

Laura climbed in beside Trisha and leaned across her, 'Allow me' she said, tugging at Trisha's seat belt, her face within a whisker of Trisha's. In that brief moment their eyes met and both women simultaneously felt a surge of passion like never before, both desperately wanting to kiss the other but not daring to make the first move for fear of rejection.

'So er' Trisha said, feeling a little awkward, 'Where we goin then?'.

Laura's mind was elsewhere but she then came to, 'Oh yes of course' she replied, starting the car, 'It's a great little bar run by some friends of mine, I hope you'll like it'.

Laura drove through the busy South London streets in a heady daze, ignoring many traffic signals and taking little notice of the flashing speed camera's. It was now Trisha's turn to cast an occasional admiring glance at Laura's shapely thigh allowing herself the wanton feelings she hadn't felt since her lustful lesbian liaison on the Spanish mainland. With their heart rates rising each could almost taste the sexual tension between them, Laura's best loved K D Lang hits oozing from the stereo helping the mood. Laura laughed as the two of them removed their hair bands and let the gusting head wind toy with their fluttering locks.

They soon arrived outside Laura's favorite haunt, Passion, a select venue for discerning clients in the back streets of Pimlico, with it's gleaming chrome columns and black smoke glass windows there was very little to suggest the nature of such an establishment. Entering the foyer the pair were greeted by a tall leggy woman dressed oddly in fishnet stockings, top hat and tails, 'Good evening Miss Laura' she said, subserviently, 'How lovely to see you again' she then gave Trisha an admiring glance, 'I don't Believe we've had the pleasure' she said, holding out her hand 'The name's Francessca, but my friends and clients call me Frankie, and you are?'.

Trisha looked over Frankie's shoulder, 'Garspin for a bleedin drink' she replied, 'Ow much is it?' she took ten pounds from her purse expecting to pay an entrance fee.

Laura pushed her hand aside, 'It's taken care of' she said, turning to Frankie, 'This is Trisha, a good friend of mine, i'll be having my usual table by the stage if that's ok'

'Of course Mistress' Frankie replied, holding a door open for the two of them and smiling politely. Laura had brought many a 'good friend' to Passion and as her brother Billy received protection payments from the bars owners she was always guaranteed a table, even when full.

Passion was London's newest and most outrageous gay and trans gender bar attracting men and women of all sexual preferences, catering for their every whim and desire from simple bondage to leather and latex fetishes and even electro sex, a process where a persons genitalia is wired to the mains and subjected to short pulsating bursts of electricity, stimulating them to a speedy climax. Such activities took place in the bar's cavernous cellar and were reserved for the bars VIP members, many of them could be found seated at the house of commons by day or parliament perhaps. Each member having to sign a document equal to the official secrets act and given a false identity to protect their reputation. All mobile phones and devices capable of recording were strictly forbidden, but such anonymity came at a price, each lustful lord or masochistic minister paying a twenty thousand pound yearly subscription to frolic with the pick of the club's hedonistic harem of young men and women, but many choosing to subject themselves to the humiliating and brutally painful punishment dealt out by the dungeon mistress herself, Princess Adora as she liked to be known, a hulking twenty eight stone beast of a woman dressed in a gargantuan vivid pink wedding dress and veil, and a pair odf studded jack boots on her feet thick black mascara could be seen through the lacy veil streaming down her face giving her the appearance of a jilted bride. In fact Princess Adora, or Kathy as she was know by day had indeed been left waiting at the alter and had vowed to seek revenge on the entire male population, and as murder came with a hefty prison sentence, sadomasochism was her only option to vent her anger.

Laura lead Trisha through a crowd of extravagantly dressed revelers adorned with flamboyant feather boa's, ultraviolet body paint and enough eye watering piercing's in private places to make Trisha wince, 'Bleedin ell!' she gasped in amazement, 'See that, there's a geezer over there with a bloody great bolt fru iz bell end!'.

Laura laughed, having seen it all before, then stopped alongside a row of men and women dressed form head to toe in black rubber with a studded lead and collar hanging from their necks and a golf ball gag firmly rammed in their mouths. 'Pick one' she told Trisha tugging hard on a tall mans choker 'You, get to my table!' she barked, the man bowed his head and scurried towards the stage.

Trisha looked a short chubby man up and down 'D'you wanna come wiv us?' she asked.

'Abuse them!' Laura called to her 'That's what they're here for!'

'Oh ok, ar get it' Trisha said, wrenching the short man from the line 'GET OVER THERE YOU FAT LITTLE FUCK OR AR'LL KICK YOUR FUCKIN ED IN!' she yelled, slapping his backside.

Laura laughed as the man sprinted to the table, 'Something along those lines!' she added.

The two rubber clad men knelt on all fours for the girls to rest their feet, 'Oooh ar like this' Trisha chuckled, digging her stiletto into his back.

Laura clicked her fingers and a butch waitress brought over two riding crops, 'If he moves, beat him' she told Trisha, who took great pleasure in tickling the mans nose with the end of the crop until he sneezed then beating him harshly about the backside 'STAY STILL YOU SHIT BAG!' she laughed 'Eeya' she said, turning to Laura, 'Me ex used to love all this kinky shit, e used to ask me to wrap im in cling film and bash iz balls wiv me Burberry brolly, e was a dirty fucker though, ar caught im wiv next doors tabby tom cat lickin tuna chunks aata the crack of iz arse, ar mean thas just wierd ain it?'.
Laura had to agree with her new friend, having seen many a strange fetish in her time, 'I suppose that's why he's your ex then Trish eh' she smirked.
'Well yeah' Trisha laughed 'That and findin im shaggin a dwarf in me nightie'
Laura looked puzzled, 'So the dwarf was wearing your nightie?'
'No ya doughnut' Trisha replied, nudging her arm, 'Me ex had me little miss naughty nighty on, the bleedin dwarf was dressed as an ewok, sick fuckers eh?' the two then burst out laughing along with their human foot stalls, 'OY!' Trisha barked, thrashing hers hard about the buttocks, 'KEEP STILL YA PERVY LITTLE PRICK!', the man moaned with pleasure, albeit muffled by his gag.
Laura whispered into a waitresses ear and soon a tray of Trisha's favorite alcopops arrived along with a magnum of expensive champagne 'Lovely jubbly!' Trisha squealed, swigging from a bottle.
Laura poured two glasses of bubbly and handed one to Trisha 'Here's to us' she said, clinking glasses,

'Yeah, why not' Trisha replied, now with a drink in each hand and loving every minute of it, 'Gawd blessya Mary Poppins'.
The two girls chatted non stop, both realizing they had more in common with one another than they first thought, like their love of marmite, mushy movies and Madonna, 'Ar made a bra like er's when ar was eight' Trisha laughed 'Aata two cornetto cones and the lastic from me nans knickers',
Laura laughed also, picturing Trisha prancing around her room singing Vogue into her hair brush.
During their conversation Trisha hardly noticed that Laura's hand had been caressing hers, and by now hadn'y a care. In a very short space of time they had formed a unique bond that had taken them both completely by surprise, Laura's usual dates being a little more dignified and sophisticated, but there was something about Trisha, something that mesmerized her. Trisha's mind was in a muddle all of a sudden and her friend Mickey's plight somehow seemed irrelevant.
Frankie took to the stage and addressed the crowd, 'Ladies and gentlemen, and those of you who haven't quite made up your mind!' her latter remark aimed at a table of gentlemen dressed in Dorothy Perkins and Dior designer dresses with plunging necklines revealing their heavily padded lacy bra's, the table of tipsy transvestites acknowledged her with a ripple of applause. 'Tonight for your delight and delectation!' Frankie continued, 'We at Passion are proud to announce the arrival of the world renowned Burlesque troupe, The Fallen Angels, please show your appreciation!'. The crowd were ecstatic, clapping and whistling loudly as the crimson velvet curtains were drawn back to reveal six beautiful girls

dressed seductively in fishnet stockings, peep hole bra's, bowler hats and an ostrich feather fan in each hand.
Amid a cloud of swirling dry ice the girls strutted their stuff to a smouldering Ella Fitzgerald melody leaving the audience speechless.
During the provocative performance Trisha noticed a queue of firtive Gentlemen at a door in a darkened corner of the room, 'Eeya pssst' she whispered, 'Are that lot going for a wee or a wank?'.
Laura looked over her shoulder, 'No no that's not the gents' she laughed, 'They're queuing to see Princess Adora, i'll take you to meet her after the show'.
Trisha turned up her nose, 'Ar'm a bit bleedin old for Dora the friggin explora!' she scoffed, 'Ar grew aata that girly shit a long time ago'
'No you don't understand' Laura said, lowering her voice, 'She's a dominatrix'
Trisha looked confused, 'What, like Keanu Reeves?' she asked, 'Oh ar loved im in them films, not as much as me nephew Marcus though' she began to ramble while Laura listened in bemusement, 'E used to prance araand the ouse in a pair of swimmin goggles and iz muvvers dressing gaan, soppy little nob reckoned e was, The one, or summink'.
Laura had heard enough and tugged at Trisha's arm, 'No, no darling that was the Matrix, Princess Adora is a Dom, a mistress, you know, for Bdsm, bondage and such things'
Trisha nodded as the penny dropped 'Oh sorry mate, yeah ar know what ya mean, me Aunty Mary tried summer that to spice fings up a bit, but er Davey tied er up in the garage and buggered off to Benidorm on a golfin oliday wiv iz mates, e brought er back two

undred fags and a sombrero but ar don't fink she see the funny side of it'

'I'm not surprised' Laura said, finding herself drawn into Trisha's tale 'What happened?'

'Well' Trisha added, 'She cut iz clubs up, max'd all iz credit cards and torched iz transit van'

'Oh my word!' Laura gasped 'His van, he must've been devastated!'

'More like cremated' Trisha chuckled, 'Since she froo im out, the silly fucker ad been kippin in it'.

As the evening went on and the drinks flowed, Trisha began to feel more at ease with Laura and her surroundings, to the point where she leaned over and planted a soft kiss on Laura's neck 'Sorry I ad to do that' she said, squeezing Laura's hand 'Ar fink iss the wicked's'

'There's no need to apologize' Laura smiled, leaning in to return the kiss, 'Mmm you smell nice'

'Fanx' Trisha smiled 'Iss DKNY, and not nunna that snide shit iver, ar got summa that daan the market last mumf an it gimme a poxy rash, ar got me money back though coz me uncle Eddy frettened to kick the geezer's ed in'.

The show eventually finished to a standing ovation with the six girls completely nude having discarded their feathers, 'Come on Trish' Laura said, leaving the table, 'I promised i'd introduce you to the Princess'

'Oh yeah, right' Trisha said, hurriedly swigging the remains of her drink.

Making her way to the front of the queue with Trisha in tow, Laura was ushered through a matt black door which lead to a dimly lit spiral staircase, 'This way' she said, taking Trisha's hand, 'Mind your step' their stilettos clanging on the iron steps.

'Bleedin dark innit' Trisha said, hobbling behind, 'There better not be no spiders in ere, ar'll shit a bleedin brick if there is'.

The cellar was also black from floor to ceiling with only a few burning torches providing light,

'Who lives daan ere?' Trisha asked, 'Uncle friggin Fester'.

Several small booths like confessionals lined the walls with curtains draped across the doorways. Muffled moans and cries could be heard coming from behind one or two of them.

'MISTRESS!' Laura called out, looking along the row of booths.

Princess Adora popped her head out of one with a length of hose in one hand, 'Laura darling, how lovely to see you!' she said, before ducking back inside to thrash her client several more times, 'I'll be out in a moment dear!' she added. She emerged red faced moments later, straightening her dress, 'Beastly man' she mumbled. 'I'm sorry dear, no rest for the wicked, you know how it is'

'Yes of course' Laura replied, 'I understand, i'd like you to meet a friend of mine, this is Trisha, Trisha may I introduce Princess Adora'.

'Blimey' Trisha said, eyeing her huge pink dress, 'Where you bin, to a bleedin pikey weddin?'

'I beg your pardon?' Princess Adora snapped, 'Do you have a problem with my atire?'.

Laura quickly stepped in to defuse a possible argument, 'So er, how's business Adora?' she asked, 'Still seeing all the regulars?'

'Yes, yes' Adora replied, sipping from a bottle of water, 'My client list is growing week by week, I had the shadow chancellor in yesterday for his ritual humiliation and the day before three premiership players requesting the anal rodding, oh and the Arch bishop of course for the nettle thrashing, so yes business is booming'. During their conversation Trisha found time to slip away and peer behind the thick black curtains, firstly coming across a member of the House of Lords trussed in leather studded straps, blindfolded and heavily marked, 'Fuck me!' she then gasped, peering in at two Police Chiefs bound together naked, save for their helmets and truncheons strategically placed. But it was the third booth that surprised her the most. 'Mr Sanjeef!' she said, ducking inside, 'Well fancy bumpin into you!'.

Mr Sanjeef, her former employer had his hands and feet bound with cable ties while his manhood hung from his open flies, attached to which was a red and black copper cable, 'What the fuck?' Trisha laughed, watching as a machine administered short pulses of low voltage electricity.

'TRISHA! WHAT ARE YOU DOING HERE?' he cried, turning away, 'IT'S NOT WHAT YOU THINK!'

'Your avin a fuckin laugh aincha!' Trisha scoffed, 'You've got ya old chap wired to the national pissin grid, what am ar spossed to fink!'.

Mr Sanjeef raised his tethered hands 'Trisha my dear' he begged, 'Please do not be telling my wife, she has only recently forgiven my wrong doings with Julie'.

'Wrong doins!' Trisha laughed, 'You mean poppin er over the safe and doin er doggy ya dirty fucker'.

Mr Sanjeef squirmed as the machine continued to shock him, 'Please Trisha I beg of you, I will see to it that you get you job back, I promise!'

'FUCK YA JOB!' Trisha barked, ramming a gag firmly into his mouth, 'I aint gonna tell your old lady, but this is for all the blinkin times you groped my arse in the stock room you dirty fucker!', Trisha flicked a switch on the machine to manual override and spun the dial to the far right giving Mr Sanjeef's penis the full two hundred and forty volts of electricity causing him to jerk and convulse, his eyes bulging in abject horror. Several second later after Trisha had had her fill of sweet revenge she switched of the machine and watched a frazzled Sanjeef slump forward in his restraints, moaning pitifully. Removing his gag Trisha looked him in the eye, 'That'll learn ya' she snarled, slapping his cheek and looking down at his blackened manhood, 'Oooh nasty' she cringed, 'Ar'll be proper surprised if you can piss aata that fing let alone pull one off, anyway gotta go, seeya!'

Trisha rejoined Laura, 'Having fun darling?' Laura asked, running her hand across Trisha's buttocks, 'Your not easily shocked I take it?'.

Trisha looked over her shoulder at Mr Sanjeefs booth, 'Not arf as easy as some people' she laughed. Having seen enough depravity, the two returned to the bar where they sipped cocktails, passing the time people watching.

'You see those two over there at the far table' Laura told Trisha, pointing to two butch lesbians with shaved heads, polo shirts and faded denims.

'Who?' Trisha said, sitting up to look, 'The Mitchell bruvvers'

'Hmmm' Laura had to agree there was a striking resemblance, 'I had the most amazing night with those two girls' she added 'We were at it for six hours straight, at one point we had to pop to the all night garage for replacement batteries'.

'Blimey thas goin some ain it' Trisha replied, wide eyed, 'Me first bloke managed free an arf hours once, at it like randy rabbits we was, ar ran out of lube in

the end and ad to grease me gusset wiv chip fat'. Laura choked on her mojito, 'Well er' she spluttered, wiping her mouth, 'If needs must I suppose'.
'Yeah' Trisha replied proudly, 'Iss the bulldog spirit ain it, make do an all that, me nan used to swear by er beef drippin, waste not want not she used to say, she even made er own love eggs out of two jersey royals and a parachute cord'.
Laura suddenly felt physically sick at such a thought, 'Beef fat and potatoes' she said, unable to finish her drink, 'That's almost a Sunday lunch'.
Trisha tugged Laura's arm 'Well ar won't tell ya what they were doin wiv the orse radish!' she said, the two girls laughed out loud.
Trisha then felt a vibration in her pocket and took out her mobile phone, hiding it from Laura and the Passion staff, Dee Dee's name was flashing on the screen. Quickly Trisha switched the phone to silent and popped it back into her pocket, a sure sign that her priority's hadshifted somewhat, having never before refused a call from her friends.
'Come on answer the fuckin phone!' Dee Dee cursed, standing outside the Wellington with Maizie, 'Dozy mare, woss she up to?'.
'Praps she's got no signal Dee' Maizie said, holding the door open, 'Try er again in a minute'.
'Yeah alright' Dee Dee agreed, 'Ar get the beers in shall I?'. The two girls disappeared inside while at Passion, Laura picked up her keys from the bar, 'Shall we go?' she asked Trisha, 'I have a gorgeous bottle of Chablis on ice back at mine'.
Trisha turned on her stool and headed for the ladies, 'Ar just av a piss an ar be right wiv ya!'. She said over her shoulder much to Laura's amusement.

Dee Dee and Maizie stood at the Wellington's beer stained bar not daring to rest their arms on it's sticky residue. Health and hygiene at the aging public house was at an all time low ever since Harry, it's elderly cleaner had been sacked for masturbating in the ladies toilets during his early morning shifts.
'Fancy a pint?' Dee Dee asked, rubbing her hands together,
'Yeah why not' Maizie smiled, 'Ar got a proper first on'.
Dee Dee summoned the barman, 'OY DICK, OVER ERE MATE!' she called out, waving a ten pound note, 'Two light and larger's geez! oh and while your at it, sort this shit out will ya' she picked up a rancid bar towel with her thumb and forefinger and tossed it over the bar, 'Aint you got another cleaner in ere yet, I erd about hand job Arry, the filthy fucker, tuggin e'z todger over the tampax machine!'.
Maizie piped up 'I erd e'z workin daan the chippy naah peelin spuds, ar do like the cod in there, don't you Dee?'
'Oh yeah!' Dee Dee laughed, pretending to masturbate an imaginary penis, 'Wiv Arry's special tartar sauce whacked all over it!'
'Oh don't Dee!' Maizie said in disgust, 'Thas put me right off it naah'.
Pouring their light ales into their glasses the two girls looked around the dilapidated baroom,
'OY BOB!' Maizie called to the end of the bar where Bobby the bet was taking wagers on two cockroaches fighting over a stale muffin on a cake stand, 'Ar'll av a fiver on the biggun' she said, joining him. But at that precise moment the smaller of the two roaches flipped the other onto it's back and sank it's teeth into it's neck. Bobby held out his hand,

'You'll never learn will ya Maizie darlin' he laughed plucking the five pounds from her hand, 'Bobby only bets on a cert you knoiw that'.
Dee Dee felt a slithering hand caress her shoulder and the familiar odour of Slippery Mick, 'Ello Dee love, wanna dance?' he asked. Mick was drunk, having spent the entire day in the Wellington annoying just about everyone with his raucous singing and staggered dancing, 'Ar put a tenner's werf of Guns n Roses on an ar'm avin it large!' he then waved his glass at the barman, 'Dicky boy, stick a large Morgans in there mate!'. Dick raised his eyebrows and reluctantly obliged.
Dee Dee brushed his hand away 'For fuck sake Mick, Get'cha bleedin and's off me will ya!' she snapped, backing away along the bar, 'You look like shit and smell twice as bleedin bad, go on, piss off'
'Suit yaself' Mick replied, sticking two fingers in the air and hobbling towards the gents, singing at the top of his voice, accompanying the jukebox, 'KNOCK KNOCK KNOCKIN ON HEAVENS DOOOOOR!'.
Dee Dee then received a text message that Trisha had sent her from the toilets at Passion reading, Don't worry Dee, arm sortin it, moments before turning her phone off. 'What the fuck does that mean?' she said to herself, dialing Trisha's number and getting the answer machine, 'Trish you dozy cow woss goin on?' she yelled, 'Gimme a ring as soon as you get this bloody message will ya'
'Did ya get er?' Maizie asked, handing Dee Dee another drink,
'No ar got er friggin voicemail, gawd knows what she's up to' Dee Dee raged.
Meanwhile Trisha and Laura were stood side by side in a glass elevator heading for the twelfth floor of

Laura's apartment block on the select Butlers wharf development, 'Blimey I aint never seen nuffin like it!' Trisha gasped, stepping out into the white marble hallway, 'Iss bloomin gorgeous ain it!'
'Yes it's quite adourable isn't it' Laura said, slipping her key into number forty six and opening the door, 'Do make yourself at home Trish, i'll get the wine' Laura disappeared into the kitchen leaving Trisha wandering round open mouthed, eventually finding herself out on the terrace overlooking the Thames, it seemed a million miles from her mother's tiny essex semi. Clinging to the rail she leaned over and closed her eyes, tasting the air as though on the bow of an ocean liner,
'There you are' Laura said, stepping out to join her with an open bottle of wine and two glasses.
'Ar love it ere' Trisha said, soaking up her surroundings, 'Your so lucky Laura'.
Laura poured the wine, handed Trisha a glass and nestled in beside her, 'Yes I am lucky aren't I' she whispered, looking Trisha up and down before planting a kiss on her lips. Trisha responded and for several seconds they were locked in a steamy sensual embrace,
'Flippin eck!' Trisha gasped, breaking away and sipping her wine, 'Ar went all giddy then'. Having had her share of childish adolescent boys and their awkward groping she soon realized what she had been missing, true emotional contact, her insides were turning sumersaults and her head was spinning, and Laura felt the same, this wasn't just another meaningless fling, this was different, this was real.
Watching the tiny boats making their way up and down the Thames, Laura and Trisha polished off a further two bottles of wine whilst engrossed in deep

and meaningful conversation. Laura took Trisha's hand, 'Stay with me tonight' she said, looking her in the eye.
Trisha's nerve's got the better of her for a moment 'What, er' she stammered, 'Kip ere, wiv you ya mean?'.
Laura nodded, 'Yes why not, it's clear we both have feelings for each other'. Before Trisha could think any further Laura took her hand and lead her inside and through to her lavish bedroom with its white deep pile carpet, tasteful sepia prints and gigantic sumptuous bed with shimmering satin sheets. 'Don't be nervous' Laura said, taking Trisha's glass, setting it down and slipping her hands around her waist.
'Oh er, arm not' Trisha replied, blushing, 'Iss er, iss just been a while thas all'
'Don't worry about a thing darling' Laura reassured her, 'We have all the time in the world'.
'Shit' Trisha said out loud, 'Look Laura ar really like ya, in fact ar really really like ya, ar mean that, but there's somefing'.
Laura put a finger to Trisha's lips, stopping her in mid sentence, 'Shhhhh we can talk later darling' she said, replacing her finger with her lips.
Trisha tried to pull away but the kiss made her melt and soon all thoughts of Black Mickey, the Tibbs's and even Dee Dee and Maizie had gone from her mind.
Tearing frantically at one anothers clothes the two girls leapt giggling onto the bed, their hands running wildly over the others bodies, biting playfully as thongs and bra's were flung across the room. In the heated moments that followed Trisha found herself experiencing levels of sexual intensity like never before, orgasm after shuddering orgasm left her

panting heavily in Laura's arms where she lay squeezing her tightly, 'Fuck me!' she eventually gasped, 'That was amazin'. Lying naked among the ruffled sheets the two girls looked deep into the other's eyes, kissing repeatedly.
'I know what you mean' Laura sighed, kissing Trisha's forehead, 'It's never been like that for me either'. Her former conquests satisfied her sexually but lacked feeling, Trisha on the other hand ticked all the boxes, she was beautiful, sexy and above all fun to be with.
Reluctantly Trisha broke the embrace and pulled away, 'Look Laura ar gotta talk to ya mate' she said, taking Laura's hand, 'Ar do really like ya, much more than I ever thought ar would'
'What's wrong?' Laura asked, 'Ar you not ready for this?'
Trisha kissed Laura's hand 'Yeah, yeah course I am, this is the nuts honest, ar really wanna be wiv ya Laura but'
'But what, what's the problem?' Laura asked, concerned. 'Please tell me'.
Trisha took a deep breath and began to explain, hoping it would not jeopardize their fledgling relationship. 'Ar got this mate' she began 'E'z names Black Mickey, e'z black, well ya probly gavered that, anyway e'z gone missin and we fink your bruvver's might av summink to do wiv it'.
Laura lay in stunned silence for a moment before leaping naked from the bed 'So your sleeping with me just to get to my brother's!' she cried, 'HOW COULD YOU!' she began to cry, 'How could you, I thought we had something, I thought we had something, I thought this was real'

'Wait Laura please!' Trisha replied, following her round the room, 'We do av somefing, Laura please let me explain will ya'
Laura shook her head, 'What's to explain, you used me Trisha, I let you into my heart and you used me, just get out!'
'Laura please!' Trisha begged.
Laura took a swing and slapped Trisha's face hard, 'I SAID GET OUT!' she screamed, climbing back into bed she pulled the sheets up around her neck and sat rocking as though her world had been torn apart. Since the death of her parents she had led a solitary life, treating other women as mere play things with no emotional attachment, and now it seems the minute she lets her guard down her feelings are trashed and trampled.
But Trisha wasn't leaving, she too had found something in Laura and wasn't about to give it up, sitting on the end of the bed she tried again to explain, 'Ar be onest wiv ya Laura' she said softly 'Yeah at first ar did string you along just to find aat abaat Mickey, me and me mates are really worried abaat im, but then everyfing changed when ar got to know ya, ar said ar really like ya an ar meant it, ar said ar wanna be wiv ya an ar meant that an'all, ar've had the most amazin time wiv you today an ar don't wonnit to end, please believe me'
Laura listened intently to the sincerity in Trisha's voice, 'Do you really mean that?' she eventually asked drying her eyes, 'Honestly'
'Yeah ar do' Trisha replied, crawling up the bed and sitting beside her, 'Onest Laura I aint never met anyone like ya, I aint been no angel, a'rve shagged araand ar'll admit that but nuffin like this, your the nuts you are, ar mean your lovely, really lovely'.

Laura stopped Trisha with a kiss 'And your the nuts too' she laughed. Trisha threw her arms round her and the two hugged tightly, 'Ar promise ar won't lie to you again' Trisha said, sobbing herself 'Never'
Laura wiped a tear from Trisha's cheek 'So this Mickey, he's a good friend of yours I take it?' she asked.
Trisha brushed away another tear 'Yeah e is' she said sniffing 'A proper mate'.
Laura handed her a box of tissues and hopped off the bed, slipping back into her clothes, 'Come on' she said, searching for her left shoe, 'I think I can help you'
'Really!' Trisha cried, gathering her own clothes, 'Oh fanx Laura, your the best you are'. The two girls left the apartment and took the elevator to the underground car park.
Back at the police station DI Pritcher was sat in his office contemplating a life back in uniform having turned up very little in the way of leads on the Sheik Abdullah case and the pressure from above was mounting. Reaching into his desk drawer he retrieved a bottle of single malt and a paper cup and proceeded to pour a large measure. Suddenly the door burst open and Detective Marsh marched in carrying a pair of ladies shoes inside a clear plastic evidence bag, 'Sir, sir I think your gonna want to see this!' he said proudly,
'For fuck sake Marsh!' the DI barked, downing his drink and flinging the cup into his waste bin, 'Ar've told you before about knocking on mar door first, now what the hell do you want'
Detective Marsh joined the DI at his desk and offered him the bag, 'Take a look at these sir' he said, prodding the bag, 'I took the liberty of sending some

of our lab guys round to the Dawson's flat and they've come up trumps'.
The DI flew into a rage, 'You went behind my back Marsh!' he snapped, 'Are you after my fucking job, is that what it is, tryna make a name for yourself by muggin me off are ya!'
'No, no not at all sir!' the Detective said, holding up his hand, 'I swear, that's why i'm bringing it straight to you guv!'.
The DI snatched the bag, 'What am I looking at Marsh?' he asked, seeing nothing more than shoes.
The Detective pointed to the heel of one shoe 'If you look closer sir' he said, excitedly, 'You'll notice small spots of blood, just there guv, what's more sir, its an exact match with the Sheiks'
'YES!' DI Pritcher yelled, leaping from his seat, 'About bloody time, get that Dawson woman back to the interview room Marsh, right now!'. As Marsh scurried from the room the DI poured himself another generous measure of whisky, grinning as he downed it to the last drop.
Moments later Detective Marsh returned, 'She's ready sir, but defiant as ever' he said, holding the door open. Carrying the evidence bag the DI marched through to where Pearl was seated with her appointed legal representative.
Pearl smirked, 'Ar'v told ya before, ar got no bleedin comment' then crossed her arms on the table.
The DI slammed the bag down in front of her 'Really!' he said, looking her in the eye, 'Can you tell me who's shoes these are?'
Pearl recognized Dee Dee's leopard print sling backs instantly, 'Er, yeah course, they're mine' she admitted, in a bid to protect her daughter 'Why woss the problem?'

The DI looked at the shoes and then at Pearl, 'There a bit slutty for a woman of your age wouldn't you say' 'What you sayin?' Pearl said, angrily, 'I ain on the bleedin game if thas what your gettin at, bleedin cheek!'.

The DI held his hands up, 'Well I got a Sheik who, if he was alive would disagree with you, you see you and two other tarts were seen going up to his apartment the night of the murder', he then looked Pearl up and down, 'Although you'd think with all his dough he could afford something a little more classy, wouldnt you say'.

'Fuckin cheek' Pearl snapped, 'Anyway like ar said, no comment'

The DI wasn't about to let up, 'What I am implying Mrs Dawson is that these shoes, which you have admitted to owning, were present at the time of Sheik Abdullah Hussain's murder in a London Hotel, the DNA match will stand up in court, so are you still saying you have no comment?'. Pearl sank back into her chair wondering what the hell Dee Dee had gotten herself into.

'Are you still saying these shoes belong to you Miss Dawson?' the DI asked again, bearing down on her, 'I must warn you that the crime of murder comes with a fifteen year minimum prison sentence, so if you are covering for someone else then now is the time to speak up'.

Pearls lawyer whispered in her ear to say nothing but she knew Dee Dee's life would be ruined with such a charge against her, 'Lark ar told ya' she added 'They're mar bleedin shoes'.

DI Pritcher placed a pen and paper in front of her, 'Are you prepared to give us a full statement Miss Dawson?' he asked, 'Namely the whereabouts of

certain documents belonging to the deceased, a large Ruby necklace and the names of your accomplices, because I don't believe for one minute that you are the mastermind behind this caper!'. Pearl pushed the pen and paper away, 'I aint sayin nuffin else' she said, defiantly, 'Ar told ya the shoes are mine, you'll av to work the rest out for yaself'
'DON'T PISS ME ABOUT DAWSON!' the DI barked, losing is temper, 'IF I DON'T GIVE ME THOSE PISSIN PAPERS I'LL THROW THE FUCKIN BOOK AT YA!'. He was then restrained from lunging at pearl by Detective Marsh,
'Guv, guv leave it!' Marsh said, with his arms around the DI's waist.
The DI pointed an accusing finger at Pearl, 'Pearl Dawson' he yelled 'I am arresting you on suspicion of murder, you do not have to say anything, but it may harm your defense if you do not mention when questioned something which you later rely on in court, anything you do say may be given in evidence, HAVE YOU GOT THAT MISS DAWSON!'
Pearl raised her middle finger which infuriated the DI further, 'Go fuck yaself!' she snarled, 'And ya can stick that in ya poxy statement!'.
DI Pritcher took Marsh by the arm, 'Get her back to the cells and get every available copper on the streets, I want to know all her known associates, family, friends' he then looked down at Pearl, 'And punters!' he added.
'Ar told you I aint on the blinkin game!' pearl replied, fiercely 'You two bob fuckers might sell yer arse for a pound note but not me!'.
The DI left the room before doing something he would later regret and returning to his desk he rang the Foreign Minister, 'Sir it's Detective Inspector

Pritcher, I have some news on the Abdullah case'. The Minister began ranting down the phone, 'Pritcher what the devil's going on man, you promised me you'd have this wrapped up within hours, you better be calling to tell me you have those papers in your possession or i'm telling you, heads will roll, NAMELY YOURS!'

The DI was taken aback by the Foreign Ministers outburst, 'Sir if you'd allow me to explain' he groveled, 'We er, we don't have the documents yet sir but we do have a suspect in custody, and i'm positive sir it's only a matter of time before they're found!'. The Minister launched a further tirade of abuse down the telephone, threatening everything from suspension to dismissal for, as he put it, the DI's imbecilic incompetence.

Nikos Papageorgiou in the meantime had been in talks with several parties interested in purchasing the famed Red Sea Ruby, a Canadian railroad magnate, a french aristocrat and two rival Japanese business men, driving the price way over the ten million pound mark. Finally Mr Nakajima, head of the infamous Nakajima crime family had emerged as a clear favorite, purely because he had threatened to send a team of sword wielding assassins to make sushi out of the pawn broker if he sold to anyone else.

Picking up the telephone Nikos dialed Dee Dee's number, 'Hello, Dee is it, or is it Dee Dee i'm not sure, it's Paps'

Dee Dee stepped outside the Wellington and cupped her phone to her ear, 'Sorry ar couldn't ear ya, who is it?'

'It's Nikos', Papageorgiou added 'Am I speaking to Dee Dee?'

'Yeah iss me' Dee Dee replied 'Wossup?'. Nikos was about to explain when Dee Dee stopped him 'Ang on a minute' she said, seeing West Ham Terry, heading her way, 'Alright Tel!' she said, lowering her phone, much to Nikos's annoyance,

'Hello, hello Dee!' he yelled, but to no avail, he could only listen to Dee Dee's muffled conversation.

Terry had an exaggerated cockney stride with his hands in his pockets scratching his balls and the collar of his harrington jacket turned up around his ears. 'Ello treacle!' he said, grinning cheekily, 'Ows it goin me old china plate?' he eyed Dee Dee's curves, 'Fuck me girl your lookin tasty' he added jostling his crotch.

Dee Dee shoved his shoulder 'You fink anyfing wiv an art beat is tasty you dirty fucker, you goin in the welly?'

'Yeah course' Terry replied, rubbing his tubby belly, 'Arv ad a cunt of a week and ar fancy gettin bladdered'.

Dee Dee could hear Nikos's faint cries, 'Dee, Dee Dee are you still there?'

'Yeah ar said ang on!' she yelled at her phone then turned back to Terry, 'Eeya, gissa fag will ya' she asked.

Terry delved into his jacket pocket 'Yeah no worries babe' he said taking out two cigarettes, lighting them both and handing one to Dee Dee, he began to get amorous as he often did in Dee Dee's company, rubbing her thigh and thrusting his hips toward her, 'Ow'z abaat me and you fuck off over the park and play ide the salami in the sand pit?'

Dee Dee pulled away, 'Er, maybe anuvva time Tel' she told him, trying to let him down gently, 'Arm on me mumflys, nart ar mean'.

Terry looked puzzled 'What you on about?' he asked, 'You was gaggin for it at Freddie Naylors party'
'Ar was fifteen!' Dee Dee laughed, 'And if ar remember you shot ya bolt before you got it aat ya bleedin traazers!'
Terry looked around furtively, 'Shut up will ya' he whispered, fearing someone would hear, 'Ar don't av that problem no more, come on babe you know you wonnit'
Dee Dee pushed him aside once more, 'Oh piss off Tel arm on the phone!' she snapped, waving her mobile, 'Maizie's in there, go and pester er'
Terry's eyes lit up as he headed for the door, mumbling to himself, 'Maizie eh, she's fit an'all, ard love to smash er back door in'.
'Ello!' Dee Dee said, taking a long drag on her cigarette and returning to Nikos, 'Yeah sorry abaat that geez, what did you want?'.
'Finally!' Nikos said, his patience wearing thin, 'Look you asked me to find a buyer for the ruby, well I have but we have to do the deal right away, the buyers flying in tonight, if I upset these people Dee Dee i'm dog meat, seriously'
Dee Dee stamped on the remainder of her cigarette, 'Well I aint doin nuffin wivaat Mickey' she told Nikos, 'Like ar said, ar'll bell ya when ar'm ready'. Dee Dee hung up and disappeared back inside the pub leaving Nikos frantically calling down the phone yet again, 'Dee Dee, Dee Dee, you don't understand, Dee Dee are you there?'.
Within a very short space of time West Ham Terry had sunk four pints of Carlsberg and three large vodka's and was now attempting to dance provocatively alongside Maizie, 'Bump and grind baby, bump and grind!' he slurred, taking off his

jacket and rubbing it like a towel between his legs, 'Come on work that booty!'.
Maizie stood with her arms folded, shaking her head, 'Your bleedin barkin you are Tel' she laughed, 'Do that chicken dance fing of yours, go on'
'Naaah later babes' Terry said, sinking his vodka, 'Giss a kiss first!' he lunged at Maizie with his lips puckered but she raised her hand and held him at bay,
'Please Tel do the dance, iss so funny, look ar put the song on' Maizie popped a pound into the jukebox and selected one of Terry's all time favorites tears of a clown, and as soon as the first few chords rang out Terry reacted 'OH FUCK YEAH!' he yelled, gyrating his hips and strutting like a chicken. One by one the drinkers at the bar turned to watch, laughing at his hilarious antics. Terry careered around the room, his little legs a bendy blur.
Dee Dee joined Maize who by now was laughing hysterically 'Oh fuckin ell Dee, e cracks me up wiv that shit, look at im e'z like a duck on drugs!' Several onlookers filmed the spectacle on their mobile phones and when the song had finished applauded loudly, patting Terry's back, 'That was the bollocks mate!' one man said, shaking his hand, 'What ya drinkin?'.

CHAPTER NINE.

The Bradley rap.

Billy Tibbs and his boys were siting round a table in the corner of the Flying Horse pub in South Bermondsey when Lenny Price, a local pot head and coke addict approached them with a crumpled ten pound note in his hand. His eyes were wide and glazed and his twitching mannerisms clearly showed he was high as a kite. Lenny dragged his twisted right foot across the floor behind him, a childhood deformity which had hindered his search for employment and thus lead to a life of benefits, petty crime and drug abuse.

'Mr Tibbs' he slurred, wiping a dribble of spit from his chin 'Ar need a score man, ya couldn't help us aat could ya'.

Billy glanced up briefly then looked away, 'Fuck off' he growled, continuing his conversation.

'Ar got money Mr Tibbs' Lenny said, placing the ten pounds on the table and pushing it towards Billy. Billy's men leaned back in their seats, giving their boss ample space, knowing full well that being treated like a small time dealer when in fact he was a major importer was an insult beyond belief.

'Bill mate!' Lenny insisted, tapping his finger on the money.
Billy stopped talking and slowly turned to look Lenny in the eye whilst sliding a large hunting knife from his right boot, then quick as a flash he thrust it through Lenny's hand, pinning him and the ten pounds to the table.
'Aaaarggh, Fuck, fuck, fuck me fuckin and!' Lenny squealed, 'Fuckin ell Bill mate what'cha do that for?'.
Billy leaned across and grabbed Lenny by the throat and dragged him across the table, 'Firtstly you fuckin scrote' he snarled 'I ain't your fuckin mate!'
Lenny looked down at his blood soaked hand and attempted to pull the knife out.
'You touch that fuckin blade!' Billy warned the addict , 'And ar'll stick it in your fuckin eye you little cunt'
Lenny sobbed, snot from his nose running down onto his top lip, 'Sorry Bill, ar'm sorry, ar'm sorry, arm really sorry!'
'And secondly' Billy added, 'You fuckin insult me by comin in ere and askin for a poxy ten pound wrap like ar'm some sorta mug', Billy looked over Lenny's shoulder at a crowd of young men at the bar who were looking over with their pints in their hands, 'Oy what the fuck are you looking at?' he asked, clinging to Lenny. The lads put their drinks down and turned for the door, 'Go on, jog on!' Billy yelled after them, 'Cunts!', Billy pulled the blade out of Lenny's hand and handed it to Jimmy, 'Jim take this fucker aat the back and cut im a new arseole', he said, swatting the money onto the floor, 'And someone clean this shit up!'. Dave the barman hurried from behind the bar and wiped the table down, 'Can ar get ya some more drinks Bill?' he asked, gathering their glasses.

'Thas very nice of ya Dave' Billy said ,grinning 'Same again ar fink, eh boys!' his men nodded while Roland rubbed his rumbling stomach,

'A'rll av free bags of twiglets, two scratching's and a pickled egg an'all' he said, tipping the remains of a packet of crisps into his mouth, 'Oh and a bag of dry roasted'.

As Lenny was being dragged towards the fire door he pleaded with the gangland boss, 'Billy please ar didn't mean it, fuckin ell Bill ar'm sorry, please Bill ar got some information for ya!'

'Get that piece of shit out of ere!' Billy barked, pointing to the door, 'And Dave' he told the barman, 'Turn them fuckin camera's off'. Dave switched off the cctv camera's to the back yard so that Lenny's punishment would go undetected.

'Bill mate honest!' Lenny begged, tears streaming down his face, 'Ar know the old bill ar gonna turn your place over!'

'WHAT!' Billy yelled, stopping his brother, 'What did you say, Jimmy bring im ere!', Jimmy dragged the trembling Lenny back to the table and held him by the hair on the back of his head,

'Bill onest mate are know summink's goin daan!'.

Billy held the knife to Lenny's throat, pushing it hard enough to break the skin, 'You better tell me what you know boy or ar'll cut your fuckin ed off right ere!'

'Iss mar sister Bill!' Lenny stammered, 'She goes out wiv a copper, ar bin stayin at er's since me mum slung me aat and I eard im talkin abaat it'

'Talkin about what?' Billy snapped, thrusting the blade harder.

'Wait Bill wait!' Lenny cried, fearing his throat would be cut at any moment, 'E works wiv that orrible pig Pritcher, an e'z a proper big ed an'all, e told me sister

they're gonna raid your gaff tomorra, seriously Bill e tells er everyfing!'.
Billy removed the knife and thought for a moment, 'Fuckin ell Bill!' Roland said, spitting morsels of crisps across the table, 'We got Mickey in the!'
Billy swatted Roland across the face, stopping him in mid sentence, 'Shut it you fuckin idiot!' he snapped, 'You lot, drink up!' he told the others, then turned his attentions to Lenny, 'You better not be fuckin me abaat boy' he said, returning his knife to his boot, 'Or believe me ar'll come and find ya and burn you aat of your sisters ouse!', Billy held his hand out, 'Jimmy gimme a wrap' he told his brother.
'Do what Bill?' Jimmy said, releasing Lenny.
'Just gimme a fuckin wrap will ya!' Billy yelled, slamming his hand down on the table. Jimmy reached into his pocket and produced a folded piece of silver paper, handing it to Billy, who threw it at Lenny, 'Eeya!' he said, getting up to leave, 'Ar don't ever wanna see you again you maggot'. Lenny pocketed the wrap then fumbled on the floor for the blood soaked ten pound note before scurrying to the door.
Billy gathered his men around him, 'We gotta get Mickey aatta the gaff asap, we'll take im daan the warehouse, less go!' Billy looked round to see Roland still seated plucking peanuts from his packet, 'Ar said less go you dick!' he said, snatching the bag from Roland's hand and hurling it across the room.
'But arm ungry Bill' Roland winged, licking his fingers, 'Carn I eat me twiglets?'
'No you fuckin can't!' Billy said, dragging his brother to his feet, 'You need to lose some weight boy, your a fuckin embarrassment'.

'Shut up Bill' Roland said, as he was shoved toward the door, 'You know iss me glands, ar carn elp it'
'Glands my arse!' Billy laughed, 'Your just a greedy fat fuck thas all'
Passing the bar, Billy held out his hand uttering a solitary word, 'Dave'
Instinctively Dave opened the till and took out the majority of the days takings, leaving very little and handed it to Billy, 'Good boy' Billy said, following his men out.
In the meantime Laura and Trisha had just arrived outside the family business, 'I think your friend is in here' Laura said, opening the door and ushering Trisha inside. Making her way to the rear, Laura was surprised to find the office door locked, 'What!' she said, pulling at the handle, 'Billy never locks this door'.
'Let me av a go' Trisha said, pulling as hard as she could.
Laura began rummaging through her desk drawer 'Wait there's a spare key i'm sure of it' she said, removing a handful of files, 'Yes here it is' she produced a brass key on a chain and handed it to a delighted Trisha, but before they had a chance to slip it in the lock they heard the screech of brakes outside, 'Shit it's Billy!' Laura cursed, grabbing Trisha by the arm, 'He'll kill me if he knew what I was doing!'. The two girls ducked behind Laura's desk and huddled together in the knee hole as Billy climbed from his car, 'Would e really kill ya?' Trisha whispered.
'I'm sure of it' Laura whispered, 'One of our cousins threatened to go to the police over my brother's business dealings, Billy had him taken to the docks in the back of a van and we never saw him again, word

is they tied him to the anchor chain of the woolwich ferry'
'Shit, really!' Trisha gasped, clinging to Laura's arm, 'E's a nasty fucker then'.
Laura nodded in agreement, then cringed hearing the key in the door, 'Shhhh' she said, holding her breath.
Billy paused before entering, noticing Laura's car parked several doors away, 'Woss that doing ere?' he said out loud.
'Ar dunno!' Jimmy replied, peering out of the door, 'Praps one of er dyke mates picked er up'.
'Mmmm' Billy said, ducking inside, 'Eeya!' he added, tossing Roland his own key, 'Get that fucker aat ere'.
Billy then sat at Laura's desk toying with her fountain pen, his feet inches from Trisha's leg, moments later Roland and one of Billy's foot soldiers returned with Mickey hanging lifeless between them, his long dreadlocks heavily frosted as were his eyebrows,
'Fuck me iss a chocolate lolly!' Billy joked.
Trisha and Laura crammed themselves into a corner as Billy's foot edged closer, with their hearts in their mouths the two girls feared they would be discovered at any moment, but instead Billy left the desk and approached his brother, 'Is e dead?' he asked.
'Nah Bill e's still breavin' Roland replied, observing Mickey's frozen breath.
Billy slapped Mickey's face hard, 'Wake up you ponce!' he snarled.
Mickey stirred, coughing and spluttering,
'Woss that Mickey?' Billy asked, stooping closer, 'You ready to talk to met yet boy'
Mickey moaned, delirious with the cold, his teeth chattering, 'Pppplease Billy ar dddon't know nuffin!' he said, struggling to speak.

'Thas bollocks Mickey!' Billy said, angrily, 'You know it and ar know it, now stop pissin me araand and tell me where that fuckin stone is or so elp me ar'll put a bullet in that fuckin black ed of yours right now' Billy held a pistol to Mickeys temple, pressing the barrel hard against his skull, but even in Mickey's semi comatose state he knew that as long as Billy thought he had the ruby he would remain alive and maybe just maybe have a chance of escape, Billy also knew that the second Mickey gave him what he wanted then he would have to disappear, permanently, possibly to a shallow forest grave or encased forever in the concrete foundations of the M25, either way, Mickey's silence was the only thing that kept him alive, but for how long under mounting pressure.

One of Billy's men tapped his arm, 'Eeya boss' he said, ushering Billy to one side out of earshot of Mickey, 'Spencer's got a sister ain e?' he whispered, 'Over at seven kings ar fink'

'Nice one Tommy' Billy smiled, 'Find aat where she lives and go pick er up'

'Ok boss' Tommy replied, leading two of his associates out the door.

Billy clicked his fingers, 'Get that fucker daan the warehouse', he told his brothers.

Trisha peered around the corner of the desk and watched them drag Mickey away, his shoes scuffing the carpet, Laura pulled her back by the shoulder, petrified they would be seen, 'Wait' she whispered.

Billy, Jimmy and Roland retrieved six black leather suitcases from the freezer, 'We gotta get this shit aat of ere an'all' Billy said, opening one on the table, Trisha could see it was crammed with bags of what looked like cocaine, in fact it was part of a shipment bound for the UK streets. Jimmy pushed his finger

through one of the polythene bags and rubbed a quantity of the drug onto his gums.
'OY!' Billy snapped, smacking his hand away, 'Leave it aat will ya, look at ya, your off ya fuckin ed as it is, you gotta take it easy on this gear ar'm tellin ya!'.
Jimmy stepped forward and threw his hands in the air, squaring up to Billy, 'Yeah well maybe ar'm sick of you tellin me what ar can and can't do!' he pushed his brother, glaring at him through wild eyes, 'Ar work mar fuckin bollocks off for this firm and you treat me like a mug, well I ain avin it no more, no more you ear, ar want an equal share!'.
Roland piped up, 'What about me?' he asked, chewing on a chocolate bar,
'Shut it you fat cunt' Jimmy growled, 'You aint werf two bob'
Billy had heard enough, he grabbed Jimmy's collar and pounded the side of his head with his clenched fist, 'You ungrateful little prick!' he yelled, thrusting him against the wall, 'You couldn't run a fuckin barf let alone this firm you stupid smack ed!'.
Jimmy tried to retaliate but he was no match for his older brother and eventually slid down the wall and cowered at Jimmy's feet, 'Alright alright!' he cried, covering his face as Billy continued to punch him, 'ENOUGH!'.
Roland grabbed his brothers wrist, 'Bill stop please your gonna kill im'.
Billy wrenched his hand free and pushed Roland back against Laura's desk almost knocking the two girls out from beneath it, 'Don't you ever touch me Rolly or you'll get in an'all, d'you ear me!'. Billy stood and straightened his jacket as his brothers licked their wounds, 'Ar run this firm, you two got that, you ever stand up to me again an ar'll bury the pair of ya,

and don't fink ar won't, now get in that fuckin mota!'. Roland pulled Jimmy to his feet and attempted to mop the blood from his mouth with his handkerchief, 'Leave me the fuck alone!' Jimmy yelled, storming out and picking on the first person he saw in an attempt to reassert himself, a young lad cycling by, 'What are you looking at?' he cried, chasing the boy along the street before hurling a dustbin after him, 'FUCKIN PRICK!' he cursed, dabbing the dripping blood from his eye.

Billy left and climbed into the passenger seat of the car, glaring at his two brothers in the rear view mirror, 'Dad'd turn in iz bleedin grave if e saw what a pair of wankers you two turned aat to be'

Jimmy and Roland sat quietly seething having lived in their older brothers shadow for the majority of their lives. Mickey was slowly thawing in the boot of the car wedged between the suitcases as it sped off along Jamaica road.

'Shit, shit, shit!' Trisha cursed, climbing out from beneath the desk, 'Naah what we gonna do?'

'I don't know' Laura replied, putting an arm around her, 'But i'm sure we'll think of something, don't worry'

Trisha took out her phone 'Ar better phone Dee' she said, tapping at the screen.

'Dee, who's Dee?' asked Laura, straightening her crooked desk, 'Is that one of your friends?'

'Yeah, one of me bestest mates' Trisha said, waiting for Dee Dee to answer, 'Oh ello Dee, iss me Trish'

Dee Dee ran into the ladies to take the call, 'Ar know iss you ya doughnut, ya name comes up, naah where the bleedin ell ya been, ar bin ringin ya'

Trisha sat at the desk and began to explain, 'Well we ad some wicked's and champagne at this great little club, oh you should see it Dee' she rambled 'Iss brilliant, Mr Sanjeef was there and a big fat bird called Princess Adora who ties blokes up and spanks their whatsits!'.

Dee Dee couldn't make head nor tale of Trisha's story, 'What the fuck are you on abaat, did you find Mickey or what?'

'Oh yeah ar faand im' Trisha replied, proudly, 'But then we lost im'

'We!' Dee Dee asked, 'What do you mean we?'

'Me and Laura' Trisha told her, 'Oh you should see er flat Dee, iss gorgeous, she's even got one of them bogs for washing yer arse in' Trisha began to ramble again, 'And a telly what comes aat the end of the bed wiv all them moody foreign channels, you know the ones where Danish birds are bangin the plumber an all that'

'TRISHA FOR FUCK SAKE!' Dee Dee screamed down the phone, 'ARE DON'T WANNA KNOW IF SHE'S GOT A TELLY IN ER BED OR A FRIGGIN ARSE WASHER, JUST TELL ME ABAAT MICKEY!'.

Trisha held the phone away from her ear, 'Alright Dee keep yer air on, ar'm gettin to that bit!'

'Well bloody get to it ya stupid bitch!' Dee Dee snapped, 'Come on urry up!'.

'Well' Trisha continued 'After me and Laura, you know, done it, we went back to the funeral place, oh did ar tell ya they got a glass lift at ers, fuck me Dee it narf wierd, ar was angin on to Laura shittin meself, you know ar'v never liked ites, ever since we went abseiling wiv the school, member that, a got stuck arf way up that bleedin great rock and that orny bloke oisted me up in iz elicopter, fuck me e was fit'

'TRISHAAAAA!' Dee Dee yelled, losing her temper, 'shut the fuck up abaat elicopters and just tell me

what appened to Mickey or so elp me when ar see ya ar'm gonne give you such a friggin slap!'.
Laura could hear Dee Dee's screams across the room, 'She's a little bit stressed' Trisha told her, covering the phone with her hand, 'Ar'v told er ar don't fink she's gettin enough vitamins, and she's up all hours and smokes far too much, it aint good for ya skin is it'. Laura shook her head, not knowing what Trisha was talking about. 'Sorry Dee where was I' Trisha said, returning to her call.
Maizie joined Dee Dee in the toilets, 'Who is it Dee, is it Trish?' she asked, 'Did she find Mickey?'.
Dee Dee thrust the phone into Maizie's hand, 'I aint got a fuckin scooby what that dozy bitch is doin, you talk to er Maize coz she's doin mar nut in!'
'Ello is that you Trish?' Maizie asked, 'Woss appnin?'
Dee Dee threw her arms in the air, 'Ar bin askin the soppy bitch that for ages, all ar got was a load of bollocks abaat glass lifts, arse scrubbers and elicopters!'.
Trisha was glad to hear Maizie's voice, 'Hiya Maizie, you alright?' she asked checking her nails, 'Oh bugger, ar broke one' she said, nibbling her little finger nail, 'Ar just ad them done an'all, oh you was wiv me wern't ya, how's yours Maize, they still alright?'.
Maizie found herself sucked into Trisha's conversation, 'Well ar fink they're shit meself, me mums ad ers a week and arf of em av fell off, stickons are crap Trish, your better off growin yer own'.
Dee Dee couldn't believe her ears, 'WHAT THE FUCK ARE YOU TALKIN ABAAT MAIZE?' she yelled, banging her head on the hand dryer, 'Your as

bleedin mad as that doughnut you are, just ask er where Mickey is before ar go ballistic will ya!'
'Oh yeah sorry Dee, yeah course' Maizie said, knowing her friend was about to blow a fuse,
'Eeya Trish mate where's Mickey?'
Trisha raised her eyebrows, 'Thas what ar bin tryna tell ya Maize, Laura told me where e was but when we come to get im er bruvva's turned up and carted im off'.
'Carted im off, where to?' Maizie asked.
'Ar dunno Maize' Trisha replied, 'But ar fink e'z in a shit loada trouble mate'
Laura put her hand on Trisha's shoulder, 'I think I know where they may have taken him' she said 'We have a warehouse by the river'.
'Ang on Maize!' Trisha said, lowering the phone, 'Can you take me there?' she asked Laura, who nodded in reply.
Dee Dee snatched the phone back from Maizie 'Trisha, Trisha you there?' she called.
Trisha returned to the phone, 'Oh ello Dee, you alright?' she asked, as though nothing had happened.
'No ar'm not alright' Dee Dee said, doing her best to remain calm, 'Just tell me where Mickey is wivaat any of your bollocks'
'Well' Trisha began, 'E was at the Tibbs's funeral place, but they come and took im away, Laura finks e'z at some warehouse by the river and she's gonna take me daan there'
'No you stay there ya doughnut!' Dee Dee barked, 'We're comin over'
'But Dee!' Trisha said, stamping her foot, 'Ar can andle it'

'JUST STAY WHERE YOU ARE!' Dee Dee yelled, 'I ain't letttin you aat of my sight again, your a bleedin nightmare you are'. Dee Dee hung up the phone. 'Woss up wiv er?' she asked Maizie, 'Was she dropped on er ed or summink?'

'You know what she like Dee' Maizie added, 'She's a bleedin fruit loop she is'.

'Right!' Dee Dee said, checking herself in the mirror, 'Give that bruvva of yours a ring, tell im to get iz arse raand ere and pick us up'. The girls headed back out into the bar with Maizie tapping at her phone, but the pair were then accosted by a drunken Terry,

'Fuck me you two bin in there for ages' he said, having waited anxiously for them, 'You bin avin a pony or summink?'

'Shut up Tel you toby' Dee Dee said, pushing him aside.

Terry leapt in front of them again, 'Don't be like that girls, lemmy buy you a drink, what you avin?' he asked brandishing a twenty pound note,

'Ar'll av a large Morgan spice' Maizie said with the phone to her ear,

'Go on then' Dee Dee told Terry 'Ar'll av a JD and coke, but it don't mean ar'm gonna suck ya cock or nuffin, d'you ear me'.

Bradley was sitting in his room watching porn when Maizie rang, not your run of the mill boy girl porn or even boy girl girl porn for that matter, this was something out of the ordinary that he had ordered from a German hard core site and had been delivered in plain brown wrapping. With English subtitles, which Bradley was having trouble following, The chicken farmer, was the tale of a randy chicken plucker who just couldn't keep his fingers or anything else for that matter out of the oven ready birds.

Bradley mauled his manhood unaware that his mobile was ringing downstairs on the kitchen table, 'BRADLEY!' his mother yelled from the kitchen sink, 'BRAAAD YA PHONE!'. But Bradley had his earphones on listening to hip hop whilst watching the filthy flic, 'BRADLEY YA PHONE!' his mother called from the foot of the stairs. She then noticed Maizie's name on the screen and answered it, 'Ello Maizie love it's mum!' she said, removing her rubber gloves, 'You alright?'

Maizie took her drink from Terry, 'Yeah ar'm ok mum, ar'm daan the welly wiv Dee, is Bradley there?'

'Ar fink e's in iz room, ang on ar get im for ya' she said, climbing the stairs.

Just as the German chicken plucker was indulging his poultry passion by adding a little stuffing of his own to the featherless flock and Bradley was close to climax and planning a trip to the supermarket for his own free range fantasy the door opened and his mother walked in, 'OH MAR GAWD!' she cried, seeing her son squirming on the bed. It took a few seconds for Bradley to notice her standing there because of the booming beat in his ears,

'MUM!' he eventually screamed, 'WHAT THE!' with a panicked expression he pulled his hand from his trousers, threw his earphones to the floor and fumbled for the remote control, 'MUM GET AAT WILL YA!' But before Bradley had a chance to switch off the television his mother turned to see the dirty plucker violating another balding bird.

'OH MAR GOOD GAWD, OH LORD JESUS WHAT THE FUCK IS THAT FILF!' she clasped her hands to her face, 'Oh gawd thas bleedin sick that is!'

Bradley quickly turned the television off, 'Mum just get aata mar room will ya!' he said, shoving her towards the door, 'Iss a documentary thas all'
'No it ain't!' his mother said, pushing Bradley away, 'Iss sick bleedin filf thas what it is, you aint right boy, just you wait till ar tell ya farva!'
Bradley tried again to usher her from his room 'What did you want anyway muvva?' he asked, trying to change the subject.
His mother threw his mobile phone onto his bed and stormed off along the landing, 'Your sisters on the bleedin phone, ar bet she don't know what sort of shit you've been watching, you just get that disgusting filf aata my ouse do you ear me Bradley, and ar mean right now!'
Bradley closed his bedroom door, 'Shit, shit shit!' he cursed, at having been caught in such a way, 'Ello, ello sis!' he said, picking up his phone, 'Yeah sorry ar didn't ear it, ar was er, doin summink'
Maizie was fending off Terry's lecherous advances with one hand whilst talking to Bradley,
'Come on girl!' Terry said, drooling, 'Me and you raand the back right now, bish bosh ow abaat it'
'D'you know what Tell' Maizie told him, leaving Bradley hanging 'As anyone ever told you your one smoov talkin fucker'
'Ar know' Terry replied, puffing out his chest, 'Ar tell ya what, ar got some quality gear back at mar gaff, proper stuff, ar don't buy off none of these two bob dealers raand ere who mix their shit with bakin powder, we can party all night babe, ar borra'd one of them video camera's off me bruvva an'all, so if your up for it we can make our own mucky movie'
'Woss that then?' Dee Dee laughed, 'Forest Gump!'

'Shut up' Terry said, attempting to assert himself 'Ar could'a done porno's ya know'
'What, wiv your stamina' Dee Dee joked, 'They'll be bleedin short films coz youd've shot your load durin the opening credits!'.
Terry picked up his drink and shuffled away, 'Poxy lezzers' he cursed.
Maize returned to Bradley, 'Sorry bruv where was I, oh yeah me and Dee need pickin up from the welly as soon as ya can'.
Bradley agreed, grabbing his keys and making his way downstairs, giving his mother a wide berth as he left the house. Putting his foot to the floor in the Nova he wheel spun away from the curb, cranking up his stereo in doing so, The trance like beat and the experience with his mother gave Bradley inspiration for an impromptu rap, 'Yeah, yeah, come on yeah' he began

'Ar fink ar'm in the shit coz me muvva caught me wankin
if she catches me again ar be gettin such a spankin,
there's nuffin wrong wiv tuggin if ya don't get caught
it aint as bad as muggin and it aint mar fault,
ar'm pullin it and shakin it and tuggin it araand
ar just love the feelin of it in my hand,
ar'm tellin ya!
there's nuffin wrong wiv tuggin if ya don't get caught
it ain't as bad as muggin an it aint mar fault,
there's nuffin wrong with tuggin
there's nuffin wrong wiv tuggin
nuffin wrong wiv tuggin if ya don't get caught!'

Bradley slapped his hand on the steering wheel 'Yeah man, das what ar'm talkin bout' he said, rocking to the beat.
Billy Tibbs and his men arrived at the Tibb's warehouse and Mickey was manhandled inside, 'Tie that fucker up!' Billy barked at Roland, who scurried around looking for anything to lash Mickey's hands with.
The warehouse was a huge cathedral like building housing stack after stack of Brazilian hardwood used in the manufacture of high end coffins. Hoists and pulleys hung from the rafters with heavy steel chains giving the place an industrial feel. Mickey was thrust into a chair and held until Roland returned with a ball of bailing twine, 'Thisa do Bill' he said, hastily tethering Mickey's hands and feet to the legs of the chair. Mickey at this point was in a bad way, slipping in and out of consciousness.
'MICKEY!' Billy yelled, 'MICKEY ARE YOU LISTENING TO ME! somebody wake this fucker up'.
Jimmy stepped forward, still seething from his altercation with his brother, 'Leave it to me' he said menacingly, taking out his knife and without hesitation he then pierced Mickey's right ear with the entire length of the blade and twisted it sadistically. The searing pain brought Mickey to his senses and he let out a gut churning cry.
'Thank you Jimmy, that'll do' Billy told his brother, but Jimmy was enjoying the feeling of power and twisted the blade a little harder causing Mickey to beg for mercy, 'Please! please stop!' he cried, his neck awash with blood.
'AR SAID ENOUGH!' Billy yelled, grabbing his brother's shoulder and pulling him away. For a split second, with the knife in his hand, Jimmy considered

plunging it into his brothers face, but Billy's Clenched fists and manic expression made him think better of it, 'Thas the second time today you've made me look like a mug Billy' Jimmy said, sulking, 'I aint gonna stand for much more of it ar tell ya'
Billy held his coat open and slapped his chest, 'You wanna stick me Jimmy!' he growled, 'Come on, naah's ya chance, come on stick me!'
Jimmy's grip on the knife increased as he contemplated a take over, it would be so easy, one thrust and he would be boss with all the respect he so eagerly craved, 'What ya waitin for?' Billy asked, smiling now, 'Just as ar fought, you ain't got the bollocks av ya!' Billy snatched the blade from Jimmy's hand, tossed it across the room and slapped his face hard which amused the others, 'Naah sit the fuck daan and behave yaself' he told his younger brother, but knowing full well that one day Jimmy mightn't be so hesitant.
As Dee Dee and Maizie waited in the Wellingtons foyer for Bradley to arrive Dee Dee glanced over her shoulder and watched the pub television through the glass door, the nightly news was broadcasting a story of a young essex man that had gotten his head stuck inside a waste bin whilst out on the town. Although she couldn't hear the commentary, the gist of the story was obvious, 'What a twat' she laughed, but then to her surprise her mothers face appeared on the screen, 'What the fuck!' Dee Dee gasped, ducking back inside in time to hear the news reader, 'An essex mother has been questioned and charged over the murder of an Arab businessman, police have overwhelming evidence linking Miss Pearl Dawson to the crime, Detective inspector Pritcher had this to say earlier' The camera switched to a

smiling DI outside his police station, 'We are pleased to announce that we have made an arrest in connection with the death of Kuwaiti Sheik Abdullah Hussain in a west London Hotel, we expect further arrests to follow as more evidence is uncovered, thank you!'
'What overwhelmin evidence?' Dee Dee said, open mouthed, 'Ar fought she'd be aat by naah' she added 'How the fuck have they pinned Abby's murder on me muvva, Mickey said that Pritcher was a slippery bastard'
'What we gonna do Dee?' Maizie asked, 'This is gettin aat of and'
Dee Dee grabbed maizie by the arms 'Ar tell ya what we aint gonna do' she snapped, 'We aint gonna panic, ar'll fink of summink don't you worry, right naah we gotta get Mickey, you got that!'
Maizie reluctantly agreed 'Ok Dee, ar just don't wanna go to prison thas all' she told her friend
'YOU AIN'T GONNA GO TO POXY PRISON!' Dee Dee yelled, then lowering her voice as several men and women looked over the rim of their glasses, 'Look we done alright so far ain't we?' she added,
Maizie was still hesitant, 'Yeah ar spose, but'.
'But nuffin' Dee Dee said, dragging her friend back out into the foyer and out of ear shot, 'Look we got a nice few quid stashed and a ruby werf a shit load more, naah I aint gonna give that up for no one, so get a fuckin grip will ya'.
Bradley then pulled up outside and sounded his horn, 'Come on' Dee Dee told Maizie ,who was still contemplating a life behind bars, 'Just get in the mota will ya'.
Maizie had been an unwilling participant in many of Dee Dee's felonious capers during their school days,

finding her difficult if not impossible to say no to. Like the time they broke into the chapel, got wasted on communion wine and urinated on the mother superiors habit, a crime that didn't go unpunished though, each of the girls receiving twenty lashes of the cane and a visit to the confessional where their sins would be heard and eventually forgiven in the eyes of the lord, but not by the mother superior who bore a grudge from that day on.

'Where you bin?' Dee Dee asked Bradley, climbing in the car 'Come on Maize urry up!'

Bradley waited for Maizie to close the door before pulling away, 'Ar do av fings to do ya know' he said, stopping at the crossroads,

'Right, where we goin?'

Dee Dee pointed to the right, 'Back to the Tibbs's and fuckin urry up, fings to do my arse, your paid to drive us you mug, so from now on you aint got nuffin else to do, d'you ear me!'

'But what abaat me music man!' Bradley replied, waving a cd, 'Ar tell ya, ar'm that close to a record deal, ar can feel it'

Dee Dee grabbed the disc and snapped it in two 'The only fing you'll be feelin you twat is my boot up yer arse if you fuck me araand'

'Oh Dee' Maizie said, leaning forward from the back seat, 'Ar fink e'z stuffs pretty good ar do, better than arf the shit on the radio'

Dee Dee had to agree, 'Ar make ya right mate, there is some crap in the charts but e'z aint no better'

'You ain erd the Bradley rap av ya Dee?' Maizie said, tapping her shoulder 'Iss wicked it is, Bradley do the Bradley rap, go on!'

'Oh fuck' Dee Dee said, sinking into her seat as Bradley rummaged in the door pocket for his backing disc,
'Buckle up you bitches, ar'm about to lay some heavy shit on ya' Bradley said, jerking his head from side to side as the pounding bass line erupted, 'Dis tunes gonna go galactic ar'm tellin ya, ar've ad free faasand and fifty hits on youtube already man!'
Maizie squealed with excitement as her brother belted out the opening verse,

'Ar'm a supersonic superstar
ar get a girl in the street ar get a girl in the bar
ar got one in my bed ar got one in my car
ar'm a supersonic superstar,

Ar'm a contract killer ar'm a loaded gun
a smokin pistol now ar'm on the run,
Ar'm in every girls sights and they love me madly
ar give em sleepless nights and mar name is Bradley,
so treat me right and ar won't treat you badly
ar give ya sleepless nights coz mar name is Bradley,

Dee Dee found herself tapping her foot in time with Bradley's rap as Maizie joined in, having heard it many times before,

Ar'm a ninja turtle ar'm a power ranger
ar'm Captain Kirk and ar fear no danger
Ar'm a Jedi knight wiv my shining sabre
Ar'm a King Kong killer and ar'm here to save ya,

Ar'm a lyrical lover in mar Mercedes Benza
ar love Anne Summer's and ar love La Senza,

ar love mar girl when she's talkin crudley
she's a big fat momma wiv a boucnin booty
she's a big fat momma and she's talkin crudely
ar love mar girl wiv her bouncin booty,
she treats me right, she don't treat me badly
ar give her sleepless nights coz mar name is Bradley,
so to all you girls who are waitin sadly
for just one kiss from the mighty Bradley,
stand in line if ya love me madly
for just one kiss from the mighty Bradley,
stand in line if ya love me madly
for just one kiss
from the mighty Bradley!'.

The ridiculous lyrics had Dee Dee in fits of laughter but she couldn't help but sing along with the other two

'Stand in line if ya love me madly
for just one kiss from the mighty Bradley
stand in line if ya love me madly
for just one kiss
just one kiss
just one kiss from the mighty Bradley'

'Iss good ain it Dee!' Maizie laughed, swaying from side to side, 'E'z gonna go on x factor wiv it'
'Well' Dee Dee said, turning the volume down, 'Iss a bit up iz own arse but yeah it aint bad mate'. Crossing the Thames in the dead of night, Dee Dee, Maizie and Bradley had no idea of the dangers that lay on the other side.
Over at Heathrow's terminal three, Virgin Atlantic flight J3941 had just touched down from Tokyo carrying Mr Nakajima and four of his most trusted

guards, each clutching a silver Samsonite case containing close to three million pounds. Mr Nakajima, a quiet unassuming man in his mid seventies was dressed in an exquisitely cut pale blue Persian silk suit with gleaming Italian leather brogues to match, anyone could be forgiven for thinking that due to his slight stature and advancing years Mr Nakajima was far beyond the prime of his life, but nothing could be further from the truth. Born in the southern province of Yamanashi in the early forties, Takashi Nakajima was the only child of the great Katsumi Nakajima, a master swordsman who knew no equal. Schooled in every aspect of armed and unarmed martial arts by his father before him, Katsumi devoted his life to ensuring his son and heir would follow in his footsteps and those of his ancestors, many of them fearless samurai warriors.

Takashi did indeed learn the ways of his proud blood line, but japan was changing and with the arrival of narcotics, fast cars and beautiful women he soon found a himself consumed with greed, eventually building a vast criminal empire around him against the strict wishes of his father. Rival gangs were dealt with swiftly and mercilessly, many beheaded, and left by the roadside with a red cross daubed on their mutilated bodies as a warning to others. The shame was too much for Katsumi to bare and after a meeting with village elders he reluctantly agreed to assassinate his wayward son, but Takashi had learned of his fathers intentions and was prepared when he came calling. What followed would be enshrined in Japanese folk law, a sword fight some say lasting up to six and a half hours, each gaining and losing the upper hand time after time. Takashi's palatial home was completely destroyed during the epic battle which spilled out onto the provinces waterlogged rice fields. After receiving a glancing slice to the right side of his face Takashi seized his chance when his father stumbled and plunged the full length of his sword through his heart and watched breathlessly as the life drained from him. Takashi buried his father with full honors knowing that from then on no man would dare oppose him, and he was right, his organization grew as did his power which reached into the very heart of the Japanese government. The scar from his fathers blade remains with Takashi to this day, a constant reminder of the ruthless extent of his psychotic nature. Takashi's governmental connections afforded him diplomatic immunity wherever and whenever he travelled, in return Takashi orchestrated the rigging of a thousand ballot boxes during the last decade ensuring his favored presidential candidate would win by a landslide at each election. He and his men each dressed in black hooded cloaks where able to bypass any airport security and baggage inspection via a side door enabling them to enter the country with not only an enormous amount of laundered cash but an arsenal of automatic weapons, knives and swords. A pre arranged black limousine swept them away from the airport, into the heart of London and then on to Hackney and Nikos Papageorgiou's dimly lit pawn shop.

Nikos was in the process of closing up for the night when he saw Takashi and his men step from the car 'Oh Fuck!' he said, ducking behind a tall display cabinet but not before slipping the bolt on the door. Nikos had dealt with Takashi on two previous occasions, once to broker a deal on a stolen Picasso and then again when the Duchess of Windsor was relieved at gunpoint of her heavily encrusted diamond tiara reportedly once owned by queen Victoria herself. On both occasions Nikos was rewarded handsomely for his efforts but had gotten the distinct impression that Takashi did not tolerate incompetence in business and was definitely not a man to be kept waiting.

Takashi pushed on the door then cursed in his native tongue when it appeared locked, after a second and third attempt and with a furious grunt he peered through the grubby glass cupping his hands to the side of his face, 'NIKOS!' he bellowed, pounding the door with his clenched fist. The petrified pawn broker hastily took out his phone and dialed Dee Dee's number,

'Come on come on!' he whispered, peering around the cabinet at an ever increasingly irate Takashi. 'Hello, hello Deborah, Debbie is that you?' he said, covering his mouth, 'Debbie it's Nikos, Nikos Papageorgiou, where the hell are you and where's the ruby, the buyer's here!.

'Oh ello Niki mate' Dee Dee replied as she, Trisha and Bradley crossed Tower bridge 'Ows it goin?' Dee Dee could barely make out what Nikos was saying with Bradley's stereo belching out a monstrous techno tune that hammered at her ear drums, 'For fuck sake turn that shit daan will ya!' she screamed over the din 'Ar carn ear a fuckin fing, aint you got any Boyzone or summink?'

Bradley reluctantly turned down the music, 'Boyzone blud!' he tutted 'I aint never heard of no Boyzone man, what are they, garage, acid house or what?'

Dee Dee now ignored Nikos at the other end of the phone who was becoming more and more

exasperated each time Takashi, who was now beside himself with rage, battered at the door.
'No ya doughnut they was a boy band weren't they' Dee Dee told Bradley, she began warbling a Boyzone classic 'Don't love me for fuuuun girl, let me be the one gir' Maize then joined in 'love me for a reeeason!'
'Ooh ar love this one Dee!' Maizie squealed 'Ar used to have that Keith wassiz face's poster on mar wall ar did, you know the one in corrie'
Nikos could hear the conversation in Bradley's car 'Will you shut up about bloody Boyzone and listen!' he said, trying to remain as quiet as he could.
'Duffy!' Dee Dee told her friend.
Maizie had lost track of the conversation momentarily 'What?'
Dee Dee raised her eyebrows and sighed, 'The paddy in corrie ya silly bitch, iz names Duffy!'. Bradley shook his head in despair as they sat in heavy traffic, 'You'z two are off yer heads man, dat shit aint music, diss is what the yoof want blud, arm tellin ya!' Bradley waved his cd under Dee Dee's nose, 'Not One bloody direction or Justin Beaver!'
'Iss Beiber' Maize said correcting her brother,
'What?' Bradley replied 'What you on abaat?'
Maizie laughed 'Iss Justin Beiber not beaver!'
'Whateve!' Bradley scoffed 'Iss all shit anyway'.
Dee Dee returned to her call 'Sorry Niki mate wossup?' she asked, ushering Bradley to turn right.
Nikos was frantic 'What's up!' he snapped 'i'll tell you what's up, i've got a Japanese psycho trying to beat my door down for a ruby that I haven't got and your swanning around with your friends talking about Boyzone and bloody beavers!'
'Iss Beiber!' Dee Dee interrupted.

'What!' Nikos growled.
'iss Beiber' Dee Dee repeated 'Not Beaver ya pillock!'
Nikos gripped his phone as though it was Dee Dee's throat 'I don't give a shit if it's beaver, Beiber or fucking beetroot, just tell me your on your way here with that bloody ruby!'
'Well not exactly' Dee Dee said, surprised at his outburst, 'We got summink to take care of first, just tell the geezer to ang on for a while, ar'll sort the stone out when we're done'.
Nikos shook his phone violently 'What, no you don't understand, Mr Nakajima won't wait!'.
But Dee Dee was having none of it 'look just tell Naka, Nakaji or whatever iz bloomin name is, if he want's the ruby he'll av to bloody wait!' with this Dee Dee hung up the phone.
'Hello, hello!' Nikos yelled 'Deborah, Deborah for god's sake!' but dee Dee had gone. Nikos then noticed that the pounding on the door had stopped and breathed a sigh of relief thinking that Takashi had left. But in fact Takashi had taken out his own gold plated phone and dialed Nikos's number. Nikos almost jumped out of his skin when his phone lit up and began to ring which alerted Takashi immediately because Nikos's ringtone was an embarrassing Jedward tune set at full volume due to his slight hearing defect. An unusual musical choice for a middle aged pawn broker but Nikos had a thing for the young twins, even insisting that many of his rent boys gel their hair to emulate the ludicrous lads. Nikos quickly covered his phone with his hand to stifle the sound but it was too late, Takashi had heard the tone and glared through the window, 'PAPAGEORGIOU!' he barked, rattling the door

handle 'Open this door or i'll break it down with my bare hands!'.
Nikos peered from behind the cabinet, 'Oh Mr. Nakajima I didn't hear you i'm sorry' he hurriedly unbolted the door, 'I was er'm, I was just er, just dusting behind the cabinet' he squirmed, seeing Takashi's furious expression, 'it's an OCD thing you see, I just cant help myself' he began to ramble nervously 'I certainly am a slave to my duster'. Takashi looked inside the grubby shop and it was clear straight away that the place hadn't seen a duster or any other cleaning product for that matter in many years.
'Get out of my way!' Takashi said, shoving Nikos aside, his men filed into the shop behind him, each of them staring expressionless at Nikos which unnerved him somewhat,
'Come in fella's, er make yourself at home' Nikos bolted the door behind them and braced himself for the tirade of abuse he was sure was coming his way, and he was right to be fearful because Takashi had never in his entire life felt as disrespected as he did at that moment, dozens if not hundreds had perished by his blade for much lessor offences.
'This is how you treat me Papageorgiou!' Takashi began, through clenched teeth, 'I come to do business and you keep me standing on the street like a stinking dog, I should have my men tear the flesh from your back for this insult!' one of Takashi's guards slid a gleaming sword from beneath his robes.
Nikos clasped his hands together in prayer 'Mr Nakajima' he pleaded 'Please accept my humble apologies, I never meant to offend you, honest I didn't, after all, we're friends aren't we!'. Nikos was

hoping the fact that their prior meeting would have somehow endeared him to the crime boss, but Takashi looked on Nikos as though he were the lowest of gods creatures,
'I have no use for friends Mr Papageorgiou!' he said menacingly 'But if I did I assure you I would not consider an odious toad like you a worthy candidate, now you know why I am here!' Takashi crossed his arms in front of him, expecting Nikos to produce the ruby at any moment. 'I have your money', the guards dropped the suitcases to the floor with a thud.
Nikos held his hands in the air and smiled a toothy grin 'Fella's, fella's what's the rush!' he said taking a box of cigars from behind the counter, 'i'm sure your all exhausted after your long journey, would you care for one of these, they're very good I can assure you'. Takashi and his men said nothing so Nikos lit one for himself and replaced the box, but as he took a long lingering drag on the cigar the sword wielding henchman lunged at him and with a lightning quick swipe of his blade cut the cigar within millimeters from Nikos's lips, 'Do not smoke in the presence of the master!' he said, in broken English.
Nikos gulped and inspected the remains of his smoke, 'Yes, yes of course!' he said, dropping the butt into an ash tray, 'Please accept my apologies Mr Nakajima, how about a cup of tea you must be thirsty surely'. Nikos then retrieved a bottle of ten year old malt whisky from beneath the counter, 'Or perhaps something a little stronger' he was half way through filling a small tumbler when Takashi swiped it across the room,
'ENOUGH!' he yelled, 'I did not come here for pleasantries, just give me the stone and ill be on my way, I cannot stand a minute longer in this, this!' he

looked around at the chaos that was Nikos's shop, 'This pig pen!'.

Nikos had no choice but to come clean and hope that Takashi would spare his miserable life, 'Look Takashi' he said, backing away slightly, then seeing the outraged look on the crime bosses face, quickly changed his approach, 'Sorry I mean Mr Nakajima, you see it's like this, I don't exactly have the stone at this precise moment' Mr Nakajima's frown intensified. 'But I assure you' Nikos quickly continued, 'I do expect delivery very soon you have my word as an honest business man'.

Takashi slammed his fist down onto the counter, 'YOU TAKE ME FOR A FOOL PAPAGEORGIOU!' he blasted, 'I've come for the ruby and I expect it now, if this is some kind of trickery to drive up the price or sell to another bidder you'll feel the edge of my steel across your miserable throat!'

Nikos clutched his neck and humbly begged for more time, 'It's not a trick honest Mr Nakajima, i've been as good as my word in the past haven't I, please just give me a few more hours to finalize things, I tell you what' he rummaged in his wallet for a business card, 'Here, my brother runs this great little hotel in Stratford, take your boys down there for the night, tell him I sent you and he'll sort you out with a couple of local whores, very nice too, eastern European all under twenty one and very flexible, if you know what I mean' Nikos gave Takashi a theatrical wink, 'Ask for Saskia' he added 'My brother tells me she can do things with a walnut whip that'll make your eyes water'.

Takashi had heard enough, with two finger thrust into a pressure point on Nikos's neck he pushed the pawn broker to his knees. 'I am not letting you out of my sight until I have what I came for, so if it will take some hours, we will wait!'

'Wait!' Nikos squealed, while in considerable pain, 'What here?'

'Yes of course!' Takashi snapped, pushing a little harder, 'I trust you have quarters here' He hoisted Nikos to his feet and pushed him toward the rear of the shop, 'I have need of rest and my men will be hungry'.

Nikos tried to resist, 'But, but you don't wanna go up there' he said, knowing the place was a mess and nowhere near fit enough for a man of Takashi's standing, 'What about the Peking palace at the end of the road, they got a wicked buffet, all you can eat for a tenner, or the Flying Horse in bishop street, that's a B and B, they got Boddingtons on draught, your lads'll love it'.

'ENOUGH YOU DOG!' Takashi barked, pulling his own sword several inches from it's sheath 'Do as I say or i'll cut out your heart and hand it too you still beating!'.

Papageorgiou relented and opened the door to the stairs, 'Ok, ok come on up then' he said leading the way 'It's er, it's a little basic, I mean not quite what your used to in your country Mr Nakajima, I er, I don't do much entertaining you see, just a few of my young friends from time to time'. By this he meant the string of teenage boys he used to fulfill his perverse desires.

Mr Nakajima and his henchmen climbed the stairs behind Nikos scuffing their shoes on the threadbare carpet and looking quizzically at the gaudy seventy's wallpaper with it's striking diagonal stripes albeit grubby, well worn and littered with graffiti written by his adolescent visitors. Takashi had no way of deciphering the scribbled street slang , words such as disasterbate meaning to masturbate after unsuccessfully attempting to pick up at a bar and mechanics arm, again a masturbatory term meaning someone who masturbates too much will end up with an arm like a mechanic.

Nikos held open the door to his first floor flat, 'Here we are' he said, toying with a broken light switch, flicking it up and down several times before the buzzing paper ball pendant light came to life, 'Like I said, it's not much but it's home' He quickly gathered up a collection of teen magazines that were strewn across the tatty chesterfield and brushed away the cake crumbs, 'Here have a seat' he added, 'I'll turn the heating on it's freezing in here at times' Nikos disappeared into the kitchen, took a hammer from the drawer and proceeded to beat the boiler in the corner of the room savagely until it whirred into life, he then tossed the hammer aside nonchalantly as though it were an everyday procedure, 'There' he said returning to the lounge where all four of Takashi's men were crammed onto the sofa, at first Nikos couldn't see their boss, 'Where's er' he asked, but then caught sight of him sitting bolt upright in the far corner of the room with his eyes closed, 'Oh there you are Mr Nakajima, i'm gonna put a pizza in the oven, are you hungry?'. There was no reply, 'Mr Nakajima' he said again, 'Mr Nakajima it's pepperoni' Nikos took a step toward Takashi and instantly had the honed tip of a samurai sword thrust at his throat. 'The master meditates' said the sword wielding guard 'He is not to be disturbed'.

'Yes, yes of course' Nikos said, edging away from the blade, 'I'll er, i'll just leave him to it, how about you guys, are you hungry?'

Each of them looked over their shoulder at their master before nodding in turn.
'Ok' Nikos said, heading back to the kitchen, 'Pepperoni it is them, how about a drink?' he added 'I've got Stella!' Nikos took six cans from the fridge and held them in the air. Again the guards checked their masters state of consciousness before nodding. Nikos handed out the drinks to the men who seemed eager to indulge, popping the ring pulls and sinking half the cans at once, 'Blimey!' Nikos gasped, 'You guys like ya beer dontcha'.
One of the guards downed his last drop and thrust the empty can into Nikos's hand 'More!' he said, sternly, the others soon followed suit.
'Right' Nikos replied, returning to the fridge, 'It's a good job i've got plenty in, the boys love it, it gets em in the mood'. One after another the four guards downed the cans in minutes and soon the premium strength larger began to take affect. They began giggling, shoving each other playfully and burping loudly, Takashi did not flinch as the mood amongst his men grew more and more raucous, soon the intoxicated ninja's were embroiled in a bizarre game of charades, rolling in fits of laughter at each pathetic attempt to describe the simplest of things.
Nikos busied himself in the kitchen preparing pizza and snacks for his guests and in his haste knocked a large baking tray from the side which clattered to the floor, 'Shit!' he whispered, peering round the door sure that Takashi would be woken, but still the Japanese mobster remained motionless, his chest barely showing signs of breathing. He had in fact mastered an ancient technique which allowed him to slow his heart rate to within a whisker of cardiac arrest and remain comatose for up to eight hours,

thus cleansing the mind, body and soul. Samurai warriors used this deep meditative process to prepare for battle and the afterlife if they were to be killed. Nikos carried the steaming pizza and potato wedges through to the guards who had discarded their robes and were parading around the room with an array of ridiculous head gear, namely a waste paper bin, turbans fashioned from Nikos's underpants that had been left to dry on the radiator and a cardboard box, 'Blimey you lot know how to enjoy yaselves!' he laughed as the ravenous men set about demolishing his snacks, 'So what's your names?'.
'I am Chin' one of them replied, lifting the pants that had slipped down over his eyes, he then introduced the others who were still giggling like school boys, 'This is Lee, that is Kim and the fool in the box is Shuji' Chin kicked an empty beer can across the floor 'We need more drink!' he said, hugging Nikos tightly, 'You have more drink?
'No more cans' Nikos said, stooping to open a walnut cupboard, 'But i've got a nice bottle of bourbon put aside if you'd like a nip'. Kim snatched the bottle from Nikos, tossed the lid aside and swigged it greedily. 'Hang on a minute!' Nikos protested 'That's a seventy pound bottle!' But the men wrestled one another for the ten year old spirit and drained the contents between them in minutes. By now chin and the others were completely inebriated, staggering clumsily arbout the room, knocking over vases and dislodging the fake Rembrandt's the hung from the peeling tongue and groove paneling.
'Hey! hey sit down will ya!' Nikos pleaded straightening the carnage behind them, 'Come on i'll put the telly on, what do you like, i've got some Bruce

Lee here somewhere that should be right up your street'.
Shuji thumbed through Nikos's dvd collection, casting them aside one by one, but he then jumped for joy waving one in the air and gesturing to his friends, 'MARY POPPINS, MARY POPPINS!' he shrieked, 'LOOK MARY POPPINS!' the others gathered around looking over Shuji's shoulder at the case, each with a huge grin on their faces ' Yes yes Mary Poppins!' Chin said, snatching the dvd and handing it to Nikos who couldn't see what all the fuss was about.
'Mary Poppins!' he said, looking it up and down, 'Are you sure, I mean i've got Jackie Chan if you'd prefer that'.
'NO!' Chin snapped 'Marry Poppins, PLAY!'. As children Chin and the others had been shown Mary Poppins in school repeatedly to help with their English, 'PLAY, PLAY!' Chin insisted as he and the others sat in readiness on the sofa, rigid with excitement,
'Ok if that's what you want' Nikos said, wishing he'd thrown away the film many years ago. The men gasped in anticipation as the opening credits rolled up the screen of Nikos's huge dated television set, they sat motionless for a time mouthing every word from Julie Andrews and the rest of the cast, but nothing could've prepared Nikos for their singing. First an awful rendition of 'a spoonful of sugar' from the swaying quartet followed by a toneless version of 'let's go fly a kite'. Nikos cringed but couldn't help but laugh at their mispronunciation of the classic 'Supercalifragilisticexpialidocious'. Later in the film the four leapt to their feet and astounded Nikos with their expertly choreographed dancing to Dick Van

dyke's hilarious 'Chim Chimeney' even if their cringe worthy cockney accents needed a little work. Lee and Kim strutted with chests puffed shrieking 'Gawd blessya Mary Poppins'. Nikos found the whole scene incredible, but after the second and third showing of the same film found himself singing along arm in arm with Chin and his friends, 'You guys are nuts!' he puffed before launching yet again into 'Um diddle diddle diddle um diddle ay!'.

CHAPTER TEN.

Two dead brothers.

Stationary at the traffic lights at Tower bridge Bradley sat scratching at his crotch as he had been doing for some time. Dee Dee had ignored the irritation until then but eventually had to intervene, 'Woss up wiv you Brad, leave the fuckin fing alone will ya, it aint right, tell im Maize!'.
Maizie leaned over her brothers shoulder, 'E'z always done that Dee, ever since e was a baby' she explained in a little more detail than Bradley would've liked, 'When e was nine e got slung aata school for tuggin it in R E, and then when e was eleven for jacking off into a plasticine fanny' Maizie clipped Bradley's ear 'Leave it alone ya mucky little bugger!' she laughed.
'Leave it aat will ya sis!' Bradley replied, ducking away 'It ain't mar fault, ar got a sick dose of that Julie man' Ever since his brothel experience Bradley had gradually become aware of a tingling sensation around his groin.
'That bitch aint clean man ar'm tellin ya' he added, pulling his trousers forward to scrutinize his balding scrotum. 'Does yer air grow back after usin that remover shit?' he asked, concerned that his present state of genital alopecia would remain with him. 'Yeah why what ya done?' Maizie asked, peering over his shoulder.
'NUFFINK!' Bradley said, sharply 'Just askin thas all'
'Wierdo' his sister replied, slipping back into her seat. Dee Dee touched up her lipstick in the visor mirror 'Ar'm not surprised yer itchin' she said, pursing her lips 'Scratty John pops raand to Julie's to empty iz

sack into er twice a week, and ya know what a dirty bastard e is'.
Bradley spun round and glared in horror at Dee Dee.
Scratty John, as he was known in the Goodmayes area was a semi vagrant with an ill fitting suit with the cancer research label still hanging from the collar. Also his odor, which resembled a festering landfill meant that John would always have at least a three meter exclusion zone around him wherever he went, which was usually The Chequers pub on a Sunday afternoon where ritually he would cough, splutter and sneeze over the roast potato freebies laid out on the bar, rendering them untouchable to the wincing customers.
'Shut up Dee!' Bradley said, shaking his head, 'Don't even joke abaat that shit blud!' Bradley's stomach churned thinking about the crusty dew drop that had hung from scratty's unwashed nose for the past month and a half.
'Ar'm not jokin' Dee Dee laughed, 'E'z a bit of a weirdo though, for an extra score she ad to lick iz sweaty pits, ar mean thas just bleedin gross ain it'.
Bradley clutched his mouth in disgust, recalling the lingering kiss Julie had given him on leaving, her probing tongue teasing his gag reflexes.
Pulling away from the green light, Bradley's mouth filled with bile and partly digested breakfast forcing him to slam on the brakes, 'Shit!' he gargled, throwing open the door and splattering the dotted line.
'Woss up wiv you ya bleedin lightweight' Maizie said, rubbing his back sympathetically, Then seeing the contents of her brothers stomach she prodded him firmly, 'Oh so it was you that nicked mar Cheerio's ya feevin git!'.

Dee Dee found this amusing and couldn't help but tease him some more, 'Eeya ar tell ya what, for a fifty the soapy fucker gets the full back sack and crack, now thas what ya call a gold wash ain it'.
Bradley vomited another steaming mouthful onto the street while Maizie turned up her nose on the back seat, 'Oh don't Dee' she cringed 'Your turning mar guts an'all, ar member when he shit imself in me uncle Davey's mini cab'.
Dee Dee smiled 'Fuck me yeah, ar member that, it put im aat of business for weeks'.
Bradley spat the last morsels from between his teeth and hoisted himself back inside, 'Will you'z two stop goin on abaat Scratty bloody John, please' he begged, wiping the beads of sweat from his top lip.
'Ok silly bollocks' Dee Dee said, tapping his knee, 'Just tell me ya never kissed er'.
Bradley said nothing, pulling away to the sound of beeping horns behind him and trying in vain to extinguish the thoughts of John and Julie's sordid sessions from his mind.
Dee Dee produced a folded piece of paper from inside her bra and sat scrutinizing it under the interior light. 'Woss that Dee?' Maizie asked, craning her neck to see.
'Wunna them papers from the safe' replied Dee Dee, looking closer, 'Summink's been buggin the fuck aatta me'. At the bottom of the document were a list of names and associated signatures, all but one were Arabic and illegible, 'Fitzroy, Fitzroy' she pondered,
'Where the fuck do ar know that name from?' she turned to her friend in the back,
'Eeya Maize your a whizz on the Google net fing aintcha'

'Do what?' Maizie replied, not knowing where the conversation was headed.
'The internet ya doughnut' Dee Dee sighed, 'That Google web your always tappin away at, by the way what are you doin on that fing all the time anyway?' she asked.
'Talkin to blokes' Maizie explained 'There's undreds on there Dee, on them datin sites, most of em are as rough as a badgers arse but there's a few orny ones'.
Dee Dee had never felt the need to trawl the net for men, preferring the direct approach, namely, grabbing a cute guy by the balls, thrusting her bosom under his nose and saying simply, 'Want some?'.
'What?' she asked, 'There's phota's on there and everyfing?'
'Yeah shit loads!' Maizie told Dee Dee, 'No cock shots or anyfing naughty like that though, ar've met a few off there I av, eeya Dee there was this hod carrier from Hoddesdon, Jesus e was fit as fuck mate ar tell ya, Darren iz name was, ar was chattin to im for a coupla weeks, you know the usual stuff, what ya wearing, how bigs ya dick and do ya fancy doggin in me dads Datsun Cherry?'.
Dee Dee high fived her friend, 'Now thas fuckin ardcore that is!' she laughed.
'Yeah not arf' Maizie chuckled, 'We done it in Asda's car park on a Saturday afternoon, it was so funny mate it was like titanic when Leo and Katie whatsername steamed up the windows, we ad four trolly dolly's an arf a dozen Romanian car washers wankin over the mota'.
Dee Dee smiled, 'Thas ardly a turtle wax is it mate' she then remembered the reason for this conversation, 'Oh yeah where was I, right get on the web and look this geezer up will ya' Dee Dee held

the document closer to the light, 'The right onorable Sir Geoffrey Fitzroy, ar wanna know what e's gotta do wiv all this and ow bad e want's these papers back'.

'Less av a look' Maizie said, taking the paper from her and tapping his name into her phone, 'Bit of a poncey name ain it'. it wasn't long before the internets powerful search engine produced several candidates, 'There's a few on ere Dee' Maizie said, zooming in on the text, 'One's a retired Australian naval captain, oh no ang on a mo' Maizie paused for a second, 'No scrub that one e's dead, got bitten in the bog by a funnel web spider apparently, oooh creepy eh, ar faand a snake in the Karzi once, it was me cousin Stewy's, bleedin great fing lookin up at me it was, like a big hissing turd' Dee Dee hadn't a clue what Maizie was going on about, but before she could scold her for going off track Maizie started up again, 'Fuckin fing was always gettin aat it was, Me nan nearly shit erself when it fell out of er baggy knickers in the ironing pile, ar never told im ar faand it though, ar just flushed the bastard daan the bog ar did, ar reckon it must've draaned in piss, but I always av a good look under the rim in case the bleeder's come back, nart ar mean'.

Dee Dee shook her head in despair , 'Ar don't give a toss if you faand a bloody octopus daan there just tell me about the bloke will ya!'.

Maizie pulled herself together, 'Oh yeah sorry Dee, where was i, eeya magine that though' she waffled on, ' An octopus wiv all them tentacle fings gropin yer arse, gives ya the creeps dunnit'.

Dee Dee waved her fist at Maizie 'Ar'll give you summink in a minute you silly bitch!' she cursed,

'Your as bad as Trisha you are, now just tell me about this Geoffrey bloke before ar lose me rag!'.
Maizie tapped at her phone, 'Oh shit ar've lost the signal naah, ang on' she frowned, waving it around the car, 'I ad it a minute ago, oh fuck now ar've dropped it' Maizie groped between her legs on the floor of the car while Dee Dee sat doing her level best to remain calm,
'When you've quite finished fuckin araand Maizie' she said, grinding her teeth.
'GOT IT!' shrieked Maizie, 'Oh look and ar got a full signal an'all, right naah let me see, Fitzroy, Fitzroy, oh yeah ere we are, Sir Geoffrey Fitzroy MP' she paused, 'Bloody ell Dee e'z in the Labor party, look there's a phota of im ere wiv that Blair geeza when e was the guvna'.
'What else does it say?' Dee Dee asked.
'Everyfing' Maizie continued, 'Where e was born, what school e went to, where e lives'
'REALLY!' Dee Dee remarked, pricking up her ears 'Where's that then?'
'Nash Terrace' Maizie replied, sounding pleased with herself, 'Regents Park, number one one five, what else d'you wanna know?'.
'Nufing fanx' Dee Dee said, snatching back the document and tucking it between her breasts once again, 'Thatta do nicely'.
Rounding the corner, Bradley stopped just short of Tibbs's undertakers, still feeling queazy he leapt from the car and scurried into an adjacent mini mart to purchase a carton of juice to wash down the sickly taste of stomach acid.
Trisha and Laura emerged from the family business straightening their clothing, having past the time fornicating in one of Tibbs's silk lined luxury

hardwood coffins. 'Alright Dee mate, ow's it goin?' Trisha cried, skipping toward the car, still in a heady romantic daze, 'This is Laura' she added proudly, 'Member ar told you about er scary lift and the arse washer fingy'.
Laura held out her hand, 'Hi you must be Dee Dee' she smiled, 'Trisha's told me all about you'.
Dee Dee ignored Laura completely, instead she leapt from the car and lunged at her friend, shaking her by the collar, 'Listen you scatty bitch!' she yelled, 'Ar bin tryna get old of you for ages, what the fuck are you playin at?'.
'Sorry Dee!' Trisha said, breaking free, 'Ar bin under cover ain I!'.
'UNDER COVER!' Dee Dee shrieked, 'AR GIVE YOU BLEEDIN UNDER COVER!'.
Laura then intervened, 'I think i'm partly to blame for Trisha's disappearance'.
Dee Dee glared at Trisha's new found love, 'I ain't talkin to you!' she snapped, 'It's coz of your friggin lot we're ere in the first place'.
Trisha stepped between them, 'Ang on a minute Dee she ain't like the uvvers, she's nice and she's gonna elp get Mickey back' she then noticed Bradley toying with his trousers, 'Woss up wiv im anyway?' she asked, diverting the attention away from Laura. Maizie gave her brother a playful pat on the back, 'Oh, scratty john give im a dose!' she said, tongue in cheek.
'WHAT!' Trisha said, knowing full well who scratty was, 'What d'ya mean e give im a dose?'
Bradley leapt to his defense, 'NO E NEVER!' he yelled, 'You'z are winding me up ar swear man!'.
Dee Dee put an arm round Bradley's shoulder and spoke calmly into his ear, 'You fink what ya like

geeza, but next time your licking iz snot off the Chequers tayters you just remember it aint the first time you've sampled his dna'.

Maizie covered her mouth, 'Oooh thas bleedin orrible that is Dee' she mumbled, 'Iss enough to put you off spuds for life'.

The sound of police sirens approaching unsettled Dee Dee, 'Get in the mota, quick!' she told the others. The five of them crammed into Bradley's hatch back and ducked down as the squad car raced by,

'Get off me Maize!' Trisha squealed as she was pinned against the door, 'Ar can't breav and your sittin on me ambag'. Trisha, Maizie and Laura jostled their backsides on the back seat of the tiny car,

'Shut up will ya!' Dee Dee snapped from the front, 'Ar'm tryna fink!'.

'Woss the plan then Dee?' Trisha asked, pushing Maizie's elbow from her ribs, 'Laura know's where Mickey is'.

'Yes' Laura added, 'But if I know my brothers then you don't have much time, that's if he isn't dead already'.

Maizie tapped Dee Dee's shoulder 'What we gonna do Dee?' she asked, fearing for her life,

'They're proper gangsters mate, probly tooled up an'all'.

'Shit yeah' Trisha agreed, 'Ar never fought abaat that, Dee what are we gonna do?'.

Dee Dee reached down between her legs and pulled the sawn off shotgun from beneath her seat, 'We're gonna get Mickey back, thas what we're gonna fuckin do' she said looking at her friends doubting faces, 'If you two want aat then open the door and piss off right naah, ar'm in this shit till the end'.

'But Dee!' Maizie added, shrugging her shoulder, 'We aint got no guns, what we gonna do, bitch slap em!'. Dee Dee rummaged again, this time producing two nine millimeter glock pistols, handing them to her fearful friends 'I aint spent all my money on Dolce and Gabbana ya know'.

'Oh ar know that' Trisha said, stroking the weighty weapon, 'You bought that dildo an'all dintcha'.

Maizie looked her piece over 'Dee I aint never used wunna these before, ar wouldn't know what to do wiv it'.

Trisha brandished her weapon confidently, 'Iss easy Maize mate' she said cocking the pistol 'Ar seen it on CSI Miami'.

Before the word 'No!' could leave Dee Dee's lips Trisha squeezed the trigger and to her complete shock and horror the gun discharged with a deafening bang.

Amid the chaotic few minutes that followed one voice could be heard above all the others, it was Bradley, 'Aaaaaaaaaaarghhh you shot me you stupid fuckin bitch, you shot my fucking leg!'.

Dee Dee, Maizie and Laura each opened their eyes to see Bradley rocking back and forth in his seat clutching his blood soaked left thigh,

'Fuck, fuck, fuck it fuckin urts man!' he cried, 'Ar can't believe you fuckin shot me!'.

Trisha flew into a blind panic, 'Oh shit, shit, shittin shit, i've shittin shot im!' she screamed, waving her arms in the air and while wildly hysterical, squeezed on the trigger once again. A second deafening bang drowned Bradley's cries momentarily, this time sending a hollow point nine millimeter bullet hurtling within a hair of Dee Dee's ear and on through the windscreen leaving a neat hole in the laminated glass in front of her.

'Jesus Trisha you stupid twat!' Dee Dee yelled, snatching the pistol from her, 'Gimmie that fuckin fing will ya before ya kill the bleedin lot of us!'.

Maizie put an arm around Bradley, 'You alright bruv' she asked trembling 'Bloody ell she really has shot you aint she, Trish you dopey fuckin mare!'.

Bradley removed his hand from the wound, 'No ar'm not alright, look at it iss pissin wiv blood and it pissin urts like shit!'.

Laura took the silk scarf from around her neck, 'Here use this as a tourniquet' she said, handing it to Dee Dee, 'We've got to get him to a hospital, Saint Barts isn't far from here'.

Dee Dee wrapped the scarf around Bradley's leg above the wound as tight as she could, 'Stay still will ya' she snapped as he hopped up and down in his seat, 'Ar'm tryna friggin elp ya!'

Laura then climbed from the back and opened Bradley's door, 'Let's get him in the back there's no way he can drive like that'. her scarf had stemmed the flow of blood from Bradley's wound but he was still in considerable pain,

'Ow! wait, wait, slow daan man!' he cried as she tugged at his arm.

Maizie helped him in the back, his joggers now heavily blood soaked, 'You'll be alright bruv' she said in a bid to calm her sibling 'The ospital'll sort you aat'.

Trisha leaned across and slapped Bradley's leg, his injured leg, 'Sorry mate' she smiled 'It just went off in me and'.

Bradley rocked back 'Aaaaaargh fuuuuuck, get away from me will ya!' he screamed, pulling his cap down over his face to mask his tears.

Dee Dee turned and glared at her clumsy friend 'For fuck sake what is it wiv you, can't you do nuffing right?'.

Trisha hung her head, sulking 'Course ar can' she mumbled, wrapping the strap of her handbag around her fingers, 'Ar won a gold rosette for me baton twirlin' she said, struggling to recall her limited achievements, 'And ar got to level eight on angry birds'

Dee Dee and Maizie, no matter how peeved couldn't help but laugh, 'You are a doughnut' Maizie said, shoving her arm.

'Ar tell ya what' Dee Dee chuckled, looking at Trisha in the rear view mirror, 'If them scientists ever get any problems wiv that space shuttle fingy ar don't fink they're gonna be bashing your door daan for the answers mate'.

Trisha looked confused 'Woss a space shuttle when iss at home?'

Dee Dee raised her eyebrows 'Exactly!' she said, knowingly.

Science and the universe was one subject that had captured Dee Dee's imagination and the fact that she found Professor Brian Cox drop dead gorgeous. Her passion for all things celestial was handed down from her doting grandfather who was perhaps the only member of the Dawson family that ever spent any real time with Dee Dee, filling her head with facts about black holes, planet formations and the birth of the universe itself. But Dee Dee's lust for boys and cheap alcohol dashed any hopes of a scientific career however promising, that and the untimely death of her beloved grandfather who suffered a massive stroke while tracking Halley's comet through the night sky. His dying wish was for his ashes to be taken into space aboard a lunar module and distributed above the earths atmosphere, but as the Dawson family was forever financially strapped, Dee Dee had to improvise. She foolishly purchased a job lot of flood damaged Taiwanese fireworks from Dutch Bobby, a wheeler dealer working from the back of his rusting transit van, offering everything from cut price Cuban cigars hand rolled in Romford to musical lavatory brushes that play Simon and Garfunkel's 'Bridge over troubled water' when immersed in the pan.

In the rear garden of her grandfathers humble two bed semi, Dee Dee attached a small bag containing his ashes to a six foot star blazer rocket that promised an electrifying thirty second show at high altitude. 'Seeya gramps' she said, lighting the firework at arms length before racing back to the patio to admire the spectacle, but instead of the glorious send off she had planned and her grandfather had wished for the rogue rocket hissed and crackled for a second or two, and then nothing, 'Oh ar don't bleedin believe it!' she cursed, 'That Dutch twat has fitted me up again!'.

Dee Dee had been duped by Bobby before when she foolishly bought a motorized Spiderman trike for her five year old nephew Dylan. A factory defect meant that the toddlers toy had a much greater top speed than the five miles per hour stated on the side of the box.

Overjoyed to receive his birthday present young Dylan insisted Dee Dee take him to the park. 'Watch me aunty Debra, watch me!' he squealed, mounting the trike and winding back the throttle. Dee Dee readied her camera for a memorable shot but instead of a sedate trundle along the tree lined path, Dylan shot off like an F1 driver in pole position. A panic stricken Dee Dee started after him but with it's faulty top speed now a staggering sixty five miles per hour she stood no chance. The terrified tot clung screaming to the handle bars, first careering through a group of startled pensioners, leaving several of them dazed and bruised and possibly needing hip replacement surgery. Unable to release his grip on the throttle, Dylan then ploughed through a bed of newly planted geraniums, across a courting couples picnic blanket before crashing headlong into an ornate stone fountain where he was tossed over the handles into the freezing weed filled water,

'Come here you!' a furious head gardener said, plucking him from the stagnant pool with his trusty rake.

Approaching the rocket cautiously Dee Dee was filled with loathing for the dodgy dealer and disappointment at having let her grandfather down, but within inches of the reject rocket Dee Dee leapt back suddenly when it spluttered into life, 'Oh shit!' she cried, turning and sprinting clear. The star blazer popped and fizzed sending a pathetic drizzle of sparks onto the lawn below. Dee Dee and the small gathering of friends and family laughed at the miserable display, but their euphoria was short lived as the firework finally showed signs of improvement with an impressive roaring flame belching from the bottom. The cheering crowd braced themselves for the aerial send off, there were 'Oooooh's!' and 'Aaaaaah's' as it left the ground on it's heavenly accent, but at approximately ten feet from the scorched earth it exploded in a gigantic ball of blinding light and began it's colorful sequence. Dee Dee and the others fell over each other fleeing to the

relative safety of the kitchen where they watched aghast from the window.
'Fuck me!' Dee Dee said, clasping her hands to her face, horrified at the havoc the defective rocket was causing. Everything in theirs and their adjacent neighbours gardens was burnt to a crisp, including two cats, a rabbit and a dozen prize koi carp boiled in their pond. The fire brigade were called to extinguish three sheds, a loft conversion, a line full of clothes and a newly laid hardwood deck, all in all an unforgettable farewell to an unforgettable man.
Laura drove the short distance to St Bartholomew's hospital with Bradley still reeling from his gun shot wound. Accident and emergency was brimming with the sick and injured with a host of ailments ranging from chronic diarrhea, festering boils, broken bones and even a young gay man with a smart phone stuck firm in his rectum, taking continuous pictures of his small intestine.
'Pull up over there!' Dee Dee told Laura who parked a short way away. Hopping out of the car she held Bradley's door open 'Come on silly nuts, aat ya get' she said, unsympathetically 'And don't tell em who shot ya'.
Bradley dragged himself out of the back seat 'You not comin in wiv me' he moaned, clutching his wound, he then turned to his sister, 'Maize you ain't just gonna leave me ere are ya?'.
Dee Dee shoved Bradley clear and climbed back inside 'Get yer arse in there ya pillock we gotta go get Mickey, we'll come back and check on ya later'.
Maizie leaned out of the window 'Go on Brad, get yaself sorted, just don't tell em it was Trisha!'.
'Nar don't say that!' Trisha added, 'Me mum'll kill me'.
Laura drove away leaving Bradley to limp into the

hospital, his leg bleeding profusely again leaving a trail behind him.

'Yes can I help' the young lady at reception asked.

'Ar bin shot innit' Bradley replied resting against the counter,

the receptionist didn't bat an eye 'Name?' she asked, tapping at her keyboard.

'What?' Bradley said, thinking it may be best for him to adopt a false identity.

'What's your name?' she said again, frustrated at the queue now forming behind him 'You do know your name don't you?'

'Oh, er yeah course! said Bradley wracking his brain and looking round for inspiration 'It's er, it's em' just then a porter crashed through the doors with a barrow, strapped to which was a bottle of liquid nitrogen, 'Das it!' Bradley gasped, 'Iss Nitro innit!' having thought long and hard for several months for a suitable stage name for himself, the would be rapper high five'd the startled porter 'Das wicked geez, cheers man!'.

The now irate and riled receptionist tapped her biro on the plate glass screen 'Sir we have people waiting, if I could just have your name!'

Bradley leaned across and smiled 'Iss Nitro babe, D J Nitro' the more he said it the more he liked it 'Nitro, yeah D J Nitro!'.

The girl looked at him in disbelief 'Nitro, your telling me your name is Nitro' she smirked.

'Yeah course innit' Bradley insisted 'Put it daan, D J Nitro'

'Ok it's just an odd name that's all' she tapping at her computer, 'Mr D J Nitro' she mumbled, raising her eyebrows 'Right now what's the nature of your visit, is it your leg?' she peered over the counter at his

sodden jogging bottoms 'What's the problem Mr er, Nitro?'
Bradley had no intention of telling her he'd been shot by a girl, that would destroy what little street cred he had, 'Ar bin Tupac'd innit' he said, using his right hand as a make shift pistol.
The young receptionist stopped typing 'I'm sorry, you've been what?' she asked, bemused.
Bradley continued 'Arm tellin ya man, they tried to take me aat in a drive by'.
'Who's they?' the girl asked.
Bradley leaned a little closer and lowered his voice 'Ar reckon it was Dizzy and Tinchy man, they put a hit on me coz of mar bitchin Lyrics'.
'You mean you've been shot' the receptionist replied, her hand hovering over the security button 'Have you informed the police?'
Bradley sucked on his teeth, 'Course not bitch I aint no snitch!' he then grabbed a pen and paper from her desk 'Hang on let me write dat daan, ar use it on me next album' he hurriedly scribbled, mumbling 'Ain't no snitch, bitch' he tossed her pen back, 'Ar'm tellin ya, das platinum dat is' he smiled 'Ar might even give you a mention if ya play ya cards right, nart ar mean' he checked out her name badge 'Kayley, yeah ar can dig dat, let me lay dis on ya girl' Bradley broke into an off the cuff rap whilst thrusting his groin at the counter,

'Me love me girl Kayley
me give it to er daily
dis way, dat way
ar cover her in Bailey's,
ar lick her like a lolly
and ar suck her like a sweet

ar lend the bitch mar brolly
when it's raining in the street,
Kayley, Kayley, ar give it to her
daily'

Bradley finished to a round of applause from the waiting room and a blushing smile from the receptionist. She pulled herself together and called for a wheelchair and then summoned security. Bradley was wheeled through two sets of double doors to a treatment room where a group of doctors and a nurse were waiting, 'Gun shot wound to the upper left thigh' the porter said, helping Bradley onto the table. The doctors hurriedly gathered their sterile instruments together and set about cutting the leg of Bradley's sweat pants,
'What ya doin blud, them's Nikey's man!' he protested.
A doctor pushed his hand away, 'I'm sorry young man but if we don't treat your wound right away, there's a good chance you could bleed to death' swabs were then hastily applied to the seeping bullet hole. A nurse handed the doctor a hypodermic syringe which he duly squirted in the air.
Bradley backed away 'What ya gonna do wiv dat man?' he asked, nervously, 'I aint avin no needles bruv!'.
The doctor put a hand on Bradley's shoulder, 'Sir you need this injection to numb the area so we can remove the bullet'
Bradley pushed the syringe away 'Fuck dat man, I aint gettin none of dat RSPCA, das proper fucked up shit man!'
'You mean MRSA' said the doctor, wrestling with Bradley, 'This is for your own good I assure you'.

'Yeah right!' Bradley scoffed, 'Me nan went into ospital for a toe job or summink, got that SMA shit from a dirty bed pan and ad to av her blinkin leg cut off, so don't be comin near me wiv no needle dat you just pulled out of a junkies arse man'.

The nurse intervened 'I assure you sir all our equipment meets strict hygiene guidelines set out by the department of health'.

'Ar don't give a shit!' Bradley said, defiantly 'You aint sticking dat scanky fing in me bitch!'

The doctor was beginning to lose his cool 'Listen!' he snapped, 'If you don't have this injection I promise you you'll be in considerable pain when we operate'.

Bradley swatted the needle from his hand 'I aint scared bro, i'z an urban warrior, just get the ting aat will ya!'

The doctor turned to his assistant, 'Will you note that the patient has refused a local anesthetic please' his assistant nodded. With Bradley smiling confidently the doctor plucked his forceps from the tray, mopped the blood clear once more and gently inserted them into the open wound.

Bradley immediately tensed up and let out an agonizing scream 'GIMME THE NEEDLE, GIMME THE FUCKIN NEEDLE MAN!'. The doctor smiled, removed the forceps and collected another syringe from the tray.

After a probing forty minute operation to remove the bullet and stitch Bradley's wound in which he, quite un-warrior like cried like a teething baby and called several times for his mummy, he was finally wheeled from the treatment room to a private ward where two police officers and a security guard were waiting to interview him.

'Mr Nitro' one of the officers said, tongue in cheek, 'Is this your real name sir?' he examined the notes on the end of Bradley's bed.

'Yeah course man!' said Bradley, proudly 'D J Nitro, cool innit blud'

'If you say so sir' the detective replied, taking out his notebook 'Right then Mr Nitro we've had reports that you've been shot, would you like to tell us exactly what happened'.

'Yeah das right' Bradley said, lifting his gown to expose his dressing 'But they was a shit shot innit, or some kind of dwarf hobbit fing dat couldn't shoot no higher'.

The officer scribbled Bradley's outlandish statement feverishly 'Ar you saying this was premeditated sir'. the second officer piped up.

'Ar weren't medicated man' Bradley protested, 'Ar don't touch dat shit bro, well maybe ar did once but ar weren't gonna let dat little ginger shit beat me in the sack race, ar took a double dose of me mums ormone tablets, set a new school record and grew three bra sizes in a week, ar tell ya man I ad some fun wiv dem puppies, two mumfs I ad em, mind you dat underwire gizmo fing takes some gettin used to ar tell ya'.

The two officers stood stunned for a moment, 'Yes well em' on of them coughed, 'It was obviously a planned hit, is there anything else you can tell us?'

'Look' Bradley sighed, 'All ar know is dat someone tried to take me aat, it was a drive by man, proper gangster stuff an'all'.

'A drive by you say' the first officer said, turning on his radio in readiness for a vehicle check on the police national computer, 'Can you give us any details, make, model, registration perhaps'.

'Yeah' Bradley replied, keen to elaborate on his concocted story, 'It was a bloody great Hummer, a stretch one like Snoop Dogs, yellow it was, wiv blacked aat winda's and bitchin wheels, ar didn't get the reg coz they JFK'd me from behind bruv'.
One of the officer sat on the end of Bradley's bed 'Do you know of anyone who would want to harm you' he asked, mulling over Bradley's ridiculous story, 'Anybody at all'.
'Well just abaat every rival rapper' Bradley explained 'Ar know they want me aat of the way man, coz ar'm a fret innit, they know when ar go up against em ar'm gonna take everyfing they got, Mobbo's, Brits, Grammy's the lot, even their smokin ollywood wives blud!'.
The officers had heard enough and turned to leave 'Ok Mr Nitro we'll be in touch if there are any developments' one of them said, following his colleague out the door, 'We'll put out a description of the vehicle, it shouldn't be too hard to find, there aren't too many yellow Hummers around with, what was it?' he checked his notes, 'Oh yeah, bitchin wheels' he laughed along with his fellow officer.
Bradley lay convalescing in hospital relishing every moment of his new found notoriety, recounting his ever exaggerated story to young gullible nurses and visiting newspaper reporters. As he saw it he was now a celebrity and the media attention would be just the catalyst he'd been waiting for to launch his music career, 'Listen!' he told the tabloid journalists, 'They got Biggy and Tupac yeah, but they didn't get Fiddy Cent and me coz we'z to fly for dem hater's ya know what ar'm sayin blud!'.

At the same time Dee Dee and the others were pulling up several car lengths from the entrance to the Tibbs's dockside warehouse,
'That's it there' Laura said, pointing to a set of black buckled wrought iron gates. The yard beyond was awash with water filled potholes from the recent rains and rampant hardy weeds sprung from the ruptured tarmac to reclaim the land.
The girls were about to step from the car when another of the Tibbs's funeral Limo's overtook them and stopped at the gates.
'Get down!' Laura yelled, recognizing her brothers gorilla's. A muscle bound monster of a man got out and undid the heavy padlock, pushed the gates aside and ushered the car inside The gates were locked behind him, but only after he had looked both ways along the road giving Bradley's car the once over. Dee Dee peered cautiously over the dashboard to see the man turn and head for the warehouse entrance.
'That was blinkin close!' Maizie said, emerging from the floor of the car brandishing her pistol, 'Ar was shittin meself Dee'.
'Yeah me an'all' Dee Dee replied, checking the bullets in her gun. It was then that she noticed a hole in the chain link fence beside them, a hole big enough for them to squeeze through, 'You wait ere' she told Laura 'Keep the mota runnin'.
'Ok' Laura nodded, secretly relieved, knowing full well what her brothers were capable of, 'If you need me though' she told Trisha 'Please call me at once, and do be careful'.
'Ar will!' Trisha replied, patting Laura's shoulder.
The three stepped from the car and huddled by the fence. 'Psssst Dee!' Trisha whispered, changing

places with Maizie, 'Can I av me gun back naah, ar might need it'.

Dee Dee took out the pistol and thrust it into Trisha's hand 'Eeeya, just be bleedin careful' she snapped, 'Remember who's on your bleedin side'. Dee Dee bent over and pushed her head and shoulders through the hole, the jagged wire tugging at her clothes, but suddenly she heard the familiar sound of a gun being cocked and turned quickly to see Trisha toying with the deadly firearm, not realizing she was pointing it at her friend, 'What the fuck are you doin?' she snapped, 'If you shoot me in the arse ar'll fuckin kill ya ya dozy cow, naah put it away till we get in there!'.

Once inside the yard the three ducked into a derelict out building and watched the entrance through a broken widow. The night was cold and damp causing the girls to shiver in their skimpy atire, 'Ar'm scared Dee' Maizie said' clinging to Dee Dee's arm 'What we gunna do?'

'Ar dunno yet' Dee Dee told her as she watched two men drag somebody from the rear of the car and manhandle them inside,

Trisha looked around and turned up her nose at the acrid stench of burnt tyres and tortured metal from the adjacent scrap yard. Dee Dee and her friends then froze as the yards ravenous Alsatian's barking pierced the eerie silence, making the hairs on their necks stand on end. The dog, which was free to roam around the piles of half dismantled cars and iron girders throughout the night had seen them and was up on it's hind legs biting savagely at the rotting timber fencing that divided the two premises, almost shaking the panels free with every menacing lunge.

'Thas it ar'm off' Maizie said, turning tail, 'Ar bleedin ate big dogs, ar was pinned to a tree and sexually assaulted by a Golden Retriever when ar was fourteen, fucked up a bleedin good pair of tights an'all, the bleeda'.

Dee Dee grabbed her arm 'Get back ere will ya!' she snapped 'We aint come all this way for you to piss ya soddin knickers at the first little fing'

'But Deeee' Maizie whimpered,

'But nuffin!' Dee Dee said before Maizie had a chance to explain 'You got a fuckin gun in yer and aincha, if the mutt comes near ya put a bullet in it's bollocks'.

'Aaaaah ya can't do that' Trisha protested, coming from an animal loving family 'You just gotta stand up to em, show em you aint scared and tap em on the nose if they're naughty'.

Dee Dee and Maizie both looked across the yard at the wild eyed slathering beast chewing chunks of wood from the fence to get at them and at the same time both said 'Fuck that!'.

Suddenly the warehouse door opened, the girls ducked out of sight as Jimmy hurled a large spanner in the dogs direction 'Shut up ya noisey fucker!' he yelled. The spanner clattered on the fence sending the petrified guard dog sprinting into the labyrinth of light iron and steel with it's tail tucked firmly between it's legs.

'Naah thas how ya tap it's bleedin nose' Dee Dee said under her breath. Jimmy stepped back inside slamming the corrugated door behind him. 'Come on you two' Dee Dee whispered making her way across the yard negotiating the puddles on the way,

Trisha and an apprehensive Maizie tottered behind her in their high heeled Gucci and Prada boots, 'Ar bet there's rats ere and everyfing' Maizie said, looking over her shoulder 'This place is probly crawlin wiv em'.

Trisha smiled 'Me cousin Tyrone ad a pet rat, e used to take daan the pub wiv im and give it a cherry brandy, Rooney e called it coz e'z a Man U supporter, anyway after five or six cherry b's the bleedin fing used to do this ilarious little rat dance on the bar, bit like that curly kid from One direction, then chase it's tail for ten minutes and crash aat in the slop tray'.

Maizie had to laugh 'You crack me up ya know that Trish' she said, stopping for a moment 'Here's us heading into gawd knows what and your chatting shit abaat rats and One direction'.

Dee Dee looked behind to see her two friends having a full blown conversation in the middle of the yard, bathed in the mid summer moonlight.

Trisha continued to ramble 'Oh but you must admit they are cute though Maize'

'What?' Maizie asked, 'One direction?'

Trisha laughed 'No ya muppet, rats, ar love their squeaky little noses don't you'.

'No ar bleedin don't' Maizie shuddered 'Orrible little bleeders, they run up ya leg and bite ya whatsit they do'.

'Ooooh whatsit's' Trisha said, her face lighting up 'Ar used to love them when ar was a baby, ar used to suck em for ages till it looked like ar'd ad a soddin spray tan'.

Dee Dee had walked back and was now within earshot of the other two 'What the fuck are you dozy pair of bitch's doin?' she said, finding it hard to restrain herself.

'Just avin a natter Dee' Trisha said, oblivious to Dee Dee's wrath 'Eeya you aint seen Tyrone's rat av ya, funny little fucker it is'
Dee Dee stared at her in disbelief 'What?' she said, feeling her blood boil 'Listen we aint got time for this bullshit just get yer arses into gear, we gotta get Mickey for fuck sake!'.
'Yeah come on she's right' Maizie said, starting after Dee Dee. The pair had only walked a few paces when they turned to see that Trisha hadn't moved and instead was tapping away at her mobile phone which lit up her face.
'Trish!' Maizie called back 'What naah?'
Trisha answered without looking up 'Arm just textin me cousin' I aint seen im in ages, see how Rooney's gettin on'.
'Rooney?' Dee Dee asked, 'Who the fuck is Rooney?'
'Iss Tyrone's rat Dee' Maizie said, knowing full well what her friends reaction would be,
'A fuckin rat!' Dee Dee growled 'Ar'm gunna kill er, ar'm gunna bloody kill er!'. Maizie quickly stepped between them preventing a livid Dee Dee from attacking Trisha, she looked over her shoulder whilst restraining Dee Dee's flaying arms 'Put the bloody phone away will ya, you soppy mare!' she told the hapless Trisha who tapped a couple more letters and then pressed send,
'There ar've done it' she smiled then looked up at her friends furious expressions, 'What?' she said innocently 'Eeya!' she then added, opening facebook 'D'ya fink ar got time to update mar status?' but then seeing the pair both lurch toward her with clenched fists and gritted teeth, she quickly popped the phone into her pocket 'Ar do it later' she said side stepping

the girls and making for the warehouse 'Well come on!' she said looking back 'We aint got all blinkin night!'.

Dee Dee and Maizie followed her, utterly incensed at her farcical behavior, having put up with it for as long as they cared to remember, 'One of these days' Dee Dee cursed 'One of these bleedin days!'

'Look at er Dee' Maizie said, watching Trisha checking her reflection in a watery hole and adjusting her hair 'Av you ever seen such a doughnut in all ya life'.

Dee Dee's temper subsided and a smile grew on her face 'No I aint mate' she told a grinning Maizie 'She's got fuck all between her ears thas for sure'. Maizie agreed and Together with Trisha they crept toward a warehouse window,

'Ar can't see' Trisha moaned, being an inch or so shorter than her friends 'Woss appnin?'.

Dee Dee and Maizie wiped the grime from the glass and peered inside 'Oh shit!' Dee Dee gasped, recognizing the figure that had been dragged from the Tibbs's car, it was Mickey's sister Marcie,

'Bleedin ell Dee!' Maizie said, turning to her friend 'This is some fucked up shit ain it'.

Inside, Marcie who was sobbing uncontrollably with a knife at her throat held by the psychotic Jimmy Tibbs begged for the savage beating of her brother to stop. Billy's patients was wearing woefully thin, 'Tell me where the fuckin stone is' he snarled 'Or trust me ar'll get mar bruvva to open your sister up like a can of pissin peaches you slag!'.

Jimmy drew the stiletto blade across Marcie's neck, 'Ar'v always wanted to do a bird Bill' he said menacingly, then whispered in Marcie's ear 'Your all gobby cunts, fit for fuckin and fuck all else'.

Roland took a half eaten pie from the warehouse fridge and a can of cola 'Result!' he said tuckin in,
'Oy fat lad!' Billy growled 'Leave it aat will ya, thas some poor fuckers lunch!'
Roland took another huge bite and put the paltry remains back into the fridge before opening the can 'But Bill me guts are rumblin, ar need me calories you know that, dad reckoned ar should've ad one of them gastric band fingys, wodda you fink?'
'Wodo ar fink?' Billy said, his hand dripping with Mickeys blood 'Ar fink you shoulda bin draaned at fuckin berf, look at the state of ya, you got more rolls than Greggs ya cunt'.
Roland looked down at his stomach, trying to suck in an inch or two, 'Ar reckon ar've lost a bit though Bill' he said proudly 'Ar'v bin eatin a lot more salad lately, ar reckon it's done me the worlda good'
Jimmy then piped up ' Yeah right!' he scoffed 'What abaat the seven paanda doner meat wrapped raand it ya toby!'
Roland took a step toward Jimmy 'Don't call me a toby Jim!' he said angrily, he then turned to Billy 'Bill tell im I aint no toby!'
Billy prodded Roland's chest with a rigid finger 'You are a mug Rolly' he said wiping the blood from his hand across the breast pocket of Roland's jacket 'You've always bin a mug and you always will be, look atcha, you aint fit to be a Tibbs'.
Roland backed away, his bottom lip quivering, 'Dad wouldn't let you say that to me' he told his brother 'He woulda took the strap to ya thas for sure'.
Billy lunged at his Brother swiping him across the face with the back of his bloody hand, having taken more than a few beatings from his ruthless father when he was alive, 'You shut your fuckin maaf boy or

so elp me they'll find your bloated arse floatin in that dock tomorra!'.
Jimmy laughed out loud 'Yeah, like Moby fuckin Dick!'.
Billy turned to Jimmy with a cold hard look of hatred 'Shut it you or you'll be bleedin joinin im' he said snatching the can from Roland's hand 'Gimme that!' he then proceeded to pour the remains over Mickeys head, washing the congealed blood into his swollen eyes.
Marcie struggled to break free from Jimmy's grip 'Let us go pleeeease!' she begged 'Whatever this is abaat we don't know nuffing honest, just don't urt him anymore'.
'Urt im' Billy laughed 'I aint even started to urt im believe me darlin'.
Marcie lost her temper 'Your all fuckin animals that's what you are!' she yelled, feeling the blade cut a little deeper in the process.
Billy stormed towards her grabbing a handful of her hair and wrenching her head back, 'Your fuckin right!' he growled 'I am a fuckin animal'.
Mickey, now semi conscious tugged at his bonds unable to speak with three broken teeth and a fractured jaw, he could only mumble and rock back and forth on his chair. 'Woss that Mickey?' Billy asked 'You tryna tell me summink, like where my fuckin ruby is by any chance, or do you want me to cut this slag a new smile'.
Marcie cleared her throat and spat into Billy's face defiantly which immediately enraged the gangland boss, 'YOU FUCKIN BITCH!' he screamed, tearing Marcie from Jimmy's grasp, peeling his right arm back and unleashing a clenched fist into her face sending her crashing into a stack of mahogany

coffins. Mickey cried out as his sisters head struck a brass handle and she was knocked unconscious. Billy wiped the spit from his face and sauntered toward Mickey 'Naah where was we?' he said, clenching his fist once more, but before he could deliver a blow he was approached by one of his men who had been standing guard, 'Eeya guv!' he said, sheepishly, 'D'ya mind if me and the lads get off, there's a big game tonight at scotch Andy's, word is some city prick's have put a shit loada dough on the table, we're gonna buy in and turn im over'.
Scotch Andy ran a crooked small time casino in Battersea luring in big spending Asian gamblers and wealthy businessmen from London's square mile with more money than brain cells.
'Yeah go on piss off' Billy said, watching them head for the door 'Don't forget ar want mar cut' he called after them.
'No worries guv, catch ya later' one of them replied closing the door behind them. Dee Dee, Maizie and Trisha ducked behind a skip and watched the heavies climb into one of the cars and leave.
'Thas better' Dee Dee whispered, assuming the odds had been narrowed in their favor.
'Oh yeah!' Maizie said, unsure 'We still got two complete nutters and Jabba the friggin utt in there don't forget'.
Peering through the window once more, Dee Dee could see Billy slapping Marcie's face and dragging her to her feet 'Come ere you!' he said, shoving her back into Jimmy's arms 'Hold er!' he added, taking out his own knife,
'Ar'm bored wiv this naah Mickey' he said, holding Marcie's left hand down on the table and in a flash

slicing off her little finger. Marcie let out a gurgling cry before fainting and slumping back onto Jimmy.
'Fuck we gotta get in there!' Dee Dee said, making for the door with a determined stride.
'Ang on Dee!' Maizie called after her 'Less fink abaat this!'
'Woss there to fink abaat' Dee Dee stopped and replied 'Marcie and Mickey'll be dead if we don't do summink quick!' then to their surprise Trisha barged past them
'You two wait ere, ar know what to do' she said, pounding on the door.
'For fuck sake Trish!' Dee Dee replied.
Trisha stopped Dee Dee in her tracks 'Dee ar can do this, onest, just be ready when ar need ya, naah get daan'. Before Dee Dee could intervene the door opened and Jimmy emerged, startled at first to see her
'What the?' he gasped, looking Trisha up and down as she struck an alluring pose.
'Ello ansum' Trisha smiled 'Want business?'
'What?' Jimmy asked again.
Billy then called from the warehouse 'Jimmy who the fuck is it?' he gripped his knife tightly for fear of intruders.
'Ar dunno!' Jimmy replied, eyeing Trisha's shapely legs 'Ar fink iss a brass'.
Billy relaxed momentarily 'Well tell er to fuck off!' he said, eager to continue Mickey's interrogation.
Trisha purred and toyed with the lapel of Jimmy's jacket 'Ar love a big strong bloke ar do'.
Jimmy looked over her shoulder across the deserted yard, 'What you doin raand ere darlin, shouldn't you be workin the west end?'.

Trisha pulled her pocket inside out 'Ar carn afford the bus fare' she told him, stretching the neck of her blouse seductively with the other hand to reveal an inch of breast 'Times are ard, and so are you' she smiled, running a finger along Jimmy's obvious bulge.
'JIMMY!' Billy barked, 'What the fucks goin on?'
Jimmy ignored his brother 'Ow much?' he asked Trisha, who thought for a moment and looked round at the Tibbs's car, 'Fifty quid' she said, 'And we can do it in ya mota!'.
'OY JIMMY!' Billy yelled, at Mickey's side 'Get rid of er and get back in ere!'.
'Ang on' Jimmy told Trisha and ducked back inside 'Look Bill' he told his brother 'Iss bin fuckin ages since I ad a shag, so ar'm gonna sort er aat in the back of the mota alright'.
Although Billy loathed his brother at times he knew that since his bitter break up with his wife, Jimmy had never looked at another woman, focusing his attention instead on drink and hard narcotics. 'Go on then but fuckin urry up!' Billy told him 'And don't forget to bag it up, you don't know who's been up them slags'.
Roland then piped up 'Can I av a go Jim?' he said, reaching beneath his hulking belly to jiggle the zip of his trousers.
'Fuck off Rolly!' Jimmy laughed 'The last time you saw your cock Elvis was alive and muvva was changing your shitty arse!'.
Billy had to laugh 'He's right fad lad' he joked 'Ar mean when was the last time you got your end away?'.

Roland tried desperately to defend himself 'That aint fair, arv ad loadsa birds I av, what about that tart from the chippy?'
'Who, greasy Jean?' Jimmy laughed 'That miserable fat bitch, your avin a laugh aintcha, she's bigger than you, stinks of chip fat and warms the saveloys in the gusset of her knickers, yeah she's a real quality bird bruv'.
Jean was as bad as Jimmy had portrayed her, with stinking sweaty pits, a prickly moustache and nicotine stained fingers. School kids had taunted her for years, standing in the doorway of the 'Codfather' chippy in Lewisham laughing and singing 'Cheer up greasy Jean' and firing wads of soaked tissue paper through straws at her.
'She aint that bad!' Roland said, throwing his arms in the air, 'Your just jealous Jim coz Gina fucked off wiv er personal trainer, what was iz name, Guy or summink poncey like that'. Roland had just overstepped the mark by a mile, Jimmy's wife had left him for her gym trainer after a torrid five year affair leaving him a broken man vowing to cut out the fitness instructors internal organs and nail his bloody carcass to the Hammersmith flyover for all to see.
'YOU FUCKIN CUNT!!' Jimmy screamed, charging towards Roland who backed away nervously, but before he could tear his brother apart Billy stepped between them, holding Jimmy back, 'Leave it!' he barked.
'Fuck off Bill!' Jimmy snarled, 'This is nuffin to do wiv you!'.
Billy pushed Jimmy toward the door 'Piss off outside and poke that whore will ya, ar'll deal with this idiot'.
Jimmy pointed a cursing finger at Roland and stormed out of the warehouse, slammed the door,

grabbed Trisha's arm and dragged her toward the car, 'Come on then' he said, still seething 'Arll give ya firty quid and no more!'.
Billy shook Roland violently by the shoulders 'One of these days he's gonna fuckin kill you you moron, ar told ya never to mention Gina didn't I, everyone knows she was a slag, fuckin ell even ar banged it but ya don't rub it in iz bleedin face'.
'Sorry Bill ar forgot' Roland squealed, fearing a beating, he then paused, 'Ang on are you sayin you done Gina, you lucky sod, ar tried it on wiv er but she wouldn't av it'.
Billy stepped back and looked at his brother 'And your actually surprised about that' he joked 'Fuck me Rolly your ficker than ar fought'.
Meanwhile Jimmy was about to throw Trisha onto the back seat of the car when he noticed the butt of her pistol sticking out of her jacket pocket, 'What the fuck?' he said, snatching it from her 'Woss this for?' he then thought for a second 'Ang on, were you gonna turn me over you fuckin bitch!'
'No, no are weren't!' Trisha replied, not knowing quite what to do.
Jimmy grinned, tossed the gun over his shoulder and unzipped his flies 'Well ar'm gonna turn you over you slag' he said, spinning her round and bending her over, forcing her face down onto the leather rear seat and tore at her knickers, Trisha kicked and screamed but Jimmy was a powerful man,
Suddenly Dee Dee and Maizie rushed from their hiding place with their guns trained on Jimmy's head, 'Get the fuck away from er!' Dee Dee barked.
Jimmy was stunned to see two more cute girls, 'What the fucks goin on?' he gasped, with his manhood still in his hand, then seeing the guns he quickly pulled

out his knife, dragged Trisha to her feet and held it at her throat. 'What ever this is you better fink seriously abaat what your doin' he told them. Dee Dee and Maizie stopped in their tracks,

'Thas better' Jimmy said, bending Trisha over once again, 'Naah put them fuckin guns daan and get in this mota, when ar'm finished wiv er your gettin some'. Jimmy then heard a familiar voice behind him and the click of a cocked pistol

'You heard her Jimmy' It was Laura who had become concerned as the three girls had been gone for some time 'Get the fuck away from her!'

'Laura!' Jimmy said, hardly believing his eyes, 'What the fuck are you doin ere?'.

Laura raised the pistol and pointed it directly at her brother 'I won't tell you again Jimmy' she threatened 'Get you hands off her'.

Jimmy had a deep hatred of women since Gina left and was now being attacked on all sides by them, 'You aint gonna use that piece Laura so piss off back to ya dyke mates, arm busy' Jimmy turned away from her and lifted Trisha's skirt once again.

'JIMMY!' Laura yelled, her hand now shaking.

Jimmy stopped a second time and turned around 'Ar said piss off' he said raising his blade to her.

Laura could feel her finger tightening on the trigger to the point of no return 'And I said get the fuck away from her' she said, closing her eyes and applying a little more pressure. The pistol jolted in her hand firing three shots in succession into Jimmy's chest, 'Oh my god!' she cried, not knowing what had just happened, opening her eyes she saw jimmy standing there looking at the blood oozing from three holes in his jacket before staggering back onto the car and

sliding along the rear wing and onto the floor, his face half submerged in an oily puddle.
Laura crumbled to her knees as Trisha hoisted up her tattered knickers and ran towards her 'Laura!' Trisha said, kneeling in front of her and throwing her arms around her 'Iss alright babe, iss alright!'.
Hearing the gun shots Billy and Roland rushed to the door 'JIMMY!' Billy shouted, seeing his brother lying beside the car, Maizie and Dee Dee instinctively turned and began firing in their direction, every shot missing by yards but enough to send the brothers fleeing back inside, 'Come on!' Dee Dee said, sprinting for the door,
Maizie followed behind, 'Trish come on!'
Trisha took the gun from Laura's shaking hands, kissed her forehead and followed her friends, the three of them bursting into the warehouse screaming at the top of their voices, which would be enough to startle the hardest of gangster.
'Shit!' Roland cried, seeing them enter. Unarmed he ran back through the kitchen striking the panic par on the fire escape door which lead to the dockside jetty, unaware that his brother had been fatally wounded. Trisha, seeing him as easy prey made after him while Dee Dee and Maizie, with their guns poised looked around the place for Billy who had taken refuge behind a pile of oak planks. Billy searched his pockets but had left his own gun in the cars glove box 'Fuck!' he cursed, looking around, he then picked up a nail gun and checked it's half loaded magazine of galvanized four inch wire nails, 'Fuck yeah' he said leaping up, holding back the safety catch and firing wildly in the direction of the girls who quickly ducked down while firing back, splintering the oak.

Maizie peered around the tool box she was tucked behind and immediately felt the stinging pain of a nail penetrating her right shoulder, 'Aaaargh fuck Deeee!' she cried, reeling back. Seeing her friend down Dee Dee stood up and walked calmly toward the wood pile firing shot after shot at it. Billy fired the last of his nails narrowly missing Dee Dee's face before hurling the gun in her direction, then did something he'd never done in his entire life, he ran toward the door like a frightened rabbit and out into the yard pursued by Dee Dee.

Laura ducked out of sight, watching her brother sprint by with Dee Dee still hot on his tail with her smoking pistol. Billy leapt into the car and fumbled for the keys and with his eyes firmly fixed on his dead brother he started the car and roared across the yard and out of the gate. Dee Dee fired the last of her bullets in his direction before sinking to her knees 'Fuck' she said, in total shock at what had just occurred, then coming to her senses she called out 'Maizie!' and ran back to the warehouse to see her friend helping Marcie to her feet with a blood soaked right arm, 'You alright mate?' she asked, rushing to her,

'Yeah ar fink so' Maizie nodded 'You get Mickey will ya'.

Dee Dee looked at Mickey's battered face, 'Shit Mick ar'm sorry mate' she said, loosening the ropes around his wrists and steadying him as he slumped forward, bruised and exhausted after his torturous ordeal.

Trisha meanwhile was gaining on Roland on the dimly lit jetty lined with cargo ships and tug boats. Roland was sweating profusely, looking over his shoulder occasionally in fear of his life. Soon he had run out of jetty and found himself with his back to a wooden rail. Throwing his arms in the air Roland begged for mercy, 'Please wait!' he cried, seeing Trisha hobbling toward him in her heels brandishing the gun 'Ar never done nuffin onest, please don't shoot!'.

Trisha stopped and pointed the gun at Roland's forehead with the thought of Mickey and Marcie's horrific wounds still fresh in her mind, 'You orrible fat fuck!' she said with a look of disgust while cocking the weapon.

Roland closed his eyes and covered his face pushing back hard against the rail which was not designed to withstand such forces. Before they both knew what was happening there was a cracking sound as the rail disintegrated sending Roland tumbling backward over the edge. 'Shit, shit elp me!' he cried, clawing hopelessly at the splintered timber as he fell. Trisha peered over the edge in time to see the screaming Tibbs brother splash down in the freezing murky Thames, sinking at first then bobbing up like a cork. Coughing and spitting out the rancid water polluted by the nearby glue factory Roland thrashed around calling out to Trisha, 'Help me please!' he begged 'Help ar can't swim!' this was true, because of his embarrassing physique Roland had never ventured inside a public baths in his life. Trisha stood and watched pondering whether to shoot him like a fish in a barrel but the turning tide had other plans for the floundering fatty, 'Elllllllp, please get elp!' he cried as the swirling river began to pull him out into deeper water where the under currents ran much faster. Roland's fate was now sealed, the Thames toyed with him for several minutes swirling him this way and that before sucking him down into it's darkened depths. Roland's reaching hand disappeared

beneath the waves just as a pleasure boat crammed with late night revelers past over the scene, all of them too drunk to notice him. Trisha smiled and headed back to her friends.
'Trish fank fuck!' Dee Dee said, on seeing her 'You alright mate?'
'Yeah course' Trisha smiled 'But ar'm afraid the big lump's aquarobics classes were a disaster' Trisha then felt a rush of emotion and raising her pistol in the air she let out a whooping cry 'WHAT A FUCKIN BUZZ!' she yelled. Dee Dee and Maizie did the same and whilst looking deep into one another's eyes the three teenage girls, for the first time in their lives felt empowered, unstoppable and most of all, united.
Dee Dee helped the battered Mickey to his feet, supporting him on her shoulder 'You shoulda told em abaat us Mick' she said, looking at his wounds 'Look at the state of ya', Mickey slipped his arm around Dee Dee's neck, shook his head and hugged her tightly knowing that she and her friends had undoubtedly saved his life and that of his sister. Mickey was an old school thief that would rather die than grass on somebody, let alone his friends, something that DI Pritcher had grown to loath about him no matter how much pressure and intimidation he applied.
Marcie ran sobbing to her brother and took him from Dee Dee 'Thank you Dee' she said, kissing his swollen cheek and cupping her bleeding hand to her chest. Dee Dee then looked over at Trisha for a moment,
'What?' Trisha said, feeling a little uneasy as though Dee Dee were about to chastise her yet again. Dee Dee had been unduly hard on her friend that day and in a rare display of emotion she held out her arms.

Trisha stood in stunned silence for a second then ran smiling into her arms like a lost and found child and squeezed her tight, their guns hanging over each other's shoulder. Dee Dee whispered into Trisha's ear 'You played a blinder there mate!' referring to her earlier brave but reckless act.

'Ahhhh fanks Dee' Trisha said, giving her a peck on the cheek.

Maizie joined her two friends in a group hug, the three of them still high on adrenalin 'You know what' Dee Dee said, in the arms of her two best friends 'We're the bollocks we are'

'Fuck yeah!' Trisha replied, kissing Maizie also,

'Eeya!' Maizie said, wiping her face 'You can save that lezzer stuff for ya mate'.

Trisha immediately broke free and ran to the door 'LAURA!' she called, forgetting that her new special friend was still out there.

Dee Dee noticed the nail embedded half way into Maizie's shoulder, the point of which narrowly missing the bone 'Shit Maize are you alright?' she asked.

'Oh yeah' Maizie said, wrapped up in the moment, 'It urt's like fuck but ar be alright, ar'm just glad we're all alive, and Trisha, bloody ell ar'm so proud of er aint you?'

'Yeah, yeah I am!' Dee Dee agreed, 'She can be a right pain in the arse and drive ya raand the bleedin twist arf the time but ar tell ya what, she's got gut's ar give her that'.

Trisha found Laura standing over her brothers lifeless body, 'You ok?' she asked, slipping her hand in Laura's who merely nodded in response. 'Ar'm sorry abaat ya bruvva' Trisha added, looking down at

Jimmy, the puddle in which he lay running with his blood.
Laura turned and looked away 'He wasn't much of a brother' she remarked 'In fact I don't think he's ever said a kind word to me, he sold my bike when I was five, broke my nose when I was twelve and raped the first girl I ever fell in love with, so he got what he deserved as far as i'm concerned, the evil bastard, in fact they're all bastards'
'Ar'm glad you said that Laura' Trisha said, hanging her head 'Coz the biggun's dead an'all'
'Roland' Laura said, without batting an eye 'He was a pathetic man hiding behind that stomach of his, blaming everybody but himself for him being a fat useless pig'. Trisha was surprised at how well Laura had taken the deaths of her brothers, but soon realized there had been absolutely no love lost.
Dee Dee rested herself against the bullet riddled hardwood planks, 'Eeya woss this?' she said, wiping off a powdery residue. On closer inspection of the timber she discovered a vast quantity of Heroin and cocaine concealed between the recently delivered shipment, an obvious ploy to fool the British customs officials as the timber's distinctive odour overpowered the drugs thus fooling the sensitive sniffer dogs. 'Maize ava look!' she said, beckoning to her friend who examined the stash,
'Naughty naughty' Maizie said, taking out her phone and photographing the drugs with a street value running into tens of millions.
A short while later Dee Dee and Maizie emerged from the warehouse supporting Mickey and his sister, both of them too weak to walk unaided. Marcie cupped her severed finger to her chest, 'GET THE MOTA!' Dee Dee shouted then looked Mickey in the

eye 'You'll be alright mate, we'll get ya to the ospital'. Laura immediately ran for Bradley's car while Trisha took Marcie from Maizie 'Fuckin ell mate' she gasped, seeing the extent of Maizie's wound close up 'You alright?'
'Ar fink so Trish mate' Maizie replied, shaking the dripping blood from her hand 'You're mad you are, that nutter coulda killed ya' she nodded in the deceased Jimmy's direction.
'Ar spose yeah' Trisha replied, the gravity of her situation finally sinking in 'Ar didn't really fink abaat it, ar just done it'.
Marcie kissed Trisha's face 'Your a star Trisha' she said, hugging her brother, 'A bloomin star'.
Trisha lapped up the adulation gratefuly as it seldom came her way.
Laura drove into the yard and stopped beside the weary bunch, 'How we all gonna get in there?' Marcie asked, and she was right to ask, there were six of them vying for a seat in Bradley's tiny Nova hatchback.
Dee Dee and Maizie both looked at the minute space in the boot beside the huge sub woofer speaker and then over at Trisha who cottoned on fast,
'Oh no!' she said, holding her hands up 'No, no, no no definitely not!'
'But Trish' Dee Dee said, slipping an arm around her waist 'You are the smallest mate'.
'Ar don't care, I aint goin in there' Trisha protested 'Ar done it last time member, and mar back aint been the same since'.
Dee Dee raised her eyebrows and sighed 'Oh bloomin ell Trish ow much longer are you gonna go on abaat that'

'Dee!' Trisha snapped 'There was nine of us in a bloomin Mini cooper goin to Glastonbury and muggins ere was in the boot, ar mean, av ya seen the boot of a bleedin Mini cooper, ar was crammed in there like a trussed up chicken wiv me ed in a tool box and a bloomin jack up me arse for free an arf hours, and anuvva fing, ow comes I ad a poxy Thomas the tank tent, it aint fair ar tell ya, I ad five faasand Foo Fighters fans in fuckin wellington boots takin the bleedin piss aata me all weekend, it was flippin umiliatin'.

Dee Dee waited for Trisha to complete her tail of woe before interjecting 'Av you finished?' she asked, abruptly. Trisha nodded. 'Right then' Dee Dee added 'Well shut up and get in then fuckin boot'.

Trisha helped Marcie into the back seat then stomped sulking to the back of the car 'A minute ago ar was a bleedin ero' she moaned 'Ar knew it wouldn't last' Trisha continued to whine whilst hitching up her short skirt, revealing her ripped little miss naughty knickers and climbing in beside Bradley's huge speaker, 'Eeya Laura!' she ranted 'Watch aat for the speed bumps will ya babe or ar'll av a bloomin great woofa fingy up me whatsit, bit like you and that golden retriever Maize!'

Maizie scowled at her from the back seat 'Oh don't remind me Trish!' she said, reliving the moment the randy pooch tried to have it's way with her in the park 'If that copper adn't pulled the bugger off ar'd av ad some fucked up kids by naah ar tell ya!'

Trisha laughed 'Yeah wiv wet noses and fluffy ears, how funny would that be?'.

Dee Dee burst out laughing also at the thought of Maizie's offspring having canine characteristics while Laura reversed the car, 'Eeya Maize' she chuckled

'Ar can just see the little bleeda's licking their own shit and draggin their arse's across the carpet'.
'Oh don't' Maizie said, covering her mouth, 'Ar'm gonna be sick, I ope they put the dirty fucker daan ar do'.
Trisha interrupted from the cramped boot 'Ahhhhhhh they can't do that it weren't iz fault' she said, defending the horny hound,
'She's right Maize' Dee Dee laughed 'It was probly that moody fur coat of yours, you looked like Cruella bleedin Deville in that shit'
'That weren't shit!' Maizie snapped, shoving Dee Dee's shoulder 'Ar got that for sixty quid at Romford market, the geezer said it was pucka Chinchilla'.
Although Mickey and Marcie were in severe pain on their journey to the hospital they couldn't help but laugh at the girls ridiculous banter.
'Chinchilla my arse!' Dee Dee said, recollecting the cut price copy manufactured in a Taiwan sweat shop 'Ar bet you got that off Bobby Pride's stall dintcha, well they don't call im Bobby snide for nuffin, me nan bought a fox fur hat off that tosser that turned out to be ginger tom, the bleedin fing stunk of piss and every time she put it daan er ten year old tabby used to fuck the arse off it'.
Maizie turned to Trisha 'What is it wiv you and dogs anyway?' she asked 'Your always sticking up for em, ar don't see what all the fuss is abaat'.
Trisha smiled from her cramped position 'Ar'v always liked dogs since ar was little' she told her friend 'We ad a yorkie called bullseye when we lived at Manor Park, e used to sleep on the end of me bed till e chewed fru me lectric blanket and frazzled imself, poor little bleeda'

Dee Dee and Maizie were used to Trisha's insane anecdotes, but Marcie and Mickey listened intently 'Then we ad Fi Fi the french bulldog' she continued 'She was lovely she was, broke my art when she snuffed it'.
'What happened to er?' Marcie asked, engrossed in the tale.
'Well it's like this' Trisha added, in somber mood 'Ar took er to the vets coz she used to suffer wiv wind summink chronic, her arse was rotten ar tell ya, she let one go in Primark once and set the bleedin sprinklers off, anyway on the way back she see a poxy cat didn't she, well the cow slipped aat of her collar, jumped over Johnny Pierce's fence and landed on his barbecue, well the poor fing was so scared it farted in the fire and the backdraft blew her to bits!'. Mickey and the others were now laughing so hard they had tears streaming down their faces, 'Fuck me Trish!' Dee Dee chuckled 'You aint ad a lotta luck wiv ya pets av ya mate, didn't you av a staff an'all, what was iz name?'
'Tyson' Trisha said, feeling a lump growing in her throat 'He was mar favrit'.
Marcie could hardly bring herself to ask 'What happened to him then?'.
Trisha now fought back her own tears 'He er' she stammered 'He climbed in the washing machine wiv me bruvva's shitty pants and ar put im on a boil wash, ar see im going raand on spin but ar couldn't open the bleedin door, ar never forget the dizzy look on iz poor little face'. Even Laura now was in fits of hysterical laughter, finding it difficult to concentrate on the road ahead.
'It aint funny!' Trisha said, angrily 'He come aat wiv a shiney coat and a pair of boxers on iz ed, we buried

im wiv the uvver's behind the shed'. Trisha's garden was fast becoming a pet cemetery with three dogs, two cats, a canary, a tortoise, a rabbit and two guinea pigs currently lying in shallow graves. 'Ar'm gonna get anuvva one wiv me money' Trisha said, feeling a little more upbeat 'Ar wanna breed Chihuahua's'

'Chihuahua's!' Dee Dee said, coming to her senses, 'What the fuck for?'

Maizie and the others were also keen to hear Trisha's explanation.

'Well ar got this idea' Trisha began, 'Ya know how blokes find it ard to talk to birds'.

'Yeaaah' Dee Dee said 'Woss that gotta do wiv Chihuahua's?'

'Ang on a minute' Trisha replied, eager to share her money spinning idea, 'Well if a geezer's got a cute little dog wiv im, ar can't resist a little stroke'

'Ar bet' Maizie laughed 'But what abaat the dog?'

'Oh shut uuup' Trisha said 'You know what are mean, anyway ar reckon ar can rent em aat to orny blokes for pickin up birds, ar'v even got a name for the business'

Dee Dee listened closely 'Oh ar gotta ear this, what is it?' she asked.

'Chihuahua for an hour' Trisha said, proudly 'Catchy ain it, iss for office bods who aint got time to av a dog of their own, ar reckon ar could charge the randy bugger's firty quid an hour, ar'll be quids in ar tell ya'.

Maizie and Dee Dee sat in stunned silence not knowing if what they had just heard was the most ridiculous business venture or the start of a multi million pound empire.

'Chihuahua for an hour' Dee Dee said, mulling it over, 'Ar must admit Trish iss got a ring to it mate'.

'Fanks' Trisha smiled, 'If ar can breed enough dogs ar reckon it could go global, ar could rent em aat to rock stars, polyticians, footballers the lot, thas mar dream, iss always been mar dream but ar never ad the dough to do anyfing abaat it'.

'Ar tell ya what Trish mate' Maizie added 'That could end up bein an ouseold name like Macdonalds or Tampax or summink'.

Laura pulled into the car park at St Barts with the girls still buzzing after their daring warehouse rescue and pondering Trisha's future canine consortium 'Yeah but Trish' Dee Dee said, climbing from the car 'You've killed every bleedin dog ya'v ever ad, d'you fink this is the business for you?'.

'Course!' Trisha said, helping Marcie out 'Ar'll av a team of dog andlers sorting the Chihuahua's, ar'll just be the brains behind it all'.

Dee Dee and Maizie looked at each other and laughed 'Just as well' Maizie said 'Your runnin out of room in the garden'.

Trisha crowbar'd herself from the tiny boot space 'Oh shut up Maize it aint that bad' she said, straightening her back.

'Wanna bet' Maizie laughed 'You've buried more bodies in your garden than Fred West'.

Dee Dee, Trisha and Laura helped their three injured friends into the hospital foyer where the sorry sight had the waiting staff stunned momentarily. 'It was a domestic' Dee Dee told the nurses rushing to assess the wounds.

'Even this?' One young nurse asked, cutting Maizie's top clear of the bloody nail. 'd I y' Dee Dee quickly added, eager for the police not to be involved, 'You know what that flat pack shit's like'.

'Yeah' Trisha piped up 'Ar bought a double wardrobe once from them Swedish gits, but by the time ar finished soddin araand wiv the bleedin bits and pieces the poxy fing looked more like a bedside cabinet'.

'You are shit at that sorta fing though Trish' Dee Dee said, turning to a pretty Asian nurse 'She tried to put a shelf up for er Westlife cd's, drilled fru the gas main and blew the back end aata the bungalow'

'Oh my god!' the nurse said, covering her mouth 'Was anybody hurt?'

'Only me dad' Trisha recalled 'He was up a ladder tryna get the bleedin cat off the roof, they faand im free doors away tangled up in a trampoline, it coulda bin a lot worse though coz the bloke next door ad a pit bull and a bloomin great greenhouse, ar'm afraid the cat was a gonna though'.

'Don't tell me' Maizie nudged her, 'You buried that in the garden an'all'

'Yeah course' Trisha said solemnly, 'Well, we scraped up the bits and managed to fill a tobacco tin, ar wanted to put er in a tuna tin coz that was her faverit but the recycle geezer's ad just been and emptied the bleedin bin'.

Maizie pulled the young nurse aside 'Mar bruvva Bradley came in earlier, d'you know where e is?' she asked, looking along the corridor.

'I'm sorry, who?' replied the nurse with a vague expression.

'Bradley!' Maizie reiterated 'Bit geeky, baseball at and a bullet in iz leg'.

The nurse then twigged 'Oh you mean DJ Nitro' she said, clasping her hand to her heart, 'Yes he's here and can I just say he's totally awesome, do you know he actually rapped for me, I can't believe it, I really can't believe it, it was amazing!'. She was referring to Bradley's latest ditty entitled 'Don't put a curse on me, put a nurse on me' with it's explicit chorus,

'I aint a batty boy, so ar don't want no geeza
give me a naughty nurse, ar show ya how to please her,
ar take her to the morgue and ar do her in the freezer
Ar'm gettin down to business when ar tease her and ar squeeze her,
Ar tease her, ar squeeze her
Ar show ya how to please her,
Ar take her to the morgue
And ar do her in the freezer!'

A second nurse then butted in, 'He wasn't rapping for you, he was rapping for me actually!'
'Don't be stupid' the first nurse exclaimed 'He was looking at me the whole time'. The two girls began a heated discussion, each insisting Bradley's affections were directed at them and not the other. Soon they were pushing and shoving each other in front of a packed waiting room, 'YOU STAY AWAY FROM HIM YOU BITCH!' one of them screamed, grabbing a fist full of the others hair and yanking her to the floor. A viscous cat fight ensued with flaying arms and gnashing teeth, by the time security reached the seen and dragged them apart their neatly turned out uniforms were shredded, their hair and make up a mess and the accident and emergency department was in complete disarray.
Dee Dee and the others looked on wondering what all the fuss was about 'They can't be fightin over your dopey bruvva!' Dee Dee laughed.

It seemed that Bradley's concocted version of events and his controversial lyrics had struck a chord with the female staff, a sign maybe that his music career was heading in only one direction. The two nurses were dragged into separate rooms to receive treatment themselves leaving Maizie, Marcie and Mickey in the hands of junior doctors.
'Dee go and find Bradley will ya' Maizie asked, wincing as a dose of antiseptic was injected into her shoulder 'OUCH YA BUGGER!' she yelled at the cute young man in white 'Aintchu got a smaller one?'.
Dee Dee leaned and slipped her hand under his white coat and cupped his manhood, much to his surprise, 'Eeya!' she laughed 'E's iver ung like a snail Maize or ar just faand iz fermometer!'.
The startled, red faced doctor clamped his legs shut and fumbled for his forceps 'Er this may hurt a little' he stammered.
'I aint sayin nuffin' Dee Dee said, avoiding the obvious double entendre for once in her life. Maizie let out a ear spitting cry and bit down on a cardboard bedpan as the doctor gripped the blood soaked nail and proceeded to extract it from her swollen shoulder. Seeing the open wound oozing clotted blood
Trisha clasped her hand to her mouth and ran from the room looking this way and that for the lavatory, 'Shit!' she gurgled as vomit entered her mouth. Now panic stricken she grabbed a waiting pensioners cloth cap from his balding head and emptied the contents of her stomach inside.
'HERE WOSS YOU BLEEDIN GAME?' he yelled angrily, lashing out with the hook of his wooden stick striking Trisha on the side of her face, which instantly

infuriated her. 'Gimme my bleedin hat back' he added, wielding his stick again'
'You wonnit back!' Trisha cried, seeing red, 'Av the fuckin fing back!' Trisha slammed the cap brimming with vomit onto his freckled head, ramming it down hard, causing the pungent puke to squelch out around his ears. Adjacent patients shuffled away along the bench seats as the petrified pensioner turned tail and hobbled out of the hospital leaving a rancid trail.
Mickey and Marcie were both whisked away to undergo corrective surgery for the injuries inflicted by the Tibbs's while Laura joined Trisha in the waiting room 'Are you ok?' she asked, rubbing Trisha's back 'You don't look too god'.
Trisha wiped the last of the vomit from her lips, 'Ar've always ated ospitals!' she said, rubbing her stomach 'Ever since ar was five and ar got Barbie's foot stuck up me bleedin nose'.
Laura had to laugh 'How on earth did you manage that?' she asked, picturing the scene 'Did you fall into your toy box?'
'Naah nuffin like that' Trisha replied, taking a sip from a water fountain 'Ar was tryna get this bugger of a bogey out with er stiletto, it was so umiliatin on the bus ar tell ya'.
Laura took her by the hand 'Listen' she said, 'Why don't you come back to my place, you need to relax after the night you've had, i'll fix us both a nice drink, how does that sound?'
'Bleedin ansum' Trisha smiled 'Ar'll just tell Dee'. Trisha popped her head back into the examination room doing her best not to look in Maizie's direction, 'Ar'm gunna get a cab back to Laura's Dee, ar'll catch ya later mate, seeya Maize!'

'Alright Trish' Dee Dee replied, still eyeing the young medics 'Be careful yeah'.
Laura waved goodbye 'Nice to have met you both, and don't worry i'll take good care of her'.
'Ar bet you will' Dee Dee said, with a knowing grin.
Trisha and Laura made there way out of the hospital where Trisha put two fingers in her mouth and whistled loudly 'OY TAXI!' she yelled, but the taxi waiting in the rank did not move 'OY TAXI OVER ERE!' she repeated angrily. The driver of the taxi appeared to be asleep so Trisha marched over to his car cursing under her breath, much to Laura's amusement, 'OY GEEZA!' she shouted, rapping her knuckles on his roof, 'STOP PLAYIN WIV YA PRICK AND PICK US UP WILL YA!'
The driver woke suddenly and sat bolt upright 'What, What, what is it?' he said rubbing his eyes.
'Iss a fuckin customer you twat thas what it is!' Trisha barked, opening the back door, 'Come on Laura, ar'v woke the nob'. Laura climbed in beside her and gave the driver her address and the pair were driven away.
'Right your good to go' the young doctor said, handing Maizie a wad of spare bandages 'You need to change the dressing twice daily and collect this prescription from the pharmacy on your way out, oh and er, no more DIY eh'.
'Yeah whateva' Maizie said, hopping down from the table 'Come on Dee less go and find Brad'.
Dee Dee reluctantly followed Maizie, allowing herself one last squeeze of the doctors bottom in passing, 'Phwoar!' she gasped 'Seeya later ansum'.
Bradley's room was simple enough to find amid the labyrinth of hospital corridors, Dee Dee and Maizie simply followed the trail of girls hurrying to catch a glimpse of him. It seemed that Bradley's exaggerated

notoriety had spread like wild fire, boosting his profile to almost god like status.

'Oy watchit!' Maizie shrieked as three teenagers and an expectant mother barged past her chattering excitedly

'Apparently he's the new Eminem!' one of them said to her friend 'I'm gonna find out where he lives and sleep outside his house till he asks me out'.

'Me too' her friend replied, trying to overtake her, 'I'm gonna buy all his stuff when it comes out, I might even get his name tattooed on my foot,, d'you think he's got a girlfriend, i'll kill her if he has'.

'What the fuck?' Dee Dee said, overhearing the swooning fans 'Scuze me, scuze me!' she said, nudging her way through the gathered crowd outside Bradley's room 'Get aat the bleedin way will ya!'.

One of the teens grabbed Dee Dee's shoulder 'Oy we were her first!' she snapped, yanking her back.

Dee Dee spun round, grabbed the girl by her school tie and tightened the knot around her neck until her face was crimson, 'Listen to me you fuckin little tart!' Dee Dee barked into her face 'You put your and on me again and ar'll rip you fuckin froat aat, you got that!'.

The terrified girl nodded and once Dee Dee had released her, ran choking along the corridor. She then stopped and called back to her friend 'Sarah are you coming?' she asked.

'No way!' Sarah shouted back 'I'm sorry Steph but nothings gonna stop me seeing Nitro!'.

'Nitro?' Maizie said, looking around, 'Who the bleedin ell's Nitro?'. Suddenly the door opened and several women and girls filed out each clutching a copy of Bradley's signature to their chest.

Bradley could be seen sitting up on the bed with his bandaged leg on show giving more adoring girls his elaborate version of events, 'So ar said to Mc Hammer yeah, ar said listen Hamerman you'z can be on me album yeah but don't be tinkin we'z bro's coz dat aint the way ar roll, ya know what ar'm sayin blud'.

The girls around him listened intently, 'Tell us how you met Puffy again Nitro' one of them asked, inching closer.

Bradley put his fist to his heart, 'Thas mar main man Diddy right there man, we'z tight man, real tight, ar take a bullet for dat dude, the mans a genius he saved my life in a knife fight at Harold Wood man'.

The girls gasped 'P Diddy came to Harold wood!' one of the shrieked 'Just to see you I suppose'.

'Yeah man ar see im all de time' Bradley explained 'Mar man Diddy digs de Essex vibe innit, dat and the wicked donner's from the Sweaty Turk, man das de bestest kebab ouse on de planet ar'm tellin ya!'.

Dee Dee pushed her way through 'OY NOB END!' she yelled 'Woss all this bollocks?'

Maizie then pulled her arm back 'Leave im Dee' she said, never having seen her brother as happy in his entire solitary life, 'Let im do this, please'.

Dee Dee relented 'Ok Maize, just for you mate' she then pushed the few remaining girls aside, Bradley immediately froze assuming Dee Dee would expose him as a fraud, but instead, to his surprise Dee Dee leant forward, unbuttoned her blouse and said, 'Can ya sign mar tit please, Nitro!'

'Er, er yeah course babe' Bradley said, not knowing what to make of the situation. Dee Dee cupped a breast in her hand and waved it in front of Bradley's mesmerized face. Snatching a pen from an adoring fan, Bradley shakily scrawled his name above Dee Dee's left nipple and then trying his luck he moved in for a kiss. 'Don't take the fuckin piss' Dee Dee whispered sternly.

Bradley pulled away and smiled to the others 'Don't you'z worry if you'z flat chested yeah coz ar do butts and beavers an'all innit'.

Maizie took Bradley's hand, 'Come on Nitro mate we got things to do' she said helping him down from the bed.

'Yeah, yeah das right' Bradley replied loud enough for everyone to hear 'We gotta cut anuvva record innit!'.

Bradley was mobbed by women and the odd homosexual all the way to the foyer where he tapped Maizie's arm 'Yo sis did ya get Mickey?' he asked whilst signing yet another autograph for a stalking fan, 'What appened to ya shoulder an'all?'

'Yeah bruv we got im, and Marcie she was there an'all' Maizie explained, handing Bradley his keys 'Are you ok to drive like that?' she asked, looking at his heavily bandaged leg 'We can leave the mota ere and get a cab if ya want'.

Bradley snatched the keys 'I aint leavin the supernova nowhere blud, this hood's full of teevs innit, they'z jack up mar ride and steal mar bangin wheels in no time!'

Driving from the hospital, Dee Dee put her hand in her pocket and took out the Red sea ruby, 'Bleedin ell Dee!' Maizie gasped 'You ad it wiv ya all the time!'

'Course' Dee Dee said, admiring the exquisite cut 'Ya don't fink arda let em kill Mickey do ya, listen if fings'd got real nasty arda give it up in an art beat'.

'Nasty!' Maizie shrieked 'Ow much nastier could itta bleedin got, poor Mickey was bashed to fuck, two of the bloomin Tibbs's are dead for gawd sake, Marcie ad er friggin finger chopped off and me, ar got shot wiv a poxy nail gun, now correct me if arm wrong here Dee but ar reckon that's abaat as nasty as it bleedin get's'.

Bradley's eyes widened as his sister recounted the evenings horrific events, 'Dat shit's propa gangster sis, you'z ho's are psycho man, flippin psycho innit!'

'Are dunno abaat you Dee' Maizie said, stretching out on the back seat 'But ar'm proper fucked mate, are need me bed'

'Yeah me an'all' Dee Dee yawned 'Ar'll crash at yours if thas ok'

Bradley's eyes lit up 'Yo Dee ar got a king size bed innit' he said, placing a hand on Dee Dee's knee 'We'z can roll araand on dat ting all night blud' he then jostled his crotch 'And if ya lucky babe' he added 'Ar'll introduce ya to the sperminator, ar know ya tempted aintcha bitch'.

Dee Dee looked down her nose at Bradley 'Ya know what nob ed' she smirked, 'I aint your bitch and I aint fuckin tempted, in fact ar'd rather shag a stinkin tramp than let you and your, sperminator or whatever it is you call your puny prick anywhere near me, you got that!'

Bradley thought for a moment 'So er' he said, putting his arm across the back of Dee Dee's seat and stroking her hair 'Thas a no then is it babe?'.

Dee Dee immediately slapped Bradley wounded leg 'Get your ands off me you twat, ar told ya I aint intrested' she then turned to Maizie 'Maize mate, what is it wiv your bruvva, is he retarded or summink?'

'No' Maizie laughed 'He's just a twat'.

'Oh yeah!' Bradley said, defending himself, 'Dat aint what dem chicks at de ospital was sayin, they'z was all over me man, ar tell ya, DJ Nitro's gonna be massive blud!'. Bradley's premonition was right, as they drove home the internet chat rooms and social networking sites were buzzing with news of a new gangster rapper on the scene, the name Nitro was on everybody's lips even before he had taken to a single stage.

Trisha spent the remainder of the night with Laura, the two of them sharing a foaming bath, sipping a crisp chilled Moselle and popping Belgian chocolates into one another's mouths, and then on to Laura's queen size bed.

Dee Dee's night wasn't so glamorous or restful for that matter, wedged against a wood chip wall at the other end of Maizie's bed with her friends big toe prodding her ear. She lay awake staring at the combed artex ceiling mulling over the days events and planning their next move, if at all there was one.

CHAPTER ELEVEN.

Billy's back.

The following morning Dee Dee and Maizie were woken by the sound of Maizie's mother Sharon's knuckles rapping on the bedroom door 'Maizie what the bleedin ell's goin on?' she yelled, 'And you Bradley!' she called along the landing 'You get aat here right naah and explain this shit!'.
'What the fuck?' Maizie moaned, rubbing her eyes 'Sod off will ya muvva iss too bleedin early!'. Sharon stormed into her daughter's bedroom followed by a weary Bradley wearing the Star wars pajamas that he'd refused to ditch since he was seven years old and that were way too small by now,
'Yeah what the fuck mum?' Bradley said, donning his baseball cap and fondling himself with the other hand.
Sharon immediately swiped the back of Bradley's head 'Ar'v told you abaat using that sort of language in this house Bradley' she snapped, 'And that goes for you an'all Maizie girl!' she then yanked Bradley's hand from his pajama bottoms 'And stop playing wiv ya wotsits ya dirty little bleeda, it aint right it aint, ar told Janice abaat it and she said er boy Clive don't do it so it must be you, your one of them perverts aintcha!'
Maizie then intervened, 'Muvva for gawd sake' she yelled, 'Ar'm tryna bleedin sleep, what do you want?'.
Sharon went to the window and threw open the curtains 'Ar want that bleedin lot to piss off, thas what are want!'.
Bradley approached the window as Dee Dee and Maizie climbed out of bed, 'Shit man, looka dat!' he cried, opening the window and peering out, 'Eeya Maize, ava look!'
Outside Sharon's humble two up two down were at least fifty teenage girls and a handful of spotty boys

with crudely made banner's featuring the Name Nitro amongst the mixed messages of love, 'There he is!' one girl shrieked 'It's DJ Nitro, oh my god i'm gonna die!' the crowd went wild, waving their banners and surging into Sharon's tiny front garden, knocking over the milk bottles and concrete meerkats. 'NITRO, NITRO WE LOVE YOU NITRO!' they chanted, many of them wearing sideways baseball caps to emulate his style.

'Fuuuck me' Dee Dee said, looking over Bradley's shoulder 'What av you done?'

'Ar told yo man' Bradley smiled, 'Dem ho's they love me blud, innit, dem's me fans mum'.

Sharon slapped Bradley's head once again 'Ar don't give a shit what they are, are want em gone right naah, looka the state of me marigolds and me poxy meerkats, ar saved up all them bloomin coupons aat the gazette for them and now look at em, not one of em's got a friggin ed!'.

Bradley waved to the ecstatic crowd 'YO ME BITCH'S!' he laughed 'ONE AT A TIME MAN, ONE AT A TIME, AR TAKE THE BLONDES FIRST DEN THE BRUNETTES INNIT, BUT IF YOU'Z A GINGA YOU MIGHT AV TO WAIT, YOU NART AR MEAN BLUD!'.

One euphoric blonde leapt up and down 'I'm a blonde, i'm a blonde!' she screamed and then promptly fainted. The crowd then began to chant 'Sing for us Nitro, sing for us Nitro' which tickled Dee Dee

'Fuck me, are they gonna be disappointed' she laughed.

'Yeah ar can do dat' Bradley yelled back before running back to his bedroom where he opened his window and pushed a huge speaker to face the screaming fans 'Ar'm gonna spit you'z some bars me bitch's!' he said, tinkering with his decks and picking up his mic. After a minute or two of pure hysteria the crowd fell silent waiting for Bradley to begin, which he did in blistering style

Yo, you'z, what can ar say
Nitro's here and ar'm here to stay,
ar'm a bitchin MC wid a brand new flavor
come worship me coz ar'm your savior
ar'll give ya summink nobody gave ya
ar'm a beat box boy wid de bad behavior,
come worship me coz ar'm here to save ya
ar'm a bitchin MC wid a brand new flavor,

Bradley pointed to several random girls in the crowd,

Ar take Sophie first den ar might do Tracey
Ruby's next wid her best mate Gracie
ar do em two at a time an ar drive dem crazy,

Don't diss me coz ar do mar own ting
ar'm a bad boy me so beware mar sting,
ar'll give ya summink nobody gave ya
ar'm a beat box boy wid de bad behavior,
ar said ar give you summink nobody gave ya
ar'm a beat box boy
ar'm a beat box boy
ar'm a beat box boy
ar'll give you summink nobody gave ya
ar'm a beat box boy wid de bad behavior.

Bradley threw his arms in the air and acknowledged the rapturous applause. Many of the frenzied fans had filmed the spectacle on their smart phones and

were busily uploading the footage to the internet for the world to see,
'Ar tell ya what' said a skeptical Dee Dee, 'For a complete moron, that weren't arf bad'.
'Your jokin aintcha!' Maizie said, clapping loudly 'That was bleedin brilliant that was, look at em Dee, they love im!'
Bradley blew the girls a kiss 'Das what ar'm talkin bout man!' he yelled. Standing there in his ill fitting child's pajamas Bradley soaked up the adulation, feeling as though his life long ludicrous musical journey was about to peak. He had climbed the mountain, vanquished the mighty Goliath, travelled the frozen wastelands of obscurity and reached the promised land. The girls that once mocked him now fell and worshiped at his feet, a true musical messiah had been born and just as Jesus preached to his people on the Mount so Bradley did from his first floor bedroom window in Essex. 'Yo you'z lot!' he addressed the crowd, 'Fanks for comin yeah, ar'm glad ya like me shit and all that, ar got plenny more where dat came from so look aat all you'z coz ar'm gonna explode on the scene like nitroglycereen innit!'. A beaming Bradley eventually closed the window on his screaming fans chanting 'NITRO! NITRO! NITRO!' and joined the others. 'Ar'z told ya blud didn't I!' he said to Dee Dee, Maizie and his mother 'Ar'z told ya me shit was sick man'.
'Sick?' his mother said, totally out of touch with the current youth speak 'You aint been watchin that disgustin chicken filf again av ya, ya dirty little bugger'
'No mum' Maizie said, quick to respond 'Sick means it's good, you know like, your roast tayters are totally sick, nart ar mean'.

'No ar don't know what ya mean' replied Sharon, leaving the room 'You kids ya all bleedin wierdo's now adays, just get them girls outta mar bleedin garden will ya!' she called from the hall 'AND GET ME SOME MORE BLOOMIN MEERKATS D'YOU HEAR ME!'

Maizie rubbed her knuckles on the top of Bradley's cap 'Blimey bruv ya've only gone and done it aintcha!'

'Too right I av sis' Bradley replied, straightening his hat 'Nobody believed in me yeah, but ar done it didn't I, ar told you'z all ar got talint, look ar prove it, i'z can rap about anyting blud'. Bradley picked up a discarded fast food menu from the Sweaty Turk.

'Your gunna rap about kebab's?' Dee Dee laughed 'Ar gotta ear this'.

Bradley beat boxed for a moment then launched into a rapid fire rap,

'Chicken and rice gotta pay the price
rum baba you know it tastes so nice,
big fat fries from a big fat guy
with a big fat belly and a big fat wife,

if a doner and kofte aint your ting
burn your botty wid mar suicide wings,
try my shish blud you won't look back
lick dem ribs from de barbecue rack'

'Yeah, yeah ok we get it' Dee Dee said, stopping Bradley in mid flow, it was then that she fully noticed his pajama's 'What the fuck are you wearin you idiot?' she asked, tugging at his bottoms 'You look a proppa cock'.

'Ar don't care blud' Bradley said, pulling away 'I aint gettin rid of dese for no one, they'z look wicked wiv me bling innit'.

Not a single soul had ever believed Bradley would make the big time or had an ounce of faith in his abilities, least of all his family, but whether through hard work, grit and determination or simply pure blind luck , Bradley had made it.

A few miles away in Hackney, Takashi Nakajima came too from his meditative slumber and saw his near naked men strewn around Nikos's dingy flat, 'GET UP!' he roared, leaping to his feet 'GET UP I SAY!'. One by one the four heavily hungover henchmen opened their eyes and looked blearily around them until they met Takashi's menacing gaze. Dressed only in their underpants and a crudely fashioned cockney neck tie made from threadbare tea towels they clambered shakily to their feet gathering up their clothes and bowing subserviently to their incensed master.

Nikos himself woke amid the commotion, emerging from his bedroom in floral house slippers and a gaudy fuchsia robe that barely covered his genitalia which swung free and loose. 'Mornin boys!' he said fondly, having thoroughly enjoyed the nights raucous proceedings 'Mornin Mr Nakajima, fancy a cuppa?'. Mr Nakajima found his joviality to be an insult and reached for his sword, 'SILENCE!' he yelled, eyeing Nikos's flamboyant attire 'YOU PATHETIC PEACOCK!' . His men stood half dressed, their eyes firmly fixed on the time worn wilton carpet. Nikos took one look at his aggressive stance and said 'Decaf' before heading through to the kitchen.

Takashi followed him, fuming at his insolent behavior,

'PAPAGEORGIOU!' he yelled, wielding his sword and bringing the blade down swiftly, slicing Nikos's red retro toaster clean in two, 'Where is my ruby?'.
Nikos jumped aside and rummaged for his phone 'I'm on it Mr Nakajima' he said, searching for Dee Dee's number and glancing at the deep gouge in his worktop made by Takashi's blade 'I'm most definitely on it' .
'Ang on it's that Nikos geezer' Dee Dee said, heading for a quiet corner of Maizie's room to take his call 'Alright Paps, woss appnin?' she asked, giving the thumbs up to Maizie 'You got the dough or what?'
'Yes, yes the money's here' Nikos replied nervously, with the tip of Takashi's sword at his throat 'Please bring the ruby over right away, Mr Nakajima is keen for a quick sale so you must hurry'.
'Listen you slag' Dee Dee snapped, perturbed at being rushed so early in the day, 'You tell Mr Nakajimmy or whatever iz bleedin name is'
'It's Nakajima' Nikos said, correcting her in mid sentence 'Mr Takashi Nakajima, he's a very important business man and I assure you he doesn't like to be kept waiting'.
'Ar don't give a flying fuck what iz bleedin name is' Dee Dee replied, getting her back up now 'You tell im to go sushi or summink, ar got a coupla fings to do first then ar'll be over, alright'.
'No, no wait!' Nikos pleaded as Dee Dee hung up the phone 'Dee Dee, Dee Dee are you still there?' he could see Mr Nakajima's disapproving glare out of the corner of his eye, so Nikos continued a phantom conversation, 'Oh there you are my dear, so you'll bring the ruby over asap am I right, that's great my dear i'll let Mr Nakajima know, and i'm sure all parties concerned will be duly satisfied'.

Takashi then grabbed the phone from Nikos and listened intently but heard nothing 'You try to deceive me Papageorgiou!' he said, clasping a strong hand around Nikos's throat and squeezing tightly 'I ought to snap your neck like a stick for such treachery'. Nikos struggled to speak with his back to the drainer, 'I'm sorry, i'm sorry what can I do?' he croaked 'I'm doing everything I can to get you the ruby you have my word Mr Nakajima, honest I am, please be patient I swear you will have it'. Takashi growled, every fibre and sinew in his body wanting to hack Nikos into a thousand pieces, making sure he was conscious throughout until the last major artery was severed and the kitchen walls ran with his traitorous blood, but Takashi craved the red sea ruby as the center piece for his mountainous collection of gems which once complete would run into tens of billions. Takashi tossed Nikos aside and stormed from the kitchen only to discover his four once trusted guards had collapsed back onto the sofa in a pathetic drunken heap only having had approximately forty five minutes sleep that night. Mary Poppins had been watched a total of nine times back to back and little did Nikos know at the time but much of the ornate cornice on the shop ceiling below had broken away and crashed down onto his dusty displays amid the clumsily choreographed chaos.

'GET UP!' Takashi roared, plunging his sword between them, piercing the dated leather sofa 'GET UP YOU DOGS BEFORE I RUN YOU THROUGH!'

Nikos popped his head round the kitchen door and smiled at the startled guards 'He's not really a morning person your guvna is he' he said, darting back inside when Takashi glared over his shoulder at him.

As Nikos kept his distance from the raging Takashi, Trisha lay in Laura's arms semi naked amid the crumpled silk sheets, each with a contented look on their slumbering faces, the sun creeping through the venetian blinds to caress their skin. suddenly there was a loud knock at the door and the two stirred,

'Wossat?' Trisha groaned through parched lips. Laura rose and gathered her robe from the floor 'Oh sorry darling' she said, stroking Trisha's face 'I took the liberty of ordering breakfast last night, there's a gorgeous little eatery round the corner that delivers to me, I do hope you like Spanish omelette'.

'Yeah ar don't mind' Trisha yawned 'But ar'd rarva av a full English though, ar like to dip me black puddin in me tea, iss bleedin ansum'.

Laura's stomach turned at the thought as she climbed from the bed 'Alright Mario i'm coming!' she said after a second louder knock and rooting through her bag 'I'm just getting my purse!'. Trisha pulled the sheet up around her neck while Laura slid back the security latch 'JESUS!' she gasped on seeing her brother Billy leaning against the door frame with blood dripping from his right sleeve and along his hand.

'Alright sis' he said, clutching his elbow, 'You gotta fix me up'

'What?' Laura replied, looking over her shoulder at the bedroom door ajar 'No Bill!' she added, barring the way 'If your hurt you gotta go to the hospital'.

'Nah fuck that' Billy said, shoving her out of the way 'Got any booze?' Billy headed straight for Laura's cocktail cabinet and rummaged amongst the bottles of cabernet and frascatti until he found a litre of scotch 'Thatta do' he coughed, unscrewing the cap with his teeth and taking a large mouthful before pouring a quantity of the whisky onto his sleeve 'Fuck!' he cursed, screwing up his face.

'Billy you can't stay here' Laura insisted 'You need a doctor to look at that, please get yourself down the hospital'.

Billy had been nicked by one of Dee Dee's bullets as he fled the warehouse, dislodging a sliver of bone which caused him immense pain when his arm was raised. 'Please Bill!' Laura said, putting herself between Billy and the bedroom door 'Come on you've been shot you need professional help'.

Billy paused for a moment 'Ar never said anyfing abaat being shot so ow the fuck do you know that?'.

Laura, realizing her mistake stood speechless 'Er, er well' she stammered 'Ar just thought, well you know'.

At that point the bedroom door opened and Trisha stood in just her lacy thong out of Billy's view 'Fuck the omelette Laura come back to bed' she said, pulling cheekily at the diamante underwear.

Billy spun round 'What the fuck?' he said, focusing first on Trisha's breasts and then her unmistakable face 'You ya bitch!' he snarled, turning on Laura, 'What the fuck's she doin ere?' he asked 'She's one of them cunts that killed ya bruvva!'.

Trisha stood mortified with nowhere to run. Laura approached her brother 'Your mistaken Billy, she's not from around here' she said, now frantic 'Just go to the hospital, please Billy'

Billy looked down at his sister with contempt 'Your in wiv em aintcha!' he snarled raising his right hand and swiping her across the face, sending her reeling backwards and a spasm of pain through his arm which enraged him even more. Trisha ran to help Laura to her feet, looking at the door as means of escape. 'Don't even fink abaat it!' Billy barked,

kicking it closed and grabbing Trisha by the hair, 'Come ere you fuckin slag' he said, dragging her to the balcony 'Your gonna av a fuckin flyin lesson'
Trisha began screaming and lashing out, but Billy drew a pistol from his pocket and rammed the barrel into her ribs and said 'Shut it you cunt or ar'll decorate this gaff wiv your guts'.
Laura tugged at her brothers arm in a futile attempt to save Trisha 'Billy please don't' she begged, wiping the dripping blood from her nose 'She hasn't done anything it was me, I killed Jimmy!'.
Billy stopped in his tracks, 'You!' he said, putting the pieces together in his head 'You killed yer own bruvva for this piece of shit' he shook Trisha violently by the arm 'Ar don't believe it, ar don't fuckin believe what your tellin me girl, Jimmy was a complete fuckin prick but e was blood you stupid fuckin dyke, ar should fro the fuckin pair of ya aat the fuckin winda!'.
Laura had an idea 'What about the ruby Billy, we can get it for ya, we know where it is!'.
Billy's expression changed slightly giving Laura a glimmer of hope 'Where the fuck is it?' he asked, flinging Trisha onto Laura's red velvet sofa 'Tell me Laura or so elp me ar'll put every bullet in this gun in your little slags ed right naah'. Billy wanted the ruby as much as Takashi, the kudos associated with a crime of it's kind would propel him to godfather status.
'Mar mates got it' Trisha said, trembling, 'We nicked it off some Arab geeza'.
Billy couldn't handle the fact that three girls had beaten him to the prize 'You're tellin me that ar was mugged off by a bunch of slags' he raged 'If that shit gets aat ar'm fucked'.

Laura sat beside Trisha and the pair covered their bare breasts with two cushions 'Bill let us go and we'll get it for you' she said in a soothing tone, 'I'll even fix up your arm before we go'.
'You two aint goin nowhere!' Billy replied menacingly, 'You're right you are gonna fix my arm and you' he said, pointing his gun at Trisha 'You ya bitch ar gonna call your fuckin mates and tell em to bring me that fuckin stone or they'll be takin your bits ome in a bucket, you got me?'. Trisha nodded and got up, 'Where you goin?' Billy asked, cocking his pistol,
'Me phones in me bag'. Trisha replied, stopping like a frightened rabbit 'Me bags in the barfroom'.
'SIT DAAN!' Billy shouted 'And don't fuckin move, Laura you get it and no fuckin abaat or your bitch gets opened up good and proper, d'you ear me?'. Trisha slipped back down onto the sofa as Laura left the room. 'You tell your mates to bring the gem to Stockwell station tonight after nine' Billy told Trisha 'They give it to me and ar'll let ya go'. Billy and his gang had a secret hideout beneath Stockwell station in an abandoned second world war deep level air raid shelter, which in it's day could house some fifteen hundred frightened Londoners. A station guard on Billy's payroll had provided him with a duplicate set of keys to the locked labyrinth and turned a blind eye to his comings and goings, which was usually directly after a big job, with it being the ideal place to lie low and divide their booty. Billy took out his own phone, wincing as he lifted his right hand to his ear 'Danny!' he said, when a member of his gang answered 'Ar need you and the boys in Stockwell tonight'. Trisha could hear Danny complaining at the other end of the phone, 'Ar don't give a fuck if your goin to the poxy dogs!' Billy yelled, spitting onto his phone 'Ar'm tellin

ya, you get the uvvers and get your arse's daan there for nine or ar'm gunna av to seriously urt the fuckin lotta ya, am I makin myself crystal!'.

'Yes boss' Danny could be heard saying 'Nine o'clock'.

Laura returned moments later carrying Trisha's bag and gave a sly wink as she handed it to her, but Billy quickly wrenched the straps from her hands 'No ya don't!' he snapped, peering inside and removing Trisha's gun 'You fink ar'm some sorta cunt don'tcha' he added, removing the remaining bullets and tossing the weapon across the room. Billy then took out Trisha's phone 'Ring em naah bitch' he said, thrusting it into her hand before removing his jacket and dragging Laura back to her feet 'And you, you sort my fuckin arm aat before ar sort you out' he said, rolling up his bloodied shirt sleeve.

Billy sat by the window within earshot of Trisha while Laura gathered towels and hot water.

'Dee iss me!' Trisha said, on hearing her friends voice 'Ar'm in a bit of bovva mate'.

Dee Dee and Maizie were sat at the kitchen table eating breakfast while Bradley strutted around the room, waving occasionally to his delirious fans outside 'Look at em man!' he said, grunting and humping the kitchen cabinets whilst eyeing the lusty teens 'Ar'z could av anyone of dem right naah ya know'.

'Shut up you plank!' said Dee Dee, putting one finger in her ear 'Woss that Trish, ar carn ear ya mate'. Bradley squeezed a Chelsea bun and rubbed his groin 'Ar gotta get me a Jacuzzi when ar'm loaded man, ar could av all of dem in it blud'.

'Oy turn it in will ya!' Dee Dee yelled 'Ar carn ear a bleedin fing wiv you chattin shit, sorry Trish go on mate'.

'Iss that Tibbs geeza, e'z ere Dee an e says e'z gonna kill me and Laura if you don't give im the ruby'.

'Oh fuck!' said Dee Dee, clasping a hand to her head 'Ar shoulda killed that prick!'.

'What is it Dee?' asked Maizie, who was also growing tired of her brothers over zealous antics 'Bradley for fuck sake!' she snapped, flinging a sausage at his head ' Piss off to your bleedin room will ya!'.

Bradley stomped from the kitchen, mumbling 'Ar don't av to take this you'z, ar'm an A list celebrity i am'

'WHATEVA!' Maizie called after him, 'Right woss appnin mate?' she asked Dee Dee.

'Iss that Billy Tibbs, e'z got Trish and Laura' Dee Dee explained 'If we don't give im the ruby e'z gunna top the pair of em'

'Shit Dee!' Maizie cried 'What we gonna do, e'z a fuckin nutter!'

Dee Dee shrugged her shoulders 'We aint got no choice, we gotta give it to im, you still there Trish?' she asked.

Trisha could see Billy watching her every word, 'Yeah Dee ar'm ere mate' she replied 'E said you gotta bring the stone to Stockwell station, you know off the Lambef road, tonight at nine o'clock then e'll let us go, you will bring it won't ya Dee'

'Course ar bleedin will mate' Dee Dee said, reassuringly, 'Don't you worry Trish ar'm gonna get you aata this shit mate ar swear, just don't do anyfing to piss im off and you'll be fine'.

'Fanks Dee' Trisha said, sobbing 'Ar'm sorry mate ar know ow much that money meant to ya'.

Dee Dee stopped Trisha in mid flow 'You shut the fuck up Trish, ar don't give a toss abaat the money, your mar mate an ar do anyfing for ya, and Maizie, ar love ya boaf, we're a team ain't we, un fuckin stoppable thas what we are, so you be careful and we'll come and get ya'.

'Ya promise' Trisha said, wiping the tears from her face.

'You fuckin bet ar do Trish' Dee Dee said, taking Maizie's hand 'No ones gunna split us up, never, d'you ear me, never, you tell im e can av iz stone, but if e lays a finger on you ar'll unt im daan and cut im a new arseole'.

Trisha found some comfort in Dee Dee's reassuring words, although deep down her gut feeling was that once Billy had what he wanted he would kill them all in an instant. Suddenly there was another knock at the door, Billy drew his pistol 'You expetin anyone?' he asked laura, wary that the authorities may be on his tail.

'It's just Mario with the breakfast Bill, that's all' Laura said, waiting for Billy's permission to answer.

'Make it quick' Billy said, grabbing Trisha and pushing her against the wall out of sight 'Any funny business and it's gonna get real messy real quick, d'you ear me'.

Laura nodded and opened the door 'Morning Mario' she said, taking the bag from him 'How much do I owe you?'.

Mario looked at his receipt 'Seven pounds thirty please Laura, call it seven pounds'.

'Thank you very much' Laura replied, digging into her purse for a handful of coins.

Mario was a regular visitor to Laura's door, a single olive skinned man, he had chatted flirtaciously with

heron many occasions, but the string of girls he had seen leaving Laura's apartment over the years convinced him she was out of his league, 'Are you ok?' he asked, noticing her reddened face from Billy's hand.
Laura turned her cheek away and pulled her hair down over the growing bruise, hearing this, Billy aimed the barrel of his gun at the door ready to kill anyone that stepped through. 'Yes, yes i'm fine thank you Mario' Laura said, wanting so badly to scream for him to go get help but knowing that her brother would put a bullet in his back before he reached the elevator. 'I er, I tripped in the bathroom that's all' Laura explained 'Shampoo on the floor I think, I really should be more careful'.
'You need to put some ice on that' Mario said, sympathetically 'It's gonna be one hell of a shiner that's for sure'.
Laura smiled at him, 'Thanks Mario, I will' she said, closing the door and listening for his footsteps along the corridor.
'Watcha got there then?' Billy asked, shoving Trisha back towards the sofa, 'Omelette Bill' Laura said, taking out two silver cartons, 'It's our breakfast'.
'Not any more it aint' Billy smiled 'Give it ere'. Laura reluctantly set both meals down in front of him then retrieved a tee shirt from her room and handed it to Trisha who pulled it over her head and covered her breasts.
'Ar was enjoying the view' Billy remarked, eyeing Trisha's legs as he tucked greedily into the omelette's.
Laura sat beside her brother and tried to reason with him, 'Billy we can't stay here all day, what about the business, we've got clients booked'

'Fuck em' Billy scoffed 'The stiffs ain't goin nowhere are they'.
Laura tended to his wound and bound his arm with a bandage, 'At least let me go and get you some proper antiseptic Bill' she said, wanting desperately to raise the alarm 'It might be infected'.
Billy pushed his sister away 'The stiffs aint goin nowhere and niver are you, so sit over there wiv ya lesbo mate and shut the fuck up'.
'I aint no lesbo' Trisha chirped up 'Ar'm just a bit bi thas all'.
'Listen!' Billy snapped, 'You bin chewin on mar sisters rug aintcha, so that makes you a bleedin lesbo in mar book, fuckin bi my arse'.
'She aint got a rug' Trisha corrected Billy.
'What?' said Billy, angrilly 'What you on abaat?'
'Ar said she aint got a rug' Trisha said again, 'She's got an Arry Hill, bald as a bleedin coot, iss more igenic ain it babe' she turned to Laura 'Ar got a landin strip ain i'.
Billy screwed up his face 'Ar don't wanna know what mar sisters got between er legs you sick bitch' he barked 'You on the uvver and can show me your landin strip anyday darlin'.
'Yeah dream on!' Trisha said, bravely 'Ar'd rarva you slung me aat the fuckin winda'.
At Maizie's house Dee Dee sat with her head in her hands wracking her brains for a solution to their predicament. 'Why don't we just call the old bill Dee?' Maizie said, pacing the room 'Trish could be dead by the time we get there'.
'Don't be daft for fuck sake Maize' Dee Dee replied 'If Tibbs even gets a whiff of the old bill e'll kill er straight away'.

'Well what are we gonna do then?' Maizie whined, 'Ar don't fink ar could go fru anuvva night like last night, ar was a baga nerves, look at me ar'm shakin naah'.
Dee Dee grabbed Maizie's arm 'You listen to me Maizie' she said, sternly 'Last night we were the bollocks, a proper firm and we don't take no shit from anyone let alone a two bob tosser like Tibbs, ar'll finka summink, but for naah less just assume we're givin im the ruby for Trisha, ok'
Maizie looked confused 'But Dee ar fought we was givin it to im'.
Dee Dee leapt to her feet and grabbed her coat from the back of the chair 'I ain't givin im fuck all unless I av to' she said, heading for the door 'Ar'm goin aat, ar be back later'
'Where ya goin Dee?' Maizie asked, following her along the hall 'What about Trish mate?'
Dee Dee stopped and shook her friend by the arms 'Look Maize ar gotta go see someone, just wait ere will ya'.
'But Dee' Maizie continued 'You promised Trish you'd get her aat, you promised er'. Dee Dee left Maizie wringing her hands in the hallway and stepped outside among the jostling teens. The girls, most of them between fifteen and sixteen looked down there noses at Dee Dee as if she were some withered hag even though she was all but a few years older than they were. One of them then began taunting Dee Dee as she stepped out of the gate 'Whore!' she yelled, assuming Dee Dee had spent the night with D J Nitro, 'He's mine you bitch!' she added, teetering on dangerously high heels.
Dee Dee stopped and turned to the crowd 'Listen you stupid bunch of slags' she snarled 'If you don't piss

off right naah those poxy meerkats won't be the only edless fuckers raand ere, now do one the lotta ya!'
While a terrified Trisha sat fearing for her life Dee Dee walked the short distance to the main road and whistled down a taxi 'Ouses of Parliament mate!' she told the Indian driver,
'Yes please miss' he replied, stroking a statuette of the Hindu god Vishnu on his dashboard for luck before they set off. En route Dee Dee helped herself to a tissue from the brightly coloured box on the back shelf and sneezed into it loudly, 'I am blessing you very much please' the driver said, looking in his rear view mirror 'And Vishnu blesses you too' , he stroked the figurine again.
'Yeah whateva' Dee Dee replied, with very little interest. She then telephoned Nikos who had been anxiously awaiting her call having spent an uncomfortable couple of hours trying to entertain the stone faced Takashi, with very little success, it would seem that the Japanese war lord's interests did not stretch to domino's or gin rummy, although his trained assassins did find the pornographic playing cards mildly amusing, each of them covertly slipping a cheeky ace into their pockets with a young lady pictured fornicating with a variety of household objects. 'Oy Nick mate listen!' she said, as they drove into the heart of London 'That Japanese geeza of yours'.
'Yes, Mr Nakajima' Nikos replied,
'Yeah if ya say so' Dee Dee continued 'You reckon e'z a nasty piece of work do ya?'
'Extremely' Nikos said, turning away from Takashi and lowering his voice 'The man's a psychopath' he explained 'He carries a flipping samurai sword round with him and so do his men'

'Men?' Dee Dee said, assuming until now that Takashi travelled alone,
Nikos glanced over at the sofa 'Yes four of them, big brutes they are and crazy with it' he said, recalling the nights events.
'Right, you tell im' Dee Dee said, hatching her plan 'If e wants the stone e'z gotta come to Stockwell station at nine and make sure e brings them bovva boys wiv im an'all'.
Nikos strummed his fingers nervously 'I er, I don't think I can hold him off for that long Dee Dee, can we please meet earlier?' the thought of spending several more hours with Takashi filled him with dread.
'No we bleedin can't!' said Dee Dee 'Ar don't care what you av to do, if you want your dough just stall im until tonight, you got that!'. Dee Dee hung up the phone once again leaving Nikos a bag of nerves.
Dee Dee's taxi stopped at the side of the road in Parliament square 'I am wanting fifteen pounds exactly please miss' the driver said as Dee Dee stepped onto the pavement.
Dee Dee thrust a twenty pound note into his open hand 'Here's a score, keep the change' she said, laughing and pointing to his beloved statuette 'Get yaself anuvva transforma or summink'.
'Thank you very much please miss' the driver replied, 'But I am happy with my Vishnu, she guides me and keeps me safe and watches over my family and helps me to keep my faith'
Dee Dee raised her eyebrows and turned away 'Yeah whateva geez' she said, leaving him extolling the virtues of the Hindu god.
Standing outside the majestic Parliament buildings Dee Dee glance up at the face of Big Ben. It was just after mid day and the hoards of eager tourists had

begun filing through the side entrance. Dee Dee tagged on the end behind an enthusiastic Dutch family, two overweight teenagers and their parents who wished to document every second of their stay in the UK with the aid of a HD camcorder, the father barking directorial instructions to the brother and sister who by now were bored senseless at having to star in yet another pointless family movie. 'Papa i'm hungry' the daughter whined, striking a lackluster pose beside the bronze statue of Baroness Thatcher, 'Shut up and smile Klara' her father snapped 'Your cousin Otto will be so jealous when he see's this' he then snatched the games console from his son's hands and shoved him toward her 'Michael go and join your sister, and wipe the chocolate from your face'.

Dee Dee left the family arguing and began to read the list of past and present MP's written in gold leaf on the wall 'Gotcha' she said to herself on seeing Sir Geoffrey Fitzroy's name at the bottom.

Following the crowd behind an aging tour guide Dee Dee paid very little attention to his informative ramblings, concentrating instead on locating the Foreign Minister. 'I'm afraid the ministerial chambers are off limits miss' the guide said, catching sight of Dee Dee trying the handle of a locked door marked official personnel only.

'Sorry mate, ar was lookin for the karzi' Dee Dee said, rejoining the group, 'Ar'm breakin me neck for a piss'.

The tour guide ushered the group along 'The ladies and gents facilities are just up ahead if any of you would like to stop' several tourists nodded and hurried along.

Dee Dee glanced over her shoulder and saw a female member of the catering staff swipe a pass through a scanner beside the locked door and open it. Dee Dee paused for a second checking that the guide was out of sight before darting through the door herself as it slowly closed with a click. Following the sound of footsteps ahead Dee Dee descended an elaborately carved staircase, quietly apprehensive at what may lie ahead. The young lady entered the House of Parliament's kitchen and busied herself preparing tea for the ministers who had just adjourned for lunch. Hiding behind a large walk in refrigerator Dee Dee watched as a selection of refreshments were placed onto a trolley, that was it, that was Dee Dee's cover, she thought. Waiting until the lady had all but finished and had stepped into the fridge to return the milk Dee Dee closed the door slowly and flicked the catch.

'What the!' the young lady was heard saying, albeit muffled by the refrigerators heavily insulated exterior 'Hey, hey open the door!' she yelled, shoving it from the inside 'Hey anybody, please I can't get out!'. Dee Dee smiled knowing that her muted cries would not be heard beyond the kitchen, and then taking a white coat from a rack she wheeled the trolley out into the corridor and closed the door behind her.

Dee Dee kept her head down pushing the tea trolley through the busy Parliament passages passing dozens of government officials huddled in groups whispering to one another and berating their opposition. After a fruitless search of the corridors of power Dee Dee stood nibbling a rich tea biscuit 'Shit' she sighed, not knowing where to turn next, then by chance a door several meters away opened and a clerk emerged

'Yes Sir Geoffrey i'll see to it right away' he said, closing the door and scurrying away with an arm full of files.
'Result!' Dee Dee said, pushing the trolley to the door. Taking a deep breath Dee Dee composed herself before turning the handle and pushing the trolley inside 'Oy fancy a cuppa geez?' she asked Sir Geoffrey who was sat at his desk reading his brief for the afternoons debate,
'I beg your pardon!' he said, lowering his glasses and looking up, completely taken aback by her brash remark.
'A cuppa!' Dee Dee said again, tapping a tea spoon on the side of a cup 'Ar got PG, happy shoppa or this poncey shit' she held up a box of Earl grey and screwed up her face.
'What, what are you talking about?' asked the dumbfounded minister 'Who are you and where's Jacqueline' he was referring to the young lady that Dee Dee had locked in the parliament freezer,
'Oh er, she's chillin aat' Dee Dee laughed, pouring two cups of tea and approaching the desk 'Ar dunno abaat you mate but ar'm garspin' she added.
Sir Geoffrey sat stunned as Dee Dee slapped the two cups down, spilling a small amount onto his cluttered leather desk top, she then pulled up a chair and slumped down into it propping her feet on Sir Geoffrey's waste paper basket ,
'Corr, bleedin ansum' she said, blowing and taking a sip.
'Get out at once!' the Foreign minister barked, slamming the palm of his hand down firmly on his desk spilling yet more tea.
'Easy tiger' Dee Dee said, producing a sample page from the stolen document from her pocket and

tossing it down in front of him ' You might wanna av a ganda at that before ya get aat ya pram'
'What on earth?' Sir Geoffrey said, unfolding the page and raising his glasses, 'Where the devil did you get this?' he asked, recognizing it instantly 'And who are you?'.
Dee Dee leaned forward in her chair 'It don't matter who I am, an ar fink you know where ar got that from, that dodgy Arab mate of yours, naah ar don't know fuck all abaat politics but ar do know that you could be in a shit load of bovva if the papers get old of this'.
Sir Geoffrey sat bolt upright at the mention of the tabloids 'What is it you want?' he asked 'Money, I trust you have the remaining pages in your possession, can I see them please?'
'First of all mate' Dee Dee said, slurping her tea loudly 'Ar don't want ya dough, an anuvva fing, ar wouldn't be dopey enough to bring the papers wiv me would I'.
Sir Geoffrey looked every inch a worried man knowing that the guttersnipe before him held all the cards, and whatever game she was wanting to play would have to be played by her rules 'Well I assume by your visit young lady' he said, feeling powerless considering his position within the present government 'That you want something from me, so what is it?'.
Dee Dee downed the last of her tea and pushed the cup onto his desk 'Naah ya talkin' she said with a cocky attitude, relishing the moment as she so often did when she had a man on his knees. 'Ar need some favor's from ya an ar need em done like yesterday if ya nart ar mean'.
'I'm listening' Sir Geoffrey replied, having very little choice.

Dee Dee began listing her demands, one of which involved her mother Pearl who was about to begin a lengthy prison sentence after a crooked conviction orchestrated by the devious D I Pritcher. When she had finished Sir Geoffrey sat shaking his head 'I'm sorry my dear but I couldn't possibly help you with any of those matters, i'm a member of parliament for heavens sake' he then opened his desk drawer and took out his cheque book and a beautifully enameled fountain pen 'I'll tell you what i'll do' he said, signing his name and dating a cheque 'You just go ahead and name your price' the foreign minister slid the cheque book across his desk toward Dee Dee avoiding the spilt tea then proceeded to mop the residue using his handkerchief with a disapproving glare.

Dee Dee shuffled her chair closer and taking his pen scrawled 'GET FUCKED' across the cheque and slid it back, 'Ar told ya' she said, slipping the fountain pen into her pocket 'Ar don't want ya dough, poke it up yer arse, you know what ar want so sort it aat'.

Sir Geoffrey then adopted a more aggressive stance, 'Young lady' he said, condescendingly, 'I suggest you accept my offer, give me back those documents and then crawl back under whichever rock from whence you came or i'll have you arrested and thrown into prison for a very long time, and if what i'm told is true of prison life your stay will be very unpleasant indeed, do I make myself clear'. Sir Geoffrey rocked back in his chair with a wry smile feeling as though the balance of power had finally swung in his favor, but Dee Dee had other ideas

'Unpleasant' she growled, looking him in the eye 'Listen when this shit its the bleedin fan you'll be the one banged up bitin ya pillow gettin butt fucked like a bitch by the body buildin batty boys mate' The image that Dee Dee had conjured filled Sir Geoffrey with dread, taking him back momentarily to his public school days where as a new boy he was subjected to a brutal initiation ceremony, sadistic to say the least and on many occasions bordering on homosexual. 'Well em, i'll see what I can do' he said, his face a little paler now, 'But i'm afraid I can't promise you anything you do understand'.

Dee Dee sprang to her feet with a smile 'Sorted!' she cried, slapping his desk and upsetting more of his tea, she then plucked a card from his open briefcase 'Ar'll give ya a bell when ar need ya' she said turning for the door and swiping another biscuit from the trolley.

Sir Geoffrey got up from his desk 'But I did say I may not be able to help'. he replied, following behind 'I have my reputation to consider after all'.

'Your avin a laugh aintcha!' Dee Dee scoffed, 'You fiddlin fuckers'd rob yer own muvver's if you ad the chance, well let me tell ya this!' she was now well and truly up on her soap box, prodding Sir Geoffrey's chest 'Mar muvva's ad er rent doubled in the last six mumfs and er disability cut by a fird, she can't pay the council tax and they stopped her heatin allowance all because some nob like you wants anuvva ouse in the country and arf a dozen Jags, so don't give me that bollocks about reputations'. having vented her frustrations on the shocked minister, Dee Dee opened the door to leave and found herself face to face with the Prime minister.

'Ahh Sir Geoffrey' he said, overlooking Dee Dee at first 'I wonder if I might have a word'.

Sir Geoffrey was still reeling from Dee Dee's outburst 'What, what oh yes of course' he said, coming to his senses 'Please do come in'.
Dee Dee brushed past the Prime minister giving his bottom a testing squeeze 'Oy ansum' she said, gesturing to the trolley 'Elp yaself to an ob nob' she then ducked out into the hall and was lost in the crowd.
The Prime minister paused for a second in disbelief, never having been treated in such a way during his political career 'Sir Geoffrey?' he said, taking a biscuit 'Who was that enchanting creature, i've never seen her before, she's a breath of fresh air that's for sure'
'Yes, quite' Sir Geoffrey replied, sounding a little less enthusiastic, 'Now what can I do for you Prime minister?'.
As Dee Dee made her way back through the historic corridors she was unaware that an eagle eyed security guard was following behind her, 'Excuse me miss' he said, within a few feet of her 'Can I see your pass?', Dee Dee then noticed that everybody around her had an ID card clipped to their jackets and quickened her step 'Miss, miss excuse me miss!' he called, fighting his way through the teaming ministers returning from lunch.
Dee Dee pushed her way between the Home secretary and the Minister for Agriculture 'Shift yer arses!' she said, ducking back into the kitchen to avoid capture and hiding behind the door. The puffing Parliament guard ran in moments behind her and scoured the room, Dee Dee's heart was in her mouth as he approached the door having exhausted all other possibilities, but as she stood considering whether to fight or flee the young lady in the

refrigerator began pounding on the door once again having all but given up hope of rescue 'Somebody please helllllllllp!' she cried, using a leg of lamb as a make shift club 'For gods sake help me i'm locked in here!'. The guard removed his hand from the door and ran to the fridge allowing Dee Dee the time to tip toe back out into the hall and up the winding staircase to the main entrance.

The frost bitten caterer was rescued shaken but unhurt and given a mug of hot soup to help thaw her before the guard resumed his search for the intruder, but Dee Dee had fled the Houses of Parliament and hopped into a waiting taxi, 'Goodmayes mate' she told the driver, slamming the door and reclining on the back seat, smiling to herself as they skirted the impressive government buildings. 'Oy turn it up geez!' she told the driver who tweaked his stereo. Dee Dee sat tapping her feet and mumbling along to the mod classic 'going underground' 'We played this at me uncle Jerry's funeral' she said, bursting into song 'Goin undergraaand, goin undergraaaand!' The driver thought it a little strange but said nothing.

The news was next which had Dee Dee pricking up her ears, 'Overnight a young Essex lad has taken the music world by storm' the presenter reported 'Calling himself DJ Nitro the boy from Goodmayes has had more than three million Youtube hits in the past twelve hours, beating the now famous clip (Charlie bit my finger) by a mile. Tipped for instant stardom with his unique urban style of rap DJ Nitro already has an army of fans including a host of high profile celebrities including JZ, Maddona, Mandella and the Obama's to name but a few. His twitter following has already surpassed that of many of his fellow musicians making him A list material and hugely marketable, music moguls from several top labels are falling over themselves to sign the young prodigy offering six figure recording contracts and global coverage, his projected earnings for the coming year are in the range of forty to fifty million pounds through album sales, personal appearances and merchandising'.

Dee Dee sat gobsmacked 'Ar don't fuckin believe it! she said, shaking her head.

'Yeah he's great ain't he' the cabbie replied, looking at Dee Dee in the rear view mirror as they stopped at a red light 'My girls are nuts about him and even the wife can't stop singing his stuff, he's from your neck of the woods isn't he?'

'You could say that ar spoze' Dee Dee replied, struggling to see what all the fuss was about.

'Do you know him then?' the driver asked 'If you do, you couldn't get us an autograph could you, the girls'd go wild'.

'Yeah ar know im' Dee Dee said, totally bored with the conversation 'But I ain't askin the twat for no autograph, not for no one'.

Rounding the corner into Maizie's road the taxi came to an abrupt halt on seeing a line of Tv transmitter vans from seven of the major channels blocking the street ahead 'Jesus what's all this then?' the driver asked, not knowing how close he was to the rapper his family adored.

'Ar dunno' Dee Dee said, opening the rear door 'Ar'll get aat ere mate, ow much?'.

'Nothing, it's on me' the driver said, handing her his card 'Just get me that autograph yeah'.

'Yeah course ar will' Dee Dee replied, screwing up the card out of sight and dropping it in the gutter 'Ar get em a pair of iz shitty pants an'all if ya like'

While the driver sat pondering how much a pair of DJ Nito's soiled briefs would fetch on the open market Dee Dee made her way through the jostling reporters 'Scuze me, comin fru'! she said, using her elbows to great effect 'Aat me way will ya!'. The ranks of supporters had swelled, spilling over into neighboring gardens, treetops and lamp posts, the exterior of the house had been daubed with messages of love scribbled on gum wrappers and text book pages. Dozens of mobile telephone numbers had been posted through the letter box with offers ranging from oral sex to full on marriage, some of which gave Bradley cause for concern, like the girl who threatened to kill herself if she couldn't have him, or another that read 'Be with me or i'll burn your house to the ground and spit on your ashes' each of them a harsh reminder of the price of fame.
Dee Dee was pulled to one side by a Chanel Four reporter as she approached the door, 'Excuse me miss are you Nitro's girlfriend?' he asked thrusting a microphone at her face. Before Dee Dee had a chance to respond a dozen more reporters hearing only the words Nitro's girlfriend surged forward dragging their cameramen with them, 'It's Nitro's girlfriend, it's his girlfriend!' many of the crowd repeated,
'This way miss, over here!' an eager cameraman called, at once some twenty to thirty lenses were pointing Dee Dee's way flashing constantly 'What's he like miss?' they asked 'How long have you two been together?'.
Dee Dee's denials could not be heard above the delirious crowd and the questions kept on coming until she finally snapped 'Oh fuck off the lotta ya!' she yelled, thumping the door until Maizie answered,

'Oh ello Dee iss you' she said, peering sheepishly around the frame 'Ar fought it was someone from the paper's again, them buggers've bin knockin ever since you went, where ya bin anyway?'.
Dee Dee hurried inside and slammed the door behind her, snapping the end off a journalists microphone in the process. 'Ar bin up London' she replied, taking off her coat 'Ar bin to see that Fitzroy geeza'.
'What, what for Dee?' Maizie asked 'Is it summink to do wiv them papers?'.
Dee Dee made her way into the kitchen and filled a kettle 'Yeah mate' she said, popping it on it's stand and taking a mug from the tree, 'D'you want one?' she asked.
'No fanks' Maizie replied, following Dee Dee around 'Ar wanna know what appened up London it's bin bleedin mental ere ar tell ya, ar went for a dump earlier and some bloody photographer bloke up a ladder took me bleedin fota, the dirty bastard'.
While Dee Dee filled Maizie in on the afternoons events things were taking a turn for the worst at Laura's penthouse flat. Three of Billy's bully boys had arrived with news that Roland's bloated body had been dragged from the Thames after becoming firmly lodged in the Greenwich flood barrier preventing one of the mighty gates from closing. Billy was beside himself with rage assuming until now that his younger brother had escaped the warehouse raid,
'Ar never killed im!' Trisha screamed as Billy dragged her to her feet 'E fell in ar swear it!'.
'You fuckin slag!' Billy raged 'Ar'll cut your fuckin eyes aat ar will!'.
Laura leapt to Trisha's defense, grabbing her brothers powerful arms as best she could 'Billy

please don't!' she cried 'She said she didn't do it and I believe her, Billy please stop!'.
Billy turned to one of his men amid the struggle 'Tommy get this cunt off me will ya!'.
Tommy prised Lara's arms away and held her tightly 'Boss wait till later!' he said, before wincing as Laura plunged the heel of her shoe into his shin bone 'For fuck sake Laura!' he warned her, 'Calm daan or ya gunna get urt!' Tommy turned back to Billy 'Boss get the stone first then do the lot of em eh'.
Billy, now purple and drooling, reluctantly agreed, throwing Trisha violently to the floor, 'That fucker's gettin it an'all!' he yelled, pointing an aggressive finger at Laura 'From now on I aint got no famly, you got that!'
'But Bill' Laura pleaded, struggling in Tommy's arms 'I'm your sister, dad told you to look after me remember'.
Billy took a wild swing at Laura and luckily for her, missed, 'Don't you dare fuckin mention mar dad you bitch!' he snarled, fists clenched 'You gave up the right to be part of this famly when you joined up wiv these fuckin whores and slaughtered mar bruvva's, ar'll kill you just as easily as ar'd kill them fucker's and ar won't lose a minutes sleep over it ar tell ya'.
It was Trisha's turn to come to Laura's aid 'She's got nuffin to do wiv this, ar killed ya bruvva's not er ya soddin bully!'.
Billy glared at Trisha with vengeful intentions 'Your right' he growled 'I am a fuckin bully, thas how ar got to be number one on this manor, by fuckin urtin people an ar don't care ow ar do it iver, bullets, blades, ammers, iss all the same to me, ar love inflictin grievous pain I always av, you could say ar got the taste for it at school when ar stoved mar

maffs teacher's ed in wiv a raander's bat for givin me a D, the wanker'

Trisha had gotten the picture by now, Billy was the nastiest piece of work ever to walk gods green earth and he relished the fact that everybody knew it.

Billy thought long and hard about killing the pair of them there and then before tugging at another of his men's arm 'Dan gissa fag for fuck sake' he said, his nerves rattled 'Or ar fink ar'm gonna do summink everyone's gonna regret'.

Danny took a cautionary step back 'But boss' he replied, clasping the cigarette packet in his pocket 'You give up remember, you told us not to'.

Billy threw his arms in the air 'Fuck what ar told ya, gimme a fag ya stupid prick!' he yelled into Danny's face.

Danny quickly offered his boss the packet 'Yeah sorry guv' he said, flicking his zippo and holding out the flame in readiness.

Meanwhile to kill time, Nikos had managed to persuade Takashi and his men to accompany him to Sheila's, his favorite greasy spoon on the Lea Bridge road, 'Mornin Sheila my love!' he said, as he and his Japanese entourage opened the door. Chin and the other guards huddled round a table by the window and eyed the dog eared menu, each of them famished after a nights heavy drinking. 'What d'ya fancy?' Nikos asked Takashi who sat bolt upright with arms folded defiantly.

Chin tapped Nikos's shoulder 'The master will not eat here, the food has not been blessed' he said 'But we are permitted'.

Sheila approached the table wearing her trademark pinny awash with egg yolk and chip fat, 'What you avin Paps?' she asked, removing the wrinkled roll up

from between her lips 'Ar gotta lovely bitta bubble on the go'.
'I bet you av Sheila' Nikos joked 'But how longs it been on the go for, that's what I wanna know'.
'Cheeky fucker!' Sheila smiled 'Ar done it fresh free days ago, naah come on don't piss me abaat what you avin?' she licked the lead of her grubby pencil that hung on a thread around her neck.
'Ar'll have the full English and a tea' Nikos said, replacing the menu 'You got any black pudding?'
'Yeah course I av' Sheila replied, looking at him fondly 'Anyfing for you Paps' she then changed the subject 'So when you takin me aat then babe, you bin promisin me for ages, ar'm free tonight and that new chipmunk films on at the Odeon'.
Nikos had been avoiding Sheila's advances for many years but her persistence was limitless 'Ar got some new suzzies an'all' she lifted the hem of her skirt to reveal the crimson lingerie wrapped around her heavily stretch marked legs 'Go on av a feel!' she added, shuffling closer 'Ar got em for you'.
Nikos buried his head in the menu 'Er, can I have a fried slice with that?' he asked, feeling pressured 'And what about you boys' he asked the hungry guards 'fancy a fry up?' they hastily agreed without actually knowing what it entailed. 'Make that five specials and tea's all round' Nikos told Sheila who stood scribbling onto her pad, each and every word spelt wrongly ,sossige and baykon being a prime example of her educational deficiency.
'Milk?' she asked, nibbling the end of her pencil, Nikos and the guards nodded but Takashi said nothing 'MILK?' she asked again, spitting the pencil splinters from her mouth 'Come on I aint got all bleedin day!'

Chin raised his hand 'Is the milk from yak?' he asked, having catered for his bosses eccentric dietary requirements for several years.
Sheila rammed the pad into her pinny pocket 'Yak my arse!' she said, stomping back to the kitchen 'Iss from bleedin Summerfield's like the rest of mar shit!' she grunted 'Fussy fuckers'.
Chin and his fellow guards were more than happy with their breakfasts, mopping every morsel from their plates and slurping down their tea greedily. Takashi on the other hand hadn't touched his cuppa, feeling out of place in the seedy east London cafe and growing tired of the loutish chatter from the scaffolders on the adjacent table.
'Ar said look babe!' one of them said loudly, puffing out his chest 'Ar know ar was bangin ya sister at the weddin but iss you ar really love ain it'. his three friends fell about laughing
'What, and she fell for that shit did she Jim?' one of them asked.
'Yeah course she did the soppy cow' Jim laughed 'She aint that bright mar Treesa, fank fuck'
'Why's that mate?' his friend asked 'How long you bin smashin er sister then?'
Jim was laughing so hard by this point he could hardly speak 'Since we got engaged back in two faasand and free, she's a pucka ride though mate!'.
One of Jim's pals leaned across to Takashi 'Oy granddad, chuck us the pepper!' he said, as his breakfast arrived in front of him, Takashi did not flinch, 'Oy Mr Miagi' the scaffolder joked 'Ar said sling us the pepper for fuck sake!'
Still Takashi sat rigid and unfazed. Nikos offered the man the condiments but he swiftly declined 'I asked the bleedin chink' he said, with a more menacing

tone 'So stay aat of it you twat'. his body language and racist slur had Takashi on edge as were his men. 'OY DIM SUM!' he added, looking at his friends for encouragement 'Ya makin me look a mug ere so just gimme the fuckin pepper before ar lose me rag and kick the shit aata ya'.

Nikos backed up against the wall on seeing Takashi's hand slip inside his robe, the final insult came when the scaffolder dipped one of his chips into the tomato sauce and flung it at Takashi's face. Quick as a flash Takashi leapt from his seat, drew his sword and brought it down swiftly and powerfully, slicing the table they were seated at in two, sending their breakfasts and beverages tumbling into their laps 'Aaaargh what the fuck?' Jim screamed, his manhood scolded 'You fuckin!' before he could finish his sentence Chin and the others each had swords at their throats 'Shit, shit, shit!' Jim's friends cried, not daring to move 'Sorry mate, sorry onest!'. The scaffolders were guided to the door on the end of the samurai swords and sent scampering on their way with beans and tea dripping from their trousers. Sheila came storming from the kitchen, hearing the commotion 'What the fucks goin on?' she said, then took a quick step back on seeing the swords, 'Jesus wept!' she gasped 'Looka mar poxy table'.

Nikos rose to his feet 'Sheila babe let me pay for the damage' he said, taking out his wallet 'It was all a big misunderstanding that's all'.

Sheila snatched a fifty pound note from Nikos's open wallet and stuffed it into her sagging bra, 'Thatta cover the table' she said, clutching her chest 'But for my emotional distress you'll av to take me to see the chipmunks, or ar'm callin the old bill'.

'No don't do that my dear!' Nikos said, placing his arm around her waist, feeling sick at the same time 'Of course i'll take you out'. Nikos then held the door open for the others 'Come on fellas, I think we need to vacate' he said, giving Sheila a half hearted wave.

CHAPTER TWELVE.

The trade.

Eight fifteen that evening, Dee Dee and Maizie sat loading their pistols, full of apprehension 'Ang on' Maizie said, her hands shaking. She reached into a kitchen cupboard and took out a bottle of brandy 'Iss bin in ere since Christmas' she said, taking two mugs from the draining board 'Ar reckon it'll elp wiv the Dutch courage, what d'ya fink?'

'Fuck yeah' Dee Dee agreed, removing the cap and holding the bottle to her nose and then half filling the mugs 'Cheers mate' she said, taking a large gulp and wiping her lips, screwing up her face in the process.
'Strong innit' Maizie laughed.
'You aint wrong Maize' said Dee Dee, refilling both mugs.
Half a bottle later any doubts that they may have had were gone and cocking their weapons with a smile the two girls drained their mugs, slamming them down on the table
'Less do this' Dee Dee said, sliding her chair back.
'Fuckin avvit!' Maizie added 'Ang on a minute Dee' she said, looking out of the window 'Ow we gonna get past that bleedin lot?'
Dee Dee joined her, Bradley's car was completely hemmed in by countless news crew vehicles 'Shit!' Dee Dee cursed then thought for a moment 'Old up ar got an idea' she said, grabbing her phone from the side and calling the police,
'What ya doin Dee?' asked Maizie,
Dee Dee raised her hand to silence her friend 'Ello is that the old bill?' she asked 'Ar wanna report a streaker'
Maizie was completely dumbfounded at this point 'What the?' she said, but Dee Dee knew that the police worked hand in hand with the media, tipping them off whenever a newsworthy story came in and thus pocketing the bungs and backhanders 'Er yeah' Dee Dee continued 'Ar just see Paris Ilton joggin butt naked in Ide Park wiv an am bag dog under er arm' Maizie could hardly believe her ears and hadn't the foggiest idea how this would help their current predicament. 'Yeah it was definitely er' Dee Dee told

the police officer before hanging up the phone and staring out of the window.

'Deeee!' Maizie said, tugging at her arm 'Woss goin on?'

'Shut up a minute' Dee Dee replied, brushing the curtain to one side. Sure enough one by one the news crews got the call from head office and raced to the Royal Park to snap the saucy celeb, soon the road outside was clear.

'Fuck me Dee, your a genius' Maizie gasped, 'But what about that lot?' the garden and pavement was still crammed with eager Nitro fans who would surely follow them wherever they went, and as Bradley was there only driver this just would not do.

'We need to disguise im' said Dee Dee, thinking out loud,

'Ar know!' Maizie said, raising her hand 'Ar got that Jack Sparra outfit in the wardrobe, ar never give it back after the Christmas party'.

'Don't be bleedin daft' Dee Dee scoffed 'E'll stand aat a blinkin mile e will, no e'z gotta look normal just like us'

'What, a girl?' Maizie said, even more lost now.

That wasn't what Dee Dee had in mind but never the less it was a brilliant idea 'Fuck yeah we'll dress im as a bird' she laughed, 'Summa your shit should fit im'.

'Ar was jokin Dee' Maizie said, thinking the plan ridiculous 'Besides e'll never go for that'

'Your jokin aintcha' Dee Dee smiled, 'That dirty little bugger'll love it, come on you get the gear ar'll sweeten im up'.

Dee Dee tapped on Bradley's door then marched straight in catching the would be superstar cavorting on his bed with five besotted babes, a ladder propped against the window ledge to gain entry. ‘Dee for god sake man!’ Bradley shrieked, covering his privates, ‘Ar need a bitta privacy blud, nart ar mean’ Bradley then gave Dee Dee a theatrical wink, hoping she would get the message and leave but Dee Dee had other ideas

‘Get rid of these slags ar need ya’ she told him.

‘Eya, who you callin a slag?’ one of the lovelies asked, pulling her top back up over her breasts ‘Who are you anyway, iz muvva?’ the other girls laughed out loud which riled Dee Dee

‘Listen you fuckin retards’ she snarled ‘If you don’t piss off you’ll be goin aat that bleedin winda wivaat a poxy ladder, d’you ear me!’

The girls leapt from the bed realizing they were no match for Dee Dee, leaving Bradley dejected ‘Yo girls don’t listen to er she’s just messin’ he said, tugging at a shapely leg ‘Dee tell em ya just messin innit’ he said, clasping his hands together in prayer.

‘I aint fuckin abaat’ Dee Dee warned, ‘Just do one before ar really spit mar dummy aat’.

One by one the teen totty hitched up their skimpy skirts and climbed back out the window much to Bradley’s dismay, ‘Ar don’t believe it man’ he sulked ‘Ar was gonna do it wiv all of em’ he crossed his arms and refused to look at Dee Dee.

‘Yeah dream on limp dick’ she laughed as Maizie entered the room carrying a selection from her wardrobe.

‘Eeya put these on’ Dee Dee said, tossing them on the bed, Bradley’s eyes immediately lit up ‘Oh ar get it’ he smiled, ‘You want dem ho’s aat the way so we can av some rude sexuality with this kinky shit, man ar’m definitely up for dat’

'Just put the bloody clothes on, you dick' Maizie said, dragging a hair brush through a brunette wig.
Bradley looked shocked as he slipped into a pair of cerise hot pants 'You aint joinin in sis' he cried, struggling with the strap on a pair of four inch heels 'I aint into that fucked up shit man so do one while me and dirty Dee get some lusty lovin goin on'.
Dee Dee and Maizie both laughed out loud 'I aint doin nuffin wiv you, you prat' said Dee Dee, tossing him one of Maizie's bra's 'You might wanna put some stuffin in that coz you aint got nuffin up top av ya'.
Bradley stood half dressed 'Ang on a minute' he said, flinging the halter neck top on the bed 'If we aint gonna do some kinky shit, what the fuck am I wearin this gear for?'.
Maizie put the wig on his head and straightened it to fit his bewildered face 'Coz we need ya to drive the mota bruv and we aint got time to fuck araand wiv that lot aat there, besides' she laughed 'I always wanted a sister'.
Bradley tore the wig from his head and threw it across the room 'No way, no way man!' he said, pacing the room 'There's no way ar'm goin aat there dressed like a blinkin slut, no way ar tell ya'.
'OY!' Maizie yelled, poking his chest 'Mar gear aint slutty, iss designer that is, proper an'all'.
Bradley sat on the end of the bed crossing his arms defiantly 'Ar don't give a monkey's what it is I aint wearin it and thas blinkin final, alright!'.
Dee Dee pinched Bradley's ear between her thumb and forefinger and hoisted him to his feet 'Listen to me you dumb fuck' she growled 'Trisha's in a shit loada trouble and she needs our elp so unless you want me to tell those bitches aat there all your gangster shit was a loada bollocks you better put that

gear on and get in touch wiv ya girly side, ar know ya got one'.
Bradley looked at his sister for support, but she merely tossed the wig back in his face 'Urry up bruv, ar do ya makeup when ya ready'.
'MAKEUP!' Bradley shrieked, 'Naah you are takin the piss!' but Bradley's futile protests fell on deaf ears as the two girls set about beautifying him, and if there was one thing the two friends knew, it was cosmetics, having spent countless hours preparing for steamy nights on the town, teasing and tantalizing the boys of east London. Maizie's magic make up box contained every product conceivable to transform the ugliest of ducklings into the most beautiful of swans.
Dee Dee had to restrain Bradley at times while false lashes and mascara were applied,
'Pukka up will ya!' Maizie said, smearing on her new red hot glitzy lipstick.
'Bleedin ell Brad' Dee Dee laughed 'You look better as a bird mate, ar tell ya'.
'Shut up will ya!' Bradley whined 'This is proper fucked up this is'.
When Maizie had finished, Bradley did in fact look stunning, 'Eeya' she said, handing him a black Dior clutch bag,
'I aint takin dat' he said, backing away,
'Why the fuck not!' Dee Dee said, assuming Bradley was about to back out 'Evry girl needs an ambag'.
Bradley pointed at his feet 'Coz it don't go wiv mar shoe's man' he said, having observed countless ladies in his time, albeit from afar 'Aint ya got nuffin in beige levva?'
'Ar knew it' Dee Dee said, slapping his bottom playfully 'Ar knew you'd love a bit of girly clobba ya saucy sod'.

Maizie retrieved a cream Chanel handbag from her room 'Ar got evry bag for evry occasion me' she said, tweaking Bradley's wig and wiping a smudge of blusher from his cheek 'Sorted!' she added, turning Bradley to face the mirror 'What d'ya fink?'.
Bradley was astounded by his transformation 'No shit man!' he cried, turning to check out his curves 'Ar look well sick, and ar love what these hotty pant fings do for me arse, ar mean just look at me crack sis, iss well fit, ar can't stop strokin it'.
'No fanks bruv' Maizie said, gathering her things 'Ar'll give that a miss'.
Dee Dee noticed the time on Bradley's Lara Croft wall clock, it was half eight and they still had to get to Stockwell, which was a good twenty to twenty five minutes away, 'Come on you two we gotta go' she told them, but Bradley, no matter ho depraved had never worn heels
'Shit this is well ard!' he said, stumbling along the hall, clinging to the banister 'Aint you got anyfink flat sis, ar'm walkin like ar'v bleedin shit meselfl'
'We aint got time!' Dee Dee snapped 'Just make do wiv them!'.
Opening the front door, the three of them were confronted with dozens and dozens of screaming girls, each expecting Nitro to appear at any moment.
'Comin fru, scuze me, comin fru!' Maize said, tactfully nudging the girls aside.
Dee Dee on the other hand showed less restraint 'Oy, get the fuck aat mar way ya dozy gits' she yelled, swatting a ten year old fan with the back of her hand 'Ar said aat the bleedin way the lotta ya!'.
On hearing this, the sea of faces parted crushing several of them against the crumbling wall.

Bradley then emerged like a roaring drunk teetering uncontrollably on the treacherous heels 'Oh shit man!' he cried, tripping on the threshold and falling face first into a fresh faced fan,
'Get off me ya silly cow!' the girl screamed, shoving Bradley aside, 'Where's D J, when's he comin out?'.
Bradley didn't dare let on it was him in drag for fear of wrecking his fledgling career, but with all that totty around he just couldn't resist squeezing a lycra clad bottom or two, 'Oy get your ands off me ya filfy dyke!' one girl yelled, slapping Bradley's face, 'That dirty cow touched me an'all' said another.
'Time to go' Dee Dee said, taking hold of Bradley's arm and dragging him out the gate.
Once in the car, Bradley had to discard the shoes and drive barefoot while Dee Dee and Maizie checked their weapons once again,
'Don't fuck araand Maize' Dee Dee told her friend 'Just shoot the fuckers if you av to, d'you ear me'.
'Ar'll try Dee' Maizie replied, hesitantly 'But I aint never killed nobody before, what if ar can't do it?'
Dee Dee spun round in her seat and pointed the barrel of her gun at Maizie's head 'Naah you listen to me Maize!' she said, glaring at her 'Them bastards av got Trisha, and they know we done two of the Tibbs's already so they aint just gonna let er go are they'
'But Dee ar fought! Maizie said, interrupting,
'You fought what!' Dee Dee snapped, 'You fought we was just gonna give em the stone and they was gonna let er go just like that, no ard feelins or nuffin'
'Well yeah' said Maizie, moving the barrel of the gun away 'Well it'd be nice wouldn't it'
'WHAT D'YA MEAN NICE?' Dee Dee stormed, waving the gun around 'These buggers aint nice,

they'd put a bullet in your ed as soon as look at ya, so ar'm tellin ya Maize, don't even esitate girl, if ya see it goin tits up you shoot any fucker that get's in ya way'.

'Ok Dee' Maizie said, her hands visibly shaking 'Shoot the fuckers, yeah right ar got it'

'You better bleedin av' Dee Dee warned her, then jabbed Bradley's leg 'Get a move on will ya, iss twenny past already'.

Bradley recoiled in his seat 'Shit Dee man thas mar shot up leg innit!' he squealed 'Ar need some more pain killers blud, iss proper stingin'.

Dee Dee waved her gun under Bradley's nose 'If you don't put your foot daan ar'll shoot the uvver bleedin leg you prat!'.

Bradley instinctively accelerated unaware he had just run a red light 'Alright, alright!' he said, rubbing his bullet wound.

Suddenly to their horror the deafening sound of sirens could be heard behind them, 'Shit!' Dee Dee cursed 'Fuck iss the old bill!'

'Oh no man ar don't believe it!' Bradley said, slowing to stop 'Thas all ar bloody need innit'

'What ya doin?' Dee Dee asked, checking the time 'Put ya friggin toe daan and lose em will ya'

'No way blud!' Bradley replied, shaking his head and checking the rear view mirror,

'They'z got a Subaru man, that ride'll piss all over mar Nova innit, besides ar got six points on me license already and two bald tyres, a dodgy brake light and no tax'.

Dee Dee laughed 'Oh your proper fucked you are, there gonna chuck the book at you mate'.

Bradley cringed at the thought of a custodial sentence.

'What we gonna do Dee?' Maizie asked, ramming her gun into her pocket 'We're tooled up and everyfink'

'Shut up!' Dee Dee snapped 'We'll av to sweet talk the buggers, push ya tits up Maize and give em an eyefull, opefully they wont notice what a piece of shit this mota is'.

'What about me man?' asked Bradley, looking down at his atire 'Ar can't go daan looking like a friggin pussycat doll'

'Well put it this way' said Dee Dee, winking at Maizie 'The faggots in Pentonville'll fink Christmas has come early when you turn up!'.

The thought of being the bitch of B wing filled Bradley with dread 'Oh shit man, shit, shit ar told ya this was fucked up didn't I'

'Shut the fuck up will ya' Dee Dee said, taking charge of the situation yet again'. The squad car driven by a lone traffic cop pulled up behind them, Dee Dee shoved her pistol into the glove box and pulled her top down almost to her nipples.

The officer approached the car with his ticket book in hand, sending a shiver down Bradley's spine 'Fuckin ell man!' he whispered 'E'z gonna nick me ar know it'.

The officer tapped on the roof of the car 'Wind your window down please Miss' he said sternly,

Bradley did so, forgetting momentarily he was dressed as a girl 'Woss up mate?' he asked. Dee Dee jabbed his leg once more and leaned across him giving the officer a birds eye view of her cleavage 'Woss the problem officer?' she asked, pouting her lips 'Was we goin too fast or summink?'. The traffic cop took a closer look at the three occupants and immediately felt a twinge in his trousers 'Well well

well, hello ladies' he said, smiling 'Off out for the night are we?'
'Yeah we're goin clubbin!' Dee Dee replied, 'And we're a bit late mate'
'Well that's no excuse for running a red light now is it' replied the officer, relishing the feeling of power over the girls 'Are you aware that not only are you putting yourselves in danger but by driving as recklessly as you were you are putting other road users in just as much danger'
Dee Dee did her best to look humble 'Sorry mate it won't appen again, onest' she said, almost choking on her words.
The officer took a particular shine to Bradley who in comparison with Dee Dee and Maizie, looked the most tarty, 'Could you step out of the vehicle please Miss' he said, opening Bradley's door
'Ay!' Bradley replied 'Ar mean pardon officer' he added in a higher pitch.
'Come on, out' the officer barked, pointing to the pavement 'Come on I haven't got all night'. but his motive was purely a selfish one, he was wanting to get a closer loom at Bradley's rear in the cerise hot pants. Bradley looked across at Dee Dee for moral support before stepping out of the car.
'Verrry nice!' said the horny officer, looking Bradley up and down, which didn't sit right with Bradley at all, 'What ya looking at?' he said, keeping his rear out of sight.
The police officer folded a page back on his ticket book 'Now i'm afraid there is the matter of this very serious traffic violation' he said, attempting to frighten Bradley.

Dee Dee leaned across a little further 'Can't ya give us a break mate, please' she said, fluttering her eyelashes 'We won't do it again, we promise'
'Yeah we promise!' Maizie reiterated 'We're good girls we are'.
The officer grinned, knowing he had them in the palm of his hand, 'Well on one hand' he said, toying with Bradley's hair 'I could issue you with a sixty pound on the spot fine and three penalty points, then go over this vehicle with a fine tooth comb and nick you for every fault, of which i'm sure there are many, or!' he paused for a moment, checking out Bradley's legs.
'Or what?' Dee Dee asked, eager to be on her way.
'Or' the officer continued, growing ever more aroused 'Your friend here could give me a little kiss'
'GET STUFFED!' Bradley cried, stepping back 'I ain't no batty boy, ar mean girl'
The officer began filling in his ticket 'Ok if that's the way you wanna play it, but I warn you we could be here for some time, right, name?'.
Dee Dee glared at Bradley 'For fuck sake brad just kiss im will ya!' she barked 'We aint got time for this shit'.
'No way blud!' Bradley said, holding his hands up 'No fuckin way man, I aint doin it ar tell ya, iss sick man!'.
The officer looked puzzled 'Brad?' he said, 'What kind of names that for a girl?'
'Iss greek!' Dee Dee told him 'Iss short for Bradelina, the goddess of cross dressers ar fink'
'Bradelina, I like that' the officer said, looking down at Bradley's bare feet 'Mmmm i've got a thing for toes i'll have you know' he told them ' So er, what's it gonna be then Bradelina honey?'

Dee Dee was growing ever impatient 'Brad just urry up and kiss im will ya, we gotta go, go on we won't tell anyone'.
Bradley could ill afford the extra points on his license but the thought of kissing another man turned his stomach 'Ar can't do it Dee, iss just too weird man!'.
Maizie wound down her window and stuck her head out 'Brad ar'm gonna give you such a fuckin slap in a minute!' she said, angrily 'Just shut yer eyes and snog the bloke will ya!'.
Bradley had nowhere to turn 'Ok!' he sulked, 'But if you'z say a word, ar mean it, ar'll murderize ya boaf'
'Yeah whateva' Dee Dee said, ushering him toward the lusty cop 'Just get on wiv it'.
Bradley drew a deep breath and screwed up his face in anticipation, both Dee Dee and maizie covered their eyes, gagging at the thought of it themselves as the officer moved in, grabbing the back of Bradley's neck and locking lips for what seemed like an age. Bradley stood mortified, his face turning white while his bottom was savagely groped. Then feeling a hand slide up his torso towards his chest he pulled away and leapt back into the car 'Can we go now?' he said, in a panic stricken tone 'Ar really wanna go please' his eyes were firmly fixed on the road ahead.
The crooked cop scribbled his number on a piece of paper and tucked it in the neck of Bradley's top through the open window 'Course you can darling' he smiled 'Listen if you ever fancy a weekend away give us a ring, i've got a caravan in Camber Sands with a king size bed in it'.
Bradley started the car, hardly daring to look in the officers direction 'Whateva geez' he said, tearing away from the kerb leaving the policemen adjusting his trousers and looking very pleased with himself, it

had been just another perk of the job to him but to Bradley it was a distressing and harrowing experience that would live with him for a very long time.

'Ow was it then?' Dee Dee asked, making conversation.

'Ow was what?' Bradley said, putting all thought of his ghastly encounter out of his head.

Dee Dee slapped his arm 'Ya snog wiv the copper' she laughed 'What d'ya fink ar mean, eeya Maize' she said, turning round, 'That copper looked like e proper enjoyed it didn't e?'

'SHUT UP WILL YA!' Bradley yelled, spitting several times out the window and wiping his tongue on his sleeve, 'Dat was gross man, ar can't believe you'z made me do it, ar feel proper sick ar do'.

Maizie tapped her brothers shoulder 'Ar bet your tempted by the caravan though aintcha' she chuckled 'You used to love Camber Sands when we was little'.

Bradley ignored his sister, trying desperately to block the thoughts of the officers snake like arms around him.

'Me nan ad a caravan at Leysdown years ago but it got struck by lightnin it did'. Dee Dee said, turning to Maizie,

'Oh no' Maizie gasped, 'Ar never knew that mate, was she in it at the time?'

'Yeah not arf!' Dee Dee said, recalling the event 'She was sittin on the chemical loo watchin Strictly, poor cow, the farmer faand her dumped upside down in a friggin edge smuvvered in er own shit!'.

Bradley forgot his recent brush with the law for a second and burst out laughing.

'It ain't bleedin funny!' Dee Dee snapped, retrieving her gun 'She's still avin counselin for it'.

At precisely Eight fifty nine Bradley pulled up outside Stockwell tube station, the Tibbs's car was parked in a side street with the lights on but nobody inside. Maizie tapped Dee Dee's shoulder 'Fuckin ell ar'm shittin meself mate' she said, her hand tightening on the butt of her pistol.
'Just remember what ar told ya' Dee Dee said, abruptly 'And don't let me daan or we're all fucked, d'you ear me'
'Yeah, yeah ar remember' Maizie replied, 'Shoot the fucker's, right'
Dee Dee stepped from the car 'Yeah thas it' she replied, then tapped on the roof 'Keep the mota runnin' she told Bradley, who looked the most nervous,
'But Dee man!' he said, looking over his shoulder 'What if the old bill come, ar mean ar'm parked on double yella's here'.
Maizie gave her brother a reassuring pat on the head 'You'll be alright bruv' she smiled 'If it's a nice lookin bobby you can tickle iz tonsils wiv ya tongue like you did that uvver geeza'.
'Oh shut up Maize!' Bradley cried, wiping his mouth once again 'Ar told ya I aint no batty boy innit!'
'Yeah wahteva bruv' Maizie laughed as she and Dee Dee headed for the station entrance with a degree of trepidation 'You loved it ya gayboy!' she called back.
'You shut up sis, ar mean it!' Bradley called after her, then quickly wound up his window as a group of lads walked by,
'Ello sweetheart!' one cocky boy said, rubbing his crotch against the car door, 'Want summa this do ya?' he slurred. His friends grabbed him around the waist and dragged him away

'Sorry love, he's wankered' his friend said, waving politely. Bradley acknowledged them with a sultry nod before locking all the doors, he then sat hunched over the wheel feeling ridiculous and most of all, vulnerable.

The station was bustling with late night commuters as the two apprehensive girls made their way inside 'What naah?' asked Maizie, looking around furtively 'Ar can't see Trish, can you?'.

Dee Dee was too tense to reply, a guard at the end of the corridor then caught her eye, he looked nervous, standing beside a wrought iron concertina door with his right foot tapping uncontrollably and his hands rammed inside his pockets. 'You here for Mr Tibbs?' he asked in a gruff voice, whilst pulling his tweed cap down over his eyes as if to hide his identity.

'Yeah where is e?' Dee Dee asked, doing her best to appear confident and assertive under the circumstances. The guard said nothing more but slid the creaking door aside and ushered them inside with a grunt. A winding staircase before them descended deep beneath the station some two hundred meters 'What, down there?' Dee Dee asked, The guard grunted again, slid the door shut behind them and scurried away clenching the hundred pounds that Billy had given him tightly in his pocket. 'Twat' Dee Dee said, peering down the stairwell which appeared bottomless.

Maizie was now a complete bag of nerves saying to herself over and over in her head, 'Shoot the fuckers, shoot the fuckers'

'Come on' Dee Dee said, leading the way, her heels clattering on the iron spiral steps.

The air grew colder the deeper the two girls descended causing them to shiver 'Ar shoulda put me leggins on' Maizie remarked, pulling her short skirt down an inch lower. The girls then stopped as the thunderous sound of a train approaching the station on the other side of the wall grew louder and louder until they could barely hear themselves think, the lights dimmed and the aging stairs shook

'Friggin ell!' Dee Dee said, clinging to the rail with one hand and covering her left ear with the other.

'What d'ya say Dee?' Maizie yelled, clasping her ears too. Soon the din subsided as the train came to a halt

'Fuck me!' Dee Dee sighed 'Ar fought the bleedin fing was comin fru the wall'

'Yeah me an'all' Maizie said, dislodging her ear wax with a probing finger.

Continuing down, moments later Dee Dee stopped sharply on seeing a pair of feet on the landing below, nudging Maizie's arm the pair proceeded with greater caution. It was Danny, Billy's hired gun waiting at the halfway point to make sure the girls were unarmed and alone. Puffing on a barely lit roll up the scouse hard man beckoned them forward as the now familiar sound of an approaching train rendered any attempt at conversation pointless. Danny gestured to Dee Dee to raise her arms to enable him to pat her down, with Maizie close behind cringing amid the deafening racket the girls inched forward,

'Shit, shit, shit' Maizie muttered, then froze as Danny reached into his pocket for his cigarette lighter after his roll up died yet again, 'OH FUCK!' Maizie screamed, fearing the henchman intended to draw a weapon. With the train roaring into the station and Dee Dee's previous warning resounding in her head Maizie yanked her pistol from her pocket, shoved

Dee Dee aside and fired five shots in rapid succession in Danny's direction, 'Aaaaaaaarhh!!' she yelled, clenching her eyes tight shut.
Dee Dee dived to the floor as the first shot rang out 'WHAT THE?' she screamed, covering her ears. After the last shot had left her gun, Maizie opened her eyes slowly and saw Danny lying slumped against the wall, all but one of Maizie's bullets had missed him by a yard, ricocheting off the Victorian porcelain tiled walls. It was the third bullet in fact that found it's target passing straight through Danny's body directly beneath his right shoulder, he was alive but reeling in agony clutching the wound, a severed artery pumping blood in time with his racing heart beat.
Dee Dee was in a state of shock herself, any one of Maizie's stray bullets could have quite easily taken her life that night 'You dozy bitch!' she cursed, clambering to her feet and shoving Maizie against the wall 'What the bleedin ell d'ya fink ya doin?'
'What ya told me Dee' Maizie replied, brandishing her pistol 'Shootin the fuckers!'.
Dee Dee was lost for words for a moment, Maizie was right of course, but some warning would have been greatly appreciated, 'Just tell me next time ya gonna shoot the bloody place up' she snapped, releasing Maize's throat, 'Ar'll wear a tin at and a bullet proof blouse'
'I aint that bad dee' Maizie said, straightening her top,
'Your avin a laugh aintcha!' Dee Dee said, recalling their childhood 'Member the fair at Central park!'
'Oh yeah' Maizie smiled 'Ar got a teddy bear for me shootin didn't I'

'Too right ya did!' Dee Dee agreed 'But they give ya that mangey fing to get rid of ya after you shot four goldfish and a bleedin coconut'.
Maizie hung her head 'It weren't mar fault Dee the sights were aat, they always are aint they'.
Danny opened his eyes and gritting his teeth he reached for his gun 'Ar don't fink so geeza!' Dee Dee said, kicking it from his hand and tapping his bloodied wound with the barrel of hers 'If ar was you ar'd get that sorted mate, coz if that keeps pissin blood like that you'll be dead in under an hour, believe me' Dee Dee's limited medical knowledge was gleaned from countless hours spent watching hospital drama's, the young doctors in white coats especially catching her eye.
Defiant, Danny reached for his mobile phone and proceeded to dial Billy's number 'Billy!' he said, hearing his bosses voice, but Dee Dee grabbed the phone from his hand and hurled it against the wall, then rammed the end of the gun barrel deep into the open wound, twisting it maliciously, causing the gangland heavy to writhe around the floor in an ever increasing pool of his own blood
'Betta make that arf hour!' Dee Dee said, grimacing.
'Ok, ok!' Danny cried, holding up his hand in defeat 'Ok ar'm goin!' He wrenched himself to his feet using the handrail and began to climb the stairs using the wall to stabilize himself and leaving a trail of blood droplets behind him.
Only when Danny was out of sight did the girls lower their weapons and breath a heavy sigh 'Jesus Dee ar fink ar've pissed meself' Maizie said, holding out her quivering hand 'I aint bin that scared since we done the weegie board at ya mums, ar couldn't sleep for weeks after that shit'

'It was me ya doughnut' Dee Dee admitted, 'Ar was movin the fingy'
Maizie stared at her friend in disbelief 'Your kiddin!' she gasped 'Oh thas out of order Dee, ar shit meself when it said ar was gonna marry geeky Pete and spend the rest of mar life metal detectin wiv im and our six spotty kids, oooh thas enough to give anyone nightmares that is, e used to look at me funny in maffs e did, bleedin wierdo!'
Dee Dee couldn't help but laugh 'E used to look at everyone funny you idiot' she said, continuing downward 'Ar fink e ad double glazed glasses or summink, the boss eyed bugger'.
Nearing the bottom of the stairwell the wind being drawn through the ventilation shafts grew stronger on the two girls faces and the tell tale sound of rats foraging amongst the debris sent a chill up their spines. Up ahead they saw a light flooding from an open door from which muffled voices could be heard,
'You ready?' Dee Dee said, concealing her gun but maintaining a tight grip on it,
'Ar fink so' replied Maizie, checking all around her feet for ravenous rodents,
Dee Dee then tapped Maizie's pocket 'You just bleedin watch what your doin wiv that shoota will ya' she said, having more than enough on her plate to worry about, what with the South London mobsters intent on revenge let alone whether her own friend was going to put a stray bullet in the back of her head.
'Yeah ok Dee' Maizie said, cocking her pistol in readiness 'Ar fink ar'v got the ang of it naah'
'Thas what ar'm worried abaat' Dee Dee said, stepping to her friends left so as to be out of the line of fire, she then pulled the giant ruby from her inside

pocket, 'OY TIBBS!' she yelled, her voice echoing through the labyrinth of drafty corridors and timeworn tunnels.

Moments later Billy emerged holding Trisha by a handful of her hair 'Well well!' he smirked, 'Nice of ya to drop by ladies'.

'You alright Trish mate?' Dee Dee asked 'E aint urt you as e?'

Trisha struggled to break free but the wrenching only caused her greater pain 'Ar'm alright Dee' she said, giving Billy a defiant stare 'Iss real good to see ya though mate, and you Maize'.

Billy shook Trisha violently 'Shut up!' he growled 'We aint ere so you slags can bitch to eachuvva, you got mar stone or what?' he asked Dee Dee who held the ruby aloft

'Yeah ar got it!' she called back, 'Let er go and ya can av it'.

Billy laughed and drew a knife from his jacket pocket, pressing the blade to Trisha's throat 'You listen to me you stupid bitch!' he snarled, almost drooling 'You don't av any say in ow this is gunna go, just give me the fuckin stone or ar'll cut this cunt in arf, d'you ear me!'.

At that point Laura came running from the room pursued by one of Billy's men 'No Bill please don't hurt her, please!' she cried,

Billy glared at his gang member as he grabbed Laura by the arm and restrained her 'Ar told you to fuckin old er you moron!' he said, venomously 'Get er back inside, naah!'

'NO!' Trisha yelled 'She goes wiv me or the deals off!'.

'No fuckin chance!' said Billy, nodding to his man to remove his sister 'She's gonna get woss comin to er, you mark mar bleedin words'.
'Dee tell im!' Trisha pleaded 'Tell im it's the ruby for the two of us, please mate we can't leave er ere'. Billy had heard enough of Trisha's bleating, raising his hand and swiping her across the face with real intent, his twenty two carat sovereign ring carving a deep gash in her left cheek,
'OY LEAVE ER YOU BASTARD!' Maizie screamed, surging forward, Dee Dee quickly pulled her back 'Ang on mate!' she told her, realizing all too soon that her friends life was in the hands of a mad man 'Alright!' she shouted 'You can av the stone!'.
Billy smiled a knowing smile and whistled for his boys to show themselves, three gun toting gorilla's sauntered from the room leaving Laura tied to a chair 'Ar told ya you don't av any say did'n I' Billy said, smiling confidently 'You see your gonna give me that stone but there's no fuckin way you bastards are leavin ere alive, not after what you done to mar bruvva's, ya know, an eye for an eye and all that shit, so chuck me the stone and ar promise mar lads'll make it quick'.
Outgunned the girls looked at each other, a long lingering look as though it would be their last 'Sorry mate' Dee Dee told Maizie who struggled to control her trembling limbs 'This is mar fault'.
Trisha turned and spat in Billy's face 'Don't you do it Dee!' she told her friend 'Don't give im the ruby, just run, the pair of ya!'.
'I aint leavin ya Trish!' Dee Dee called back.
Billy snarled and wiped his face 'You slag!' he said, peeling back his clenched fist so as to plunge his knife deep into her stomach,

'EEYAR!' Dee Dee yelled, waving the ruby above her head 'Take it!'
Billy paused, seeing the precious stone glinting in the half light, 'Gimme it!' he said eagerly.
Maize stood frozen to the spot, unable to run as Dee Dee pulled her arm back to toss the ruby to Billy, once their one and only bargaining chip had gone their fate would surely be sealed. But fate hadn't finished with the three amigo's because Dee Dee suddenly felt a hand clasp around hers,
'I believe that is mine' Takashi said, stepping from the shadows and pocketing the gem, 'Step aside please' he then told Dee Dee 'We will handle this, oh and your money, it is safe with Nikos'.
'Result' Dee said, taking Maizie's hand and ducking behind a hoarding.
'Who the fuck are you?' Billy asked, brandishing his knife 'And what the fuck are you doin wiv mar rock?'
Takashi stood beneath a flickering light with his hands in the sleeves of his robe 'I am Takashi Nakajima' he said, abruptly 'And you and your men should savor what precious seconds of life you have left'.
Billy took a moment to process Takashi's threat before bursting out laughing 'You've got some bollocks you av' he chuckled, 'Comin down ere and fretenin me and mar firm, who d'you fink you are, Bruce flippin Lee or summink, go on, leave the stone and fuck off back to ya noodle shop before ar get mar lads ere to go to work on ya, and trust me me old china, it won't be pleasant'. Billy and his men laughed confidently but then stopped abruptly as Takashi's four assassins stepped into the light to join him.
'So ya've come for a row av ya!' Billy said, puffing out his chest in a show of bravado, 'Well you just made

the biggest mistake of your life geeza, this is mar manor and ar'm gonna keep it that way, so you enjoy your last fuckin seconds' he turned to his men 'Kill these cunts!' he barked. Billy's three gunmen drew their weapons and began firing a volley of bullets towards Takashi and his men who merely stepped aside with blistering speed, avoiding shot after shot without flinching. Takashi himself drew his sword and swatted several bullets like angry wasps with the shimmering blade.

Billy stood dumbfounded as his men emptied their entire magazines in Takashi's direction and not a single bullet had hit it's mark 'Come on you slags!' he barked at his boys 'Fuckin kill em!'. While his men reloaded frantically Takashi approached them with stealth and precision hacking the backs of their ankles, thus severing their Achilles tendons causing them to drop to the floor, unable to support their body weight.

'Arrrrgh fuck fuuuuck!' each of them cried, trying to stem the flow of blood.

Shell shocked, Billy backed away still clutching Trisha's hair and wondering in the back of his mind if he had maybe bitten off more than he could chew, 'Get up you useless pricks!' he screamed at his men who inched away on their backs from the menacing Takashi who towered above them with blood dripping from his blade.

Dee Dee and Maizie watched from the relative safety of their bolt hole still fearful for their friends safety 'E don't fuck abaat does e' Maize said, clinging to Dee Dee's arm, 'GET OUR MATE WILL YA MISTER!' she called out to Takashi.

Billy looked Trisha up and down and smiled 'You want this bitch!' he said, gripping his knife tightly,

'You can fuckin av er!' with this he plunged the full seven inches of cold steel into Trisha's side,
'NO, FUCK NO!' Dee Dee screamed, dashing into the light. Trisha let out a pitiful cry before slipping from Billy's grasp and collapsing with a thud on the rough concrete floor, the south London crime boss stood wielding his bloodied blade snarling at Takashi and his men
'Come on you fuckin wankers, less avit' he yelled, having faced greater odds in the past and emerged victorious, fending off skinhead and Yardie gangs who dared encroach on his turf, it had gotten to such a point that he and even his men believed he led a charmed life or maybe even an immortal one. 'COME ON!' he roared again as Trisha lay limp and lifeless at his feet.
Takashi grabbed Dee Dee by the arm as she raced toward her dying friend 'NO, NO LET ME GO!' she cried, 'TRISHA, TRISHA!' she wrestled to break free but Takashi's grip was strong 'TRIIISH!' .
Maizie sat in floods of tears watching a pool of crimson blood grow at Trisha's side and the color drain from her battered face. Dee Dee buried her face in Takashi's shoulder sobbing and screaming her friends name. Takashi had never been shown compassion neither had he shown it to another, but something came over him that night, he found himself slipping an arm around Dee Dee however awkward it made him feel, then with a nod of his head he let his dogs loose, sending his four faithful warriors to tackle the head of the Tibbs empire. With acrobatic perfection Chin and the others tumbled and rolled towards Billy putting him off guard with their aireal agility,

'What the fuck?' Billy said, taking a step back, but before he knew what was happening the guards dropped at his feet, raised their swords above their heads and thrust them downwards simultaneously through his chest and stood looking him in the eye. Billy stood in a state of deep shock for several seconds, staring at the four gilded hilts protruding from his jacket, 'That was the nuts ar give ya that' he said, gargling blood and showing the men a modicum of respect, his eyes then fluttered as he went into cardiac arrest, staggering backwards until his legs buckled beneath him.

Maizie leapt to her feet and rushed to Trisha's side 'Trisha, Trisha!' she said, trying desperately to rouse her, but Trisha's internal hemorrhaging and punctured lung meant that without immediate hospital treatment she would undoubtedly die.

Dee Dee tore herself from Takashi's clutches and joined Maizie at her side 'Shit no Trish!' she said, feeling powerless for the first time in her life, she then turned to Takashi 'Please elp us!' she said, pulling Trisha's head to her chest 'Please mister, please ar'm beggin ya!'

Maizie rocked back and forth caressing Trisha's hand mumbling 'No, no, no ,no' and feeling empty inside. Chin and the others looked first to Takashi who nodded in agreement then stooped and gathered Trisha in their arms and headed for the stairs with Dee Dee and Maizie following quickly behind, clinging desperately to one another.

Takashi took a moment to gather his thoughts, looking with contempt at Billy's mutilated men cowering at his feet and then at the villain himself. Billy was always destined to die by the sword, figuratively speaking. His grip on the south side of the river was finally at an end and without a shadow of a doubt there would be more cause for celebration amongst the residents now that his oppressive regime had been crushed.

Takashi was about to follow the others when he heard a muffled cry coming from the side room, it was Laura gagged and bound to a chair. She had heard the commotion outside but saw nothing of her brothers brutal slaying, but what she really didn't expect to see was a Japanese war lord with a blood spattered samurai sword enter the room. 'NO, NO!' she mumbled, edging her chair back across the room, fearing Billy had sent Takashi to kill her. Takashi reached behind the now hysterical girl and slashed her bonds, freeing her hands and feet.

Laura leapt to her feet and backed into a corner wrenching the oily rag from her mouth, 'Please don't kill me!' she begged, clasping her rope burnt hands together 'I've done nothing wrong, please!'.

Takashi held out a hand 'Come' he said 'You are free' he wiped the blood from his blade and slipped it beneath his robe 'Come you friend needs you'.

Laura knew instinctively that it was Trisha who was in trouble, 'Trisha, where is she?' she cried, running from the room and past the stricken gangsters without giving them a second look. 'Trisha!' she called, sprinting up the stairs two at a time until she finally caught up with them at the landing, 'What's happened?' she said, seeing her lovers lifeless body in the arms of Chin and his associates .

'She's bin stabbed' Dee Dee told her 'By that bastard bruvva of yours!'.

'Billy!' Laura said, looking back down the stairs, her heart in her mouth 'Where is he?'

'This lot shish kebab'd im!' Maizie said with a bitter tone 'Good job an'all, I ope e rots in ell'.

Laura deduced by this that her elder brother was dead, but oddly enough she felt no sorrow 'I can't say he didn't deserve it' she said emotionless 'When I think back at all the people he's hurt over the years, many of them undeserving, I am ashamed to bare the same name'. The three of them hurried after the Japanese guards, up and out of the busy station where shocked men and women stood and stared at the bloody mess that was once a beautiful bubbly young girl.

Bradley was sat listening to the nightly news in his car, secretly fondling his stuffed bra and blowing kisses to himself in the mirror. He was feeling particularly pleased with himself as the newsreader had just reported that D J Nitro's youtube clip had had more hits than the recent top ten put together and that music giants Sony were about to make him a seven figure offer for his next five albums. 'Booyaka!' he said, clenching his fist 'Das what ar'm talkin bout blud!', but then seeing Trisha's body being carried from the station he leapt from the car 'Shit man woss appened?' he asked, seeing the trail of blood behind her, 'Maize woss appened to er?'

'She's bin stabbed in the guts bruv' Maizie said with a worried look on her face 'Iss bad bruv, real bad ar fink'.

'Is she gonna die?' Bradley asked, trying to flick a piece of chewing gum from the soul of his foot.

'NO SHE FUCKIN AINT!' Dee Dee yelled, shaking him by the scruff of his neck,

'She aint gonna die d'you ear me, she fuckin aint ar tell ya!'.

As Kim and Lee slipped Trisha onto the back seat of their hired Limo Nikos leaned over from the front 'Oh my god!' he said, never having seen so much blood 'The poor girl, we need to get her to a hospital, hurry by the looks of things we don't have much time!'.
'We'll folla ya!' Dee Dee told him, dragging Bradley back to his car 'Come on urry up!' she told Laura, who stood in a state of shock, 'You gettin in or what?' Laura climbed in beside Bradley and sat with her head in her hands, unable to speak. Dee Dee and Maizie sat huddled together on the back seat watching as Takashi joined the others in the limo and it sped away from the station forecourt. Both girls knew but would not dare say that Trisha's chances of survival having lost over half of her body's blood supply were slim to none. Squeezing each others hands to the point of pain they willed their friend to live.
Bradley approached a red light 'GO FRU IT!' Maizie shouted, slapping his back 'Ar don't care ow many coppers you gotta kiss you keep up wiv that fuckin mota, d'you ear me!'.
Bradley didn't dare refuse glancing in his rear view mirror at the two manic faces behind him, 'Yeah no probs sis' he said, accelerating to catch Takashi's car. After six flashing speed camera's the Limo and Nova skidded to a stop outside St Bartholomew's, 'Quick get aat!' Dee Dee told Maizie, who fumbled with the door handle 'Come on for fuck sake'.
Nikos hurried around the car to open the door for Chin and the others, 'NURSE PLEASE HELP US!' he called, to two girls outside on their break, 'HURRY PLEASE, SHE'S BEEN STABBED!'. One of the nurses ran to help while the other hurried inside to

inform the crash team who, moments later emerged with a trolley.
'What's happened?' a doctor asked, finding it hard to locate the entry wound amid the congealed blood 'Where has she been stabbed, did anybody see it?'
'There ar fink' Dee Dee said, pointing to Trisha's side 'Please you gotta elp er' she added, grabbing the doctors arm.
'We'll do the best we can' he replied reassuringly, 'But by the looks of things your friend has lost a lot of blood, we'll have to check that we have enough stock to replace it'.
'Just do it will ya' Dee Dee said, looking down at her friends face 'You gotta save er, tell me your gonna save er, tell me!'.
The doctor removed Dee Dee's hand from his arm and led the way into the hospital 'like I said miss' he told her 'We'll do everything we can, now please, let us do our job, after all, time is of the essence here'.
'E'z right Dee mate' Maize said, putting an arm around Dee Dee 'These lot know what they're doin''.
Takashi stepped from the car and approached the two girls as Laura followed the doctors inside 'I must go' he told Dee Dee, taking her hand 'I hope your friend lives and recovers well' he added.
Dee Dee choked back the tears 'Yeah so do I mate!' she replied, flinging her arms around his neck, which made him feel a little uneasy, 'Fanks for what ya done' she whispered, then looking over his shoulder she smiled at Chin and the others 'And you blokes, you were brilliant!'.
Takashi pulled away and took a small card from his pocket 'Somehow I think our paths will cross again one day' he said, handing it to her.

Dee Dee looked at the strange Japanese markings on it which meant nothing to her, but at the bottom was Takashi's private telephone number. 'Fanks' she said, slipping it in her jacket pocket, 'Ar text ya sometime'.

Takashi clapped his hands and his men climbed back into their car, 'Goodbye, and thank you for the ruby' he said, pulling his robe around his legs and climbing in beside Shuji, 'Now go to your friend' he added as his blackened window closed and the limo pulled away leaving Dee Dee and Maizie waving goodbye.

'How did you do it?' Nikos asked, standing beside Dee Dee.

'Do what?' she replied, watching the limo disappear out of sight,

'Mr Nakajima is a psychopath' Nikos explained 'But somehow you seemed to have tamed him'.

Dee Dee took Maizie's hand once again 'Ar dunno' she said 'Ar reckon we're two of a kind or summink' she then prodded Nikos's chest, 'So if you fuck us for our dough, you know what's comin dontcha!'

Nikos had seen enough of Dee Dee to know she was deadly serious 'My dear I simply wouldn't dream of it' he told her 'Come by my place tomorrow and i'll have it ready for you, now run along and make sure your friend is ok' Nikos hailed a waiting cab and hopped inside, smiling at the thought of being at least three million pounds richer and knowing there would be no rebuke from the infamous Tibbs brothers.

'Yeah come on Dee' Maizie said, running into the hospital in time to see Trisha's trolley being wheeled into an elevator,

'OY OLD UP!' Dee Dee yelled, racing to her 'Woss appnin, where you takin er?'

'Up to theatre' the doctor replied, pressing the third floor button 'You'll have to wait here, i'm sorry' Dee Dee and Maizie watched helplessly as the elevator doors slowly closed, fixing their gaze on their critically ill friend to the last.

'She is gonna be alright ain't she Dee?' Maizie said, looking her friend in the eye.

'Ar dunno Mate' Dee Dee replied, taking a seat by the coffee machine 'Ar really don't know'. Bradley and Laura joined them, each not uttering a word during the next three hours while a team of brilliant surgeons, the best in fact that the cash strapped NHS had at it's disposal, led by doctor Charles Klyne who's god like gift had saved countless Trauma victims just like Trisha.

During the tense operation Trisha's weakened heart stopped beating five times sending her into immediate cardiac arrest, the team worked tirelessly to save her, shocking her fragile torso with the defibrillator to regain a pulse, however weak, much of the time the beeping cardiograph kept a slow irregular tone in the background.

Dee Dee and the others took turns to pace the corridors with a thousand memories of their beloved bungling friend racing through their minds, like the time she stampeded a heard of camels at a watering hole with her phones screeching ringtone while out on a desert excursion in Sharm El Sheikh. The three girls and their arab guides were forced to walk thirty five miles in scorching temperatures back to the resort. Dee Dee and Maizie, both badly sunburnt refused to talk to Trisha for three days during their Egyptian holiday, but somehow the pair could never remain angry with her for too long, Trisha was like that, her infectious smile and blundering cavalier attitude to life had won her many friends, each of their lives enriched in some small way for having met her.

Doctor Klyne struggled to stem the flow of blood from Trisha's ruptured artery with clamps and dozens of swabs, each of the team knowing in their hearts that their efforts were futile. While her friends agonized downstairs Trisha went into arrest yet again,

'CLEAR!' doctor Klyne yelled, shocking her chest, he and the nurses stared at the flat line on the cardiograph, willing it to beep, but nothing, 'Come on' he said, shocking her again 'Come on young lady' again and again he shocked her while a nurse mopped his sodden brow, but still nothing.

The nurses one by one glanced up at the clock on the wall, 'Doctor' one of them said, taking his hand,

'You should stop' but doctor Klyne was a tenacious man, flinging the paddles aside he began to administer CPR pressing rhythmically on Trisha's chest 'Come on, come on!' he said, through gritted teeth.

'Doctor please' one of his senior assistants said, shaking his head, 'We should call time'.

Doctor Klyne slowly removed his tired and bloodied hands from Trisha's chest and stared at her face for a moment, he had saved many more patients than he had lost during his long career but never the less each fatality took a heavy toll on him, 'Two forty three am' he said, looking each of his staff in the eye, they nodded in solemn reply. Removing his hat and gown Doctor Klyne stepped back from the table, visibly shaken 'Close her up' he told his assistant 'I'll inform her friends'

'Would you like me to do it doctor?' a young nurse asked, wishing to spare him the burden,

'No, no, i'll do it' he replied, backing slowly out of the theatre, 'Be sure to clean her' he told his staff, knowing that friends and family would wish to view her body before she was laid to rest.
Dee Dee was sat with her head in her hands when the door opened and Doctor Klyne approached them with his head bowed 'No' Dee Dee said, rising to her feet 'No, no don't you say it!'
'I'm so sorry' Doctor Klyne said, wringing his hands 'We did all we could, i'm really am so sorry'. Dee Dee turned to Maizie who dropped to her knees, wailing hysterically, clasping her head, unable to comprehend what had just been said. Laura sprang to her feet and ran from the hospital in floods of tears while Bradley sat beating his head gently against the coffee machine.
'No, no I aint avin it!' Dee Dee said, clenching her fists 'I aint avin it ar tell ya, you get back up there and save mar mate, go on, get back and save er!'.
Doctor Klyne stood with a deadened look in his eyes as he had done before, watching loved ones crumble before him at the news of a passing, 'She was just too weak' he told them 'You have my deepest condolences, she obviously meant a great deal to all of you'.
'She's our mate!' Dee Dee cried, fighting to catch her breath 'Please, please, please try again, she's our mate, she's our mate ar tell ya, please save er!' Dee Dee's knee's then buckled beneath her as the enormity of the situation hit her.
Doctor Klyne caught her as she fell towards him, her eyes puffed and swollen with tears. Suddenly everything they had strived for, the money, the clothes, the chance of a better life meant nothing without Trisha, a hollow aching pain filled their

hearts. Dee Dee pounded on the Doctor's shoulder with her fist as he hugged her tight 'You gotta save er, please!' she cried.

Bradley helped his sister to her feet and wrapped his arms around her 'Ar can't believe it sis' he said, licking the tears from his top lip.

'Ar know' Maizie sobbed 'Tell me it aint appnin Brad, please tell me this aint appnin'.

While Trisha's friends slowly came to terms with the fact that the miracle they had prayed so hard for was not coming and that in fact the friend they loved and cherished so dearly had gone from their lives, the nurses and assistants set about the grim task of making her body presentable. She lay on the table, the green sheets that covered her, heavily blood soaked 'Poor girl!' one male nurse remarked, he then looked over at the cardiograph that was still letting out a continuous beeeeeeeeeeeeeeeeeeep! 'Turn that off!' he told a nurse, removing his mask.

As the nurse approached the machine her finger barely touched the switch to turn it off when there was the faintest of beeps and the flat line twitched ever so slightly causing her to step back as if she'd seen a ghost, then there was another tiny beep and a twitch, the other nurses and assistants approached the machine in disbelief as the beep grew louder and the twitching line grew stronger. Each of them in turn turned slowly and stared at Trisha's stricken body detecting the faintest of movements on her chest, 'Get Doctor Klyne!' one assistant told the nurses 'Get him, NOW!'

An ecstatic nurse fled the room, bounding down the stairs completely disregarding her own safety and burst out into the lobby, momentarily annoying the Doctor who was offering Dee Dee Maizie and

Bradley a few words of comfort. 'DOCTOR, DOCTOR KLYNE IT'S THE GIRL!' she yelled, 'IT'S THE GIRL DOCTOR, SHE'S BACK!'
'WHAT!' Doctor Klyne snapped, still peeved at her intrusion 'What are you talking about?'
'We have a beat sir!' she told him 'We have a pulse!'.
'That's impossible!' replied the Doctor, adopting a realistic attitude 'Have you checked the cardiograph?'
'Yes sir, it's working fine' she said, excitedly, 'You have to come back Doctor, she's alive!'.
Dee Dee looked up into the Doctors eyes, her head a mess of emotions 'Well what the fuck are you waitin for?' she smiled 'Get yer arse back up there and elp mar mate!'
'Yes, yes!'. Doctor Klyne said, helping Dee Dee to her seat and hurrying after the nurse.
'Is she really gonna be alright?' Maizie asked Dee Dee, wiping her face 'Is she Dee?'
'You fuckin bet she is!' Dee Dee said, crossing her fingers tightly, 'She's a bleedin fighter she is'.
Maizie clasped her hands together and looked to the tiled ceiling 'Come on Trish mate, you can do it' she begged, 'Come on we need ya!'
'She's gonna be alright! Dee Dee said 'Ar can feel it' she then stood and punched the air 'COME ON TRISHA YOU FUCKIN BEAUTY!' she screamed, willing her friend with every ounce of her being to fight for her life 'COME ON TRISHA MATE, YOU CAN DO IT!'.
Doctor Klyne replaced his mask and rejoined his dumbstruck team in the operating theatre, 'My god it's true' he gasped, seeing that Trisha's heart was beating slowly but unaided, 'Right team!' he said, scrubbing up 'Seeing as how this young lady refuses to die I suggest we give her every possible chance to

live, what do you say?' his elated team all nodded and set about their work.

Meanwhile Dee Dee was growing restless downstairs and started up the stairs 'Where ya goin Dee?' Maizie called after her 'We're supposed to wait ere!'

'Fuck that!' Dee Dee replied 'Trish's up there and she needs us, you comin or what?' Maizie looked at Bradley and the two of them ran to join Dee Dee. Locating the theatre the three of them stood with their noses pressed firmly against the glass, hoping and praying that Trisha was strong enough to pull through,

'Come on girl!' Dee Dee mumbled.

A further ninety minutes of frantic surgery followed, but this time the team performed with a renewed confidence, pulling out all the stops and working through exhaustion and hunger to save this little bloodied miracle that lay before them. Eventually doctor Klyne emerged slipping off his hat and mask, the next few seconds of silence seemed more like hours to Dee Dee and the others as they waited intently and diligently for the news they so desperately craved.

'She's stable' Doctor Klyne said, smiling 'For the life of me I don't know how but your friend is stable' these epic words washed over the three friends like an emotional tidal wave and had Dee Dee and Maizie leaping into one another's arms

'Yes, yes fuckin yes!' Dee Dee cried,

'Bleedin ell Dee!' Maizie added 'Does this mean she's gonna make it, is she really gonna be ok?'. Bradley slid down the wall and sat with his face in his hands quietly sobbing, the past few hours had been all too much for him.

Doctor Klyne was almost bowled over by the jubilant girls as the flung themselves at him, 'Fank you, fanx doc!' Dee Dee laughed, 'Your a bleedin genius you are!'.
'Well she's not quite out of the woods yet i'm afraid' Doctor Klyne told them 'The next twenty four hours are going to be critical to her chances of ever leading a normal life again, so we'll have to keep a close eye on her'.
'She aint never led a normal life!' Maizie laughed, 'So ow we gonna tell the bloomin diffrence?' she then stooped and helped Bradley to his feet 'Oh bruv, bruv don't cry' she said, hugging him.
'Bruv?' Doctor Klyne remarked, looking Bradley up and down, his mascara had run and one of his false boobs had slipped a great deal lower than the other.
'Oh er yeah' Dee Dee said, struggling for an explanation 'He's got issues thas all, nart ar mean'.
'Yes, quite' the Doctor replied 'Now if you'll excuse me I must get back inside'
'Oh yeah crack on!' Dee Dee said, holding the door open for him.
Whether it be divine intervention, the dogged determination of the tireless NHS surgeons or just plain unadulterated luck that saved Trisha that night, the truth of the matter is, it just wasn't her time. She was eventually moved to the intensive care unit where nurses could closely monitor her progress.
'You go home bruv' Maizie told a tired looking Bradley 'Me and Dee'll stay and keep an eye on er'
'Ok sis if your sure' Bradley yawned 'Ar'm totally fucked, gimme a call in the mornin yeah, let me know woss appnin'. Bradley left his sister and Dee Dee at Trisha's bedside and drove home craving a bath, his bed and most of all his own clothes.

Dee Dee and Maize spent the next hour caressing their friends hands and talking softly to her, although she was heavily sedated,
'You ad us goin there Trish mate' Dee Dee told her, still fighting back a tear or two 'If you'da left us ard'a give you such a bleedin slap ar would'
'Yeah me an'all' Maizie smiled 'Coz ya still owe me fifty quid for me iPod fingy ya broke, ya doughnut'
'What, you an'all' Dee Dee asked Maizie, having lent Trisha hers the week before 'The dozy mare managed to wipe evry bitta music I ad off mine and get me edphone wires in a major fucked up knot'. The two girls began a lengthy conversation discussing the pitfalls of being a friend of Trisha while she lay unconscious before them,
'Ar lent er me bike to go to the chippy once' Maizie reminisced, 'The brake cable snapped goin daan Bluebell hill, she mounted the friggin kerb and crashed into me uncle Alfie's veg stall, it was in the gazette an evryfing'.
'Yeah ar member that' Dee Dee laughed, 'What abaat that copper in Corfu she tried to set me up wiv?'
'Oh yeah, e was fit as fuck e was' Maizie said 'What appened, did ya cop off wiv im?'
'Did I fuck!' Dee Dee said angrily 'Silly nuts ere said leave it to er coz she could speak the lingo, lingo my arse, she ended up tellin im e'z a filfy dago twat and to go fuck iz cousin wiv a courgette, so no ar didn't cop off wiv im fanx to er'.
Maizie looked at her bed ridden friend with fondness 'Ya gotta love er though aintcha Dee' she smiled 'She's totally barkin but fings wouldn't be the same wivaat er would they?'. Dee Dee was forced to agree and after a brief discussion on Trisha's finer qualities

the pair of them drifted off to sleep with their heads resting on Trisha's bed.

Throughout the night and much of the following morning the hospital staff busied themselves at Trisha's bedside while Dee Dee and Maizie slept.

A further three days drifted by with very little change, but the on the fourth day around ten thirty am, Trisha stirred 'Doctor Klyne, doctor Klyne I think she's awake!' a nurse called out,

The Doctor hurried to her side 'Good morning young lady' he said as Trisha raised her eyelids, unable to focus at first 'You gave us all quite a scare you know' he added, checking the strength of her pulse 'Your a very remarkable girl' he told her 'I've never known a trauma patient come back from the brink in the way that you did and go from strength to strength in such a short space of time, it really is astonishing'.

Trisha looked down and saw her dozing friends at her side 'Dee' she said, still very weak 'Maize'.

'They've been here all the time you were unconscious' the Doctor said, adding to her charts, 'They've been worried sick about you, the pair of them'.

Trisha stretched out her arms as best she could and ran her fingers gently through Dee Dee and Maizie's hair, 'They're good mates they are' she said, fondly.

Dee Dee stirred, rubbed her eyes and wiped her mouth 'Trish!' she said, taking her hand 'Trish mate your awake, oh shit mate ar'm so glad, Maize wake up for fuck sake' Dee Dee shook Maize violently 'Oy ya silly bitch wake up will ya'.

Maizie was a notoriously heavy sleeper at the best of times but after having very little sleep the night before she would require a more proactive approach, Dee Dee quickly grabbed the daffodils from the elderly ladies vase on her bedside locker beside them and beat her friend around the head with them, showering her with petals 'Oy Maizie wake up will ya you arse wipe, Trisha's up!'

'Steady on there' Doctor Klyne said, intervening and snatching the stalks from her and replacing them in the vase as the old lady slept.

Maizie came too, rubbing her head, 'Woss up Dee, wod'ya wake me for?' she asked, frowning.

'Alright Maize' Trisha said, managing a smile 'Ad a good kip av ya?'

Maizie came to her senses, flinging her arms around Trisha's neck 'Trish mate fank fuck!' she cried, squeezing her tightly.

'Ow, ow careful Maize' Trisha said, wincing, 'That bleedin urts'.

'Sorry mate' Maizie replied, backing off 'Ar'm just so glad to see ya thas all'.

Trisha tugged at the tubes in her right arm 'Whatta mar doin ere?' she asked 'What appened Dee ar don't remember a fing'. Trisha's brush with death had left several side effects, least of all being a spell of amnesia.

'You was kidnapped by that arsehole Billy Tibbs' Dee Dee explained, 'We was gonna give im the ruby to get ya back but some Japanese geeza turned up wiv some kick arse ninja's and killed im, but the bugger stabbed ya first'.

'What!' Trisha cried, peering under the sheets at her dressing 'Bleedin ell, was it bad?'. Dee Dee and Maizie couldn't bring themselves to tell her she had died several times on the operating table 'Nar just a scratch ar fink' Dee Dee said, winking at the doctor 'Eh doc'

'Well a little more than a scratch i'd say' Doctor Klyne remarked, ever the professional 'But I don't see any cause for concern at this stage, get plenty of rest and i'll be back to check on you later'. with this he hung Trisha's notes on the end if her bed and continued his rounds

'Fanks again doc!' Dee Dee called after him.

'Yeah cheers mate!' Maizie added, shaking the daffodil petals from her hair.

The girls chatted until Trisha, still weak from her ordeal, drifted off to sleep again 'Come on Maize' Dee Dee said, picking up her handbag, 'Less bugger off and let er sleep' she then tugged a nurses sleeve, 'Scuze me' she said 'When our mate wakes up tell er we've gone ome to get changed and we'll be back up later'.

'Yes of course' the nurse replied 'Visiting time are between two and four'

'Yeah whatever' Dee Dee told her as she and Maizie left the ward.

That afternoon when Dee Dee and Maizie had recovered from their emotionally draining few days they took a taxi to Hackney to visit Nikos, 'Alright Niky boy!' Dee Dee said, entering the shop.

'One moment ladies' Nikos replied, seeing to an elderly chap at the counter who was attempting to pawn his first world war medals to pay his over inflated council tax and his heating bill. 'Well there's not a lot of call for these nowadays' Nikos told him, always on the look out for a bargain 'I tell you what, i'll give you thirty quid for the lot'.

The mans face dropped 'Thirty pounds!' he said, his bottom lip quivering as he remembered the harrowing circumstances in which the medals had been earned. Under heavy mortar fire he and a small group of men had stormed an enemy gun emplacement thus allowing allied troops to advance unhindered, but his regiment had suffered heavy losses, including three of his best friends and his beloved twin brother Charlie who had died in his arms at the bottom of a water logged trench, 'Well I suppose that will have to do' he said, choking back a tear.

'Ang on a minute!' Dee Dee said, intervening, 'What ya sellin ya medals for geez?' she asked, her great grandfather had served in North Africa during world war two and used to fill her head with stories of battlefield heroics.

'Well needs must and all that my dear ' the man said, rubbing the medals fondly in the palm of his hand.

'Ar tell ya what' Dee Dee said, putting a hand on his shoulder 'Ar'll give ya ten grand to keep em'.

The man smiled assuming she was joking and turned to Nikos 'Ok i'll take the thirty pounds if that's all your offering' he said laying the medals of valor down on the counter. Nikos was about to snatch them when Dee Dee slammed her hand down over them

'Get aat of it ya feevin fucker!' she snapped 'They aint for sale!'

'But, but' the man said, desperate for the cash 'I don't have any choice'

'Yeah ya do' Dee Dee told him, pinning the medals to his chest and holding out her hand,

'Gimme ten grand Niky' she said, giving Nikos a determined stare 'Ar know ya got it'

'Are you serious?' Nikos replied 'Those medals are worthless' he added.

'To you maybe ya maggot' Dee Dee snarled, 'Just gimme the fuckin dough will ya, are know ya minted now after our caper'.

Nikos's share from the sale of the red sea ruby was well in excess of two million pounds making him a very wealthy man indeed, never the less he still couldn't resist driving a hard bargain 'I tell you what' he told the old man 'I'll make it a hundred and that's far more than they're actually worth and leaves me absolutely no margin for profit'.

Dee Dee leaned across and grabbed Nikos by his paisley tie 'Profit you slag!' she said, angrily 'You've ad enough profit outta me to last a friggin lifetime, naah give im ten grand or you and me are gonna fall aat, big time!'. Maizie took a step back , having seen her friend lose her cool on many occasions.

Nikos prised his tie from Dee Dee's grasp 'Ok, ok i'll get him the money!' he said, ducking beneath the counter and spinning the dial on his heavily fortified safe, 'There you are' he said, counting out ten one thousand pound bundles, 'Seven, eight, nine, ten thousand'.

'Cheers' Dee Dee said, stuffing the cash into the startled old mans pockets 'There ya go mate' she told him 'That should see ya alright, just don't let me catch ya tryna flog them medals again, d'you ear me'. The old man was speechless at first, having had to scrape by on his pathetic war pension for so many years,

'Gawd blessya darlin' he said, drying his eyes 'Gawd blessya, ar mean that'.

Dee Dee saw him to the door 'Go on off ya go' she said, patting his back 'Go and get yaself summink nice for tea'.

'Ar will' the man said, waving goodbye 'Ar might get meself a tin of spam and a rice puddin, oooh ar can't wait'

'You do that gramps' Dee Dee called after him 'Coz thas proppa rock and roll that is'. Dee Dee closed the shop door and turned the sign to closed 'Right Niky you dodgy fuck' she said, approaching the counter 'You'll be glad to know our mate's alrights so you got our dough or what?'
'Yeah' Maizie added, peering behind the counter 'Come on, and it over!'.
Nikos produced an open laptop from behind the counter 'My dears I can do better than that' he said, tapping at the keyboard 'I took the liberty of depositing your share into three offshore accounts, thats just over three million pounds each, all you need do is enter your details here now and a courier will deliver your platinum cards within the hour'
'That saands a bit moody to me' Maizie said, expecting a large bundle of cash.
Dee Dee studied the screen 'Ow do we know this is kosher?' she asked.
Nikos explained to the girls how the rich and famous use such accounts to avoid the UK's hefty tax levy 'I assure you this is all above board girls, I have an account myself'
'Ar bet you do you slippry fucker' Dee Dee said, thinking it over 'Ar spoze iss better than a bleedin great wad in ya pocket, what do you recon Maize, shall we max the plastic or what?'
Maizie was a little unsure but trusted her friends instincts 'If you fink iss pukka Dee then yeah ar'm up for it, ar know Trisha's details'
'Yeah ok Niky' Dee Dee said, turning the laptop to face her 'But you know ar'll kick yer arse if this is moody'
'Yes, yes of course' Nikos replied 'But I promise you it's absolutely perfect for people in our position'

'What, feefs ya mean?' Maizie asked, tapping her name and date of birth into the computer.
'Well I like to think of myself as an entrepreneur' Nikos told her with a devilish grin 'A shrewd business man with my finger on the pulse'.
Dee Dee looked him in the eye 'Yeah well you won't av a bleedin pulse if you fuck us over' she said, entering her own details 'A'll put your address daan Maizie' she told her friend 'Coz ar can't go back to the flat' It then suddenly dawned on her that she was finally free of the gruesome tower block that had been her home for so many years.
'What about ya mum Dee?' Maizie asked, 'The poor cows banged up coz of us'
'Yeah ar know' Dee Dee said, the thought of her mother behind bars weighing heavily on her mind 'Ar just ope that fucker Fitzroy get's iz finger aat' she sighed,
With their money safely stashed Dee Dee and Maizie left Nikos and returned home, 'Fuck me Dee, we're propper minted ain't we' Maizie said, stepping from the taxi and fighting her way through the hoards of adoring Nitro fans once again, many of them now wearing their own pajama's and bling as Bradley had done previously. Maizie was about to slip her key in the lock when the door opened and Bradley appeared followed by two men in suits 'Alright bruv, woss up?' she asked.
Bradley had a broad smile across his face, 'Guess what sis!' he said, hugging her, 'Dese geeza's just signed me to there label man, ar got a mill up front and a bitchin record deal, ar made it sis, ar propper made it!'. Bradley's recording contract would indeed make him a very wealthy young man with a chance to travel the world and perform alongside many of his

childhood hero's 'We'z just goin to a press conference or summink so ar catch ya later yeah' he was mobbed by the screaming girls all the way to the waiting limo which whisked him off to central London where he would be formally introduced to the worlds media. Many of the fans chased his car to the end of the road while the others stole trophies from his mothers garden, the headless meerkats and even the rusting gate,

'OY YA FEEVIN FUCKERS!' Sharon screamed, waving a rolled up radio times in the air 'COME BACK WIV MAR FRIGGIN GATE!' one remaining young girl was about to flee when Sharon swiped the back of her head with the magazine 'And that's for me bleedin meerkats' she yelled 'Go on piss off!'.

Later that afternoon, as promised a motorcycle courier delivered a package containing three platinum cards with Dee Dee, Maizie and Trisha's names on them 'D'you reckon these are pukka?' Maizie asked, slipping hers into her purse,

'There's only one way to find aat' Dee Dee smiled 'Less go shop!'.

Hopping into a Taxi, the two girls hit London's west end with more money at their disposal than they had ever dreamed of, 'Ar dunno what to buy!' Maizie said, standing in Oxford Street surrounded by designer stores that were once off limits to her.

A beautiful diamond Cartier watch had caught Dee Dee's eye 'Ar'm avin that' she said, with her nose pressed against the glass 'Ar'v ad enough of snides, ar'll get one for Trish an'all'. Venturing inside the store Dee Dee was apprehensive at first

'Can I help you madam' the tall well dressed assistant said, looking her up and down 'Perhaps you'd like to see something from our discount range'.

'No ar bleedin wouldn't' Dee Dee replied, taking his comment to heart 'Ar want to av a look at that watch in the winda, the one wiv the gold face and the diamonds on it'.
Again the assistant looked down at her 'Madam that's a nineteen hundred pound limited editiontime piece' he told her, expecting a shocked response.
'Thas alright' Dee Dee said, producing her card 'Ar'll av two of em'
The assistant recognized the card instantly 'Yes, yes of course madam' he said, changing his tone 'If you'd like to take a seat i'll bring them right out'. Entering her pin number Dee Dee held her breath for a second or two, wondering if the transaction would be accepted, 'That's fine madam' the assistant said, handing her back her card and the watches 'If I can be of any further assistance, please don't hesitate to ask'.
'Bleedin ell Maize!' Dee Dee gasped 'Ar could get propper used to this'
'Ar gotta try mine!' an ecstatic Maize said, skipping from the jewellry store and heading for the boutiques where a stunning red leather jacket simply cried out for her to buy it. At two and a half thousand pounds, the hand made one off was a must have for any would be socialite, 'OY!' Maizie yelled at the nattering sales girl 'Stick that in a bag will ya, ar'll av it!'
'Really madam' the sales girl smirked 'You do realize that's a Suzzie Wong original, with if I might add, quite a hefty price tag attached'.
Maizie waved her card under the girls nose, 'Listen ya dopey bitch!' she said, sharply, 'Don't gimme any of that pretty woman bollocks, ar got the dough an ar wonnit, alright!'

The store manager arrived having seen the glinting platinum card 'I'll take care of this Sandra' she told the girl 'The stock room needs sweeping if you wouldn't mind'.
'Yeah jog on' Maizie said, watching the disgruntled girl scurry away.
'Thank you madam' the manager said, taking Maizie's card 'Will there be anything else?'
'Yeah' Maizie smiled, like a kid in a sweet shop 'Ar'll av that belt, two of them bags and that Burberry at'
'Excellent choices madam' the manager replied, totting up over five thousand pounds of sales 'I'll have them bagged for you right away'.
Dee Dee and Maize spent the next two hours hitting many of the major west end stores in a heady haze of retail bliss before taking a taxi back to the hospital where they showered Trisha's bed with expensive gifts 'We done it Trish, we got the dough!' Maizie squealed, 'We're bloomin loaded!'
'Ar don't believe it' Trisha replied, still sore from the operation.
Dee Dee handed Trisha her platinum card 'There ya go mate, there's over free million quid on that' she told her 'And you deserve evry penny of it mate'.
Trisha clutched the card to her chest, almost speechless for once 'We aint never gotta work no more av we' she said, taking Dee Dee's hand.
'No we ain't Trish' Dee Dee replied, putting a hand on her friends shoulder 'Soon as your aat of ere we're all gonna live the good life, ar seen this pukka villa in Marbella ar might buy, iss got two swimmin pools, a private beech and a bath big enough for six'.
Maizie inched closer 'Ar'v always wanted to live somewhere ot' she said, day dreaming, 'We can all get gaffs aat there eh Dee'.

Dee Dee was about to reply when Bradley came waltzing onto the ward with a page three stunner on his arm, a huge gold letter N on a hefty chain around his neck and a pink box with a lacy bow in his hands 'Yo me bitch's!' he smirked 'You'z now lookin at the next Ice T blud!'
'More like lemon tea' Dee Dee laughed, 'Who's the bird wiv the tits then?'.
Bradley's date smiled sheepishly, pushing up her double D falsies. 'Diss is Chantelle' Bradley said, affectionately 'She's a massive fan of the Nitro innit'
Bradley set the box down on Trisha's lap 'Ar'z got ya summink Trish' he said, tugging at the bow 'Coz ar neva fought ya'd make it man'.
'Ahhhhh thas really sweet Bradley, fanx' Trisha said, lifting the lid and peering inside, 'Oh mar gawd, oh bleedin ell!' she gasped, lifting out two gorgeous Chihuahua puppies.
'They'z a boy and girl Chihuahua' Bradley told her 'Ar fought you could start off ya business wiv em, you know, renting em aat to sad geeza's what can't get a bird'.
Trisha cradled the puppies in her arms 'Ahhhh their bloomin beautiful Brad, ar dunno what to say' she said, kissing them both 'Ar'm gonna call em Dave and Doris after me great aunt and uncle who died at sea before are was born'.
'Ahhh thas nice' Maizie said, stroking the puppies 'Was they on the Titanic or summink?'
'Nahhh' Trisha said, with a lump in her throat 'A pedalo offa Walton on the Naze, bleedin tragic it was, they got caught in the shipping lanes and was dragged over four faasand miles by a Shanghai tanker'.

Bradley then noticed Dee Dee's Cartier watch 'Wo man das some quality bling Dee' he said, taking her hand, 'Is it real?'

'Course it is ya muppet!' Dee Dee said, snatching her hand away 'We got paid aat for that caper didn't we'

'Yeah bruv' Maizie said, holding up her department store bags 'We're minted naah and we're all pissin off to Spain, ya comin?'.

Bradley looked round at his new girlfriends pouting lips and heaving chest 'Ar can't sis' he replied 'Ar'm on the Jonafon Wossy show tonight and Richard and Judy in the mawnin, den ar'm in the studio wiv Elton doin some duet for skinny African kids or summink'. Bradley's managerial team had the new star booked solidly for the coming months with a grueling schedule of recording, touring and personal appearances. He was the hottest of hot properties and everyone wanted a piece of him. He turned back to his girlfriend 'Where am I after dat babe?' he asked her.

'Well!' she said, thinking hard 'You gotta do Party in the Park in a coupla weeks then the Queens jubilee gig babe'

'Don't tell me your singin for the Queen' Dee Dee said, totally aghast 'You!'

'Yeah blud!' Bradley laughed 'Ar bin workin on me Lizzy rap, check it aat' with this Bradley began beat boxing yet again,

'Yo mar bitch Lizzy, here's lookin at you
you bin on dat frone since fifty two,
lookin kinda fresh in ya diamonds and pearls
better dan da Sugarbabes and all de uvver girls,
better dan da Spice girls, Britney and Beyonce
Gimme arf a chance Lizzy, ar'll be your fiance,
Gimme arf a chance girl ya better than Beyonce

Gimme arf a chance Lizzy, ar'll be your fiance'

'If you were mine Lizzy, i'd treat ya right good
i'd treat ya so fine ya'd give me a knight hood,
ar mean ya no harm and ar mean ya no malice
here's to you marm in ya Buckingham Palace'
Yo mar bitch Lizzy iss ya jubilee
if ar fink abaat you, will ya fink abaat me
sittin on ya frone on ya jubilee
if ar fink abaat you, will ya fink abaat me'

Dee Dee, Maize, Trisha and just about everybody within earshot applauded Bradley,
'Just a few bars for mar girl Lizzy innit' Bradley said, acknowledging the applause, 'Ar'm still workin on it though, nart ar mean, and don't worry sis, ar come visit ya soon as ar can yeah'
'You make sure you do bruv' Maizie told him, 'Don't be a bleedin stranger d'you ear me'. Then to everyone's surprise Mickey Spencer came hobbling in on a pair of crutches
'Alright Trish babe' he said, parking his crutches and taking a seat beside her 'I eard you was in ere, you ok mate?'
'Ello Mickey' the three girls said simultaneously, 'Not too bad Mickey' Trisha added 'Ar got bleedin stabbed up didn't I, but ar'm on the mend'.
'Shit, who dunnit?' Mickey asked 'That nutter Billy Tibbs was it?'
'Yeah' Dee Dee said, interrupting 'But the arse wipe got what e was due thas for sure'
'Eh!' Mickey gasped 'You killed Billy Tibbs?'
'Not exactly' Dee Dee explained 'It was a mate of ours and iz boys, they propper done im an'all!'.

‘Good’ Mickey said, remembering the savage beating he had endured from Billy and his brothers ‘Shame someone don’t do the same to that bastard copper Pritcher’

‘Why woss up Mickey?‘ Maizie asked, ‘You ad a visit av ya?’

‘Yeah the fucker’s just bin in’ Mickey replied, angrily ‘Reckons e’z gonna fit me up for every unsolved crime on iz books for the last ten years when ar get aat of ere, and that slag’ll do it an’all, e bleedin ates me’.

‘E can’t do that can e?’ asked Dee Dee,

‘Wanna bet Dee‘ Mickey told her ‘D I Pritcher’s just abaat as bent as any copper can be, if e’z got it in for ya, basically your fucked’.

‘Right thas it!‘ Dee Dee said, assertively,‘You’re comin wiv us Mick, we’re off to the Costa’s, tommorra if ar can get a flight, bring Marcie an’all, ow is she by the way?

‘She’s taken a turn for the worse Dee mate, mentally ar mean’ Mickey said, clambering to his feet ‘The docs reckon it’s delayed shock or summink after that fucker cut er finger off, apparently it could be weeks even months before she snaps aat of it’.

Dee Dee took Mickeys hand and handed him his crutches ‘Don’t worry abaat a fing mate’ she told him ‘A bitta sun on er back and she’a be as right as rain believe me, give er mar love and the pair of ya get the fuc aat of ere and meet us at eafrow airport at nine he mornin’.

‘ e mate, fanks’ Mickey said, kissing her cheek er, see ya later girls and you Brad, I eard you spital radio fing this mornin bro, man that shit blud!’

'Fanks Mickey man!', Bradley said, touching knuckles with Mickey 'Later's yeah'. Mickey hobbled out of the door and back to his sisters bedside leaving Bradley to say his goodbyes to his sister, Dee Dee and Trisha. 'Ar gotta go girls coz the suits want me in the studio innit' he told them 'Ar catch'ya later yeah, look after yaselves' Bradley kissed each of them
'Sorry for shootin ya' Trisha whispered, returning his kiss,
'Don't worry abaat it babe' Bradley replied, out of earshot of his girlfriend who stood applying glitter polish to her nails, 'You done me a proper favor innit'
'Cheers geez' Dee Dee said, giving Bradley a firm standoffish pat on the back 'Maybe you aint such a twat after all'
'Fanks Dee' Bradley replied, eyeing her chest yet again 'If you'z ever wanna get it on yeah, ar reckon ar could fit you in babe'.
Dee Dee pulled him closer 'Not if you was the last dick on the planet ya numpty' she smirked, 'Naah go on, piss off and enjoy yaself'
Bradley turned to his sister 'Ar know she's nuts abaat me Maize' he said 'She just won't give in to er feelins innit'
'She's right brad' Maizie told him, giving him a loving hug 'You are a numpty but ar do love ya, ar'm really glad fingsa workin aat for ya, you got talent bruv and don't let anyone tell you uvverwise, d'you ear me'.
'Fanks si!' Bradley said, turning to leave 'Ar catch you all later yeah, come on Chantelle babe' he said, taking his girlfriends hand 'Ar gotta room in one of them poncey Park Lane otels, iss got cider in the fridge an everyfink'
Dee Dee winked at Chantelle 'You've landed on ya feet aintcha' she laughed 'Two minutes in the sack

and a can of white lightnin, ar mean e'z ardley George flippin Cloony is e'.
Chantelle nestled her cheek in alongside Bradley's 'Ahhh, he's lovely he is' she said, in a high pitched tone 'He's like a little fluffy bunny wunny aren't you thumper, that's my pet name for him, coz he bangs his foot on the floor every time he wants a shag'
'Chantelle!' Bradley snapped 'Ar told ya that stuffs private innit, ar'm supposed to be a bad boy rapper ain I!'
'You are a bad boy' Chantelle replied, cheekily 'A very bad boy, and when mummy gets you home she's gonna punish you again and again and again'
Bradley, now red faced dragged Chantelle from the ward.
'Oooh er!' Dee Dee laughed 'Looks like there'll be tears before bedtime and no bot bot for Bradley by the looksa fings'.
Bradley could be heard chastising Chantelle all the way down the corridor 'But you said you liked it my little love bunny' Chantelle moaned,
'Yeah ar do babe!' Bradley complained 'But it aint good for me image man, ar mean, ya don't hear mar man Dizzy being called no love hamster or summink do ya?'
'No I spoze not' Chantelle replied, hanging her head 'Sorry lover, i'll make it up to you I promise'
'Now ya talkin sweet cheeks' Bradley said, rubbing his hands together at the thought of a lusty afternoon in his penthouse apartment.
Tr sha suddenly sat bolt upright in bed and looked und 'Dee mate!' she said, quizzically 'Where's a?'
shit!' Dee Dee gasped 'She finks ya dead, oh give us er number ar'll give er a ring'.

Trisha took out her phone and scoured the address book 'Nar ar'll do it!' she said, waiting for a reply, 'Come on answer the bleedin phone' she added, biting a nail, 'Ello babe iss me Trish!' there was a moment of silence and then a scream that could be heard all around Trisha's bed, 'Calm daan babe' Trisha said, smiling 'Ar'm alright, really'.
Laura had spent the last few days in floods of tears, lashing out at inanimate objects as though they were to blame, 'They, they told me you were dead' she sobbed 'Oh my god, oh my god Trisha is it really you, it is isn't it, oh god tell me i'm not dreaming'.
'Yeah iss me alright' Trisha replied, choking back a tear herself 'Come up and see me will ya'.
'I will, I will!' Laura said, frantically searching for her car keys 'I'm leaving right now, don't go anywhere i'm on my way'. Laura raced from her flat leaving the front door wide open and thumped the elevator buttons 'Come on, come on!' she said, fidgeting impatiently.
After an emotional reunion during which Dee Dee and Maizie slipped away to the cafeteria Trisha explained to Laura that she and her friends were leaving the country the very next day 'Come wiv us' Trisha begged 'Ar got enough dough for the two of us'.
As tempting as it sounded to Laura and after much deliberation she reluctantly declined Trisha's idyllic offer, 'This'll tear me apart I know' she said, squeezing Trisha's hand 'But i've got a business to run and i'm going to do my damnedest to make sure it's a respectable one, for far too long the Tibbs name has been a blight on our community, but I aim to change all that, am I making any sense?'

'Yeah ar know what ya sayin' Trisha said with a heavy heart 'But it aint gonna be easy sayin goodbye to ya'.
'Look at it this way' Laura said, trying to soften the blow for the both of them 'I'll have somewhere to stay when I go on holiday now, won't I?'.
Trisha's face lit up 'Oh yeah, ar never foughta that' she said, jubilantly, 'Opefully ar'll av me Jacuzzi by then'.
'Mmm, sounds wonderful' Laura said 'I really can't wait'. The two chatted for a while longer before Dee Dee and Maizie returned, 'Oh I er, I really should be going' Laura said, hugging Trisha 'You have my number, so do call me won't you'
'Yeah course ar will' Trisha said, attempting to climb from her bed,
'No please don't get up you'll hurt yourself' Laura told her,
'She's bleedin right ya doughnut' Dee Dee added, pushing her friend back down 'Ya need all the rest ya can get if we're buggerin off tommora'.
Laura blew Trisha a kiss 'I'll see you, I promise' she said heading for the door.
'Yeah see ya babe!' Trisha replied, craning her neck to catch a final glimpse of her 'Bye!'.
'Ar brought you a brew' Dee Dee said, setting the vending cup down on Trisha's bedside table 'An a baga wine gums, ar know ya love em'. Trisha hadn't heard a word Dee Dee had said, still staring along the now empty corridor. Dee Dee nudged Trisha's arm, 'Oy Trish ar got ya wine gums!',
'Eh, oh fanks' Trisha said, snapping out of her daze 'Ya know they're me favrit dontcha'
'Yeah thas why we got em ya dopey cow' Maizie laughed.

Trisha tore at the packet, 'Eeya, when ar was little' she said, popping two into her mouth 'We used to lick em and stick em to me granddad's ed when e was asleep, that and marshmallow's, e used to kick right off when e woke up and we used to shout buckarooooooo!'
'E did av proper naughty temper your granddad' Dee Dee said, sipping her tea 'Member when e caught you shaggin shifty Mick in iz pottin shed, ya done im on the flymo dintcha?'
'Yeah ar did' Trisha recollected, 'Apparently iss a lot less bovva when ya bangin on a hovva, me granddad went mental e did, e chased shifty Mick up the garden wiv a rusty rake and fretened to tell me nan'.
'Did e tell er?' Maizie asked, knowing what a typically fiery catholic woman she was.
Trisha shook her head 'Nah course not' she said, smiling 'Ar told im ar knew e was givin it to Gladiss at number ferty two on a friday afternoon, e tells me nan e'z just mowin er grass'
'Sounds like e's trimmin er bush an'all' Dee Dee laughed, 'The randy old sod'
'No, really!' Maizie gasped, being a close friend of the family 'What, ya mean e'z bin doin the dirty on ya nan, that aint nice is it'.
'Well e aint gettin it at ome thas for sure' Trisha explained 'E reckons im and me nan aint ad sex since the war, some doodlebug fingy landed on the shelter they were shaggin in and put im off iz stride, she got the ump and as ad er legs shut ever since, so ar don't really blame im for shaggin araand, ar fink it's quite sweet'. The girls spent the remainder of the day reminiscing and trying to keep the Chihuahua's out of sight of hospital staff, pulling the curtain around the bed for privacy,

'Listen Trish we better be off mate' Dee Dee eventually said 'You get some kip, we'll be back to get ya tommora' Dee Dee and Maizie said their goodbyes leaving Trisha to doze off with her dogs.

'Come on Maize mate' Dee Dee said, leaving the hospital 'Less go down the Welly and get wankered, one last time eh'

'Yeah go on then, less av it!' Maizie agreed 'Ya never know ar might give Terry a blowy as a goin away present'

'Who, chicken legs!' Dee Dee said, referring to West Ham Terry 'That melt!' Melt being urban slag for a complete fucking idiot,

'Ahh e aint that bad Dee' Maizie said, defending the lovable drunk 'E might be ung like a snail but ar'v erd e knows what to do wiv it'.

'Ar'll tell im what to do wiv it if e comes near me' Dee Dee sneered, having fought off Terry's intoxicated lecherous advances on all too many occasions 'E can stick it up iz arse thas what e can do wiv it, fuckin melt'.

CHAPTER THIRTEEN

The getaway.

The next morning Dee Dee and Maizie, a little hung over and bleary eyed from a heavy night at the Wellington gathered up their passports and a few personal items and returned to the hospital to collect Trisha 'Me mum was a bit teary when ar left' Maizie said as they entered the foyer 'Ar told er me and you ad a summer job in Magaloof and ar see er at the end of the season, and to keep er sweet ar left er twenny grand in the biscuit tin an a note sayin I ad a win on the orses, what about your muvva Dee, you erd anyfink?'
'Naaah' Dee Dee sighed 'Ar left a message on that Fitzroy geeza's fone this mornin fretenin all sorts if e don't elp er, but I aint oldin me breff!'
'Ello Dee, Maize, you alright?' Trisha said, sitting up in bed 'I aint slept a bleedin wink all night, ar bin so excited'. Dave and Doris were fast asleep beside her
'Alright Trish mate, what did the nurses say about the dogs bein in ere, ar bet they weren't too pleased'.
'They was well pissed off' Trisha replied, looking lovingly at her new pets 'But ar sweetened em up by promisin to buy em anuvva breast cancer screenin fingy'
'Ahhh thas nice of ya' Maize said, sitting beside her 'Me Auntie Rita ad a dose of that shit, they lopped off

a tit and drugged er up, but iss bin ten years naah and she's still ere gawd bless er, we ad a wicked party for er when she got the all clear'.

Doctor Klyne was doing his morning rounds and noticed Dee Dee and Maizie helping Trisha out of bed 'What on earth do you think your doing?' he asked, flinging his clipboard down on an adjacent bed 'Get back in bed this instant'

'Ang on Doc' Dee Dee said, standing between them, 'We're flying out of Eafrow this mornin, all of us'.

'Absolutely not!' Doctor Klyne snapped 'This young lady is in no fit state to travel, you'll have to leave without her i'm afraid'.

'No way!' Trisha said, slipping into the clothes that Maizie had brought her 'Just dose me up wiv pain killers ar be alright'.

'Pain killers, are you out of your mind?' asked the doctor, standing firmly in their way, 'This isn't a bout of period pains we're talking about here, may I remind you you were admitted to this hospital with a near fatal stab wound, you are very lucky to be alive at this moment in time, you need rest and plenty of it!'

'Ar be gettin plenny of that by the pool over there wun I' Trisha replied.

'Listen geez' Dee Dee said, taking Doctor Klyne to one side 'We're takin er aat of ere wevva you like it or not, don't worry ar make sure she's ok, even if I av to fly a team of docs aat wiv us, so just give er summink to num the pain for naah and ar promise ya, soon as land we'll take er somewhere and get er s

Klyne knew that if Trisha wished to discharge here was very little he could do to stop her, e best interests of his patient he reluctantly

agreed to help, 'Ok, but I insist you let me check you over first' he said, sitting her back on the bed.
After a thorough examination, Doctor Klyne was still unhappy with the situation but asked one of his nurses to prepare a strong pain reliving injection that would hopefully ease any discomfort Trisha may have until they arrived in Spain. 'Fanks doc' Trisha said, planting a slobbering kiss on his cheek 'Fanks a lot'.
'Just look after yourself' the doctor said, pulling away 'And see a doctor as soon as you land, d'you hear me'
'Yeah ar promise' Trisha replied, taking a pair of crutches from the nurse 'Can ya get Dave and Doris Maize?' Trisha asked, hooking her handbag on the handle of her crutch 'Right off we go!' she said, leading the way, albeit shakily 'Cor blimey these fings take some bleedin gettin used to don't they' she added. The three girls met Mickey and Marcie in the corridor and headed for the exit with them
'You alright Marce?' Dee Dee asked, but Marcie stared blankly ahead,
'She's alright Dee' Mickey told her 'She just needs a bit of time to get over it thas all'
'Ar fink a coupla Pina colada's by the pool'll sort that aat Mick' Maizie said, linking arms with him 'Ar fink it'a sort us all aat'.
Queuing at the check in desk the girls were growing more and more excited 'Ar can't wait to check aat the pecs on the beach' Trisha laughed 'And the tits an'all'
'You dirty bitch' Maizie chuckled.
Safely in the terminal, Dee Dee and the others cruised the duty free shops trying on ridiculous sunglasses and taking embarrassing photographs with the disposable cameras before replacing them

on the stand, and after a spot of lunch they settled down waiting to board their plane, but after only five minutes Mickey felt a firm hand on his shoulder
'Mr Spencer' a member of airport security said 'Could you come with me sir'.
'What?' a startled Mickey said, spinning round 'Woss the problem?'
'Yeah woss up?' Dee Dee said, springing to her feet 'Woss all this abaat?'
'We'd just like a few words in private' the guard said, pointing the way to the security offices 'If you could accompany me right away sir, i'd be grateful'
'E aint goin nowhere!' Dee Dee barked, 'We're flyin in a minute'.
The guard was then joined by two of his colleagues 'I'm afraid you won't be flying anywhere Mr Spencer, until this is sorted'.
Mickey relented and followed the men 'Ar be alright Dee, wait for me will ya'
'Fuck that ar'm comin wiv ya' Dee Dee said, trotting after them 'Me an'all, and me!' Maize and Trisha said, helping Marcie to her feet
'Come on Marce, you better come an'all' Maizie said, holding her hand.
Mickeys passport had triggered an alert on the police national computer and DI Pritcher had gotten wind of it, 'That slag aint doin a bunk' he said, as he and his team raced to the airport.
'Goin somewhere Mickey?' the D I said, storming into the office 'Wivaat even sayin goodbye'
Mickeys heart sank when he saw the D I, 'Pritcher!' he gasped 'What the fuck are you doin ere?'.
D I Pritcher sat on the edge of the desk, grinning like a Cheshire cat 'Makin sure villains like you Mickey' he said 'Don't bugger off to some sandy beach when

they should be on lockdaan in a shitty Pentonville piss ole, thas what ar'm doin ere me old son'.
One of the D I's officers looked Dee Dee, Maize and Trisha up and down before whispering in his bosses ear 'Sir these three fit the descriptions of the young ladies seen entering Sheik Abdullah's hotel suite the night he was murdered'.
The D I pricked up his ears, 'Really!' he said, checking them out for himself 'Well this just get's betta and betta' he smirked 'Four slags for the price of one, 'Jones cuff the bleedin lot of em'.
'You slimy bastard!' Dee Dee yelled' knowing the life of sun, sex and sangria that she had come so close to was about to be cruelly denied her.
Maizie was the first to be shackled 'Ar fought it was too good to be true' she sighed, accepting her fate.
Next it was Trisha's turn, 'Not so tight ya kinky fucker!' she told the officer.
'Oy careful wiv er!' Dee Dee yelled 'She's just ad a bloomin operation'.
D I Pritcher grabbed Dee Dee by the shoulder 'Will somebody cuff this gobby bitch!' he snapped at his team 'Come on get ya fingers aat yer arses!'.
Dee Dee was eventually cuffed and read her rights 'Anything you say will be taken down and used as evidence' a WPC informed her.
'Anyfing ar say?' Dee Dee asked, struggling in her restraints 'Well take this daan and shove it!' she said 'PRITCHER YOUR A PRICK!' she added at the top of her voice, determined to make her feelings known before her liberty and freedom were taken from her.
'You aint wrong there love' the WPC said under her breath.
Dee Dee and the others were frog marched through the busy terminal and out where a metropolitan

police van was waiting. 'Sorry Mickey mate' Dee Dee said as he was being bundled in the back.
'Don't worry abaat it Dee' Mickey smiled 'You get used to it after a while, and the grub ain't arf bad eeva'.
Trisha, Maizie and Marcie were also helped aboard and their cuffs secured to the side of the van 'What abaat Dave and Doris Dee?' Trisha asked,
'They're already on the blinkin plane!'.
'Dave and Doris?' the D I said 'Who are they then, more of your shitty little firm ar spoze'
'Nah ya dick ed' Trisha sneered, 'They're me Chihuahua's, you gotta get em off!'
'I ain't gotta do nuffing' the D I smiled 'Looks like the little bleeda's'll be goin to sunny Spain wivoucha, tough eh'.
Dee Dee glared at him 'You really are a werfless wanker aint'cha' she snarled.
Enraged by her remark the D I shoved Dee Dee against the rear of the van 'Go on get in there you slag!' he growled, eager to see the lot of them behind bars.
Mickey tried to get to his feet but was pushed back down 'Marcie aint done nuffing man, let er go!' he said, hoping the D I had even the slightest shred of decency, but he was wasting his time,
'Shut the fuck up Mickey' the D I said, pointing a stiff finger at him 'If she's anyfing to do wiv you she's gotta be a villain, and even if she aint, ar'll pin sumink on er just for the fun of it'.
Climbing aboard with the rest of her friends, Dee Dee looked at their empty expressions but had no words of comfort to offer them.
The D I, pleased with his mornings work was about to slam the doors shut when a gleaming silver chauffeur

driven Daimler swept alongside the kerb behind him. The rear door opened and Lord Fitzroy stepped out onto the pavement, he then reached back inside and took a woman's hand and helped her out,

'Mum!' Dee Dee yelled, pushing the van door open,

'Ello love, you alright?' Pearl replied.

'What's she doin ere?' The D I stormed, assuming Pearl was safely locked up at her majesty's pleasure 'What's goin on?'.

Lord Fitzroy approached the D I and began whispering in his ear 'NO WAY!' the D I said, backing away 'No way, no bleedin way am ar lettin these slags go!'.

Lord Fitzroy had used his political connections to secure pearl's release in exchange for the damming documents which could destroy him, 'My dear Detective inspector' the minister said, calmly 'If you don't do as I say I can promise you you'll be a parking attendant before this day is out, do I make myself clear!'. D I Pritcher paced up and down seething 'This is bang aat of order!' he cursed, but he knew his hands were well and truly tied, 'HENSHAW!' he barked 'Get these fucker's aat of mar van!'.

A smiling Dee Dee and the others were helped from the back and released from their handcuffs, 'You ok mum?' Dee Dee asked, giving her mother a hug, 'They bin treatin you alright av they?'

'Oh yeah ar bin fine love' Pearl replied 'I ad a telly an all me Sudoku mags, oh and guess what, I aint ad a drink since they banged me up, and I aint missed it neeva'.

'Ar'm really glad' Dee Dee said, kissing her cheek 'You don't know ow much ar'v wanted to av me old mum back, you was such a laugh before the booze'.

'Ar know an ar'm sorry babe' Pearl said, hanging her head 'I aint bin much of a muvva to ya since ya dad buggered off av I?'
'Oh shut up mum' Dee Dee said, looking her mother in the eye 'You done a pukka job of bringin me up on yer own an ar love ya for it, but naah iss mar turn to look after you'.
Lord Fitzroy looked over in Dee Dee's direction and cleared his throat 'I believe you have something for me' he said, expectantly 'I trust you have it'
'Ang on mum ar gotta sort summink' Dee Dee told her mother, 'Yeah ar got it' she replied, stepping to one side with the minister and reaching inside her jacket 'Ow do ar know you aint gonna bang us up soon as you got it?' she asked.
Lord Fitzroy answered her question with one of his own 'My dear, how do I know you haven't made several copies of these documents?'
'Ya don't' Dee Dee said, realizing the two of them had a mutual understanding.
'Precisely' the minister replied, slipping the documents into his attaché case 'I'm hoping we never have cause to meet again young lady' he told Dee Dee 'Now I suggest you and your, friends, board that plane and think twice about ever returning, do I make myself clear'.
Any other time Dee Dee would have torn a strip off the minister for threatening her in such a way, but seeing the excited smiles on her friends faces and knowing she was so close to her dream she felt it best not to muddy the waters' Don't worry mate ar bin tryna get aat of ere me ole life' she told the minister 'Ar'v ad the crap naah ar want the cream, nart ar mean'

'Yes, quite' Lord Fitzroy said, struggling with the language barrier 'Right I must be off' he told Dee Dee 'I have a meeting with the PM in an hour'.
'Tell im ar said ello' Dee Dee replied, tongue in cheek, 'Oh and tell the bleeda to sort aat the old age pension an'all, me great Aunt Alice as ad to let out er box room to arf a dozen Ukrainian brickies just to keep a roof over er ed, she's takin in washin, does a paper raand, two shifts at the Flyin Orse and she props up a friggin lollypop at St Winifreds, ar mean, give the poor cow a break will ya, stop shellin aat shit loads of cash to bone idol benefit ponce's and scroungers and give it to them that bleedin deserves it, people like me Aunty Alice are the bleedin backbone of this country and don't you forget it mate!'.
This was the second time the minister had been on the receiving end of a political barracking from Dee Dee, not even the most fearsome of opposition back benchers had attacked him with such venom. 'Alice you say?' the minister said, touched by her plight.
'Yeah thas right' Dee Dee said, proudly 'And don't you dare say 'who the fuck is Alice' or ar'll slap ya'
'I wouldn't dream of it my dear' the minister said, checking his wrist watch 'She sounds like quite a remarkable woman, i'll mention your concerns to the PM personally'.
'Yeah you do that' Dee Dee said, turning to rejoin her friends,
'Listen to me you slag!' D I Pritcher said, stopping Dee Dee in her tracks 'You fink ya'v got the better of me dontcha, well let me tell ya this, you just made the top of mar shit list and you and your firm are goin daan ar can promise ya that, iss just a matter of time thas all'.

Dee Dee took Trisha's arm and helped her back toward the terminal 'Dream on Pritcher you mug!' she called back 'You'll always be a mug and from what ar'v erd ya'v always bin a bleedin mug, ta daa!'
'Yeah laters dip shit!' Maizie added before hurrying inside.
The D I flew into a violent rage, 'AR'LL FUCKIN AV YOU, YOU SLAGS!' he screamed 'AN AR'LL FUCKIN BURY THE LOT OF YA!' his temper increased when he noticed a number of his officers laughing behind their helmets 'Get back to work you morons!' he yelled 'Or ar'll av you all up on a fuckin charge, you see if ar don't!' the officers quickly donned their helmets and leapt into their vehicles leaving the D I raging, 'ARRRRRGH FUCK!' he roared, kicking the side of the police van as hard as he could, stubbing his big toe in the process 'Shit, shit, shit!' he cursed, hopping on one foot.
'You alright sir?' a young WPC said, sheepishly.
It was all the D I could do to stop himself lunging at the girl 'NO I'M NOT!' he cried, resting against the van 'NAAH FUCK OFF AND DO SOME WORK WILL YA!'.
Dee Dee and the others boarded the plane unhindered and settled in their seats 'We're really goin aint we Dee' Trisha said as they taxied along the runway.
'Yeah we are mate' Dee Dee replied, looking out of the window at the country she was about to leave behind, 'And there aint nuffin to stop us naah, nuffin'.
Maizie sat trembling in her seat with her eyes clenched tightly shut 'Oh fuck, oh fuck, oh fuck!' she wailed 'Ar bleedin ate this bit ar do'.
Mickey patted her back 'Iss alright Maizie girl iss perfectly safe' he said, attempting to calm her rattled

nerves 'Me fly backwards and forwards to Jamaica all the time and nuttin ever happened to me ya know' but as the pilot pulled back on the throttles and the planes nose rose from the tarmac, Maizie wrenched at her seat belt 'Ar gotta get off, Dee ar gotta get off mate, ar can't do this!' she sobbed.
'Shuuut up you dopey cow' Dee Dee said, adopting a less diplomatic approach 'We aint stoppin naah, not for you, not for no one'
Trisha raised her hand 'Ar get a dicky tummy when ar fly ar do!' she said, crossing her legs.
'Oh for fuck sake, don't you bleedin start!' Dee Dee snapped, glaring across at Trisha, 'Iss bad enough wiv silly nuts ere'
'It aint mar fault Dee!' Maizie moaned 'I aint ad me tablits'
'Ar really need the Karzi' Trisha said, wriggling in her seat 'Ar fink ar got a toucha squirts'.
Dee Dee now had a whinging friend on either side of her and quite frankly she had had enough of their belly aching. 'If you two don't shut the fuck up ar'll give you bofe such a bleedin slap, Maizie we aint gonna bleedin crash and Trish, you can wait five minutes till you splatter the friggin pan, ok!'.
A scolded Maizie and Trisha sat in silence for several moment until Trisha piped up 'Ar read a book about a plane crash once' she said, oblivious to Maizie's feelings 'Most of the poor bleeda's on board died and the rest got eaten by bears, good it was!'.
Maizie began to hyperventilate and thrash around in her seat 'We're gonna die, we're gonna die ar know it!' she screamed.
Dee Dee leaned across, grabbed Maizie by the scruff and slapped her face hard, 'Shut it will ya, your doin my ed in, and you Trisha, shut up abaat friggin plane

crashes or ar'll stab ya meself!'. As the airplane broke through the cloud layer Dee Dee sat back believing she had finally taken control of the situation until Trisha opened her mouth yet again

'Anyone seen Snakes on a plane wiv Samuel L whatsisface?'. Maizie and the surrounding passengers began instinctively looking under their seats,

'TRISHA!' Dee Dee yelled 'What the fuck did ar tell ya, eh?'.

The seat belt sign eventually went out and a stewardess approached the girls 'Excuse me is there a problem?' she asked, leaning between the seats.

'Yeah!' Dee Dee said, abruptly 'That dopey mare over there!'.

'What?' Trisha lsaid leaping from her seat, grabbing her crutches and hobbling quickly to the lavatory clutching her backside,'Iss comin, iss comin ar can feel it!' she cried, kicking the door open.

Dee Dee clutched the stewardesses sleeve 'Get me a large JD will ya before ar frottle mar two mates, they're proper doin mar nut in'

'Certainly madam the refreshment cart will be along shortly' the stewardess replied 'And can I get something for your friend' she looked over at Maizie who clung to her seatbelt.

'Yeah a friggin parachute!' Dee Dee smirked, 'Coz if she keeps this shit up ar'll open the bloody door and fuck er off aat meself, ar mean it!'

At that moment Trisha came staggering back with a drained expression, 'Fuuuck me!' she gasped 'That come aat like me Gran's gravy it did' she tapped the stewardess on the shoulder 'Er, you might wanna run a mop raad the rim in there love, ar didn't av time to get it all in the pan, nart ar mean' but before the bewildered stewardess could react there was a loud thud behind them as a wealthy arab business woman dressed in a full length jet black burka with the tiniest of slits for her eyes, entered the lavatory and immediately slipped on the remains of Trisha's recent visit, 'Oooooh nasty!' Trisha cringed watching the woman, who was half in and half out of the cubicle thrash around on the floor screaming 'Allah help me, help me please!' whilst coating her clothing in the stinking liquefied excrement. 'Forget the mop!' Trisha laughed 'looks like she's done it for ya!'.

The frantic stewardess and her colleagues ran to the woman's aid, screwing up their faces in disgust, and after an extensive clean up operation the angry Arab was forced to sit out the remainder of her journey dressed in a British airways uniform with a crudely made veil across her face fashioned from a sick bag.

Maizie calmed down some what once the plane reached cruising altitude and Trisha, still heavily medicated, drifted off to sleep leaving Dee Dee to enjoy several double JD's listening to Westlife on her MP3 player 'Ar'm flyin wivaaaat wiiiiings!' she sang, with a moth full of ice.

Hearing this, Maizie pressed her nose against the window checking that the wings were in fact still attached to the airplane.

Three hours later the plane touched down at Malaga airport, a taxi ride away from the resort of Marbella where Dee Dee's dream villa was situated 'Flippin ell, ain it ot!' Trisha said as she and the rest of her friends stepped out into the blistering midday sun, 'Yeah, pukka ain it' Dee Dee smiled, closing her eyes and feeling the heat radiate on her face. The party took a taxi along the Costa Del Sol coastline to the millionaires paradise resort of Marbella where many of the worlds most influential figures owned an idyllic retreat and maybe a yacht or two in the glamorous marina.

Booking into the five star Don Carlos Hotel they each relaxed in the luxurious surroundings, a far cry from the grubby Essex streets they had grown up on. 'Iss like a bloody dream' Trisha said, reclining by the pool with a tall margarita in her hand and a handsome waiter by her side to cater to her every whim.

Mickey and his sister strolled barefoot along the coral sand hand in hand, 'Thank you Mickey' Marcie said, resting her head on his shoulder 'For always being there for me'

Mickey was taken aback at first because Marcie hadn't uttered a single word for the past three days, 'You welcome sis, anytime you know that' he told her 'Fings are gonna be different naah for both of us, ar promise'.

Dee Dee left her mother enjoying a relaxing Massage, sipping pineapple juice with a contented smile on her face whilst she and Maizie wandered through the palm tree lined streets, eyeing the Porsche's and Lamborghini's parked outside the bars and coffee shops. Soon they came across an estate agent specializing in luxury villas, 'Oy geeza!' Dee Dee said, producing a photograph of her dream villa from her pocket, 'Ar wanna buy this gaff, d'you know where it is?'

'Excuse me?' the owner said in broken English, peering at the crumpled photo 'Ar yes, this villa is on our books, please take a seat and I will show you'. Within half an hour the deal was done, Dee Dee was now the proud owner of a one point two million pound waterfront villa, 'Your key's Senorita' the estate agent said, politely 'Turn to the right at the end of the marina and your new home is the second on the left'. 'Fanks mate' Dee Dee said, grinning at Maizie 'Ar got it Maize, ar fuckin got it!' The two of them hurried toward the marina giggling with excitement 'Oh mar gawd Maizie!' Dee Dee gasped as they rounded the corner and her new home came into sight 'Look at it Maize, look at the bleedin size of it!' The gleaming white beachside property was arguably one of the biggest and best on the complex with electric gates, a sweeping drive and immaculately manicured lawns and hedges,

'Can I help you Miss?' a gardener tending to the flower beds asked,

'Yeah!' Dee Dee said, waving the keys above her head 'Ar just bought this gaff so open the bloody gate mate!'

The gardner hurriedly rummaged in his pocket for the gate key 'Sorry Miss, yes of course, welcome, welcome both of you!'

Dee Dee stood and admired his handy work 'D'you do all this yaself?' she asked, noticing his callused hands and sweat soaked shirt,

'Yes miss' the gardener replied, bowing his head subserviently.

'Fuckin lovely ain it' Maizie added, looking around.

'Woss your name?' asked Dee Dee, lifting the gardeners chin to make eye contact 'And don't bovva wiv nunna that bowing shit, I aint the bleedin queen muvva!'

'Alfonso' the gardener replied, 'My name is Alfonso Miss'

'Well Alfie me old son, ow much is your firm payin ya for this?'

Alfonso wiped his sweaty hands on his handkerchief 'Thirty euros per day miss' he told her 'I work from seven in the morning until six in the evening with a twenty minute break'

'Not any more ya don't' Dee Dee said, putting an arm around him 'Tell em to poke their job, you work for me naah Alfie, ar give ya sixty euros a day and you work from nine till three wiv an hours break, alright!'

'For real?' Alfonso asked, hardly believing his ears 'For real Miss?'

'Yeah Alfie mate' Dee Dee laughed 'And me names Dee Dee so bleedin use it, naah take the rest of the day off, go for a paddle or summink'

'Thank you, thank you Miss Dee Dee' Alfonso smiled, with this he collected his tools together and scurried across the lawn.

'Oy Alfie!' Dee Dee called after him,

'Yes Miss Dee Dee!' Alfonso said, stopping abruptly and screwing his hat in his hands,

'D'you drive?' Dee Dee asked,

Alfonso produced his drivers license from his wallet 'Yes Miss Dee Dee, I drive very well!' he said, eager to please.

'Good!' Dee Dee yelled 'Coz tommora we're gonna buy a mota, a big flash fucker an'all!'

'Yes, yes I know just the place' Alfonso told her, 'My cousin has a Ferrari dealership on the edge of town, I will take you'

'Sorted!' Dee said, waving 'Ar double ya money again to drive me raand ok, ar see ya tommora then!'. Alfonso left them beaming from ear to ear.

Dee Dee's hand trembled as she slipped the key into the lock of the huge entrance door, the gleaming white marble tiles at their feet illuminating the underside of their eager faces. The door swung smoothly and quietly open unlike that of Dee Dee's previous home on the Bircham estate which creaked like a churchyard gate, 'Oh mar gawd!' Dee Dee gasped, the photographs she had seen of the villa did it no justice what so ever and with a solid lump in her throat and a single tear creeping from the corner of her eye she stepped cautiously inside as though she were an uninvited guest.

'Jesus Dee, iss beautiful!' Maizie said, awestruck 'Eeya, d'ya reckon iss got wunna them arse washers Trisha was on abaat?'

'Ar friggin ope so' Dee Dee replied, running her hand along the perfectly plastered ivory walls. The palatial living room complete with domed ceiling, crystal chandelier and seventy two inch plasma tv took their breath away. Dee Dee pinched at the sumptuous cream leather six seater sofa in a daze and was momentarily lost for words.

'Shit Dee, look at the pool!' Maizie gasped, approaching the sliding patio doors. The two girls stepped out onto the sun deck and stood in amazement staring at the thirty meter shimmering pool beautifully tiled in cobalt blue mosaics with a white dolphin in the center. Without saying a word, the two friends who had been through so much together looked at each other for a moment, nodded and sprinted across the patio to the waters edge and leapt into the air, arms raised and fists clenched and a smile that said, we made it, on their faces. After a huge splash which sent a surge of water across the garden, Dee Dee and Maizie surfaced embracing and laughing raucously,

'FUCK YEAH!' Dee Dee cried, punching the air. Frolicking in the pool for a further twenty minutes the girls then sat drying in the sun on mahogany loungers sipping champagne retrieved from the villas well stocked bar, and it was at that moment that the weight they had carried throughout their deprived upbringing was finally lifted from their shoulders.

SIX MONTHS LATER.

Having settled into her glamorous new home with her mother safely housed in the poolside chalet Dee Dee decided to throw a lavish party for her nearest and dearest. Gourmet caterers were hired to provide the finest of foods while florists hurried about the place tweaking vases of exotic flowers. Alfonso in his perfectly tailored chauffeurs uniform ran a duster over Dee Dee's two Ferrari's parked outside, one red and the other diamond white.

The first to arrive and be greeted by Dee Dee on the drive were Mickey and Marcie who now lived a stones throw away in a state of the art apartment overlooking the sea, 'Lookin sharp Mickey mate!' Dee Dee said, with her arms outstretched, 'And you Marce babe, that dress is bleedin gawjuss'

'Cheers Dee' the brother and sister said together, kissing Dee Dee's cheek

'Go on in' Dee Dee told them 'Elp yaself to a drink, me mums aat the back' Dee Dee then smiled as a yellow Jaguar sports swept through the gates with the top down 'Alright Maize!' she said, waving.

Maizie lifted her Gucci glasses and waved back from the passenger seat 'Alright Dee, this is Enrique' she said, stepping from the car 'Enrique this is wunna mar bestest mates Dee'.

Enrique Fetolini was an Italian formula one driver that Maizie had met in Monaco the previous week and had fallen madly in love with. Clinging together like newly weds the two kissed Dee Dee and followed the others inside.

Dee Dee stood on the drive checking her diamond encrusted watch but suddenly the peace and tranquility was shattered by the sound of Bradley's approaching black stretch Hummer belting out a deafening drum and base beat, 'Yo Dee!' Bradley yelled, stepping from the back and helping Chantelle out 'Nice crib girl!' he said, looking the villa over. The music stopped and the two embraced, Bradley giving Dee Dee's bottom a playful squeeze, 'Niiiice!' he smiled,

'Cheeky fucker!' Dee Dee said, pulling away,

'Woss appnin then Brad?' she asked 'Or is it friggin Nitro, ar don't know these days'.

'Ar just gone platnum in five country's innit!' Bradley said, slipping his arm around Chantelle's waist 'Ar got two Grammy's for me new track 'Bitches' and mar record company just bought me a Lea jet man, can you believe it Dee, ar got a flippin plane blud!'.

Bradley's music career had indeed rocketed, putting him head and shoulders above some of the biggest names in the industry.

'Ar'm glad Brad mate' Dee Dee said, 'You alright Chantelle babe?' she asked,

'Yeah ar'm great fanks Dee!' Chantelle replied, flashing a diamond ring 'Me and thumper are gettin engaged next week'

'Nice one' Dee Dee said as Bradley dragged his girlfriend away

'Ar told ya not to call me that babycakes, ar'm a flippin bad boy rapper ain I!' he said, angrily.

'Not to me your not' Chantelle said, kissing his cheek 'You're mar little fluffy bunny wunny'.

Dee Dee laughed, watching the two of them enter the villa and again checked her watch, 'Come on ya dozy bitch, where are ya?' she said several moments later, but then a shocking pink Rolls crept sedately through the gates, stopping at Dee Dee's feet. The rear door swung open and Trisha stepped out dressed in a

stunning white latex cat suit 'Alright Dee, ow's it goin?' she said, flinging her arms around Dee Dee's neck. Her chauffeur then stepped from the car, a gorgeous brunette wearing a similar cat suit and clutching Dave and Doris, Trisha's Chihuahua's,
'Stunnin aint she?' Trisha said,
Dee Dee looked the car over 'Yeah nice wheels!' she agreed'
'No ya doughnut!' Trisha said, slapping her Chauffeurs bottom 'Ar meant Martina, she's a cracker aint she'
Dee Dee hugged her friend again 'You are a dirty bitch aint'cha' she whispered,
Trisha broke away and took Dee Dee's hand 'Oh look at this Dee' she said, taking her to the rear of the car where a logo was emblazoned across the boot which read Chihuahua for an hour dot com, 'Ar got dogs in six country's naah and ar got a fleet of motorcycle couriers deliverin em like pizza's to sad fuckers desperate for a bird, ar made arf a mill in the last two days Dee!'.
Trisha's Chihuahua rental business had gone from strength to strength with a global network spanning all continents, 'And it all started wiv these randy little bugger's' Trisha said, stroking Dave and Doris's chins 'They just can't stop shagghin, the orny little bleeda's!'
'Ar wonder where they get that from!? Dee Dee laughed, ushering them inside, she then turned to Alfonso 'Oy Alfie, get yaself inside and av a drink mate' she told him, 'And try summa that lobster an'all!'
'Thank you Miss Dee' Alfonso replied, taking a glass of champagne from the caterer at the door.

Dee Dee stood outside for a moment collecting her thoughts before entering her villa and making her way to the rear. Stepping onto the sun deck she smiled, seeing her mother and her closest friends standing in a line to greet her. Grinning from ear to ear Maizie raised her hands and began a slow rhythmic clap of appreciation, one by one the others joined her, acknowledging Dee Dee's outstanding leadership qualities that had brought them so far from their humble beginnings. The clapping grew in intensity until it was a full blown round of applause. Dee Dee raised her glass and saluted each and every one of them and then looking skywards quietly said,

'Yes!'......

49402829R00243

Made in the USA
Charleston, SC
24 November 2015